Dear Jo

From Laura coyn

FAMOUS FIVE ADVENTURE COLLECTION

FAMOUS FIVE ADVENTURE COLLECTION

ENID BLYTON

Hodder
Children's
Books

a division of Hodder Headline Limited

This collection first published in Great Britain in 2004 by
Hodder Children's Books
Five On a Treasure Island first published in Great Britain in 1942
Five Go Adventuring Again first published in Great Britain in 1942
Five Go to Billycock Hill first published in Great Britain in 1957

For further information on Enid Blyton please contact
www.blyton.com

2

A Catalogue record for this book is available
from the British Library

ISBN 0 340 89362 1

Typeset by Hewer Text Limited, Edinburgh
Printed and bound in Great Britain by
Clays Ltd, St Ives plc

The paper used in this book is a natural recyclable product
made from wood grown in sustainable forests.
The hard coverboard is recycled.

Hodder Children's Books
a division of Hodder Headline Limited
338 Euston Road
London NW1 3BH

CONTENTS

FIVE ON A TREASURE ISLAND
1

FIVE GO ADVENTURING AGAIN
169

FIVE GO TO BILLYCOCK HILL
339

FIVE ON A TREASURE ISLAND

CONTENTS

1 A GREAT SURPRISE   5
2 THE STRANGE COUSIN   12
3 A PECULIAR STORY – AND A NEW
     FRIEND   21
4 AN EXCITING AFTERNOON   31
5 A VISIT TO THE ISLAND   41
6 WHAT THE STORM DID   52
7 BACK TO KIRRIN COTTAGE   61
8 EXPLORING THE WRECK   69
9 THE BOX FROM THE WRECK   79
10 AN ASTONISHING OFFER   90
11 OFF TO KIRRIN ISLAND   97
12 EXCITING DISCOVERIES   106
13 DOWN IN THE DUNGEONS   117
14 PRISONERS!   127
15 DICK TO THE RESCUE!   135
16 A PLAN – AND A NARROW ESCAPE   144
17 THE END OF THE GREAT ADVENTURE   156

CHAPTER ONE

A great surprise

'MOTHER, HAVE you heard about our summer holidays yet?' said Julian, at the breakfast-table. 'Can we go to Polseath as usual?'

'I'm afraid not,' said his mother. 'They are quite full up this year.'

The three children at the breakfast-table looked at one another in great disappointment. They did so love the house at Polseath. The beach was so lovely there, too, and the bathing was fine.

'Cheer up,' said Daddy. 'I dare say we'll find somewhere else just as good for you. And anyway, Mother and I won't be able to go with you this year. Has Mother told you?'

'No!' said Anne. 'Oh, Mother – is it true? Can't you really come with us on our holidays? You always do.'

'Well, this time Daddy wants me to go to Scotland with him,' said Mother. 'All by ourselves! And as you are really getting big enough to look after yourselves now, we thought it would be rather fun for you to have a holiday on your own too. But now that you can't go to Polseath, I don't really quite know where to send you.'

'What about Quentin's?' suddenly said Daddy. Quentin was his brother, the children's uncle. They had only seen him once, and had been rather frightened of him. He was a very tall, frowning man, a clever scientist who spent all his time studying. He lived by the sea – but that was about all that the children knew of him!

'Quentin?' said Mother, pursing her lips. 'Whatever made you think of him? I shouldn't think he'd want the children messing about in his little house.'

'Well,' said Daddy, 'I had to see Quentin's wife in town the other day, about a business matter – and I don't think things are going too well for them. Fanny said that she would be quite glad if she could hear of one or two people to live with her for a while, to bring a little money in. Their house is by the sea, you know. It might be just the thing for the children. Fanny is very nice – she would look after them well.'

'Yes – and she has a child of her own too, hasn't she?' said the children's mother. 'Let me see – what's her name – something funny – yes, Georgina! How old would she be? About eleven, I should think.'

'Same age as me,' said Dick. 'Fancy having a cousin we've never seen! She must be jolly lonely all by herself. I've got Julian and Anne to play with – but Georgina is just one on her own. I should think she'd be glad to see us.'

'Well, your Aunt Fanny said that her Georgina would love a bit of company,' said Daddy. 'You know, I really think that would solve our difficulty, if we telephone to Fanny and arrange for the children to go there. It would help Fanny, I'm sure, and Georgina would love to have someone to play with in the holidays. And we should know that our three were safe.'

The children began to feel rather excited. It would be fun to go to a place they had never been to before, and stay with an unknown cousin.

'Are there cliffs and rocks and sands there?' asked Anne. 'Is it a nice place?'

'I don't remember it very well,' said Daddy. 'But I feel

6

sure it's an exciting kind of place. Anyway, you'll love it! It's called Kirrin Bay. Your Aunt Fanny has lived there all her life, and wouldn't leave it for anything.'

'Oh Daddy, do telephone to Aunt Fanny and ask her if we can go there!' cried Dick. 'I just feel as if it's the right place somehow. It sounds sort of adventurous!'

'Oh, you always say that, wherever you go!' said Daddy, with a laugh. 'All right – I'll ring up now, and see if there's any chance.'

They had all finished their breakfast, and they got up to wait for Daddy to telephone. He went out into the hall, and they heard him dialling.

'I hope it's all right for us!' said Julian. 'I wonder what Georgina's like. Funny name, isn't it? More like a boy's than a girl's. So she's eleven – a year younger than I am – same age as you, Dick – and a year older than you, Anne. She ought to fit in with us all right. The four of us ought to have a fine time together.'

Daddy came back in about ten minutes' time, and the children knew at once that he had fixed up everything. He smiled round at them.

'Well, that's settled,' he said. 'Your Aunt Fanny is delighted about it. She says it will be awfully good for Georgina to have company, because she's such a lonely little girl, always going off by herself. And she will love looking after you all. Only you'll have to be careful not to disturb your Uncle Quentin. He is working very hard, and he isn't very good-tempered when he is disturbed.'

'We'll be as quiet as mice in the house!' said Dick.

'Honestly we will. Oh, goody, goody – when are we going, Daddy?'

'Next week, if Mother can manage it,' said Daddy.

Mother nodded her head. 'Yes,' she said, 'there's nothing much to get ready for them – just bathing suits and jerseys and jeans. They all wear the same.'

'How lovely it will be to wear jeans again,' said Anne, dancing round. 'I'm tired of wearing school tunics. I want to wear shorts, or a bathing suit, and go bathing and climbing with the boys.'

'Well, you'll soon be doing it,' said Mother, with a laugh. 'Remember to put ready any toys or books you want, won't you? Not many, please, because there won't be a great deal of room.'

'Anne wanted to take all her fifteen dolls with her last year,' said Dick. 'Do you remember, Anne? Weren't you funny?'

'No, I wasn't,' said Anne, going red. 'I love my dolls, and I just couldn't choose which to take – so I thought I'd take them all. There's nothing funny about that.'

And do you remember the year before, Anne wanted to take the rocking-horse?' said Dick, with a giggle.

Mother chimed in. 'You know, I remember a little boy called Dick who put aside one teddy bear, three toy dogs, two toy cats and his old monkey to take down to Polseath one year,' she said.

Then it was Dick's turn to go red. He changed the subject at once.

'Daddy, are we going by train or by car?' he asked.

'By car,' said Daddy. 'We can pile everything into the boot. Well – what about Tuesday?'

'That would suit me well,' said Mother. 'Then we could take the children down, come back, and do our own packing at leisure, and start off for Scotland on the Friday. Yes – we'll arrange for Tuesday.'

8

A GREAT SURPRISE

So Tuesday it was. The children counted the days eagerly, and Anne marked one off the calendar each night. The week seemed a very long time in going. But at last Tuesday did come. Dick and Julian, who shared a room, woke up at about the same moment, and stared out of the nearby window.

'It's a lovely day, hurrah!' cried Julian, leaping out of bed. 'I don't know why, but it always seems very important that it should be sunny on the first day of a holiday. Let's wake Anne.'

Anne slept in the next room. Julian ran in and shook her. 'Wake up! It's Tuesday! And the sun's shining.'

Anne woke up with a jump and stared at Julian joyfully. 'It's come at last!' she said. 'I thought it never would. Oh, isn't it an exciting feeling to go away for a holiday!'

They started soon after breakfast. Their car was a big one, so it held them all very comfortably. Mother sat in front with Daddy, and the three children sat behind, their feet on two suitcases. In the luggage-place at the back of the car were all kinds of odds and ends, and one small trunk. Mother really thought they had remembered everything.

Along the crowded London roads they went, slowly at first, and then, as they left the town behind, more quickly. Soon they were right into the open country, and the car sped along fast. The children sang songs to themselves, as they always did when they were happy.

'Are we picnicking soon?' asked Anne, feeling hungry all of a sudden.

'Yes,' said Mother. 'But not yet. It's only eleven o'clock. We shan't have lunch till at least half-past twelve, Anne.'

'Oh, gracious!' said Anne. 'I know I can't last out till then!'

So her mother handed her some chocolate, and she and the boys munched happily, watching the hills, woods and fields as the car sped by.

The picnic was lovely. They had it on the top of a hill, in a sloping field that looked down into a sunny valley. Anne didn't very much like a big brown cow which came up close and stared at her, but it went away when Daddy told it to. The children ate enormously, and Mother said that instead of having a tea-picnic at half-past four they would have to go to a tea-house somewhere, because they had eaten all the tea sandwiches as well as the lunch ones!

'What time shall we be at Aunt Fanny's?' asked Julian, finishing up the very last sandwich and wishing there were more.

'About six o'clock with luck,' said Daddy. 'Now who wants to stretch their legs a bit? We've another long spell in the car, you know.'

The car seemed to eat up the miles as it purred along. Tea-time came, and then the three children began to feel excited all over again.

'We must watch out for the sea,' said Dick. 'I can smell it somewhere near!'

He was right. The car suddenly topped a hill – and there was the shining blue sea, calm and smooth in the evening sun. The three children gave a yell.

'There it is!'

'Isn't it marvellous!'

'Oh, I want to bathe this very minute!'

'We shan't be more than twenty minutes now, before we're at Kirrin Bay,' said Daddy. 'We've made good time. You'll see the bay soon – it's quite a big one – with a funny sort of island at the entrance of the bay.'

A GREAT SURPRISE

The children looked out for it as they drove along the coast. Then Julian gave a shout.

'There it is – that must be Kirrin Bay. Look, Dick – isn't it lovely and blue?'

'And look at the rocky little island guarding the entrance of the bay,' said Dick. 'I'd like to visit that.'

'Well, I've no doubt you will,' said Mother. 'Now, let's look out for Aunt Fanny's house. It's called Kirrin Cottage.'

They soon came to it. It stood on the low cliff overlooking the bay, and was a very old house indeed. It wasn't really a cottage, but quite a big house, built of old white stone. Roses climbed over the front of it, and the garden was full of flowers.

'Here's Kirrin Cottage,' said Daddy, and he stopped the car in front of it. 'It's supposed to be about three hundred years old! Now – where's Quentin? Hallo, there's Fanny!'

11

CHAPTER TWO

The strange cousin

THE CHILDREN'S aunt had been watching for the car. She came running out of the old wooden door as soon as she saw it draw up outside. The children liked the look of her at once.

'Welcome to Kirrin!' she cried. 'Hallo, all of you! It's lovely to see you. And what big children!'

There were kisses all round, and then the children went into the house. They liked it. It felt old and rather mysterious somehow, and the furniture was old and very beautiful.

'Where's Georgina?' asked Anne, looking round for her unknown cousin.

'Oh, the naughty girl! I told her to wait in the garden for you,' said her aunt. 'Now she's gone off somewhere. I must tell you, children, you may find George a bit difficult at first – she's always been one on her own, you know, and at first may not like you being here. But you mustn't take any notice of that – she'll be all right in a short time. I was very glad for George's sake that you were able to come. She badly needs other children to play with.'

'Do you call her "George"?' asked Anne, in surprise. 'I thought her name was Georgina.'

'So it is,' said her aunt. 'But George hates being a girl, and we have to call her George, as if she were a boy. The naughty girl won't answer if we call her Georgina.'

The children thought that Georgina sounded rather

12

exciting. They wished she would come. But she didn't. Their Uncle Quentin suddenly appeared instead. He was a most extraordinary looking man, very tall, very dark, and with a rather fierce frown on his wide forehead.

'Hallo, Quentin!' said Daddy. 'It's a long time since I've seen you. I hope these three won't disturb you very much in your work.'

'Quentin is working on a very difficult book,' said Aunt Fanny. 'But I've given him a room all to himself on the other side of the house. So I don't expect he will be disturbed.'

Their uncle looked at the three children, and nodded to them. The frown didn't come off his face, and they all felt a little scared, and were glad that he was to work in another part of the house.

'Where's George?' he said, in a deep voice.

'Gone off somewhere again,' said Aunt Fanny, vexed. 'I told her she was to stay here and meet her cousins.'

'She wants a good talking to,' said Uncle Quentin. The children couldn't quite make out whether he was joking or not. 'Well, children, I hope you have a good time here, and maybe will knock a little common-sense into George!'

There was no room at Kirrin Cottage for Mother and Daddy to stay the night, so after a hurried supper they left to stay at a hotel in the nearest town. They would drive back to London immediately after breakfast the next day. So they said good-bye to the children that night.

Georgina still hadn't appeared. 'I'm sorry we haven't seen Georgina,' said Mother. 'Just give her our love and tell her we hope she'll enjoy playing with Dick, Julian and Anne.'

Then Mother and Daddy went. The children felt a little

bit lonely as they saw the big car disappear round the corner of the road, but Aunt Fanny took them upstairs to show them their bedrooms, and they soon forgot to be sad.

The two boys were to sleep together in a room with slanting ceilings at the top of the house. It had a marvellous view of the bay. The boys were really delighted with it. Anne was to sleep with Georgina in a smaller room, whose windows looked over the moors at the back of the house. But one side-window looked over the sea, which pleased Anne very much. It was a nice room, and red roses nodded their heads in at the window.

'I do wish Georgina would come,' Anne said to her aunt. 'I want to see what she's like.'

'Well, she's a funny little girl,' said her aunt. 'She can be very rude and haughty – but she's kind at heart, very loyal and absolutely truthful. Once she makes friends with you, she will always be your friend – but she finds it very difficult indeed to make friends, which is a great pity.'

Anne suddenly yawned. The boys frowned at her, because they knew what would happen next. And it did!

'Poor Anne! How tired you are! You must all go to bed straight away, and have a good night. Then you will wake up quite fresh tomorrow,' said Aunt Fanny.

'Anne, you *are* an idiot,' said Dick, crossly, when his aunt had gone out of the room. 'You know quite well what grown-ups think as soon as we yawn. I did want to go down on the beach for a while.'

'I'm so sorry,' said Anne. 'Somehow I couldn't help it. And anyway, *you're* yawning now, Dick – and Julian too!'

So they were. They were as sleepy as could be with their long drive. Secretly all of them longed to cuddle down into bed and shut their eyes.

'I wonder where Georgina is,' said Anne, when she said good-night to the boys, and went to her own room. 'Isn't she odd – not waiting to welcome us – and not coming in to supper – and not even in yet! After all, she's sleeping in my room – goodness knows what time she'll be in!'

All the three children were fast asleep before Georgina came up to bed! They didn't hear her open Anne's door. They didn't hear her get undressed and clean her teeth. They didn't hear the creak of her bed as she got into it. They were so tired that they heard nothing at all until the sun awoke them in the morning.

When Anne awoke she couldn't at first think where she was. She lay in her little bed and looked up at the slanting ceiling, and at the red roses that nodded at the open window – and suddenly remembered all in a rush where she was! 'I'm at Kirrin Bay – and it's the holidays!' she said to herself, and screwed up her legs with joy.

Then she looked across at the other bed. In it lay the figure of another child, curled up under the bed-clothes. Anne could just see the top of a curly head, and that was all. When the figure stirred a little, Anne spoke.

'I say! Are you Georgina?'

The child in the opposite bed sat up and looked across at Anne. She had very short curly hair, almost as short as a boy's. Her face was burnt a dark-brown with the sun, and her very blue eyes looked as bright as forget-me-nots in her face. But her mouth was rather sulky, and she had a frown like her father's.

'No,' she said. 'I'm not Georgina.'

'Oh!' said Anne, in surprise. 'Then who are you?'

'I'm George,' said the girl. 'I shall only answer if you call me George. I hate being a girl. I won't be. I don't like

15

doing the things that girls do. I like doing the things that boys do. I can climb better than any boy, and swim faster too. I can sail a boat as well as any fisher-boy on this coast. You're to call me George. Then I'll speak to you. But I shan't if you don't.'

'Oh!' said Anne, thinking that her new cousin was most extraordinary. 'All right! I don't care what I call you. George is a nice name, I think. I don't much like Georgina. Anyway, you look like a boy.'

'Do I really?' said George, the frown leaving her face for a moment. 'Mother was awfully cross with me when I cut my hair short. I had hair all round my neck; it was awful.'

The two girls stared at one another for a moment. 'Don't you simply hate being a girl?' asked George.

'No, of course not,' said Anne. 'You see – I do like pretty frocks – and I love my dolls – and you can't do that if you're a boy.'

'Pooh! Fancy bothering about pretty frocks,' said George, in a scornful voice. 'And dolls! Well, you *are* a baby, that's all I can say.'

Anne felt offended. 'You're not very polite,' she said. 'You won't find that my brothers take much notice of you if you act as if you know everything. They're *real* boys, not pretend boys, like you.'

'Well, if they're going to be nasty to me I shan't take any notice of *them*,' said George, jumping out of bed. 'I didn't want any of you to come, anyway. Interfering with my life here! I'm quite happy on my own. Now I've got to put up with a silly girl who likes frocks and dolls, and two stupid boy-cousins!'

Anne felt that they had made a very bad beginning. She said no more, but got dressed herself too. She put on her grey jeans and a red jersey. George put on jeans too, and a boy's jersey. Just as they were ready the boys hammered on their door.

'Aren't you ready? Is Georgina there? Cousin Georgina, come out and see us.'

George flung open the door and marched out with her head high. She took no notice of the two surprised boys at all. She stalked downstairs. The other three children looked at one another.

'She won't answer if you call her Georgina,' explained Anne. 'She's awfully funny, I think. She says she didn't want us to come because we'll interfere with her. She laughed at me, and was rather rude.'

Julian put his arm round Anne, who looked a bit doleful. 'Cheer up!' he said. 'You've got us to stick up for you. Come on down to breakfast.'

They were all hungry. The smell of bacon and eggs was very good. They ran down the stairs and said good-morning to their aunt. She was just bringing the breakfast to the table. Their uncle was sitting at the head, reading his paper. He nodded at the children. They sat down without a word, wondering if they were allowed to speak at meals. They always were at home, but their Uncle Quentin looked rather fierce.

George was there, buttering a piece of toast. She scowled at the three children.

'Don't look like that, George,' said her mother. 'I hope you've made friends already. It will be fun for you to play together. You must take your cousins to see the bay this morning and show them the best places to bathe.'

'I'm going fishing,' said George.

Her father looked up at once.

'You are not,' he said. 'You are going to show a few good manners for a change, and take your cousins to the bay. Do you hear me?'

'Yes,' said George, with a scowl exactly like her father's.

'Oh, we can go to the bay by ourselves all right, if George is going fishing,' said Anne, at once, thinking that it would be nice not to have George if she was in a bad temper.

'George will do exactly as she's told,' said her father. 'If she doesn't, I shall deal with her.'

So, after breakfast, four children got ready to go down to the beach. An easy path led down to the bay, and they ran down happily. Even George lost her frown as she felt the warmth of the sun and saw the dancing sparkles on the blue sea.

'You go fishing if you want to,' said Anne when they were down on the beach. 'We won't tell tales on you. We don't want to interfere with you, you know. We've got ourselves for company, and if you don't want to be with us, you needn't.'

'But we'd like you, all the same, if you'd like to be with us,' said Julian, generously. He thought George was rude and ill-mannered, but he couldn't help rather liking the look of the straight-backed, short-haired little girl, with her brilliant blue eyes and sulky mouth.

George stared at him. 'I'll see,' she said. 'I don't make friends with people just because they're my cousins, or something silly like that. I only make friends with people if I like them.'

'So do we,' said Julian. 'We may not like *you*, of course.'

'Oh!' said George, as if that thought hadn't occurred to her. 'Well – you may not, of course. Lots of people don't like me, now I come to think of it.'

Anne was staring out over the blue bay. At the entrance to it lay a curious rocky island with what looked like an old ruined castle on the top of it.

'Isn't that a funny place?' she said. 'I wonder what it's called.'

'It's called Kirrin Island,' said George, her eyes as blue as the sea as she turned to look at it. 'It's a lovely place to

19

go to. If I like you, I may take you there some day. But I don't promise. The only way to get there is by boat.'

'Who does the funny island belong to?' asked Julian.

George made a most surprising answer. 'It belongs to *me*,' she said. 'At least, it *will* belong to me – some day! It will be my very own island – and my very own castle!'

CHAPTER THREE

A peculiar story – and a new friend

THE THREE children stared at George in the greatest surprise.

George stared back at them.

'What do you mean?' said Dick, at last. 'Kirrin Island can't belong to you. You're just boasting.'

'No, I'm not,' said George. 'You ask Mother. If you're not going to believe what I say I won't tell you another word more. But I don't tell untruths. I think it's being a coward if you don't tell the truth – and I'm not a coward.'

Julian remembered that Aunt Fanny had said that George was absolutely truthful, and he scratched his head and looked at George again. How could she be possibly telling the truth?

'Well, of course we'll believe you if you tell us the truth,' he said. 'But it does sound a bit extraordinary, you know. Really, it does. Children don't usually own islands, even funny little ones like that.'

'It *isn't* a funny little island,' said George, fiercely. 'It's lovely. There are rabbits there, as tame as can be – and the big cormorants sit on the other side – and all kinds of gulls go there. The castle is wonderful too, even if it *is* all in ruins.'

'It sounds fine,' said Dick. 'How does it belong to you, Georgina?'

George glared at him and didn't answer.

21

'Sorry,' said Dick, hastily. 'I didn't mean to call you Georgina. I meant to call you George.'

'Go on, George – tell us how the island belongs to you,' said Julian, slipping his arm through his sulky little cousin's.

She pulled away from him at once.

'Don't do that,' she said. 'I'm not sure that I want to make friends with you yet.'

'All right, all right,' said Julian, losing patience. 'Be enemies or anything you like. We don't care. But we like your mother awfully, and we don't want her to think we won't make friends with you.'

'Do you like my mother?' said George, her bright blue eyes softening a little. 'Yes – she's a dear, isn't she? Well – all right – I'll tell you how Kirrin Castle belongs to me. Come and sit down here in this corner where nobody can hear us.'

They all sat down in a sandy corner of the beach. George looked across at the little island in the bay.

'It's like this,' she said. 'Years ago my mother's family owned nearly all the land around here. Then they got poor, and had to sell most of it. But they could never sell that little island, because nobody thought it worth anything, especially as the castle has been ruined for years.'

'Fancy nobody wanting to buy a dear little island like that!' said Dick. 'I'd buy it at once if I had the money.'

'All that's left of what Mother's family owned is our own house, Kirrin Cottage, and a farm a little way off – and Kirrin Island,' said George. 'Mother says when I'm grown-up it will be mine. She says she doesn't want it now,

22

either, so she's sort of given it to me. It belongs to me. It's my own private island, and I don't let anyone go there unless they get my permission.'

The three children stared at her. They believed every word George said, for it was quite plain that the girl was speaking the truth. Fancy having an island of your very own! They thought she was very lucky indeed.

'Oh, Georgina – I mean George!' said Dick. 'I do think you're lucky. It looks such a nice island. I hope you'll be friends with us and take us there one day soon. You simply can't imagine how we'd love it.'

'Well – I might,' said George, pleased at the interest she had caused. 'I'll see. I never have taken anyone there yet, though some of the boys and girls round here have begged me to. But I don't like them, so I haven't.'

There was a little silence as the four children looked out over the bay to where the island lay in the distance. The tide was going out. It almost looked as if they could wade over to the island. Dick asked if it was possible.

'No,' said George. 'I told you – it's only possible to get to it by boat. It's farther out than it looks – and the water is very, very deep. There are rocks all about too – you have to know exactly where to row a boat, or you bump into them. It's a dangerous bit of coast here. There are a lot of wrecks about.'

'Wrecks!' cried Julian, his eyes shining. 'I say! I've never seen an old wreck. Are there any to see?'

'Not now,' said George. 'They've all been cleared up. Except one, and that's the other side of the island. It's deep down in the water. You can just see the broken mast if you row over it on a calm day and look down into the water. That wreck really belongs to me too.'

This time the children really could hardly believe George. But she nodded her head firmly.

'Yes,' she said, 'it was a ship belonging to one of my great-great-great-grandfathers, or someone like that. He was bringing gold – big bars of gold – back in his ship – and it got wrecked off Kirrin Island.'

'Oooh – what happened to the gold?' asked Anne, her eyes round and big.

'Nobody knows,' said George. 'I expect it was stolen out of the ship. Divers have been down to see, of course, but they couldn't find any gold.'

'Golly – this does sound exciting,' said Julian. 'I wish I could see the wreck.'

'Well – we might perhaps go this afternoon when the tide is right down,' said George. 'The water is so calm and clear today. We could see a bit of it.'

'Oh, how wonderful!' said Anne. 'I do so want to see a real live wreck!'

The others laughed. 'Well, it won't be very alive,' said Dick. 'I say, George – what about a bathe?'

'I must go and get Timothy first,' said George. She got up.

'Who's Timothy?' said Dick.

'Can you keep a secret?' asked George. 'Nobody must know at home.'

'Well, go on, what's the secret?' asked Julian. 'You can tell us. We're not sneaks.'

'Timothy is my very greatest friend,' said George. 'I couldn't do without him. But Mother and Father don't like him, so I have to keep him in secret. I'll go and fetch him.'

She ran off up the cliff path. The others watched her go.

They thought she was the most peculiar girl they had ever known.

'Who in the world can Timothy be?' wondered Julian. 'Some fisher-boy, I suppose, that George's parents don't approve of.'

The children lay back in the soft sand and waited. Soon they heard George's clear voice coming down from the cliff behind them.

'Come on, Timothy! Come on!'

They sat up and looked to see what Timothy was like. They saw no fisher-boy – but instead a big brown mongrel dog with an absurdly long tail and a big wide mouth that really seemed to grin! He was bounding all round George, mad with delight. She came running down to them.

'This is Timothy,' she said. 'Don't you think he is simply perfect?'

As a dog, Timothy was far from perfect. He was the wrong shape, his head was too big, his ears were too pricked, his tail was too long and it was quite impossible to say what kind of a dog he was supposed to be. But he was such a mad, friendly, clumsy, laughable creature that every one of the children adored him at once.

'Oh, you darling!' said Anne, and got a lick on the nose.

'I say – isn't he grand!' said Dick, and gave Timothy a friendly smack that made the dog bound madly all round him.

'I wish *I* had a dog like this,' said Julian, who really loved dogs, and had always wanted one of his own. 'Oh, George – he's fine. Aren't you proud of him?'

The little girl smiled, and her face altered at once, and became sunny and pretty. She sat down on the sand and her dog cuddled up to her, licking her wherever he could find a bare piece of skin.

'I love him awfully,' she said. 'I found him out on the moors when he was just a pup, a year ago, and I took him home. At first Mother liked him, but when he grew bigger he got terribly naughty.'

'What did he do?' asked Anne.

'Well, he's an awfully chewy kind of dog,' said George. 'He chewed up everything he could – a new rug Mother had bought – her nicest hat – Father's slippers – some of his papers, and things like that. And he barked too. I liked his bark, but Father didn't. He said it nearly drove him mad. He hit Timothy and that made me angry, so I was awfully rude to him.'

'Did you get told off?' said Anne. 'I wouldn't like to be rude to your father. He looks fierce.'

George looked out over the bay. Her face had gone sulky again. 'Well, it doesn't matter what punishment I got,' she said, 'but the worst part of all was when Father said I couldn't keep Timothy any more, and Mother backed Father up and said Tim must go. I cried for days – and I never do cry, you know, because boys don't and I like to be like a boy.'

'Boys do cry sometimes,' began Anne, looking at Dick, who had been a bit of a cry-baby three or four years back. Dick gave her a sharp nudge, and she said no more.

George looked at Anne.

'Boys don't cry,' she said, obstinately. 'Anyway, I've never seen one, and I always try not to cry myself. It's so babyish. But I just couldn't help it when Timothy had to go. He cried too.'

The children looked with great respect at Timothy. They had not known that a dog could cry before.

'Do you mean – he cried real tears?' asked Anne.

'No, not quite,' said George. 'He's too brave for that. He cried with his voice – howled and howled and looked so miserable that he nearly broke my heart. And then I knew I couldn't possibly part with him.'

'What happened then?' asked Julian.

'I went to Alf, a fisher-boy I know,' said George, 'and I asked him if he'd keep Tim for me, if I paid him all the pocket-money I get. He said he would, and so he does.

That's why I never have any money to spend – it all has to go on Tim. He seems to eat an awful lot – don't you, Tim?'

'Woof!' said Tim, and rolled over on his back, all his shaggy legs in the air. Julian tickled him.

'How do you manage when you want any sweets or ice-creams?' said Anne, who spent most of her pocket-money on things of that sort.

'I don't manage,' said George. 'I go without, of course.'

This sounded awful to the other children, who loved ice-creams, chocolates and sweets, and had a good many of them. They stared at George.

'Well – I suppose the other children who play on the beach share their sweets and ices with you sometimes, don't they?' asked Julian.

'I don't let them,' said George. 'If I can never give them any myself it's not fair to take them. So I say no.'

The tinkle of an ice-cream man's bell was heard in the distance. Julian felt in his pocket. He jumped up and rushed off, jingling his money. In a few moments he was back again, carrying four fat chocolate ice-cream bars. He gave one to Dick, and one to Anne, and then held out one to George. She looked at it longingly, but shook her head.

'No, thanks,' she said. 'You know what I just said. I haven't any money to buy them, so I can't share mine with you, and I can't take any from you. It's mean to take from people if you can't give even a little back.'

'You can take from us,' said Julian, trying to put the ice into George's brown hand. 'We're your cousins.'

'No, thanks,' said George again. 'Though I do think it's nice of you.'

She looked at Julian out of her blue eyes and the boy

28

frowned as he tried to think of a way to make the obstinate little girl take the ice. Then he smiled.

'Listen,' he said, 'you've got something we badly want to share – in fact you've got a lot of things we'd like to share, if only you'd let us. You share those with us, and let us share things like ices with you. See?'

'What things have I got that you want to share?' asked George, in surprise.

'You've got a dog,' said Julian, patting the big brown mongrel. 'We'd love to share him with you, he's such a darling. And you've got a lovely island. We'd be simply thrilled if you'd share it sometimes. And you've got a wreck. We'd like to look at it and share it too. Ices and sweets aren't so good as those things – but it would be nice to make a bargain and share with each other.'

George looked at the brown eyes that gazed steadily into hers. She couldn't help liking Julian. It wasn't her nature to share anything. She had always been an only child, a lonely, rather misunderstood little girl, fierce and hot-tempered. She had never had any friends of her own. Timothy looked up at Julian and saw that he was offering something nice and chocolatey to George. He jumped up and licked the boy with his friendly tongue.

'There you are, you see – Tim wants to be shared,' said Julian, with a laugh. 'It would be nice for him to have three new friends.'

'Yes – it would,' said George, giving in suddenly, and taking the chocolate bar. 'Thank you, Julian. I will share with you. But promise you'll never tell anyone at home that I'm still keeping Timothy?'

'Of course we'll promise,' said Julian. 'But I can't imagine that your father or mother would mind, so long

29

as Tim doesn't live in their house. How's the ice? Is it nice?'

'Ooooh – the loveliest one I've ever tasted!' said George nibbling at it. 'It's so cold. I haven't had one this year. It's simply DELICIOUS!'

Timothy tried to nibble it too. George gave him a few crumbs at the end. Then she turned and smiled at the three children.

'You're nice,' she said. 'I'm glad you've come after all. Let's take a boat out this afternoon and row round the island to have a look at the wreck, shall we?'

'Rather!' said all three at once – and even Timothy wagged his tail as if he understood!

CHAPTER FOUR

An exciting afternoon

THEY ALL had a bathe that morning, and the boys found that George was a much better swimmer than they were. She was very strong and very fast, and she could swim under water, too, holding her breath for ages.

'You're jolly good,' said Julian, admiringly. 'It's a pity Anne isn't a bit better. Anne, you'll have to practise your swimming strokes hard, or you'll never be able to swim out as far as we do.'

They were all very hungry at lunch-time. They went back up the cliff-path, hoping there would be lots to eat – and there was! Cold meat and salad, plum-pie and custard, and cheese afterwards. How the children tucked in!

'What are you going to do this afternoon?' asked George's mother.

'George is going to take us out in a boat to see the wreck on the other side of the island,' said Anne. Her aunt looked most surprised.

'*George* is going to take you!' she said. 'Why, George – what's come over you? You've never taken a single person before, though I've asked you to dozens of times!'

George said nothing, but went on eating her plum-pie. She hadn't said a word all through the meal. Her father had not appeared at the table, much to the children's relief.

'Well, George, I must say I'm pleased that you want to try and do what your father said,' began her mother again. But George shook her head.

31

'I'm not doing it because I've got to,' she said. 'I'm doing it because I want to. I wouldn't have taken anyone to see my wreck, not even the Queen of England, if I didn't like them.'

Her mother laughed. 'Well, it's good news that you like your cousins,' she said. 'I hope they like you!'

'Oh yes!' said Anne, eagerly, anxious to stick up for her strange cousin. 'We do like George – and we like Ti . . .'

She was just about to say that they liked Timothy too, when she got such a kick on her ankle that she cried out in pain and the tears came into her eyes. George glared at her.

'George! Why did you kick Anne like that when she was saying nice things about you?' cried her mother. 'Leave the table at once. I won't have such behaviour.'

George left the table without a word. She went out into the garden. She had just taken a piece of bread and cut herself some cheese. It was all left on her plate. The other three stared at it in distress. Anne was upset. How could she have been so silly as to forget she mustn't mention Tim?

'Oh, please call George back!' she said. 'She didn't mean to kick me. It was an accident.'

But her aunt was very angry with George. 'Finish your meal,' she said to the others. 'I expect George will go into a sulk now. Dear, dear, she *is* such a difficult child!'

The others didn't mind about George going into a sulk. What they did mind was that George might refuse to take them to see the wreck now!

They finished the meal in silence. Their aunt went to see if Uncle Quentin wanted any more pie. He was having his meal in the study by himself. As soon as she had gone out of the room, Anne picked up the bread and cheese from George's plate and went out into the garden.

The boys didn't scold her. They knew that Anne's tongue very often ran away with her – but she always tried to make up for it afterwards. They thought it was very brave of her to go and find George.

George was lying on her back under a big tree in the garden. Anne went up to her. 'I'm sorry I nearly made a mistake, George,' she said. 'Here's your bread and cheese. I've brought it for you. I promise I'll never forget not to mention Tim again.'

George sat up. 'I've a good mind not to take you to see the wreck,' she said. 'Stupid baby!'

Anne's heart sank. This was what she had feared. 'Well,' she said, 'you needn't take me, of course. But you might take the boys, George. After all, they didn't do anything silly. And anyway, you gave me an awful kick. Look at the bruise.'

George looked at it. Then she looked at Anne. 'But wouldn't you be miserable if I took Julian and Dick without you?' she asked.

'Of course,' said Anne. 'But I don't want to make them miss a treat, even if *I* have to.'

Then George did a surprising thing for her. She gave Anne a hug! Then she immediately looked most ashamed of herself, for she felt sure that no boy would have done that! And she always tried to act like a boy.

'It's all right,' she said, gruffly, taking the bread and cheese. 'You were nearly very silly – and I gave you a kick – so it's all square. Of course you can come this afternoon.'

Anne sped back to tell the boys that everything was all right – and in fifteen minutes' time four children ran down to the beach. By a boat was a brown-faced fisher-boy, about fourteen years old. He had Timothy with him.

'Boat's all ready, George,' he said with a grin. 'And Tim's ready, too.'

'Thanks,' said George, and told the others to get in. Timothy jumped in, too, his big tail wagging nineteen to the dozen. George pushed the boat off into the surf and then jumped in herself. She took the oars.

She rowed splendidly, and the boat shot along over the

blue bay. It was a wonderful afternoon, and the children loved the movement of the boat over the water. Timothy stood at the prow and barked whenever a wave reared its head.

'He's funny on a wild day,' said George, pulling hard. 'He barks madly at the big waves, and gets so angry if they splash him. He's an awfully good swimmer.'

'Isn't it nice to have a dog with us?' said Anne, anxious to make up for her mistake. 'I do so like him.'

'Woof,' said Timothy, in his deep voice and turned round to lick Anne's ear.

'I'm sure he knew what I said,' said Anne in delight.

'Of course he did,' said George. 'He understands every single word.'

'I say – we're getting near to your island now,' said Julian, in excitement. 'It's bigger than I thought. And isn't the castle exciting?'

They drew near to the island, and the children saw that there were sharp rocks all round about it. Unless anyone knew exactly the way to take, no boat or ship could possibly land on the shore of the rocky little island. In the very middle of it, on a low hill, rose the ruined castle. It had been built of big white stones. Broken archways, tumbledown towers, ruined walls – that was all that was left of a once beautiful castle, proud and strong. Now the jackdaws nested in it and the gulls sat on the topmost stones.

'It looks awfully mysterious,' said Julian. 'How I'd love to land there and have a look at the castle. Wouldn't it be fun to spend a night or two here!'

George stopped rowing. Her face lit up. 'I say!' she said, in delight. 'Do you know, I never thought how lovely that would be! To spend a night on my island! To be there all alone, the four of us. To get our own meals, and pretend we really lived there. Wouldn't it be grand?'

'Yes, rather,' said Dick, looking longingly at the island. 'Do you think – do you suppose your mother would let us?'

'I don't know,' said George. 'She might. You could ask her.'

'Can't we land there this afternoon?' asked Julian.

'No, not if you want to see the wreck,' said George. 'We've got to get back for tea today, and it will take all the time to row round to the other side of Kirrin Island and back.'

'Well – I'd like to see the wreck,' said Julian, torn between the island and the wreck. 'Here, let me take the oars for a bit, George. You can't do all the rowing.'

'I can,' said George. 'But I'd quite enjoy lying back in the boat for a change! Look – I'll just take you by this rocky bit – and then you can take the oars till we come to another awkward piece. Honestly, the rocks around this bay are simply dreadful!'

George and Julian changed places in the boat. Julian rowed well, but not so strongly as George. The boat sped along rocking smoothly. They went right round the island, and saw the castle from the other side. It looked more ruined on the side that faced the sea.

'The strong winds come from the open sea,' explained George. 'There's not really much left of it this side, except piles of stones. But there's a good little harbour in a little cove, for those who know how to find it.'

George took the oars after a while, and rowed steadily out a little beyond the island. Then she stopped and looked back towards the shore.

'How do you know when you are over the wreck?' asked Julian, puzzled. 'I should never know!'

'Well, do you see that church tower on the mainland?' asked George. 'And do you see the tip of that hill over there? Well, when you get them exactly in line with one another, between the two towers of the castle on the island, you are pretty well over the wreck! I found that out ages ago.'

The children saw that the tip of the far-off hill and the church tower were practically in line, when they looked at them between the two old towers of the island castle. They looked eagerly down into the sea to see if they could spy the wreck.

The water was perfectly clear and smooth. There was hardly a wrinkle. Timothy looked down into it too, his head on one side, his ears cocked, just as if he knew what he was looking for! The children laughed at him.

'We're not exactly over it,' said George, looking down too. 'The water's so clear today that we should be able to see quite a long way down. Wait, I'll row a bit to the left.'

'Woof!' said Timothy, suddenly, and wagged his tail – and at the same moment the three children saw something deep down in the water!

'It's the wreck!' said Julian, almost falling out of the boat in his excitement. 'I can see a bit of broken mast. Look, Dick, look!'

All four children and the dog, too, gazed down earnestly into the clear water. After a little while they could make out the outlines of a dark hulk, out of which the broken mast stood.

'It's a bit on one side,' said Julian. 'Poor old ship. How it must hate lying there, gradually falling to pieces.

George, I wish I could dive down and get a closer look at it.'

'Well, why don't you?' said George. 'You've got your swimming trunks on. I've often dived down. I'll come with you, if you like, if Dick can keep the boat round about here. There's a current that is trying to take it out to sea. Dick, you'll have to keep working a bit with this oar to keep the boat in one spot.'

The girl stripped off her jeans and jersey and Julian did the same. They both had on bathing costumes underneath. George took a beautiful header off the end of the boat, deep down into the water. The others watched her swimming strongly downwards, holding her breath.

After a bit she came up, almost bursting for breath. 'Well, I went almost down to the wreck,' she said. 'It's just the same as it always is – seaweedy and covered with limpets and things. I wish I could get right into the ship itself. But I never have enough breath for that. You go down now, Julian.'

So down Julian went – but he was not so good at swimming deep under water as George was, and he couldn't go down so far. He knew how to open his eyes under water, so he was able to take a good look at the deck of the wreck. It looked very forlorn and strange. Julian didn't really like it very much. It gave him rather a sad sort of feeling. He was glad to go to the top of the water again, and take deep breaths of air, and feel the warm sunshine on his shoulders.

He climbed into the boat. 'Most exciting,' he said. 'Golly, wouldn't I just love to see that wreck properly – you know – go down under the deck into the cabins and look around. And oh, suppose we could really find the boxes of gold!'

'That's impossible,' said George. 'I told you proper divers have already gone down and found nothing. What's the time? I say, we'll be late if we don't hurry back now!'

They did hurry back, and managed to be only about five minutes late for tea. Afterwards they went for a walk over the moors, with Timothy at their heels, and by the time that bedtime came they were all so sleepy that they could hardly keep their eyes open.

'Well, good-night, George,' said Anne, snuggling down into her bed. 'We've had a lovely day – thanks to you!'

'And *I've* had a lovely day, too,' said George, rather gruffly. 'Thanks to *you*. I'm glad you all came. We're going to have fun. And won't you love my castle and my little island!'

'Oooh, yes,' said Anne, and fell asleep to dream of wrecks and castles and islands by the hundred. Oh, when would George take them to her little island?

CHAPTER FIVE

A visit to the island

THE CHILDREN'S aunt arranged a picnic for them the next day, and they all went off to a little cove not far off where they could bathe and paddle to their hearts' content. They had a wonderful day, but secretly Julian, Dick and Anne wished they could have visited George's island. They would rather have done that than anything!

George didn't want to go for the picnic, not because she disliked picnics, but because she couldn't take her dog. Her mother went with the children, and George had to pass a whole day without her beloved Timothy.

'Bad luck!' said Julian, who guessed what she was brooding about. 'I can't think why you don't tell your mother about old Tim. I'm sure she wouldn't mind you letting someone else keep him for you. I know my mother wouldn't mind.'

'I'm not going to tell anybody but you,' said George. 'I get into awful trouble at home always. I dare say it's my fault, but I get a bit tired of it. You see, Daddy doesn't make much money with the learned books he writes, and he's always wanting to give mother and me things he can't afford. So that makes him bad-tempered. He wants to send me away to a good school but he hasn't got the money. I'm glad. I don't want to go away to school. I like being here. I couldn't bear to part with Timothy.'

'You'd like boarding school,' said Anne. 'We all go. It's fun.'

'No, it isn't,' said George obstinately. 'It must be awful to be one of a crowd, and to have other girls all laughing and yelling round you. I should hate it.'

'No, you wouldn't,' said Anne. 'All that is great fun. It would be good for you, George, I should think.'

'If you start telling me what is good for me, I shall hate you,' said George, suddenly looking very fierce. 'Mother and Father are always saying that things are good for me – and they are always the things I don't like.'

'All right, all right,' said Julian, beginning to laugh. 'My goodness, how you do go up in smoke! Honestly, I believe anyone could light a cigarette from the sparks that fly from your eyes!'

That made George laugh, though she didn't want to. It was really impossible to sulk with good-tempered Julian.

They went off to bathe in the sea for the fifth time that day. Soon they were all splashing about happily, and George found time to help Anne to swim. The little girl hadn't got the right stroke, and George felt really proud when she had taught her.

'Oh, thanks,' said Anne, struggling along. 'I'll never be as good as you – but I'd like to be as good as the boys.'

As they were going home, George spoke to Julian. 'Could you say that you want to go and buy a stamp or something?' she said. 'Then I could go with you, and just have a peep at old Tim. He'll be wondering why I haven't taken him out today.'

'Right!' said Julian. 'I don't want stamps, but I *could* do with an ice. Dick and Anne can go home with your mother and carry the things. I'll just go and tell Aunt Fanny.'

He ran up to his aunt. 'Do you mind if I go and buy

some ice-creams?' he asked. 'We haven't had one today. I won't be long. Can George go with me?'

'I don't expect she will want to,' said his aunt. 'But you can ask her.'

'George, come with me!' yelled Julian, setting off to the little village at a great pace. George gave a sudden grin and ran after him. She soon caught him up and smiled gratefully at him.

'Thanks,' she said. 'You go and get the ice-creams, and I'll have a look at Tim.'

They parted, Julian bought four ice-creams, and turned to go home. He waited about for George, who came running up after a few minutes. Her face was glowing.

'He's all right,' she said. 'And you can't imagine how pleased he was to see me! He nearly jumped over my head! I say – another ice-cream for me. You really are a sport, Julian. I'll have to share something with you quickly. What about going to my island tomorrow?'

'Golly!' said Julian, his eyes shining. 'That would be marvellous. Will you really take us tomorrow? Come on, let's tell the others!'

The four children sat in the garden eating their ices. Julian told them what George had said. They all felt excited. George was pleased. She had always felt quite important before when she had haughtily refused to take any of the other children to see Kirrin Island – but it felt much nicer somehow to have consented to row her cousins there.

'I used to think it was much, much nicer always to do things on my own,' she thought, as she sucked the last bits of her ice. 'But it's going to be fun doing things with Julian and the others.'

The children were sent to wash themselves and to get tidy before supper. They talked eagerly about the visit to the island next day. Their aunt heard them and smiled.

'Well, I really must say I'm pleased that George is going to share something with you,' she said. 'Would you like to take your dinner there, and spend the day? It's hardly worthwhile rowing all the way there and landing unless you are going to spend some hours there.'

'Oh, Aunt Fanny! It would be marvellous to take our dinner!' cried Anne.

George looked up. 'Are you coming too, Mother?' she asked.

'You don't sound at all as if you want me to,' said her mother, in a hurt tone. 'You looked cross yesterday, too, when you found I was coming. No – I shan't come tomorrow – but I'm sure your cousins must think you are an odd girl never to want your mother to go with you.'

George said nothing. She hardly ever did say a word when she was scolded. The other children said nothing too. They knew perfectly well that it wasn't that George didn't want her mother to go – it was just that she wanted Timothy with her!

'Anyway, I couldn't come,' went on Aunt Fanny. 'I've some gardening to do. You'll be quite safe with George. She can handle a boat like a man.'

The three children looked eagerly at the weather the next day when they got up. The sun was shining, and everything seemed splendid.

'Isn't it a marvellous day?' said Anne to George, as they dressed. 'I'm so looking forward to going to the island.'

'Well, honestly, I think really we oughtn't to go,' said George, unexpectedly.

A VISIT TO THE ISLAND

'Oh, but why?' cried Anne, in dismay.

'I think there's going to be a storm or something,' said George, looking out to the south-west.

'But, George, why do you say that?' said Anne, impatiently. 'Look at the sun – and there's hardly a cloud in the sky!'

'The wind is wrong,' said George. 'And can't you see the little white tops of the waves out there by my island? That's always a bad sign.'

'Oh, George – it will be the biggest disappointment of our lives if we don't go today,' said Anne, who couldn't bear any disappointment, big or small. 'And besides,' she added, artfully, 'if we hang about the house, afraid of a storm, we shan't be able to have dear old Tim with us.'

'Yes, that's true,' said George. 'All right – we'll go. But mind – if a storm does come, you're not to be a baby. You're to try and enjoy it and not be frightened.'

'Well, I don't much like storms,' began Anne, but stopped when she saw George's scornful look. They went down to breakfast, and George asked her mother if they could take their dinner as they had planned.

'Yes,' said her mother. 'You and Anne can help to make the sandwiches. You boys can go into the garden and pick some ripe plums to take with you. Julian, you can go down to the village when you've done that and buy some bottles of lemonade or ginger-beer, whichever you like.'

'Ginger-pop for me, thanks!' said Julian, and everyone else said the same. They all felt very happy. It would be marvellous to visit the strange little island. George felt happy because she would be with Tim all day.

They set off at last, the food in two kit-bags. The first thing they did was to fetch Tim. He was tied up in the fisher-boy's backyard. The boy himself was there, and grinned at George.

''Morning, Master George,' he said. It seemed so funny to the other children to hear Georgina called 'Master George'! 'Tim's been barking his head off for you. I guess he knew you were coming for him today.'

'Of course he did,' said George, untying him. He at once went completely mad, and tore round and round the children, his tail down and his ears flat.

'He'd win any race if only he were a greyhound,' said Julian, admiringly. 'You can hardly see him for dust. Tim! Hey, Tim! Come and say "Good-morning".'

Tim leapt up and licked Julian's left ear as he passed on his whirlwind way. Then he sobered down and ran lovingly by George as they all made their way to the beach. He licked George's bare legs every now and again, and she pulled at his ears gently.

They got into the boat, and George pushed off. The fisher-boy waved to them. 'You won't be very long, will you?' he called. 'There's a storm blowing up. Bad one it'll be, too.'

'I know,' shouted back George. 'But maybe we'll get back before it begins. It's pretty far off yet.'

George rowed all the way to the island. Tim stood at each end of the boat in turn, barking when the waves reared up at him. The children watched the island coming closer and closer. It looked even more exciting than it had the other day.

'George, where are you going to land?' asked Julian. 'I simply can't imagine how you know your way in and out of these awful rocks. I'm afraid every moment we'll bump into them!'

A VISIT TO THE ISLAND

'I'm going to land at the little cove I told you about the other day,' said George. 'There's only one way to it, but I know it very well. It's hidden away on the east side of the island.'

The girl cleverly worked her boat in and out of the rocks, and suddenly, as it rounded a low wall of sharp rocks, the children saw the cove she had spoken of. It was like a natural little harbour, and was a smooth inlet of water running up to a stretch of sand, sheltered between high rocks. The boat slid into the inlet, and at once stopped rocking, for here the water was like glass, and had hardly a wrinkle.

'I say – this is fine!' said Julian, his eyes shining with delight. George looked at him and her eyes shone too, as bright as the sea itself. It was the first time she had ever taken anyone to her precious island, and she was enjoying it.

They landed on the smooth yellow sand. 'We're really on the island!' said Anne, and she capered about, Tim joining her and looking as mad as she did. The others laughed. George pulled the boat high up on the sand.

'Why so far up?' said Julian, helping her. 'The tide's almost in, isn't it? Surely it won't come as high as this.'

'I told you I thought a storm was coming,' said George. 'If one does, the waves simply tear up this inlet and we don't want to lose our boat, do we?'

'Let's explore the island, let's explore the island!' yelled Anne, who was now at the top of the little natural harbour, climbing up the rocks there. 'Oh do come on!'

They all followed her. It really was a most exciting place. Rabbits were everywhere! They scuttled about as the children appeared, but did not go into their holes.

47

'Aren't they awfully tame?' said Julian, in surprise.

'Well, nobody ever comes here but me,' said George, 'and I don't frighten them. Tim! Tim, if you go after the rabbits, I'll be furious.'

Tim turned big sorrowful eyes on to George. He and George agreed about every single thing except rabbits. To Tim rabbits were made for one thing – to chase! He never could understand why George wouldn't let him do this. But he held himself in and walked solemnly by the children, his eyes watching the lolloping rabbits longingly.

'I believe they would almost eat out of my hand,' said Julian.

But George shook her head.

'No, I've tried that with them,' she said. 'They won't. Look at those baby ones. Aren't they lovely?'

'Woof!' said Tim, agreeing, and he took a few steps towards them. George made a warning noise in her throat, and Tim walked back, his tail down.

'There's the castle!' said Julian. 'Shall we explore that now? I do want to.'

'Yes, we will,' said George. 'Look – that is where the entrance used to be – through that big broken archway.'

The children gazed at the enormous old archway, now half-broken down. Behind it were ruined stone steps leading towards the centre of the castle.

'It had strong walls all round it, with two towers,' said George. 'One tower is almost gone, as you can see, but the other is not so bad. The jackdaws build in that every year. They've almost filled it up with their sticks!'

As they came near to the better tower of the two the jackdaws circled round them with loud cries of 'Chack, chack, chack!' Tim leapt into the air as if he thought he could get them, but they only called mockingly to him.

'This is the centre of the castle,' said George, as they entered through a ruined doorway into what looked like a great yard, whose stone floor was now overgrown with grass and other weeds. 'Here is where the people used to live. You can see where the rooms were – look, there's one almost whole there. Go through that little door and you'll see it.'

They trooped through a doorway and found themselves in a dark, stone-walled, stone-roofed room, with a space at one end where a fireplace must have been. Two slit-like windows lit the room. It felt very strange and mysterious.

'What a pity it's all broken down,' said Julian, wandering out again. 'That room seems to be the only one quite whole. There are some others here – but all of them seem to have either no roof, or one or other of the walls gone. That room is the only livable one. Was there an upstairs to the castle, George?'

'Of course,' said George. 'But the steps that led up are gone. Look! You can see part of an upstairs room there, by the jackdaw tower. You can't get up to it, though, because I've tried. I nearly broke my neck trying to get up. The stones crumble away so.'

'Were there any dungeons?' asked Dick.

'I don't know,' said George. 'I expect so. But nobody could find them now – everywhere is so overgrown.'

It was indeed overgrown. Big blackberry bushes grew here and there, and a few gorse bushes forced their way into gaps and corners. The coarse green grass sprang everywhere, and pink thrift grew its cushions in holes and crannies.

'Well, I think it's a perfectly lovely place,' said Anne. 'Perfectly and absolutely lovely!'

'Do you really?' said George, pleased. 'I'm so glad. Look! We're right on the other side of the island now, facing the sea. Do you see those rocks, with those peculiar big birds sitting there?'

The children looked. They saw some rocks sticking up, with great black shining birds sitting on them in strange positions.

'They are cormorants,' said George. 'They've caught plenty of fish for their dinner, and they're sitting there digesting it. Hallo – they're all flying away. I wonder why?'

She soon knew – for, from the south-west there suddenly came an ominous rumble.

'Thunder!' said George. 'That's the storm. It's coming sooner than I thought!'

CHAPTER SIX

What the storm did

THE FOUR children stared out to sea. They had all been so interested in exploring the exciting old castle that not one of them had noticed the sudden change in the weather.

Another rumble came. It sounded like a big dog growling in the sky. Tim heard it and growled back, sounding like a small roll of thunder himself.

'My goodness, we're in for it now,' said George, half-alarmed. 'We can't get back in time, that's certain. It's blowing up at top speed. Did you ever see such a change in the sky?'

The sky had been blue when they started. Now it was overcast, and the clouds seemed to hang very low indeed. They scudded along as if someone was chasing them – and the wind howled round in such a mournful way that Anne felt quite frightened.

'It's beginning to rain,' said Julian, feeling an enormous drop spatter on his outstretched hand. 'We had better shelter, hadn't we, George? We shall get wet through.'

'Yes, we will in a minute,' said George. 'I say, just look at these big waves coming! My word, it really *is* going to be a storm. Golly – what a flash of lightning!'

The waves were certainly beginning to run very high indeed. It was amazing to see what a change had come over them. They swelled up, turned over as soon as they came to rocks, and then rushed up the beach of the island with a great roar.

'I think we'd better pull our boat up higher still,' said George suddenly. 'It's going to be a very bad storm indeed. Sometimes these sudden summer storms are worse than a winter one.'

She and Julian ran to the other side of the island where they had left the boat. It was a good thing they went, for great waves were already racing right up to it. The two children pulled the boat up almost to the top of the low cliff and George tied it to a stout gorse bush growing there.

By now the rain was simply pelting down, and George

and Julian were soaked. 'I hope the others have been sensible enough to shelter in that room that has a roof and walls,' said George.

They were there all right, looking rather cold and scared. It was very dark there, for the only light came through the two slits of windows and the small doorway.

'Could we light a fire to make things a bit more cheerful?' said Julian, looking round. 'I wonder where we can find some nice dry sticks?'

Almost as if they were answering the question a small crowd of jackdaws cried out wildly as they circled in the storm. 'Chack, chack, chack!'

'Of course! There are plenty of sticks on the ground below the tower!' cried Julian. 'You know – where the jackdaws nest. They've dropped lots of sticks there.'

He dashed out into the rain and ran to the tower. He picked up an armful of sticks and ran back.

'Good,' said George. 'We'll be able to make a nice fire with those. Anyone got any paper to start it – or matches?'

'I've got some matches,' said Julian. 'But nobody's got paper.'

'Yes,' said Anne, suddenly. 'The sandwiches are wrapped in paper. Let's undo them, and then we can use the paper for the fire.'

'Good idea,' said George. So they undid the sandwiches, and put them neatly on a broken stone, rubbing it clean first. Then they built up a fire, with the paper underneath and the sticks arranged criss-cross on top.

It was fun when they lit the paper. It flared up and the sticks at once caught fire, for they were very old and dry. Soon there was a fine cracking fire going and the little ruined room was lit by dancing flames. It was very dark outside now, for the clouds hung almost low enough to touch the top of the castle tower! And how they raced by! The wind sent them off to the north-east, roaring behind them with a noise like the sea itself.

'I've never, never heard the sea making such an awful noise,' said Anne. 'Never! It really sounds as if it's shouting at the top of its voice.'

What with the howling of the wind and the crashing of the great waves all round the little island, the children could hardly hear themselves speak! They had to shout at one another.

'Let's have our dinner!' yelled Dick, who was feeling terribly hungry as usual. 'We can't do anything much while this storm lasts.'

'Yes, let's,' said Anne, looking longingly at the ham sandwiches. 'It will be fun to have a picnic round the fire in this dark old room. I wonder how long ago other people had a meal here? I wish I could see them.'

'Well, I don't,' said Dick, looking round half-scared as if he expected to see the old-time people walk in to share their picnic. 'It's quite a strange enough day without wanting things like that to happen.'

They all felt better when they were eating the sandwiches and drinking the ginger-beer. The fire flared up as more and more sticks caught, and gave out quite a pleasant warmth, for now that the wind had got up so strongly, the day had become cold.

'We'll take it in turns to fetch sticks,' said George. But Anne didn't want to go alone. She was trying her best not to show that she was afraid of the storm – but it was more than she could do to go out of the cosy room into the rain and thunder by herself.

Tim didn't seem to like the storm either. He sat close by George, his ears cocked, and growled whenever the thunder rumbled. The children fed him with titbits and he ate them eagerly, for he was hungry too.

All the children had four biscuits each. 'I think I shall give all mine to Tim,' said George. 'I didn't bring him any of his own biscuits, and he does seem so hungry.'

'No, don't do that,' said Julian. 'We'll each give him a biscuit – that will be four for him – and we'll still have three left each. That will be plenty for us.'

'You are really nice,' said George. 'Tim, don't you think they are nice?'

Tim did. He licked everyone and made them laugh. Then he rolled over on his back and let Julian tickle him underneath.

The children fed the fire and finished their picnic. When it came to Julian's turn to get more sticks, he disappeared out of the room into the storm. He stood and looked around, the rain wetting his bare head.

The storm seemed to be right overhead now. The lightning flashed and the thunder crashed at the same moment. Julian was not a bit afraid of storms, but he couldn't help feeling rather over-awed at this one. It was so magnificent. The lightning tore the sky in half almost every minute, and the thunder crashed so loudly that it sounded almost as if mountains were falling down all around!

The sea's voice could be heard as soon as the thunder stopped – and that was magnificent to hear too. The spray flew so high into the air that it wetted Julian as he stood in the centre of the ruined castle.

'I really must see what the waves are like,' thought the

boy. 'If the spray flies right over me here, they must be simply enormous!'

He made his way out of the castle and climbed up on to part of the ruined wall that had once run all round the castle. He stood up there, looking out to the open sea. And what a sight met his eyes!

The waves were like great walls of grey-green! They dashed over the rocks that lay all around the island, and spray flew from them, gleaming white in the stormy sky. They rolled up to the island and dashed themselves against it with such terrific force that Julian could feel the wall beneath his feet tremble with the shock.

The boy looked out to sea, marvelling at the really great sight he saw. For half a moment he wondered if the sea might come right over the island itself! Then he knew that couldn't happen, for it would have happened before. He stared at the great waves coming in – and then he saw something rather strange.

There was something else out on the sea by the rocks besides the waves – something dark, something big, something that seemed to lurch out of the waves and settle down again. What could it be?

'It can't be a ship,' said Julian to himself, his heart beginning to beat fast as he strained his eyes to see through the rain and the spray. 'And yet it looks more like a ship than anything else. I hope it isn't a ship. There wouldn't be anyone saved from it on this dreadful day!'

He stood and watched for a while. The dark shape heaved into sight again and then sank away once more. Julian decided to go and tell the others. He ran back to the firelit room.

'George! Dick! There's something strange out on the

rocks beyond the island!' he shouted, at the top of his voice. 'It looks like a ship – and yet it can't possibly be. Come and see!'

The others stared at him in surprise, and jumped to their feet. George hurriedly flung some more sticks on the fire to keep it going, and then she and the others quickly followed Julian out into the rain.

The storm seemed to be passing over a little now. The rain was not pelting down quite so hard. The thunder was rolling a little farther off, and the lightning did not flash so often. Julian led the way to the wall on which he had climbed to watch the sea.

Everyone climbed up to gaze out to sea. They saw a great tumbled, heaving mass of grey-green water, with waves rearing up everywhere. Their tops broke over the rocks and they rushed up to the island as if they would gobble it whole. Anne slipped her arm through Julian's. She felt rather small and scared.

'You're all right, Anne,' said Julian, loudly. 'Now just watch – you'll see something strange in a minute.'

They all watched. At first they saw nothing, for the waves reared up so high that they hid everything a little way out. Then suddenly George saw what Julian meant.

'Gracious!' she shouted. 'It *is* a ship! Yes, it is! Is it being wrecked? It's a big ship – not a sailing-boat, or fishing-smack!'

'Oh, is anyone in it?' wailed Anne.

The four children watched and Tim began to bark as he saw the strange dark shape lurching here and there in the enormous waves. The sea was bringing the ship nearer to shore.

'It will be dashed on to those rocks,' said Julian, suddenly. 'Look – there it goes!'

As he spoke there came a tremendous crashing, splintering sound, and the dark shape of the ship settled down on to the sharp teeth of the dangerous rocks on the south-west side of the island. It stayed there, shifting only slightly as the big waves ran under it and lifted it a little.

'She's stuck there,' said Julian. 'She won't move now. The sea will soon be going down a bit, and then the ship will find herself held by those rocks.'

As he spoke, a ray of pale sunshine came wavering out

between a gap in the thinning clouds. It was gone almost at once. 'Good!' said Dick, looking upwards. 'The sun will be out again soon. We can warm ourselves then and get dry – and maybe we can find out what that poor ship is. Oh, Julian – I do so hope there was nobody in it. I hope they've all taken to boats and got safely to land.'

The clouds thinned out a little more. The wind stopped roaring and dropped to a steady breeze. The sun shone out again for a longer time, and the children felt its welcome warmth. They all stared at the ship on the rocks. The sun shone on it and lighted it up.

'There's something odd about it somehow,' said Julian, slowly. 'Something awfully odd. I've never seen a ship quite like it.'

George was staring at it with a strange look in her eyes. She turned to face the three children, and they were astonished to see the bright gleam in her blue eyes. The girl looked almost too excited to speak.

'What is it?' asked Julian, catching hold of her hand.

'Julian – oh, Julian – it's my wreck!' she cried, in a high excited voice. 'Don't you see what's happened? The storm has lifted the ship up from the bottom of the sea, and has lodged it on those rocks. It's my wreck!'

The others saw at once that she was right. It was the old wrecked ship! No wonder it looked peculiar. No wonder it looked so old and dark, and such a strange shape. It was the wreck, lifted high out of its sleeping-place and put on the rocks nearby.

'George! We shall be able to row out and get into the wreck now!' shouted Julian. 'We shall be able to explore it from end to end. We may find the boxes of gold. Oh, *George*!'

CHAPTER SEVEN

Back to Kirrin Cottage

THE FOUR children were so tremendously surprised and excited that for a minute or two they didn't say a word. They just stared at the dark hulk of the old wreck, imagining what they might find. Then Julian clutched George's arm and pressed it tightly.

'Isn't this wonderful?' he said. 'Oh, George, isn't it an extraordinary thing to happen?'

Still George said nothing, but stared at the wreck, all kinds of thoughts racing through her mind. Then she turned to Julian.

'If only the wreck is still mine now it's thrown up like this!' she said. 'I don't know if wrecks belong to the queen or anyone, like lost treasure does. But after all, the ship did belong to our family. Nobody bothered much about it when it was down under the sea – but do you suppose people will still let me have it for my own now it's thrown up?'

'Well, don't let's tell anyone!' said Dick.

'Don't be silly,' said George. 'One of the fishermen is sure to see it when his ship goes slipping out of the bay. The news will soon be out.'

'Well, then, we'd better explore it thoroughly ourselves before anyone else does!' said Dick, eagerly. 'No one knows about it yet. Only us. Can't we explore it as soon as the waves go down a bit?'

'We can't wade out to the rocks, if that's what you

61

mean,' said George. 'We might get there by boat – but we couldn't possibly risk it now, while the waves are so big. They won't go down today, that's certain. The wind is still too strong.'

'Well, what about tomorrow morning, early?' said Julian. 'Before anyone has got to know about it? I bet if only *we* can get into the ship first, we can find anything there is to find!'

'Yes, I expect we could,' said George. 'I told you divers had been down and explored the ship as thoroughly as they could – but of course it is difficult to do that properly under water. We might find something they've missed. Oh, this is like a dream. I can't believe it's true that my old wreck has come up from the bottom of the sea like that!'

The sun was now properly out, and the children's wet clothes dried in its hot rays. They steamed in the sun, and even Tim's coat sent up a mist too. He didn't seem to like the wreck at all, and growled deeply at it.

'You are funny, Tim,' said George, patting him. 'It won't hurt you! What do you think it is?'

'He probably thinks it's a whale,' said Anne with a laugh. 'Oh, George – this is the most exciting day of my life! Oh, can't we possibly take the boat and see if we can get to the wreck?'

'No, we can't,' said George. 'I only wish we could. But it's quite impossible, Anne. For one thing, I don't think the wreck has quite settled down on the rocks yet, and maybe it won't till the tide has gone down. I can see it lifting a little still when an extra big wave comes. It would be dangerous to go into it yet. And for another thing I don't want my boat smashed to bits on the rocks, and us thrown into that wild water! That's what would happen.

We must wait till tomorrow. It's a good idea to come early. I expect lots of grown-ups will think it's their business to explore it.'

The children watched the old wreck for a little time longer and then went all round the island again. It was certainly not very large, but it really was exciting, with its rocky little coast, its quiet inlet where their boat was, the ruined castle, the circling jackdaws, and the scampering rabbits everywhere.

'I do love it,' said Anne. 'I really do. It's just small enough to *feel* like an island. Most islands are too big to feel like islands. I mean, Britain is an island, but nobody living on it could possibly know it unless they were told. Now this island really *feels* like one because wherever you are you can see to the other side of it. I love it.'

George felt very happy. She had often been on her island before, but always alone except for Tim. She had always vowed that she never, never would take anyone there, because it would spoil her island for her. But it hadn't been spoilt. It had made it much nicer. For the first time George began to understand that sharing pleasures doubles their joy.

'We'll wait till the waves go down a bit then we'll go back home,' she said. 'I rather think there's some more rain coming, and we'll only get soaked through. We shan't be back till tea-time as it is, because we'll have a long pull against the out-going tide.'

All the children felt a little tired after the excitements of the morning. They said very little as they rowed home. Everyone took turns at rowing except Anne, who was not strong enough with the oars to row against the tide. They looked back at the island as they left it. They couldn't see

63

the wreck because that was on the opposite side, facing the open sea.

'It's just as well it's there,' said Julian. 'No one can see it yet. Only when a boat goes out to fish will it be seen. And we shall be there as early as any boat goes out! I vote we get up at dawn.'

'Well, that's pretty early,' said George. 'Can you wake up? I'm often out at dawn, but you're not used to it.'

'Of course we can wake up,' said Julian. 'Well – here we are back at the beach again – and I'm jolly glad. My arms are awfully tired and I'm so hungry I could eat a whole larderful of things.'

'Woof,' said Tim, quite agreeing.

'I'll have to take Tim to Alf,' said George, jumping out of the boat. 'You get the boat in, Julian. I'll join you in a few minutes.'

It wasn't long before all four were sitting down to a good tea. Aunt Fanny had baked new scones for them, and had made a ginger cake with black treacle. It was dark brown and sticky to eat. The children finished it all up and said it was the nicest they had ever tasted.

'Did you have an exciting day?' asked their aunt.

'Oh yes!' said Anne, eagerly. 'The storm was grand. It threw up . . .'

Julian and Dick both kicked her under the table. George couldn't reach her or she would most certainly have kicked her too. Anne stared at the boys angrily, with tears in her eyes.

'Now what's the matter?' asked Aunt Fanny. 'Did somebody kick you, Anne? Well, really, this kicking under the table has got to stop. Poor Anne will be covered with bruises. What did the sea throw up, dear?'

'It threw up the most enormous waves,' said Anne, looking defiantly at the others. She knew they had thought she was going to say that the sea had thrown up the wreck – but they were wrong! They had kicked her for nothing!

'Sorry for kicking you, Anne,' said Julian. 'My foot sort of slipped.'

'So did mine,' said Dick. 'Yes, Aunt Fanny, it was a magnificent sight on the island. The waves raced up that little inlet, and we had to take our boat almost up to the top of the low cliff there.'

'I wasn't really afraid of the storm,' said Anne. 'In fact, I wasn't really as afraid of it as Ti . . .'

Everyone knew perfectly well that Anne was going to mention Timothy, and they all interrupted her at once, speaking very loudly. Julian managed to get a kick in again.

'Oooh!' said Anne.

'The rabbits were so tame,' said Julian, loudly.

'We watched the cormorants,' said Dick and George joined in too, talking at the same time.

'The jackdaws made such a noise, they said "Chack, chack, chack," all the time.'

'Well, really, you sound like jackdaws yourselves, talking all at once like this!' said Aunt Fanny, with a laugh. 'Now, have you all finished? Very well, then, go and wash your sticky hands – yes, George, I know they're sticky, because *I* made that gingerbread, and you've had three slices! Then you had better go and play quietly in the other room, because it's raining, and you can't go out. But don't disturb your father, George. He's very busy.'

The children went to wash. 'Idiot!' said Julian to Anne. 'Nearly gave us away twice!'

'I didn't mean what you thought I meant the first time!' began Anne indignantly.

George interrupted her.

'I'd rather you gave the secret of the wreck away than my secret about Tim,' she said. 'I do think you've got a careless tongue.'

'Yes, I have,' said Anne, sorrowfully. 'I think I'd better not talk at meal-times any more. I love Tim so much I just can't seem to help wanting to talk about him.'

They all went to play in the other room. Julian turned a table upside down with a crash. 'We'll play at wrecks,' he said. 'This is the wreck. Now we're going to explore it.'

The door flew open and an angry, frowning face looked in. It was George's father!

'What was that noise?' he said. 'George! Did you over-turn that table?'

'I did,' said Julian. 'I'm sorry. I quite forgot you were working.'

'Any more noise like that and I shall keep you all in tomorrow!' said his uncle Quentin. 'Georgina, keep your cousins quiet.'

The door shut and Uncle Quentin went out. The children looked at one another.

'Your father's awfully fierce, isn't he?' said Julian. 'I'm sorry I made that row. I didn't think.'

'We'd better do something really quiet,' said George. 'Or he'll keep his word – and we'll find ourselves inside tomorrow just when we want to explore the wreck.'

This was a terrible thought. Anne went to get one of her dolls to play with. She had managed to bring quite a number after all. Julian fetched a book. George took up a beautiful little boat she was carving out of a piece of wood.

Dick lay back on a chair and thought of the exciting wreck. The rain poured down steadily, and everyone hoped it would have stopped by the morning.

'We'll have to be up most awfully early,' said Dick, yawning. 'What about going to bed in good time tonight? I'm tired with all that rowing.'

In the ordinary way none of the children liked going to bed early – but with such an exciting thing to look forward to, early bed seemed different that night.

'It will make the time go quickly,' said Anne, putting down her doll. 'Shall we go now?'

'Whatever do you suppose Mother would say if we went just after tea?' said George. 'She'd think we were all ill. No, let's go after supper. We'll just say we're tired with rowing – which is perfectly true – and we'll get a good night's sleep, and be ready for our adventure tomorrow morning. And it *is* an adventure, you know. It isn't many people that have the chance of exploring an old, old wreck like that, which has always been at the bottom of the sea!'

So, by eight o'clock, all the children were in bed, rather to Aunt Fanny's surprise. Anne fell asleep at once. Julian and Dick were not long – but George lay awake for some time, thinking of her island, her wreck – and, of course, her beloved dog!

'I must take Tim too,' she thought, as she fell asleep. 'We can't leave old Tim out of this. He shall share in the adventure too!'

CHAPTER EIGHT

Exploring the wreck

JULIAN WOKE first the next morning. He awoke just as the sun was slipping over the horizon in the east, and filling the sky with gold. Julian stared at the ceiling for a moment, and then, in a rush, he remembered all that had happened the day before. He sat up straight in bed and whispered as loudly as he could.

'Dick! Wake up! We're going to see the wreck! Do wake up!'

Dick woke and grinned at Julian. A feeling of happiness crept over him. They were going on an adventure. He leapt out of bed and ran quietly to the girls' room. He opened the door. Both the girls were fast asleep, Anne curled up like a dormouse under the sheet.

Dick shook George and then dug Anne in the back. They awoke and sat up. 'Buck up!' whispered Dick. 'The sun is just rising. We'll have to hurry.'

George's blue eyes shone as she dressed. Anne skipped about quietly, finding her few clothes – just a bathing suit, jeans and jersey – and rubber shoes for her feet. It wasn't many minutes before they were all ready.

'Now, not a creak on the stairs – not a cough or a giggle!' warned Julian, as they stood together on the landing. Anne was a dreadful giggler, and had often given secret plans away by her sudden explosive choke. But this time the little girl was as solemn as the others, and as careful. They crept down the stairs and undid the little

69

front door. Not a sound was made. They shut the door quietly and made their way down the garden path to the gate. The gate always creaked, so they climbed over it instead of opening it.

The sun was now shining brightly, though it was still low in the eastern sky. It felt warm already. The sky was so beautifully blue that Anne couldn't help feeling it had been freshly washed! 'It looks just as if it had come back from the laundry,' she told the others.

They squealed with laughter at her. She did say odd things at times. But they knew what she meant. The day had a lovely new feeling about it – the clouds were so pink in the bright blue sky, and the sea looked so smooth and fresh. It was impossible to imagine that it had been so rough the day before.

George got her boat. Then she went to get Tim, while the boys hauled the boat down to the sea. Alf, the fisher-boy, was surprised to see George so early. He was about to go with his father, fishing. He grinned at George.

'You going fishing, too?' he said to her. 'My, wasn't that a storm yesterday! I thought you'd be caught in it.'

'We were,' said George. 'Come on, Tim! Come on!'

Tim was very pleased to see George so early. He capered round her as she ran back to the others, almost tripping her up as she went. He leapt into the boat as soon as he saw it, and stood at the stern, his red tongue out, his tail wagging violently.

'I wonder his tail keeps on,' said Anne, looking at it. 'One day, Timothy, you'll wag it right off.'

They set off to the island. It was easy to row now, because the sea was so calm. They came to the island, and rowed around it to the other side.

EXPLORING THE WRECK

And there was the wreck, piled high on some sharp rocks! It had settled down now and did not stir as waves slid under it. It lay a little to one side, and the broken mast, now shorter than before, stuck out at an angle.

'There she is,' said Julian, in excitement. 'Poor old wreck! I guess she's a bit more battered now. What a noise she made when she went crashing on to those rocks yesterday!'

'How do we get to her?' asked Anne, looking at the mass of ugly, sharp rocks all around. But George was not at all dismayed. She knew almost every inch of the coast around her little island. She pulled steadily at the oars and soon came near to the rocks in which the great wreck rested.

The children looked at the wreck from their boat. It was big, much bigger than they had imagined when they had peered at it from the top of the water. It was encrusted with shellfish of some kind, and strands of brown and green seaweed hung down. It smelt funny. It had great holes in its sides, showing where it had battered against rocks. There were holes in the deck too. Altogether, it looked a sad and forlorn old ship – but to the four children it was the most exciting thing in the whole world.

They rowed to the rocks on which the wreck lay. The tide washed over them. George took a look round.

'We'll tie our boat up to the wreck itself,' she said. 'And we'll get on to the deck quite easily by climbing up the side. Look, Julian! – throw this loop of rope over that broken bit of wood there, sticking out from the side.'

Julian did as he was told. The rope tightened and the boat was held in position. Then George clambered up the side of the wreck like a monkey. She was a marvel at climbing. Julian and Dick followed her, but Anne had to be helped up. Soon all four were standing on the slanting deck. It was slippery with seaweed, and the smell was very strong indeed. Anne didn't like it.

'Well, this was the deck,' said George, 'and that's where the men got up and down.' She pointed to a large hole. They went to it and looked down. The remains of an iron ladder were still there. George looked at it.

'I think it's still strong enough to hold us,' she said. 'I'll go first. Anyone got a torch? It looks pretty dark down there.'

EXPLORING THE WRECK

Julian had a torch. He handed it to George. The children became rather quiet. It was mysterious somehow to look down into the dark inside of the big ship. What would they find? George switched on the torch and then swung herself down the ladder. The others followed.

The light from the torch showed a very strange sight. The under-parts of the ship were low-ceilinged, made of thick oak. The children had to bend their heads to get about. It seemed as if there were places that might have been cabins, though it was difficult to tell now, for everything was so battered, sea-drenched and seaweedy. The smell was really horrid, though it was mostly of drying seaweed.

The children slipped about on the seaweed as they went round the inside of the ship. It didn't seem so big inside after all. There was a big hold under the cabins, which the children saw by the light of their torch.

'That's where the boxes of gold would have been kept, I expect,' said Julian. But there was nothing in the hold except water and fish! The children couldn't go down because the water was too deep. One or two barrels floated in the water, but they had burst open and were quite empty.

'I expect they were water-barrels, or barrels of pork or biscuit,' said George. 'Let's go round the other part of the ship again – where the cabins are. Isn't it strange to see bunks there that sailors have slept in? – and look at that old wooden chair. Fancy it still being here after all these years! Look at the things on those hooks too – they are all rusty now, and covered with seaweedy stuff – but they must have been the cook's pans and dishes!'

It was a very weird trip round the old wreck. The

children were all on the look-out for boxes which might contain bars of gold – but there didn't seem to be one single box of any kind anywhere!

They came to a rather bigger cabin than the others. It had a bunk in one corner, in which a large crab rested. An old bit of furniture looking rather like a table with two legs, all encrusted with greyish shells, lay against the bunk. Wooden shelves, festooned with grey-green seaweed, hung crookedly on the walls of the cabin.

'This must have been the captain's own cabin,' said Julian. 'It's the biggest one. Look, what's that in the corner?'

'An old cup!' said Anne, picking it up. 'And here's half of a saucer. I expect the captain was sitting here having a cup of tea when the ship went down.'

This made the children feel rather uneasy. It was dark and smelly in the little cabin, and the floor was wet and slippery to their feet. George began to feel that her wreck was really more pleasant sunk under the water than raised above it!

'Let's go,' she said, with a shiver. 'I don't like it much. It *is* exciting, I know – but it's a bit frightening too.'

They turned to go. Julian flashed his torch round the little cabin for the last time. He was about to switch it off and follow the others up to the deck above when he caught sight of something that made him stop. He flashed his torch on to it, and then called to the others.

'I say! Wait a bit. There's a cupboard here in the wall. Let's see if there's anything in it!'

The others turned back and looked. They saw what looked like a small cupboard set in level with the wall of the cabin. What had caught Julian's eye was the keyhole. There was no key there, though.

'There just *might* be something inside,' said Julian. He
tried to prise open the wooden door with his fingers, but it
wouldn't move. 'It's locked,' he said. 'Of course it would
be!'

'I expect the lock is rotten by now,' said George, and she
tried too. Then she took out her big strong pocket-knife
and inserted it between the cupboard door and the cabin-
wall. She forced back the blade – and the lock of the

cupboard suddenly snapped! As she had said, it was quite rotten. The door swung open, and the children saw a shelf inside with a few curious things on it.

There was a wooden box, swollen with the wet sea-water in which it had lain for years. There were two or three things that looked like old, pulpy books. There was some sort of glass drinking-vessel, cracked in half – and two or three funny objects so spoilt by sea-water that no one could possibly say what they were.

'Nothing very interesting – except the box,' said Julian, and he picked it up. 'Anyway, I expect that whatever is inside is ruined. But we may as well try and open it.'

He and George tried their best to force the lock of the old wooden box. On the top of it were stamped initials – H.J.K.

'I expect those were the captain's initials,' said Dick.

'No, they were the initials of my great-great-great-grandfather!' said George, her eyes shining suddenly. 'I've heard all about him. His name was Henry John Kirrin. This was his ship, you know. This must have been his very private box in which he kept his old papers or diaries. Oh – we simply *must* open it!'

But it was quite impossible to force the lid up with the tools they had there. They soon gave it up, and Julian picked up the box to carry it to the boat.

'We'll open it at home,' he said, his voice sounding rather excited. 'We'll get a hammer or something, and get it open somehow. Oh, George – this really is a find!'

They all of them felt that they really had something mysterious in their possession. Was there anything inside the box – and if so, what would it be? They longed to get home and open it!

They went up on deck, climbing the old iron ladder. As soon as they got there they saw that others besides themselves had discovered that the wreck had been thrown up from the bottom of the sea!

'Golly! Half the fishing-smacks of the bay have discovered it!' cried Julian, looking round at the fishing-boats that had come as near as they dared to the wreck. The fishermen were looking at the wreck in wonder. When they saw the children on board they halloo-ed loudly.

'Ahoy there! What's that ship?'

'It's the old wreck!' yelled back Julian. 'She was thrown up yesterday in the storm!'

'Don't say any more,' said George, frowning. 'It's *my* wreck. I don't want sightseers on it!'

So no more was said, and the four children got into their boat and rowed home as fast as they could. It was past their breakfast-time. They might get a good scolding. They might even be sent to bed by George's fierce father – but what did they care? They had explored the wreck – and had come away with a box which *might* contain – well, if not bars of gold, one *small* bar, perhaps!

They did get a scolding. They had to go without half their breakfast, too, because Uncle Quentin said that children who came in so late didn't deserve hot bacon and eggs – only toast and marmalade. It was very sad.

They hid the box under the bed in the boys' room. Tim had been left with the fisher-boy – or rather, had been tied up in his backyard, for Alf had gone out fishing, and was even now gazing from his father's boat at the strange wreck.

'We can make a bit of money taking sightseers out to this wreck,' said Alf. And before the day was out scores of interested people had seen the old wreck from the decks of motor-boats and fishing-smacks.

George was furious about it. But she couldn't do anything. After all, as Julian said, anybody could have a look!

CHAPTER NINE

The box from the wreck

THE FIRST thing that the children did after breakfast was to fetch the precious box and take it out to the tool-shed in the garden. They were simply longing to force it open. All of them secretly felt certain that it would hold treasure of some sort.

Julian looked round for a tool. He found a chisel and decided that would be just the thing to force the box open. He tried, but the tool slipped and jabbed his fingers. Then he tried other things, but the box obstinately refused to open. The children stared at it crossly.

'I know what to do,' said Anne at last. 'Let's take it to the top of the house and throw it down to the ground. It would burst open then, I expect.'

The others thought over the idea. 'It might be worth trying,' said Julian. 'The only thing is it might break or spoil anything inside the box.'

But there didn't seem any other way to open the box, so Julian carried it up to the top of the house. He went to the attic and opened the window there. The others were down below, waiting. Julian hurled the box out of the window as violently as he could. It flew through the air and landed with a terrific crash on the crazy paving below.

At once the french window there opened and their Uncle Quentin came out like a bullet from a gun.

'Whatever are you doing?' he cried. 'Surely you aren't

79

throwing things at each other out of the window? What's this on the ground?'

The children looked at the box. It had burst open and lay on the ground, showing a tin lining that was waterproof. Whatever was in the box would not be spoilt! It would be quite dry!

Dick ran to pick it up.

'I said, what's this on the ground?' shouted his uncle and moved towards him.

THE BOX FROM THE WRECK

'It's – it's something that belongs to us,' said Dick, going red.

'Well, I shall take it away from you,' said his uncle. 'Disturbing me like this! Give it to me. Where did you get it?'

Nobody answered. Uncle Quentin frowned till his glasses nearly fell off. 'Where did you get it?' he barked, glaring at poor Anne, who was nearest.

'Out of the wreck,' stammered the little girl, scared.

'Out of the *wreck*!' said her uncle, in surprise. 'The old wreck that was thrown up yesterday? I heard about that. Do you mean to say you've been in it?'

'Yes,' said Dick. Julian joined them at that moment, looking worried. It would be too awful if his uncle took the box just as they got it open. But that was exactly what he did do!

'Well, this box may contain something important,' he said, and he took it from Dick's hands. 'You've no right to go prying about in that old wreck. You might take something that mattered.'

'Well, it's my wreck,' said George, in a defiant tone. 'Please, Father, let us have the box. We'd just got it opened. We thought it might hold – a gold bar – or something like that!'

'A gold bar!' said her father, with a snort. 'What a baby you are! This small box would never hold a thing like that! It's much more likely to contain particulars of what happened to the bars! I have always thought that the gold was safely delivered somewhere – and that the ship, empty of its valuable cargo, got wrecked as it left the bay!'

'Oh, Father – please, please let us have our box,' begged George, almost in tears. She suddenly felt certain that it did contain papers that might tell them what had happened to the gold. But without another word her father turned and went into the house, carrying the box, burst open and cracked, its tin lining showing through under his arm.

Anne burst into tears. 'Don't blame me for telling him we got it from the wreck,' she sobbed. 'Please don't. He glared at me so. I just had to tell him.'

'All right, Baby,' said Julian, putting his arm round Anne. He looked furious. He thought it was very unfair of his uncle to take the box like that. 'Listen – I'm not going to stand this. We'll get hold of that box somehow and look into it. I'm sure your father won't bother himself with it, George – he'll start writing his book again and forget all about it. I'll wait my chance and slip into his study and get it, even if it means a telling off if I'm discovered!'

'Good!' said George. 'We'll all keep a watch and see if Father goes out.'

So they took it in turns to keep watch, but most annoyingly their Uncle Quentin remained in his study all the morning. Aunt Fanny was surprised to see one or two children always about the garden that day, instead of down on the beach.

'Why don't you all keep together and bathe or do something?' she said. 'Have you quarrelled with one another?'

'No,' said Dick. 'Of course not.' But he didn't say why they were in the garden!

'Doesn't your father *ever* go out?' he said to George, when it was her turn to keep watch. 'I don't think he leads a very healthy life.'

'Scientists never do,' said George, as if she knew all

about them. 'But I tell you what – he may go to sleep this afternoon! He sometimes does!'

Julian was left behind in the garden that afternoon. He sat down under a tree and opened a book. Soon he heard a curious noise that made him look up. He knew at once what it was!

'That's Uncle Quentin snoring!' he said in excitement. 'It is! Oh – I wonder if I could possibly creep in at the french window and get our box!'

He stole to the windows and looked in. One was a little way open and Julian opened it a little more. He saw his uncle lying back in a comfortable armchair, his mouth a little open, his eyes closed, fast asleep! Every time he took a breath, he snored.

'Well, he really does look sound asleep,' thought the boy. 'And there's the box, just behind him, on that table. I'll risk it. I bet I'll get an awful telling off if I'm caught, but I can't help that!'

He stole in. His uncle still snored. He tiptoed by him to the table behind his uncle's chair. He took hold of the box.

And then a bit of the broken wood of the box fell to the floor with a thud! His uncle stirred in his chair and opened his eyes. Quick as lightning the boy crouched down behind his uncle's chair, hardly breathing.

'What's that?' he heard his uncle say. Julian didn't move. Then his uncle settled down again and shut his eyes. Soon there was the sound of his rhythmic snoring!

'Hurrah!' thought Julian. 'He's off again!'

Quietly he stood up, holding the box. On tiptoe he crept to the french window. He slipped out and ran softly down the garden path. He didn't think of hiding the box. All he wanted to do was to get to the other children and show them what he had done!

He ran to the beach where the others were lying in the sun. 'Hi!' he yelled. 'Hi! I've got it! I've got it!'

They all sat up with a jerk, thrilled to see the box in Julian's arms. They forgot all about the other people on the beach. Julian dropped down on the sand and grinned.

'Your father went to sleep,' he said to George. 'Tim, don't lick me like that! And George, I went in – and a bit of the box dropped on the floor – and it woke him up!'

'Golly!' said George. 'What happened?'

'I crouched down behind his chair till he went to sleep again,' said Julian. 'Then I fled. Now – let's see what's in here. I don't believe your father's even tried to see!'

He hadn't. The tin lining was intact. It had rusted with the years of lying in the wet, and the lid was so tightly fitted down that it was almost impossible to move it.

But once George began to work at it with her pocket-knife, scraping away the rust, it began to loosen – and in about a quarter of an hour it came off!

The children bent eagerly over it. Inside lay some old papers and a book of some kind with a black cover. Nothing else at all. No bar of gold. No treasure. Everyone felt a little bit disappointed.

'It's all quite dry,' said Julian, surprised. 'Not a bit damp. The tin lining kept everything perfect.'

He picked up the book and opened it. 'It's a diary your great-great-great-grandfather kept of the ship's voyages,' he said. 'I can hardly read the writing. It's so small and funny.'

George picked up one of the papers. It was made of thick parchment, quite yellow with age. She spread it out on the sand and looked at it. The others glanced at it too, but they couldn't make out what it was at all. It seemed to be a kind of map.

'Perhaps it's a map of some place he had to go to,' said Julian. But suddenly George's hands began to shake as she held the map, and her eyes gleamed brilliantly as she looked up at the others. She opened her mouth but didn't speak.

'What's the matter?' said Julian, curiously. 'What's up? Have you lost your tongue?'

George shook her head and then began to speak with a rush. 'Julian! Do you know what this is? It's a map of my old castle – of Kirrin Castle – when it wasn't a ruin. And it shows the dungeons! And look – just look what's written in this corner of the dungeons!'

She put a trembling finger on one part of the map. The others leaned over to see what it was – and, printed in old-fashioned letters was a curious word.

INGOTS

'Ingots!' said Anne, puzzled. 'What does that mean? I've never heard that word before.'

But the two boys had. 'Ingots!' cried Dick. 'Why – that must be the bars of gold. They were called ingots.'

'Most bars of metal are called ingots,' said Julian, going red with excitement. 'But as we know there is gold missing from that ship, then it really looks as if ingots here meant bars of gold. Oh golly! To think they may still be hidden somewhere under Kirrin Castle. George! George! Isn't it terribly, awfully exciting?'

George nodded. She was trembling all over with excitement. 'If only we could find it!' she whispered. 'If only we could!'

'We'll have a jolly good hunt for it,' said Julian. 'It will be awfully difficult because the castle is in ruins now, and so overgrown. But somehow or other we'll find those ingots. What a lovely word. Ingots! Ingots! Ingots!'

It sounded somehow more exciting than the word gold. Nobody spoke about gold any more. They talked about the ingots. Tim couldn't make out what the excitement was at all. He wagged his tail and tried hard to lick first

one and then another of the children, but for once not one
of them paid any attention to him! He simply couldn't
understand it, and after a while he went and sat down by
himself with his back to the children, and his ears down.

'Oh, do look at poor Timothy!' said George. 'He can't
understand your excitement. Tim! Tim, darling, it's all
right, you're not in disgrace or anything. Oh, Tim, we've
got the most wonderful secret in the whole world.'

Tim bounded up, his tail wagging, pleased to be taken

notice of once more. He put his big paw on the precious map, and the four children shouted at him at once.

'Golly! We can't have that torn!' said Julian. Then he looked at the others and frowned. 'What are we going to do about the box?' he said. 'I mean – George's father will be sure to miss it, won't he? We'll have to give it back.'

'Well, can't we take out the map and keep it?' said Dick. 'He won't know it was there if he hasn't looked in the box. And it's pretty certain he hasn't. The other things don't matter much – they are only that old diary and a few letters.'

'To be on the safe side, let's take a copy of the map,' said Julian. 'Then we can put the real map back and replace the box.'

They all voted that a very good idea. They went back to Kirrin Cottage and traced out the map carefully. They did it in the tool-shed because they didn't want anyone to see them. It was a strange map. It was in three parts.

'This part shows the dungeons under the castle,' said Julian. 'And this shows a plan of the ground floor of the castle – and this shows the top part. My word, it was a fine place in those days! The dungeons run all under the castle. I bet they were pretty awful places. I wonder how people got down to them.'

'We'll have to study the map a bit more and see,' said George. 'It all looks rather muddled to us at present – but once we take the map over to the castle and study it there, we may be able to make out how to get down to the hidden dungeons. Ooooh! I don't expect any children ever had such an adventure as this.'

Julian put the traced map carefully into his jeans pocket. He didn't mean it to leave him. It was very precious. Then he put the real map back into the box and looked towards the house. 'What about putting it back now?' he said. 'Maybe your father is still asleep, George.'

But he wasn't. He was awake. Luckily he hadn't missed the box! He came into the dining-room to have tea with the family, and Julian took his chance. He muttered an excuse, slipped away from the table, and replaced the box on the table behind his uncle's chair!

He winked at the others when he came back. They felt relieved. They were all scared of Uncle Quentin, and were not at all anxious to be in his bad books. Anne didn't say one word during the whole of the meal. She was so terribly afraid she might give something away, either about Tim or the box. The others spoke very little too. While they were at tea the telephone rang and Aunt Fanny went to answer it.

She soon came back. 'It's for you, Quentin,' she said. 'Apparently the old wreck has caused quite a lot of excitement, and there are men from a London paper who want to ask you questions about it.'

'Tell them I'll see them at six,' said Uncle Quentin. The children looked at one another in alarm. They hoped that their uncle wouldn't show the box to the newspaper men. Then the secret of the hidden gold might come out!

'What a mercy we took a tracing of the map!' said Julian, after tea. 'But I'm jolly sorry now we left the real map in the box. Someone else may guess our secret!'

CHAPTER TEN

An astonishing offer

THE NEXT morning the papers were full of the extraordinary way in which the old wreck had been thrown up out of the sea. The newspaper men had got out of the children's uncle the tale of the wreck and the lost gold, and some of them even managed to land on Kirrin Island and take pictures of the old ruined castle.

George was furious. 'It's *my* castle!' she stormed to her mother. 'It's *my* island. You said it could be mine. You did, you did!'

'I know, George dear,' said her mother. 'But you really must be sensible. It can't hurt the island to be landed on, and it can't hurt the castle to be photographed.'

'But I don't want it to be,' said George, her face dark and sulky. 'It's mine. And the wreck is mine. You said so.'

'Well, I didn't know it was going to be thrown up like that,' said her mother. 'Do be sensible, George. What can it possibly matter if people go to look at the wreck? You can't stop them.'

George couldn't stop them, but that didn't make her any the less angry about it. The children were astonished at the interest that the cast-up wreck caused, and because of that, Kirrin Island became an object of great interest too. Sightseers from the places all around came to see it, and the fishermen managed to find the little inlet and land the people there. George sobbed with rage, and Julian tried to comfort her.

'Listen, George! No one knows our secret yet. We'll wait till this excitement has died down, and then we'll go to Kirrin Castle and find the ingots.'

'If someone doesn't find them first,' said George, drying her eyes. She was furious with herself for crying, but she really couldn't help it.

'How could they?' said Julian. 'No one has seen inside the box yet! I'm going to wait my chance and get that map out before anyone sees it!'

But he didn't have a chance, because something dreadful happened. Uncle Quentin sold the old box to a man who bought antique things! He came out from his study, beaming, a day or two after the excitement began, and told Aunt Fanny and the children.

'I've struck a very good bargain with that man,' he said to his wife. 'You know that old tin-lined box from the wreck? Well, this fellow collects curious things like that, and he gave me a very good price for it. Very good indeed. More even that I could expect for the writing of my book! As soon as he saw the old map there and the old diary he said at once that he would buy the whole collection.'

The children stared at him in horror. The box was sold! Now someone would study that map and perhaps jump to what 'ingots' meant. The story of the lost gold had been put into all the newspapers now. Nobody could fail to know what the map showed if they studied it carefully.

The children did not dare to tell Uncle Quentin what they knew. It was true he was all smiles now, and was promising to buy them new shrimping-nets, and a raft for themselves – but he was such a changeable person. He might fly into a furious temper if he heard that Julian had taken the box and opened it himself, while his uncle was sleeping.

When they were alone the children discussed the whole matter. It seemed very serious indeed to them. They half-wondered if they should let Aunt Fanny into the secret – but it was such a precious secret, and so marvellous, that they felt they didn't want to give it away to anyone at all.

'Now listen!' said Julian, at last. 'We'll ask Aunt Fanny if we can go to Kirrin Island and spend a day or two there – sleep there at night too, I mean. That will give us a little time to poke round and see what we can find. The sightseers won't come after a day or two, I'm sure. Maybe we'll get in before anyone tumbles to our secret. After all, the man who bought the box may not even guess that the map shows Kirrin Castle.'

They felt more cheerful. It was so awful to do nothing. As soon as they had planned to act, they felt better. They decided to ask their aunt the next day if they might go and spend the weekend at the castle. The weather was gloriously fine, and it would be great fun. They could take plenty of food with them.

When they went to ask Aunt Fanny, Uncle Quentin was with her. He was all smiles again, and even clapped Julian on the back. 'Well!' he said. 'What's this deputation for?'

'We just wanted to ask Aunt Fanny something,' said Julian, politely. 'Aunt Fanny, as the weather is so fine, do you think you would let us go for the weekend to Kirrin Castle, please, and spend a day or two there on the island? You can't think how we would love to!'

'Well – what do you think, Quentin?' asked their aunt, turning to her husband.

'If they want to, they can,' said Uncle Quentin. 'They won't have a chance to, soon. My dears, we have had a marvellous offer for Kirrin Island! A man wants to buy it, rebuild the castle as a hotel, and make it into a proper holiday place! What do you think of that?'

All four children stared at the smiling man, shocked and horrified. Somebody was going to buy the island! Had their secret been discovered? Did the man want to buy the castle because he had read the map, and knew there was plenty of gold hidden there?

George gave a curious choke. Her eyes burned as if they were on fire. 'Mother! You can't sell my island! You can't sell my castle! I won't let them be sold.'

Her father frowned. 'Don't be silly, Georgina,' he said. 'It isn't really yours. You know that. It belongs to your mother, and naturally she would like to sell it if she could. We need the money very badly. You will be able to have a great many nice things once we sell the island.'

'I don't want nice things!' cried poor George. 'My castle and my island are the nicest things I could ever have. Mother! Mother! You know you said I could have them. You know you did! I believed you.'

'George dear, I did mean you to have them to play on, when I thought they couldn't possibly be worth anything,' said her mother, looking distressed. 'But now things are different. Your father has been offered quite a good sum, far more than we ever thought of getting – and we really can't afford to turn it down.'

'So you only gave me the island when you thought it wasn't worth anything,' said George, her face white and angry. 'As soon as it is worth money you take it away again. I think that's horrid. It – it isn't honourable.'

'That's enough, Georgina,' said her father, angrily. 'Your mother is guided by me. You're only a child. Your mother didn't really mean what she said – it was only to please you. But you know well enough you will share in the money we get and have anything you want.'

'I won't touch a penny!' said George, in a low choking voice. 'You'll be sorry you sold it.'

The girl turned and stumbled out of the room. The others felt very sorry for her. They knew what she was feeling. She took things so very seriously. Julian thought she didn't understand grown-ups very well. It wasn't a bit of good fighting grown-ups. They could do exactly as they liked. If they wanted to take away George's island and castle, they could. If they wanted to sell it, they could! But what Uncle Quentin didn't know was the fact that there might be a store of gold ingots there! Julian stared at his uncle and wondered whether to warn him. Then he decided not to. There was just a chance that the four children could find the gold first!

'When are you selling the island, Uncle?' he asked quietly.

'The deeds will be signed in about a week's time,' was the answer. 'So if you really want to spend a day or two there, you'd better do so quickly, for after that you may not get permission from the new owners.'

'Was it the man who bought the old box who wants to buy the island?' asked Julian.

'Yes,' said his uncle. 'I was a little surprised myself, for I thought he was just a buyer of old things. It was astonishing to me that he should get the idea of buying the island to rebuild the castle as a hotel. Still, I dare say there will be big money in running a hotel there – very romantic, staying on a little island like that – people will like it. I'm no businessman myself, and I certainly shouldn't care to invest my money in a place like Kirrin Island. But I should think he knows what he is doing all right.'

'Yes, he certainly does,' thought Julian to himself, as he went out of the room with Dick and Anne. 'He's read that map – and has jumped to the same idea that we did – the store of hidden ingots is somewhere on that island – and he's going to get it! He doesn't want to build a hotel! He's after the treasure! I expect he's offered Uncle Quentin some silly low price that poor old uncle thinks is marvellous! Oh dear – this is a horrible thing to happen.'

He went to find George. She was in the tool-shed, looking quite green. She said she felt sick.

'It's only because you're so upset,' said Julian. He slipped his arm round her. For once George didn't push it away. She felt comforted. Tears came into her eyes, and she angrily tried to blink them away.

'Listen, George!' said Julian. 'We mustn't give up hope. We'll go to Kirrin Island tomorrow, and we'll do our very, very best to get down into the dungeons somehow and find the ingots. We'll jolly well stay there till we do. See? Now cheer up, because we'll want your help in planning everything. Thank goodness we took a tracing of the map.'

George cheered up a little. She still felt angry with her father and mother, but the thought of going to Kirrin Island for a day or two, and taking Timothy too, certainly seemed rather good.

'I do think my father and mother are unkind,' she said.

'Well, they're not really,' said Julian, wisely. 'After all, if they need money badly, they would be silly not to part with something they think is quite useless. And you know, your father did say you could have anything you want. I know what I would ask for, if I were you!'

'What?' asked George.

'Timothy, of course!' said Julian. And that made George smile and cheer up tremendously!

CHAPTER ELEVEN

Off to Kirrin Island

JULIAN AND George went to find Dick and Anne. They were waiting for them in the garden, looking rather upset. They were glad to see Julian and George and ran to meet them.

Anne took George's hands. 'I'm awfully sorry about your island, George,' she said.

'So am I,' said Dick. 'Bad luck, old girl – I mean, old boy!'

George managed to smile. 'I've been behaving like a girl,' she said, half-ashamed. 'But I did get an awful shock.'

Julian told the others what they had planned. 'We'll go tomorrow morning,' he said. 'We'll make out a list of all the things we shall need. Let's begin now.'

He took out a pencil and notebook. The others looked at him.

'Things to eat,' said Dick at once. 'Plenty because we'll be hungry.'

'Something to drink,' said George. 'There's no water on the island – though I believe there was a well or something, years ago, that went right down below the level of the sea, and was fresh water. Anyway, I've never found it.'

'Food,' wrote down Julian, 'and drink.' He looked at the others.

'Spades,' he said solemnly, and scribbled the word down.

Anne stared in surprise.

'What for?' she asked.

'Well, we'll want to dig about when we're hunting for a way down to the dungeons,' said Julian.

'Ropes,' said Dick. 'We may want those too.'

'And torches,' said George. 'It'll be dark in the dungeons.'

'Oooh!' said Anne, feeling a pleasant shiver go down her back at the thought. She had no idea what dungeons were like, but they sounded thrilling.

'Rugs,' said Dick. 'We'll be cold at night if we sleep in that little old room.'

Julian wrote them down. 'Mugs to drink from,' he said. 'And we'll take a few tools too – we may perhaps need them. You never know.'

At the end of half an hour they had quite a nice long list, and everyone felt pleased and excited. George was beginning to recover from her rage and disappointment. If she had been alone, and had brooded over everything, she would have been in an even worse sulk and temper – but somehow the others were so calm and sensible and cheerful. It was impossible to sulk for long if she was with them.

'I think I'd have been much nicer if I hadn't been on my own so much,' thought George to herself, as she looked at Julian's bent head. 'Talking about things to other people does help a lot. They don't seem so dreadful then; they seem more bearable and ordinary. I like my three cousins awfully. I like them because they talk and laugh and are always cheerful and kind. I wish I were like them. I'm sulky and bad-tempered and fierce, and no wonder Father doesn't like me and scolds me so often. Mother's a dear, but I understand now why she says I am difficult. I'm different from my cousins – they're easy to understand, and everyone likes them. I'm glad they came. They are making me more like I ought to be.'

This was a long thought to think, and George looked very serious while she was thinking it. Julian looked up and caught her blue eyes fixed on him. He smiled.

'Penny for your thoughts!' he said.

'They're not worth a penny,' said George, going red. 'I was just thinking how nice you all are – and how I wished I could be like you.'

'You're an awfully nice person,' said Julian, surprisingly. 'You can't help being an only child. They're always a bit odd, you know, unless they're mighty careful. You're a most interesting person, I think.'

George flushed red again, and felt pleased. 'Let's go and take Timothy for a walk,' she said. 'He'll be wondering what's happened to us today.'

They all went off together, and Timothy greeted them at the top of his voice. They told him all about their plans for the next day, and he wagged his tail and looked up at them out of his soft brown eyes as if he understood every single word they said!

'He must feel pleased to think he's going to be with us for two or three days,' said Anne.

It was very exciting the next morning, setting off in the boat with all their things packed neatly at one end. Julian checked them all by reading out aloud from his list. It didn't seem as if they had forgotten anything.

'Got the map?' said Dick, suddenly.

Julian nodded.

'I put on clean jeans this morning,' he said, 'but you

may be sure I remembered to pop the map into my pocket. Here it is!'

He took it out – and the wind at once blew it right out of his hands! It fell into the sea and bobbed there in the wind. All four children gave a cry of utter dismay. Their precious map!

'Quick! Row after it!' cried George, and swung the boat round. But someone was quicker than she was! Tim had seen the paper fly from Julian's hand, and had heard and understood the cries of dismay. With an enormous splash he leapt into the water and swam valiantly after the map.

He could swim well for a dog, for he was strong and powerful. He soon had the map in his mouth and was swimming back to the boat. The children thought he was simply marvellous!

George hauled him into the boat and took the map from his mouth. There was hardly the mark of his teeth on it he had carried it so carefully! It was wet, and the children looked anxiously at it to see if the tracing had been spoilt. But Julian had traced it very strongly, and it was quite all right. He placed it on a seat to dry, and told Dick to hold it there in the sun.

'That was a narrow squeak!' he said, and the others agreed.

George took the oars again, and they set off once more for the island, getting a perfect shower-bath from Timothy when he stood up and shook his wet coat. He was given a big biscuit as a reward, and crunched it up with great enjoyment.

George made her way through the reefs of rocks with a sure hand. It was marvellous to the others how she could slide the boat in between the dangerous rocks and never get a scratch. They thought she was really wonderful. She brought them safely to the little inlet, and they jumped out on to the sand. They pulled the boat high up, in case the tide came far up the tiny cove, and then began to unload their goods.

'We'll carry all the things to that little stone room,' said Julian. 'They will be safe there and won't get wet if it rains. I hope nobody comes to the island while we are here, George.'

'I shouldn't think they would,' said George. 'Father said it would be about a week before the deeds were signed, making over the island to that man. It won't be his till then. We've got a week, anyhow.'

'Well, we don't need to keep a watch in case anyone else arrives then,' said Julian, who had half thought that it would be a good idea to make someone stay on guard at the inlet, to give a warning to the others in case anyone else arrived. 'Come on! You take the spades, Dick. I'll take the food and drink with George. And Anne can take the little things.'

The food and drink were in a big box, for the children did not mean to starve while they were on the island! They had brought loaves of bread, butter, biscuits, jam, tins of fruit, ripe plums, bottles of ginger-beer, a kettle to make tea, and anything else they could think of! George and Julian staggered up the cliff with the heavy box. They had to put it down once or twice to give themselves a rest!

They put everything into the little room. Then they went back to get the collection of blankets and rugs from the boat. They arranged them in the corners of the little room, and thought that it would be most exciting to spend the night there.

'The two girls can sleep together on this pile of rugs,' said Julian. 'And we two boys will have this pile.'

George looked as if she didn't want to be put with Anne, and classed as a girl. But Anne didn't wish to sleep alone in her corner, and she looked so beseechingly at George that the bigger girl smiled at her and made no objection. Anne thought that George was getting nicer and nicer!

'Well, now we'll get down to business,' said Julian, and

he pulled out his map. 'We must study this really carefully, and find out exactly under which spot the entrances to the dungeons are. Now – come around and let's do our best to find out! It's up to us to use our brains – and beat that man who's bought the island!'

They all bent over the traced map. It was quite dry now, and the children looked at it earnestly. It was plain that in the old days the castle had been a very fine place.

'Now look,' said Julian, putting his finger on the plan of the dungeons. 'These seem to run all along under the castle – and here – and – here – are the marks that seem to be meant to represent steps or stairs.'

'Yes,' said George. 'I should think they are. Well, if so, there appear to be two ways of getting down into the dungeons. One lot of steps seems to begin somewhere near this little room – and the other seems to start under the tower there. And what do you suppose this thing is here, Julian?'

She put her finger on a round hole that was shown not only in the plan of the dungeons, but also in the plan of the ground floor of the castle.

'I can imagine what that is,' said Julian, puzzled. 'Oh yes, I know what it might be! You said there was an old well somewhere, do you remember? Well, that may be it, I should think. It would have to be very deep to get fresh water right under the sea – so it probably goes down through the dungeons too. Isn't this thrilling?'

Everyone thought it was. They felt happy and excited. There was something to discover – something they could and must discover within the next day or two.

They looked at one another. 'Well,' said Dick,' what are we going to start on? Shall we try to find the entrance to

103

the dungeons – the one that seems to start round about this little room? For all we know there may be a big stone we can lift that opens above the dungeon steps!'

This was a thrilling thought, and the children jumped up at once. Julian folded up the precious map and put it into his pocket. He looked round. The stone floor of the little room was overgrown with creeping weeds. They must be cleared away before it was possible to see if there were any stones that looked as if they might be moved.

'We'd better set to work,' said Julian, and he picked up a spade. 'Let's clear away these weeds with our spades – scrape them off, look, like this – and then examine every single stone!'

They all picked up spades and soon the little stone room was full of a scraping sound as the four of them chiselled away at the close-growing weeds with their spades. It wasn't very difficult to get the stones clear of them, and the children worked with a will.

Tim got most excited about everything. He hadn't any idea at all what they were doing, but he joined in valiantly. He scraped away at the floor with his four paws, sending earth and plants flying high into the air!

'Hi, Tim!' said Julian, shaking a clod of earth out of his hair. 'You're being a bit too vigorous. My word, you'll send the stones flying into the air too, in a minute. George, isn't Tim marvellous the way he joins in everything?'

How they all worked! How they all longed to find the entrance to the underground dungeons! What a thrill that would be.

CHAPTER TWELVE

Exciting discoveries

SOON THE stones of the little room were clear of earth, sand and weeds. The children saw that they were all the same size – big and square, fitted well together. They went over them carefully with their torches, trying to find one that might move or lift.

'We should probably find one with an iron ring handle sunk into it,' said Julian. But they didn't. All the stones looked exactly the same. It was most disappointing.

Julian tried inserting his spade into the cracks between the various stones, to see if by any chance he could move one. But they couldn't be moved. It seemed as if they were all set in the solid ground. After about three hours' hard work the children sat down to eat a meal.

They were very hungry indeed, and felt glad to think there were so many things to eat. As they ate they discussed the problem they were trying to solve

'It looks as if the entrance to the dungeons was not under this little room after all,' said Julian. 'It's disappointing – but somehow I don't think now that the steps down to the dungeon started from here. Let's measure the map and see if we can make out exactly where the steps do start. It may be, of course, that the measurements aren't correct and won't be any help to us at all. But we can try.'

So they measured as best they could, to try and find out in exactly what place the dungeon steps seemed to begin. It was impossible to tell, for the plans of the three floors seemed to be done to different scales. Julian stared at the map, puzzled. It seemed rather hopeless. Surely they wouldn't have to hunt all over the ground floor of the castle! It would take ages.

'Look,' said George, suddenly, putting her finger on the hole that they all thought must be meant to represent the well. 'The entrance to the dungeons seems to be not very far off the well. If only we could find the well, we could hunt around a bit for the beginning of the dungeon steps. The well is shown in both maps. It seems to be somewhere about the middle of the castle.'

'That's a good idea of yours,' said Julian, pleased. 'Let's go out into the middle of the castle – we can more or less guess where the old well ought to be, because it definitely seems to be about the middle of the old yard out there.'

Out they all went into the sunshine. They felt very important and serious. It was marvellous to be looking for lost ingots of gold. They all felt perfectly certain that they really were somewhere beneath their feet. It didn't occur to any of the children that the treasure might not be there.

They stood in the ruined courtyard that had once been the centre of the castle. They paced out the middle of the yard and then stood there, looking around in vain for anything that might perhaps have been the opening of an old well. It was all so overgrown. Sand had blown in from the shore, and weeds and bushes of all kinds grew there. The stones that had once formed the floor of the big courtyard were now cracked and were no longer lying flat. Most of them were covered with sand or weeds.

'Look! There's a rabbit!' cried Dick, as a big sandy rabbit lolloped slowly across the yard. It disappeared into a hole on the other side. Then another rabbit appeared, sat up and looked at the children, and then vanished too. The children were thrilled. They had never seen such tame rabbits before.

A third rabbit appeared. It was a small one with absurdly big ears, and the tiniest white bob of a tail. It didn't even look at the children. It bounded about in a playful way, and then, to the children's enormous delight, it sat up on its hind legs, and began to wash its big ears, pulling down first one and then the other.

But this was too much for Timothy. He had watched the other two bound across the yard and then disappear without so much as barking at them. But to see this youngster actually sitting there washing its ears under his very nose was really too much for any dog. He gave an excited yelp and rushed full-tilt at the surprised rabbit.

For a moment the little thing didn't move. It had never been frightened or chased before, and it stared with big eyes at the rushing dog. Then it turned itself about and tore off at top speed, its white bobtail going up and down as it bounded away. It disappeared under a gorse bush near the children. Timothy went after it, vanishing under the big bush too.

Then a shower of sand and earth was thrown up as Tim tried to go down the hole after the rabbit and scraped and scrabbled with his strong front paws as fast as he could. He yelped and whined in excitement, not seeming to hear George's voice calling to him. He meant to get that rabbit! He went almost mad as he scraped at the hole, making it bigger and bigger.

'Tim! Do you hear me! Come out of there!' shouted

George. 'You're not to chase the rabbits here. You know you mustn't. You're very naughty. Come out!'

But Tim didn't come out. He just went on and on scraping away madly. George went to fetch him. Just as she got up to the gorse bush the scraping suddenly stopped. There came a scared yelp – and no more noise was heard. George peered under the prickly bush in astonishment.

Tim had disappeared! He just simply wasn't there any more. There was the big rabbit-hole, made enormous by Tim – but there was no Tim.

'I say, Julian – Tim's gone,' said George in a scared voice. 'He surely can't have gone down the rabbit's hole, can he? I mean – he's such a big dog!'

The children crowded round the big gorse bush. There came the sound of a muffled whine from somewhere below it. Julian looked astonished.

'He *is* down the hole!' he said. 'How funny! I never heard of a dog really going down a rabbit-hole before. How ever are we going to get him out?'

'We'll have to dig up the gorse bush, to begin with,' said George, in a determined voice. She would have dug up the whole of Kirrin Castle to get Tim back, that was certain! 'I can't have poor old Tim whining for help down there and not do what we can to help him.'

The bush was far too big and prickly to creep underneath. Julian was glad they had brought tools of all kinds. He went to fetch an axe. They had brought a small one with them and it would do to chop away the prickly branches and trunk of the gorse bush. The children slashed at it and soon the poor bush began to look a sorry sight.

109

It took a long time to destroy it, for it was prickly, sturdy and stout. Every child's hands were scratched by the time the bush had been reduced to a mere stump. Then they could see the hole quite well. Julian shone his torch down it.

He gave a shout of surprise. 'I know what's happened! The old well is here! The rabbits had a hole at the side of it – and Tim scraped away to make it bigger and uncovered a bit of the well-hole – and he's fallen down the well!'

'Oh no, oh no,' cried George, in panic. 'Oh Tim, Tim, are you all right?'

A distant whine came to their ears. Evidently Tim was there somewhere. The children looked at one another.

'Well, there's only one thing to do,' said Julian. 'We must get out spades now and dig out the hole of the well. Then maybe we can let a rope down or something and get Tim.'

They set to work with their spades. It was not really difficult to uncover the hole, which had been blocked only by the spreading roots of the big gorse bush, some fallen masonry, earth, sand and small stones. Apparently a big slab had fallen from part of the tower across the well-hole, and partly closed it. The weather and the growing gorse bush had done the rest.

It took all the children together to move the slab. Underneath was a very rotten wooden cover, which had plainly been used in the old days to protect the well. It had rotted so much that when Tim's weight had been pressed on it, it had given just there and made a hole for Tim to fall through.

Julian removed the old wooden cover and then the children could see down the well-hole. It was very deep and very dark. They could not possibly see the bottom. Julian took a stone and dropped it down. They all listened for the splash. But there was no splash. Either there was no longer any water there, or the well was too deep even to hear the splash!

'I think it's too deep for us to hear anything,' said Julian. 'Now – where's Tim?'

He shone his torch down – and there was Tim! Many years before a big slab had fallen down the well itself and had stuck a little way down, across the well-hole – and on this old cracked slab sat Tim, his big eyes staring up in fright. He simply could not imagine what had happened to him.

There was an old iron ladder fastened to the side of the well. George was on it before anyone else could get there! Down she went, not caring if the ladder held or not, and reached Tim. Somehow she got him on to her shoulder and, holding him there with one hand, she climbed slowly up again. The other three hauled her out and Tim jumped round her, barking and licking for all he was worth!

'Well, Tim!' said Dick. 'You shouldn't chase rabbits – but you've certainly done us a good turn, because you've found the well for us! Now we've only got to look around a little to find the dungeon entrance!'

They set to work again to hunt for the dungeon entrance. They dug about with their spades under all the bushes. They pulled up crooked stones and dug their spades into the earth below, hoping that they might suddenly find them going through into space! It was really very thrilling.

And then Anne found the entrance! It was quite by accident. She was tired and sat down to rest. She lay on her front and scrabbled about in the sand. Suddenly her fingers touched something hard and cold in the sand. She uncovered it – and lo and behold, it was an iron ring! She gave a shout and the others looked up.

'There's a stone with an iron ring in it here!' yelled Anne, excitedly. They all rushed over to her. Julian dug about with his spade and uncovered the whole stone. Sure enough, it did have a ring in it – and rings are only set into stones that need to be moved! Surely this stone must be the one that covered the dungeon entrance!

All the children took turns at pulling on the iron ring, but the stone did not move. Then Julian tied two or three turns of rope through it and the four children put out their full strength and pulled for all they were worth.

The stone moved. The children distinctly felt it stir. 'All together again!' cried Julian. And all together they pulled. The stone stirred again and then suddenly gave way. It moved upwards – and the children fell over on top of one another like a row of dominoes suddenly pushed down! Tim darted to the hole and barked madly down it as if all the rabbits of the world lived there!

Julian and George shot to their feet and rushed to the opening that the moved stone had disclosed. They stood there, looking downwards, their faces shining with delight. They *had* found the entrance to the dungeons! A steep flight of steps, cut out of the rock itself, led downwards into deep darkness.

'Come on!' cried Julian, snapping on his torch. 'We've found what we wanted! Now for the dungeons!'

The steps down were slippery. Tim darted down first, lost his footing and rolled down five or six steps, yelping with fright. Julian went after him, then George, then Dick and then Anne. They were all tremendously thrilled. Indeed, they quite expected to see piles of gold and all kinds of treasure everywhere around them!

It was dark down the steep flight of steps, and smelt very musty. Anne choked a little.

'I hope the air down here is all right,' said Julian. 'Sometimes it isn't good in these underground places. If anyone feels a bit funny they'd better say so and we'll go up into the open air again.'

But however funny they might feel, nobody would have said so. It was all far too exciting to worry about feeling strange.

The steps went down a long way. Then they came to an end. Julian stepped down from the last rock-stair and flashed his torch around. It was a weird sight that met his eyes.

The dungeons of Kirrin Castle were made out of the rock itself. Whether there were natural caves here, or whether they had been hollowed out by man the children could not tell. But certainly they were very mysterious, dark and full of echoing sounds. When Julian gave a sigh of excitement it fled into the rocky hollows and swelled out and echoed around as if it were a live thing. It gave all the children a very peculiar feeling.

'Isn't it strange?' said George, in a low voice. At once the echoes took up her words, and multiplied them and made them louder – and all the dungeon caves gave back the girl's words over and over again. 'Isn't it strange, ISN'T IT STRANGE, ISN'T IT STRANGE.'

Anne slipped her hand into Dick's. She felt scared. She didn't like the echoes at all. She knew they *were* only echoes – but they did sound exactly like the voices of scores of people hidden in the caves!

'Where do you suppose the ingots are?' said Dick. And at once the caves threw him back his words. INGOTS! INGOTS ARE! INGOTS ARE! ARE! ARE!

Julian laughed – and his laugh was split up into dozens of different laughs that came out of the dungeons and spun round the listening children. It really was the strangest thing.

'Come on,' said Julian. 'Maybe the echoes won't be so bad a little farther in.'

'FARTHER IN, said the echoes at once. 'FARTHER IN!'

They moved away from the end of the rocky steps and explored the nearby dungeons. They were really only rocky cellars stretching under the castle. Maybe wretched prisoners had been kept there many, many years before, but mostly they had been used for storing things.

'I wonder which dungeon was used for storing the ingots,' said Julian. He stopped and took the map out of his pocket. He flashed his torch on to it. But although it showed him quite plainly the dungeon where INGOTS were marked, he had no idea at all of the right direction.

'I say – look – there's a door here, shutting off the next dungeon!' suddenly cried Dick. 'I bet this is the dungeon we're looking for! I bet there are ingots in here!'

CHAPTER THIRTEEN

Down in the dungeons

FOUR TORCHES were flashed on to the wooden door. It was big and stout, studded with great iron nails. Julian gave a whoop of delight and rushed to it. He felt certain that behind it was the dungeon used for storing things.

But the door was fast shut. No amount of pushing or pulling would open it. It had a great keyhole – but no key there! The four children stared in exasperation at the door. Bother it! Just as they really thought they were near the ingots, this door wouldn't open!

'We'll fetch the axe,' said Julian, suddenly. 'We may be able to chop round the keyhole and smash the lock.'

'That's a good idea!' said George, delighted. 'Come on back!'

They left the big door, and tried to get back the way they had come. But the dungeons were so big and so rambling that they lost their way. They stumbled over old broken barrels, rotting wood, empty bottles and many other things as they tried to find their way back to the big flight of rock-steps.

'This is sickening!' said Julian, at last. 'I simply haven't any idea at all where the entrance is. We keep on going into one dungeon after another, and one passage after another, and they all seem to be exactly the same – dark and smelly and mysterious.'

'Suppose we have to stay here all the rest of our lives!' said Anne, gloomily.

117

'Idiot!' said Dick, taking her hand. 'We shall soon find the way out. Hallo! – what's this?'

They all stopped. They had come to what looked like a chimney shaft of brick, stretching down from the roof of the dungeon to the floor. Julian flashed his torch on to it. He was puzzled.

'I know what it is!' said George, suddenly. 'It's the well, of course! You remember it was shown in the plan of the dungeons, as well as in the plan of the ground floor. Well, that's the shaft of the well going down and down. I wonder if there's any opening in it just here – so that water could be taken into the dungeons as well as up to the ground floor.'

They went to see. On the other side of the well-shaft was a small opening big enough for one child at a time to put his head and shoulders through and look down. They shone their torches down and up. The well was so deep that it was still impossible to see the bottom of it. Julian dropped a stone down again, but there was no sound of either a thud or a splash. He looked upwards, and could see the faint gleam of daylight that slid round the broken slab of stone lying a little way down the shaft – the slab on which Tim had sat, waiting to be rescued.

'Yes,' he said, 'this is the well all right. Isn't it weird? Well – now we've found the well we know that the entrance to the dungeons isn't very far off!'

That cheered them all up tremendously. They held hands and hunted around in the dark, their torches making bright beams of light here and there.

Anne gave a screech of excitement. 'Here's the entrance! It must be, because I can see faint daylight coming down!'

The children rounded a corner and sure enough, there

was the steep, rocky flight of steps leading upwards. Julian took a quick look round so that he might know the way to go when they came down again. He didn't feel at all certain that he would find the wooden door!

They all went up into the sunshine. It was delicious to feel the warmth on their heads and shoulders after the cold air down in the dungeons. Julian looked at his watch and gave a loud exclamation.

'It's half-past six! *Half-past six!* No wonder I feel hungry. We haven't had any tea. We've been working, and wandering about those dungeons for hours.'

'Well, let's have a kind of tea-supper before we do anything else,' said Dick. 'I don't feel as if I've had anything to eat for about twelve months.'

'Well, considering you ate about twice as much as anyone else at dinner-time,' began Julian, indignantly. Then he grinned. 'I feel the same as you,' he said. 'Come on! – let's get a really good meal. George, what about boiling a kettle and making some cocoa, or something? I feel cold after all that time underground.'

It was fun boiling the kettle on a fire of dry sticks. It was lovely to lie about in the warmth of the evening sun and munch bread and cheese and enjoy cake and biscuits. They all enjoyed themselves thoroughly. Tim had a good meal too. He hadn't very much liked being underground, and had followed the others very closely indeed, his tail well down. He had been very frightened, too, of the curious echoes here and there.

Once he had barked, and it had seemed to Tim as if the whole of the dungeons were full of other dogs, all barking far more loudly than he could. He hadn't even dared to whine after that! But now he was happy again, eating the tit-bits that the children gave him, and licking George whenever he was near her.

It was past eight o'clock by the time that the children had finished their meal and tidied up. Julian looked at the others. The sun was sinking, and the day was no longer so warm.

'Well,' he said, 'I don't know what you feel. But I don't somehow want to go down into those dungeons again today, not even for the sake of smashing in that door with the axe and opening it! I'm tired – and I don't like the thought of losing my way in those dungeons at night.'

The others heartily agreed with him, especially Anne, who had secretly been dreading going down again with the night coming on. The little girl was almost asleep; she was so tired out with hard work and excitement.

'Come on, Anne!' said George, pulling her to her feet. 'Bed for you. We'll cuddle up together in the rugs on the floor of that little room – and in the morning when we wake we'll be simply thrilled to think of opening that big wooden door.'

All four children, with Tim close behind, went off to the little stone room. They curled up on their piles of rugs, and Tim crept in with George and Anne. He lay down on them, and felt so heavy that Anne had to push him off her legs.

He sat himself down on her again, and she groaned, half-asleep. Tim wagged his tail and thumped it hard against her ankles. Then George pulled him on to her own legs and lay there, feeling him breathe. She was very happy. She was spending the night on her island. They had almost found the ingots, she was sure. She had Tim with her, actually sleeping on her rugs. Perhaps everything would come right after all – somehow.

DOWN IN THE DUNGEONS

She fell asleep. The children felt perfectly safe with Tim on guard. They slept peacefully until the morning, when Tim saw a rabbit through the broken archway leading to the little room, and sped away to chase it. He awoke George as he got up from the rugs, and she sat up and rubbed her eyes.

'Wake up!' she cried to the others. 'Wake up, all of you! It's morning! And we're on the island!'

They all awoke. It was really thrilling to sit up and remember everything. Julian thought of the big wooden door at once. He would soon smash it in with his axe, he felt sure. And then what would they find?

They had breakfast, and ate just as much as ever. Then Julian picked up the axe they had brought and took everyone to the flight of steps. Tim went too, wagging his tail, but not really feeling very pleased at the thought of going down into the strange places where other dogs seemed to bark, and yet were not to be found. Poor Tim would never understand echoes!

They all went down underground again. And then, of course, they couldn't find the way to the wooden door! It was most tiresome.

'We shall lose our way all over again,' said George, desperately. 'These dungeons are about the most rambling spread-out maze of underground caves I've ever known! We shall lose the entrance again too!'

Julian had a bright idea. He had a piece of white chalk in his pocket, and he took it out. He went back to the steps, and marked the wall there. Then he began to put chalk-marks along the passages as they walked in the musty darkness. They came to the well, and Julian was pleased.

121

'Now,' he said, 'whenever we come to the well we shall at least be able to find the way back to the steps, because we can follow my chalk-marks. Now the thing is – which is the way next? We'll try and find it and I'll put chalk-marks along the walls here and there – but if we go the wrong way and have to come back, we'll rub out the marks, and start again from the well another way.'

This was really a very good idea. They did go the wrong way, and had to come back, rubbing out Julian's marks. They reached the well, and set off in the opposite direction. And this time they did find the wooden door!

There it was, stout and sturdy, its old iron nails rusty and red. The children stared at it in delight. Julian lifted his axe.

Crash! He drove it into the wood and round about the keyhole. But the wood was still strong, and the axe only went in an inch or two. Julian drove it in once more. The axe hit one of the big nails and slipped a little to one side. A big splinter of wood flew out – and struck poor Dick on the cheek!

He gave a yell of pain. Julian jumped in alarm, and turned to look at him. Dick's cheek was pouring with blood!

'Something flew out of the door and hit me,' said poor Dick. 'It's a splinter, or something.'

'Golly!' said Julian, and he shone his torch on to Dick. 'Can you bear it a moment if I pull the splinter out? It's a big one, and it's still sticking into your poor cheek.'

But Dick pulled it out himself. He made a face with the pain, and then turned very white.

'You'd better get up into the open air for a bit,' said Julian. 'And we'll have to bathe your cheek and stop it

122

bleeding somehow. Anne's got a clean hanky. We'll bathe it and dab it with that. We brought some water with us, luckily.'

'I'll go with Dick,' said Anne. 'You stay here with George. There's no need for us all to go.'

But Julian thought he would like to see Dick safely up into the open air first, and then he could leave him with Anne while he went back to George and went on with the smashing down of the door. He handed the axe to George.

'You can do a bit of chopping while I'm gone,' he said.
'It will take some time to smash that big door in. You get
on with it – and I'll be down in a few minutes again. We
can easily find the way to the entrance because we've only
got to follow my chalk-marks.'

'Right!' said George, and she took the axe. 'Poor old
Dick – you do look a sight.'

Leaving George behind with Tim, valiantly attacking
the big door, Julian took Dick and Anne up to the open
air. Anne dipped her hanky into the kettle of water and
dabbed Dick's cheek gently. It was bleeding very much, as
cheeks do, but the wound was not really very bad. Dick's
colour soon came back, and he wanted to go down into
the dungeons again.

'No, you'd better lie down on your back for a little,' said
Julian. 'I know that's good for nose-bleeding – and maybe
it's good for cheek-bleeding too. What about Anne and
you going out on the rocks over there, where you can see
the wreck, and staying there for half an hour or so? Come
on – I'll take you both there, and leave you for a bit. You'd
better not get up till your cheek's stopped bleeding, old
boy.'

Julian took the two out of the castle yard and out on to
the rocks on the side of the island that faced the open sea.
The dark hulk of the old wreck was still there on the rocks.
Dick lay down on his back and stared up into the sky,
hoping that his cheek would soon stop bleeding. He didn't
want to miss any of the fun!

Anne took his hand. She was very upset at the little
accident, and although she didn't want to miss the fun
either, she meant to stay with Dick till he felt better. Julian
sat down beside them for a minute or two. Then he went

back to the rocky steps and disappeared down them. He followed his chalk-marks, and soon came to where George was attacking the door.

She had smashed it well round the lock – but it simply would *not* give way. Julian took the axe from her and drove it hard into the wood.

After a blow or two something seemed to happen to the lock. It became loose, and hung a little sideways. Julian put down his axe.

'I think somehow that we can open the door now,' he said, in an excited voice. 'Get out of the way, Tim, old fellow. Now then, push, George!'

They both pushed – and the lock gave way with a grating noise. The big door opened creakingly, and the two children went inside, flashing their torches in excitement.

The room was not much more than a cave, hollowed out of the rock – but in it was something quite different from the old barrels and boxes the children had found before. At the back, in untidy piles, were curious, brick-shaped things of dull yellow-brown metal. Julian picked one up.

'George!' he cried. 'The ingots! These are real gold!' Oh, I know they don't look like it – but they are, all the same. George, oh George, there's a small fortune here in this cellar – and it's yours! We've found it at last!'

CHAPTER FOURTEEN

Prisoners!

GEORGE COULDN'T say a word. She just stood there, staring at the pile of ingots, holding one in her hands. She could hardly believe that these strange brick-shaped things were really gold. Her heart thumped fast. What a wonderful, marvellous find!

Suddenly Tim began to bark loudly. He stood with his back to the children, his nose towards the door – and how he barked!

'Shut up, Tim!' said Julian. 'What can you hear? Is it the others coming back?'

He went to the door and yelled down the passage outside. 'Dick! Anne! Is it you? Come quickly, because we've found the ingots! We've found them! Hurry! Hurry!'

Tim stopped barking and began to growl. George looked puzzled. 'Whatever *can* be the matter with Tim?' she said. 'He surely can't be growling at Dick and Anne.'

Then both children got a most tremendous shock – for a man's voice came booming down the dark passage, making strange echoes all around.

'Who is here? Who is down here?'

George clutched Julian in fright. Tim went on growling, all the hairs on his neck standing up straight. 'Do be quiet, Tim!' whispered George, snapping off her torch. But Tim simply would *not* be quiet. He went on growling as if he were a small thunderstorm.

The children saw the beam of a powerful torchlight

coming round the corner of the dungeon passage. Then the light picked them out, and the holder of the torch came to a surprised stop.

'Well, well, well!' said a voice. 'Look who's here! Two children in the dungeons of my castle.'

'What do you mean, *your* castle!' cried George.

'Well, my dear little girl, it *is* my castle, because I'm in the process of buying it,' said the voice. Then another voice spoke, more gruffly.

PRISONERS!

'What are you doing down here? What did you mean when you shouted out "Dick" and "Anne", and said you had found the ingots? What ingots?'

'Don't answer,' whispered Julian to George. But the echoes took his words and made them very loud in the passage. 'DON'T ANSWER! DON'T ANSWER!'

'Oh, so you won't answer,' said the second man, and he stepped towards the children. Tim bared his teeth, but the man didn't seem at all frightened of him. The man went to the door and flashed his torch inside the dungeon. He gave a long whistle of surprise.

'Jake! Look here!' he said. 'You were right. The gold's here all right. And how easy to take away! All in ingots – my word, this is the most amazing thing we've ever struck.'

'This gold is mine,' said George, in a fury. 'This island and the castle belong to my mother – and so does anything found here. This gold was brought here and stored by my great-great-great-grandfather before his ship got wrecked. It's not yours, and never will be. As soon as I get back home I shall tell my father and mother what we've found – and then you may be sure you won't be able to buy the castle or the island! You were very clever, finding out from the map in the old box about the gold – but just not clever enough for us. We found it first!'

The men listened in silence to George's clear and angry voice. One of them laughed. 'You're only a child,' he said. 'You surely don't think you can keep us from getting our way? We're going to buy this island – and everything in it – and we shall take the gold when the deeds are signed. And if by any chance we couldn't buy the island, we'd take the gold just the same. It would be easy enough to bring a ship

129

here and transfer the ingots from here by boat to the ship. Don't worry – we shall get what we want all right.'

'You will not!' said George, and she stepped out of the door. 'I'm going straight home now – and I'll tell my father all you've said.'

'My dear little girl, you are not going home,' said the first man, putting his hands on George and forcing her back into the dungeon. 'And, by the way, unless you want me to shoot this unpleasant dog of yours, call him off, will you?'

George saw, to her dismay, that the man had a shining revolver in his hand. In fright she caught hold of Tim's collar and pulled him to her. 'Be quiet, Tim,' she said. 'It's all right.'

But Tim knew quite well that it wasn't all right. Something was very wrong. He went on growling fiercely.

'Now listen to me,' said the man, after he had had a hurried talk with his companion. 'If you are going to be sensible, nothing unpleasant will happen to you. But if you want to be obstinate, you'll be very sorry. What we are going to do is this – we're going off in our motor-boat, leaving you nicely locked up here – and we're going to get a ship and come back for the gold. We don't think it's worthwhile buying the island now we know where the ingots are.'

'And you are going to write a note to your companions above, telling them you've found the gold and they are to come down and look for it,' said the other man. 'Then we shall lock up all of you in this dungeon, with the ingots to play with, leaving you food and drink till we come back. Now then – here is a pencil. Write a note to Dick and Anne, whoever they are, and send your dog up with it. Come on.'

'I won't,' said George, her face furious. 'I won't. You can't make me do a thing like that. I won't get poor Dick and Anne down here to be made prisoners. And I won't let you have my gold, just when I've discovered it.'

'We shall shoot your dog if you don't do as you're told,' said the first man, suddenly. George's heart sank down and she felt cold and terrified.

'No, no,' she said in a low, desperate voice.

'Well, write the note then,' said the man, offering her a pencil and paper. 'Go on. I'll tell you what to say.'

'I can't!' sobbed George. 'I don't want to get Dick and Anne down here to be made prisoners.'

'All right – I'll shoot the dog then,' said the man, in a cold voice and he levelled his revolver at poor Tim. George threw her arms round her dog and gave a scream.

'No, no! I'll write the note. Don't shoot Tim, don't shoot him!'

The girl took the paper and pencil in a shaking hand and looked at the man. 'Write this,' he ordered. ' "Dear Dick and Anne. We've found the gold. Come on down at once and see it." Then sign your name, whatever it is.'

George wrote what the man had said. Then she signed her name. But instead of writing 'George' she put 'Georgina'. She knew that the others would feel certain she would never sign herself that – and she hoped it would warn them that something odd was up. The man took the note and fastened it to Tim's collar. The dog growled all the time, but George kept telling him not to bite.

'Now tell him to go and find your friends,' said the man.

'Find Dick and Anne,' commanded George. 'Go on, Tim. Find Dick and Anne. Give them the note.'

Tim did not want to leave George, but there was something very urgent in her voice. He took one last look at his mistress, gave her hand a lick and sped off down the passage. He knew the way now. Up the rocky steps he bounded and into the open air. He stopped in the old yard, sniffing. Where were Dick and Anne?

He smelt their footsteps and ran off, his nose to the ground. He soon found the two children out on the rocks. Dick was feeling better now and was sitting up. His cheek had almost stopped bleeding.

'Hallo,' he said in surprise, when he saw Tim. 'Here's

132

Timothy! Why, Tim, old chap, why have you come to see
us? Did you get tired of being underground in the dark?'

'Look, Dick – he's got something twisted into his
collar,' said Anne, her sharp eyes seeing the paper there.
'It's a note. I expect it's from the others, telling us to go
down. Isn't Tim clever to bring it?'

Dick took the paper from Tim's collar. He undid it and
read it.

' "Dear Dick and Anne," ' he read out aloud. ' "We've
found the gold. Come on down at once and see it.
Georgina." '

'Oooh!' said Anne, her eyes shining. 'They've found it.
Oh, Dick – are you well enough to come now? Let's hurry.'

But Dick did not get up from the rocks. He sat and
stared at the note, puzzled.

'What's the matter?' said Anne, impatiently.

'Well, don't you think it's funny that George should
suddenly sign herself "Georgina"?' said Dick, slowly.
'You know how she hates being a girl, and having a girl's
name. You know how she will never answer if anyone calls
her Georgina. And yet in this note she signs herself by the
name she hates. It does seem a bit funny to me. Almost as
if it's a kind of warning that there's something wrong.'

'Oh, don't be so silly, Dick,' said Anne. 'What could be
wrong? Do come on.'

'Anne, I'd like to pop over to that inlet of ours to make
sure there's no one else come to the island,' said Dick.
'You stay here.'

But Anne didn't want to stay there alone. She ran round
the coast with Dick, telling him all the time that she
thought he was very silly.

But when they came to the little harbour, they saw that

there was another boat there, as well as their own. It was a motor-boat! Someone else *was* on the island!

'Look,' said Dick, in a whisper. 'There *is* someone else here. And I bet it's the men who want to buy the island. I bet they've read that old map and know there's gold here. And they've found George and Julian and want to get us all together down in the dungeons so that they can keep us safe till they've stolen the gold. That's why they made George send us that note – but she signed it with a name she never uses – to warn us! Now – we must think hard. What are we going to do?'

CHAPTER FIFTEEN

Dick to the rescue!

DICK CAUGHT hold of Anne's hand and pulled her quickly away from the cove. He was afraid that whoever had come to the island might be somewhere about and see them. The boy took Anne to the little stone room where their things were and they sat down in a corner.

'Whoever has come has discovered Julian and George smashing in that door, I should think,' said Dick, in a whisper. 'I simply can't think what to do. We mustn't go down into the dungeons or we'll most certainly be caught. Hallo – where's Tim off to?'

The dog had kept with them for a while but now he ran off to the entrance of the dungeons. He disappeared down the steps. He meant to get back to George, for he knew she was in danger. Dick and Anne stared after him. They had felt comforted while he was there, and now they were sorry he had gone.

They really didn't know what to do. Then Anne had an idea. 'I know!' she said. 'We'll row back to the land in our boat and get help.'

'I'd thought of that,' said Dick, gloomily. 'But you know perfectly well we'd never know the way in and out of those awful rocks. We'd wreck the boat. I'm sure we're not strong enough either to row all the way back. Oh, dear – I do wish we could think what to do.'

They didn't need to puzzle their brains long. The men came up out of the dungeons and began to hunt for the

135

two children! They had seen Tim when he came back and had found the note gone. So they knew the two children had taken it – and they couldn't imagine why they had not obeyed what George had said in the note, and come down to the dungeons!

Dick heard their voices. He clutched hold of Anne to make her keep quiet. He saw through the broken archway that the men were going in the opposite direction.

'Anne! I know where we can hide!' said the boy, excitedly. 'Down the old well! We can climb down the ladder a little way and hide there. I'm sure no one would ever look there!'

Anne didn't at all want to climb down the well even a little way. But Dick pulled her to her feet and hurried her off to the middle of the old courtyard. The men were hunting around the other side of the castle. There was just time to climb in. Dick slipped aside the old wooden cover of the well and helped Anne down the ladder. She was very scared. Then the boy climbed down himself and slipped the wooden cover back again over his head, as best he could.

The old stone slab that Tim had sat on when he fell down the well was still there. Dick climbed down to it and tested it. It was immovable.

'It's safe for you to sit on, Anne, if you don't want to keep clinging to the ladder,' he whispered. So Anne sat shivering on the stone slab across the well-shaft, waiting to see if they were discovered or not. They kept hearing the voices of the men, now near at hand and now far-off. Then the men began to shout for them.

'Dick! Anne! The others want you! Where are you? We've exciting news for you.'

'Well, why don't they let Julian and George come up and tell us then?' whispered Dick. 'There's something wrong, I know there is. I do wish we could get to Julian and George and find out what has happened.'

The two men came into the courtyard. They were angry. 'Where have those kids got to?' said Jake. 'Their boat is still in the cove, so they haven't got away. They must be hiding somewhere. We can't wait all day for them.'

'Well, let's take some food and drink down to the two

we've locked up,' said the other man. 'There's plenty in that little stone room. I suppose it's a store the children brought over. We'll leave half in the room so that the other two kids can have it. And we'll take their boat with us so that they can't escape.'

'Right,' said Jake. 'The thing to do is to get the gold away as quickly as possible, and make sure the children are prisoners here until we've made a safe getaway. We won't bother any more about trying to buy the island. After all, it was only the idea of getting the ingots that put us up to the idea of getting Kirrin Castle and the island.'

'Well – come on,' said his companion. 'We will take the food down now, and not bother about the other kids. You stay here and see if you can spot them while I go down.'

Dick and Anne hardly dared to breathe when they heard all this. How they hoped that the men wouldn't think of looking down the well! They heard one man walk to the little stone room. It was plain that he was getting food and drink to take down to the two prisoners in the dungeons below. The other man stayed in the courtyard, whistling softly.

After what seemed a very long time to the hidden children, the first man came back. Then the two talked together, and at last went off to the cove. Dick heard the motor-boat being started up.

'It's safe to get out now, Anne,' he said. 'Isn't it cold down here? I'll be glad to get out into the sunshine.'

They climbed out and stood warming themselves in the hot summer sunshine. They could see the motor-boat streaking towards the mainland.

'Well, they're gone for the moment,' said Dick. 'And they've not taken our boat, as they said. If only we could rescue Julian and George, we could get help, because George could row us back.'

'Why *can't* we rescue them?' cried Anne, her eyes shining. 'We can go down the steps and unbolt the door, can't we?'

'No – we can't,' said Dick. 'Look!'

Anne looked to where he pointed. She saw that the two men had piled big, heavy slabs of broken stone over the dungeon entrance. It had taken all their strength to put the big stones there. Neither Dick nor Anne could hope to move them.

'It's quite impossible to get down the steps,' said Dick. 'They've made sure we shan't do that! And you know we haven't any idea where the second entrance is. We only know it was somewhere near the tower.'

'Let's see if we can find it,' said Anne eagerly. They set off to the tower on the right of the castle – but it was quite clear that whatever entrance there might have been once, it was gone now! The castle had fallen in very much just there, and there were piles of old broken stones every-where, quite impossible to move. The children soon gave up the search.

'Blow!' said Dick. 'How I do hate to think of poor old Julian and George prisoners down below, and we can't even help them! Oh, Anne – can't *you* think of something to do?'

Anne sat down on a stone and thought hard. She was very worried. Then she brightened up a little and turned to Dick.

'Dick! I suppose – I suppose we couldn't *possibly* climb down the well, could we?' she asked. 'You know it goes past the dungeons – and there's an opening on the dun-geon floor from the well-shaft, because don't you remember we were able to put in our heads and shoulders and look right up the well to the top? Could we get past that slab, do you think – the one that I sat on just now, that has fallen across the well?'

Dick thought it all over. He went to the well and peered down it. 'You know, I believe you are right, Anne,' he said at last. 'We might be able to squeeze past that slab. There's just about room. I don't know how far the iron ladder goes down though.'

'Oh, Dick – do let's try,' said Anne. 'It's our only chance of rescuing the others!'

'Well,' said Dick, 'I'll try it – but not you, Anne. I'm not going to have you falling down that well. The ladder might be broken half-way down – anything might happen. You must stay up here and I'll see what I can do.'

'You will be careful, won't you?' said Anne, anxiously. 'Take a rope with you, Dick, so that if you need one you won't have to climb all the way up again.'

'Good idea,' said Dick. He went to the little stone room and got one of the ropes they had put there. He wound it round and round his waist. Then he went back to Anne.

'Well, here goes!' he said, in a cheerful voice. 'Don't worry about me. I'll be all right.'

Anne was rather white. She was terribly afraid that Dick might fall right down to the bottom of the well. She watched him climb down the iron ladder to the slab of stone. He tried his best to squeeze by it, but it was very difficult. At last he managed it and after that Anne could see him no more. But she could hear him, for he kept calling up to her.

'Ladder's still going strong, Anne! I'm all right. Can you hear me?'

'Yes,' shouted Anne down the well, hearing her voice

echo in a funny hollow manner. 'Take care, Dick. I do hope the ladder goes all the way down.'

'I think it does!' yelled back Dick. Then he gave a loud exclamation. 'Blow! It's broken just here. Broken right off. Or else it ends. I'll have to use my rope.'

There was a silence as Dick unwound the rope from his waist. He tied it firmly to the last but one rung of the ladder, which seemed quite strong.

'I'm going down the rope now!' he shouted to Anne. 'Don't worry. I'm all right. Here I go!'

Anne couldn't hear what Dick said after that, for the well-shaft made his words go crooked and she couldn't make out what they were. But she was glad to hear him shouting even though she didn't know what he said. She yelled down to him too, hoping he could hear her.

Dick slid down the rope, holding on to it with hands, knees and feet, glad that he was so good at gym at school. He wondered if he was anywhere near the dungeons. He seemed to have gone down a long way. He managed to get out his torch. He put it between his teeth after he had switched it on, so that he might have both hands free for the rope. The light from the torch showed him the walls of the well around him. He couldn't make out if he was above or below the dungeons. He didn't want to go right down to the bottom of the well!

He decided that he must have just passed the opening into the dungeon-caves. He climbed back up the rope a little way and to his delight saw that he was right. The opening on to the dungeons was just by his head. He climbed up till he was level with it and then swung himself to the side of the well where the small opening was. He managed to get hold of the bricked edge, and then tried to scramble through the opening into the dungeon.

It was difficult, but luckily Dick was not very big. He
managed it at last and stood up straight with a sigh of relief.
He was in the dungeons! He could now follow the chalk-
marks to the room or cave where the ingots were – and
where he felt sure that George and Julian were imprisoned!

He shone his torch on the wall. Yes – there were the
chalk-marks. Good! He put his head into the well-opening
and yelled at the top of his voice.

'Anne! I'm in the dungeons! Watch out that the men
don't come back!'

142

Then he began to follow the white chalk-marks, his heart beating fast. After a while he came to the door of the store-room. As he had expected, it was fastened so that George and Julian couldn't get out. Big bolts had been driven home at the top and bottom, and the children inside could not possibly get out. They had tried their hardest to batter down the door, but it was no good at all.

They were sitting inside the store-cave, feeling angry and exhausted. The man had brought them food and drink, but they had not touched it. Tim was with them, lying down with his head on his paws, half-angry with George because she hadn't let him fly at the men as he had so badly wanted to. But George felt certain that Tim would be shot if he tried biting or snapping.

'Anyway, the other two had sense enough not to come down and be made prisoners too,' said George. 'They must have known there was something funny about that note when they saw I had signed myself Georgina instead of George. I wonder what they are doing. They must be hiding.'

Tim suddenly gave a growl. He leapt to his feet and went to the closed door, his head on one side. He had heard something, that was certain.

'I hope it's not those men back again already,' said George. Then she looked at Tim in surprise, flashing her torch on to him. He was wagging his tail!

A great bang at the door made them all jump out of their skins! Then came Dick's cheerful voice. 'Hi, Julian! Hi, George! Are you here?'

'Wuffffff!' barked Tim joyfully, and scratched at the door.

'Dick! Open the door!' yelled Julian in delight. 'Quick, open the door!'

CHAPTER SIXTEEN

A plan – and a narrow escape

DICK UNBOLTED the door at the top and bottom and flung it open. He rushed in and thumped George and Julian happily on the back.

'Hallo!' he said. 'How does it feel to be rescued?'

'Fine!' cried Julian, and Tim barked madly round them. George grinned at Dick.

'Good work!' she said. 'What happened?'

Dick told them in a few words all that had happened. When he related how he had climbed down the old well, George and Julian could hardly believe their ears. Julian slipped his arm through his younger brother's.

'You're a brick!' he said. 'A real brick! Now quick – what are we going to do?'

'Well, if they've left us our boat I'm going to take us all back to the mainland as quickly as possible,' said George. 'I'm not playing about with men who brandish revolvers all the time. Come on! Up the well we go and find the boat.'

They ran to the well-shaft and squeezed through the small opening one by one. Up the rope they went and soon found the iron ladder. Julian made them go up one by one in case the ladder wouldn't bear the weight of all three at once.

It really wasn't very long before they were all up in the open air once more, giving Anne hugs, and hearing her exclaim gladly, with tears in her eyes, how pleased she was to see them all again.

'Now come on!' said George after a minute. 'Off to the boat. Quick! Those men may be back at any time.'

They rushed to the cove. There was their boat, lying where they had pulled it, out of reach of the waves. But what a shock for them!

'They've taken the oars!' said George, in dismay. 'The beasts! They know we can't row the boat away without oars. They were afraid you and Anne might row off, Dick – so instead of bothering to tow the boat behind them, they just grabbed the oars. Now we're stuck. We can't possibly get away.'

It was a great disappointment. The children were almost ready to cry. After Dick's marvellous rescue of George and Julian, it had seemed as if everything was going right – and now suddenly things were going wrong again.

'We must think this out,' said Julian, sitting down where he could see at once if any boat came in sight. 'The men have gone off – probably to get a ship from somewhere in which they can put the ingots and sail away. They won't be back for some time, I should think, because you can't charter a ship all in a hurry – unless, of course, they've got one of their own.'

'And in the meantime we can't get off the island to get help, because they've got our oars,' said George. 'We can't even signal to any passing fishing-boat because they won't be out just now. The tide's wrong. It seems as if all we've got to do is wait here patiently till the men come back and take my gold! And we can't stop them.'

'You know – I've got a sort of plan coming into my head,' said Julian, slowly. 'Wait a bit – don't interrupt me. I'm thinking.'

The others waited in silence while Julian sat and frowned, thinking of his plan. Then he looked at the others with a smile.

'I believe it will work,' he said. 'Listen! We'll wait here in patience till the men come back. What will they do? They'll drag away those stones at the top of the dungeon entrance, and go down the steps. They'll go to the store-room, where they left us – thinking we are still there – and they will go into the room. Well, what about one of us being hidden down there ready to bolt *them* into the room?

A PLAN – AND A NARROW ESCAPE

Then we can either go off in their motor-boat or our own boat if they bring back our oars – and get help.'

Anne thought it was a marvellous idea. But Dick and George did not look so certain. 'We'd have to go down and bolt that door again to make it seem as if we are still prisoners there,' said George. 'And suppose the one who hides down there doesn't manage to bolt the men in? It might be very difficult to do that quickly enough. They will simply catch whoever we plan to leave down there – and come up to look for the rest of us.'

'That's true,' said Julian, thoughtfully. 'Well – we'll suppose that Dick, or whoever goes down, doesn't manage to bolt them in and make them prisoners – and the men come up here again. All right – while they are down below we'll pile big stones over the entrance, just as they did. Then they won't be able to get out.'

'What about Dick down below?' said Anne, at once.

'I could climb up the well again!' said Dick, eagerly. 'I'll be the one to go down and hide. I'll do my best to bolt the men into the room. And if I have to escape I'll climb up the well-shaft again. The men don't know about that. So even if they are not prisoners in the dungeon room, they'll be prisoners underground!'

The children talked over this plan, and decided that it was the best they could think of. Then George said she thought it would be a good thing to have a meal. They were all half-starved and, now that the worry and excitement of being rescued was over, they were feeling very hungry!

They fetched some food from the little room and ate it in the cove, keeping a sharp look-out for the return of the men. After about two hours they saw a big fishing-smack

147

appear in the distance, and heard the chug-chug-chug of a motor-boat too.

'There they are!' said Julian, in excitement, and he jumped to his feet. 'That's the ship they mean to load with the ingots, and sail away in safety – and there's the motor-boat bringing the men back! Quick, Dick, down the well you, go and hide until you hear them in the dungeons!'

Dick shot off. Julian turned to the others. 'We'll have to hide,' he said. 'Now that the tide is out we'll hide over there, behind those uncovered rocks. I don't somehow think the men will do any hunting for Dick and Anne – but they might. Come on! Quick!'

They all hid themselves behind the rocks, and heard the motor-boat come chugging into the tiny harbour. They could hear men calling to one another. There sounded to be more than two men this time. Then the men left the inlet and went up the low cliff towards the ruined castle.

Julian crept behind the rocks and peeped to see what the men were doing. He felt certain they were pulling away the slabs of stone that had been piled on top of the entrance to prevent Dick and Anne going down to rescue the others.

'George! Come on!' called Julian in a low tone. 'I think the men have gone down the steps into the dungeons now. We must go and try to put those big stones back. Quick!'

George, Julian and Anne ran softly and swiftly to the old courtyard of the castle. They saw that the stones had been pulled away from the entrance to the dungeons. The men had disappeared. They had plainly gone down the steps.

The three children did their best to tug at the heavy stones to drag them back. But their strength was not the same as that of the men, and they could not manage to get any very big stones across. They put three smaller ones, and Julian hoped the men would find them too difficult to move from below. 'If only Dick has managed to bolt them into that room!' he said to the others. 'Come on, back to the well now. Dick will have to come up there, because he won't be able to get out of the entrance.'

They all went to the well. Dick had removed the old wooden cover, and it was lying on the ground. The children leaned over the hole of the well and waited anxiously. What was Dick doing? They could hear nothing from the well and they longed to know what was happening.

There was plenty happening down below! The two men, and another, had gone down into the dungeons, expecting, of course, to find Julian, George and the dog still locked up in the store-room with the ingots. They passed the well-shaft not guessing that an excited small boy was hidden there, ready to slip out of the opening as soon as they had passed.

A PLAN – AND A NARROW ESCAPE

Dick heard them pass. He slipped out of the well-opening and followed behind quietly, his feet making no sound. He could see the beams made by the men's powerful torches, and with his heart thumping loudly he crept along the smelly old passages, between great caves, until the men turned into the wide passage where the store-cave lay.

'Here it is,' Dick heard one of the men say, as he flashed his torch on to the great door. 'The gold's in there – so are the kids!'

The men unbolted the door at top and bottom. Dick was glad that he had slipped along to bolt the door, for if he hadn't done that before the men had come they would have known that Julian and George had escaped, and would have been on their guard.

The man opened the door and stepped inside. The second man followed him. Dick crept as close as he dared, waiting for the third man to go in too. Then he meant to slam the door and bolt it!

The first man swung his torch round and gave a loud exclamation. 'The children are gone! How strange! Where are they?'

Two of the men were now in the cave – and the third stepped in at that moment. Dick darted forward and slammed the door. It made a crash that went echoing round and round the caves and passages. Dick fumbled with the bolts, his hand trembling. They were stiff and rusty. The boy found it hard to shoot them home in their sockets. And meanwhile the men were not idle!

As soon as they heard the door slam they spun round. The third man put his shoulder to the door at once and heaved hard. Dick had just got one of the bolts almost into

151

its socket. Then all three men forced their strength against the door, and the bolt gave way!

Dick stared in horror. The door was opening! He turned and fled down the dark passage. The men flashed their torches on and saw him. They went after the boy at top speed.

Dick fled to the well-shaft. Fortunately the opening was on the opposite side, and he could clamber into it without being seen in the light of the torches. The boy only just had time to squeeze through into the shaft before the three men came running by. Not one of them guessed that the runaway was squeezed into the well-shaft they passed! Indeed, the men did not even know that there was a well there.

Trembling from head to foot, Dick began to climb the rope he had left dangling from the rungs of the iron ladder. He undid it when he reached the ladder itself, for he thought that perhaps the men might discover the old well and try to climb up later. They would not be able to do that if there was no rope dangling down.

The boy climbed up the ladder quickly, and squeezed round the stone slab near the top. The other children were there, waiting for him.

They knew at once by the look on Dick's face that he had failed in what he had tried to do. They pulled him out quickly. 'It was no good,' said Dick, panting with his climb. 'I couldn't do it. They burst the door open just as I was bolting it, and chased me. I got into the shaft just in time.'

'They're trying to get out of the entrance now!' cried Anne, suddenly. 'Quick! What shall we do? They'll catch us all!'

'To the boat!' shouted Julian, and he took Anne's hand to help her along. 'Come along! It's our only chance. The men will perhaps be able to move those stones.'

The four children fled down the courtyard. George darted into the little stone room as they passed it, and caught up an axe. Dick wondered why she bothered to do that. Tim dashed along with them, barking madly.

They came to the cove. Their own boat lay there without oars. The motor-boat was there too. George jumped into it and gave a yell of delight.

'Here are our oars!' she shouted. 'Take them, Julian, I've got a job to do here! Get the boat down to the water, quick!'

Julian and Dick took the oars. Then they dragged their boat down to the water, wondering what George was doing. All kinds of crashing sounds came from the motor-boat!

'George! George! Buck up. The men are out!' suddenly

154

yelled Julian. He had seen the three men running to the cliff that led down to the cove. George leapt out of the motor-boat and joined the others. They pushed their boat out on to the water, and George took the oars at once, pulling for all she was worth.

The three men ran to their motor-boat. Then they paused in the greatest dismay – for George had completely ruined it! She had chopped wildly with her axe at all the machinery she could see – and now the boat could not possibly be started! It was damaged beyond any repair the men could make with the few tools they had.

'You wicked girl!' yelled Jake, shaking his fist at George. 'Wait till I get you!'

'I'll wait!' shouted back George, her blue eyes shining dangerously. 'And you can wait too! You won't be able to leave my island now!'

CHAPTER SEVENTEEN

The end of the great adventure

THE THREE men stood at the edge of the sea, watching George pull away strongly from the shore. They could do nothing. Their boat was quite useless.

'The fishing-smack they've got waiting out there is too big to use in that little inlet,' said George, as she pulled hard at her oars. 'They'll have to stay there till someone goes in with a boat. I guess they're as wild as can be!'

Their boat had to pass fairly near to the big fishing-boat. A man hailed them as they came by.

'Ahoy there! Have you come from Kirrin Island?'

'Don't answer,' said George. 'Don't say a word.' So no one said anything at all, but looked the other way as if they hadn't heard.

'AHOY THERE!' yelled the man, angrily. 'Are you deaf? Have you come from the island?'

Still the children said nothing at all, but looked away while George rowed steadily. The man on the ship gave it up, and looked in a worried manner towards the island. He felt sure the children had come from there – and he knew enough of his comrades' adventures to wonder if everything was right on the island.

'He may put out a boat from the smack and go and see what's happening, said George. 'Well, he can't do much except take the men off – with a few ingots! I hardly think they'll dare to take any of the gold though, now that we've escaped to tell our tale!'

Julian looked behind at the ship. He saw after a time that the little boat it carried was being lowered into the sea. 'You're right,' he said to George. 'They're afraid something is up. They're going to rescue those three men. What a pity!'

Their little boat reached land. The children leapt out into the shallow water and dragged it up to the beach. Tim pulled at the rope too, wagging his tail. He loved to join in anything that the children were doing.

'Shall you take Tim to Alf?' asked Dick.

George shook her head. 'No,' she said, 'we haven't any time to waste. We must go and tell everything that has happened. I'll tie Tim up to the fence in the front garden.'

They made their way to Kirrin Cottage at top speed. Aunt Fanny was gardening there. She stared in surprise to see the hurrying children.

'Why,' she said, 'I thought you were not coming back till tomorrow or the next day! Has anything happened? What's the matter with Dick's cheek?'

'Nothing much,' said Dick.

The others chimed in.

'Aunt Fanny, where's Uncle Quentin? We have something important to tell him!'

'Mother, we've had such an adventure!'

'Aunt Fanny, we've an awful lot to tell you! We really have!'

Aunt Fanny looked at the untidy children in amazement. 'Whatever has happened?' she said. Then she turned towards the house and called 'Quentin! Quentin! The children have something to tell us!'

Uncle Quentin came out, looking rather cross, for he was in the middle of his work. 'What's the matter?' he asked.

'Uncle, it's about Kirrin Island,' said Julian, eagerly. 'Those men haven't bought it yet, have they?'

'Well, it's practically sold,' said his uncle. 'I've signed my part, and they are to sign their part tomorrow. Why? What's that to do with you?'

'Uncle, those men won't sign tomorrow,' said Julian. 'Do you know why they wanted to buy the island and the castle? Not because they really wanted to build an hotel or anything like that – but because they knew the lost gold was hidden there!'

'What nonsense are you talking?' said his uncle.

'It isn't nonsense, Father!' cried George indignantly. 'It's all true. The map of the old castle was in that box you sold – and in the map was shown where the ingots were hidden by my great-great-great-grandfather!'

George's father looked amazed and annoyed. He simply didn't believe a word! But his wife saw by the solemn and serious faces of the four children that something important really had happened. And then Anne suddenly burst into loud sobs! The excitement had been too much for her and she couldn't bear to think that her uncle wouldn't believe that everything was true.

'Aunt Fanny, Aunt Fanny, it's all true!' she sobbed. 'Uncle Quentin is horrid not to believe us. Oh, Aunt Fanny, the man had a revolver – and oh, he made Julian and George prisoners in the dungeons – and Dick had to climb down the well to rescue them. And George has smashed up their motor-boat to stop them escaping!'

Her aunt and uncle couldn't make head or tail of this, but Uncle Quentin suddenly seemed to think that the matter was serious and worth looking into. 'Smashed up a motor-boat!' he said. 'Whatever for? Come indoors. I shall have to hear the story from beginning to end. It seems quite unbelievable to me.'

They all trooped indoors. Anne sat on her aunt's knee and listened to George and Julian telling the whole story. They told it well and left nothing out. Aunt Fanny grew quite pale as she listened, especially when she heard about Dick climbing down the well.

'You might have been killed,' she said. 'Oh, Dick! What a brave thing to do!'

Uncle Quentin listened in the utmost amazement. He

had never had much liking or admiration for any children
– he always thought they were noisy, tiresome, and silly.
But now, as he listened to Julian's tale, he changed his
mind about these four children at once!

'You've been very clever,' he said. 'And very brave too.
I'm proud of you. Yes, I'm very proud of you all. No
wonder you didn't want me to sell the island, George,
when you knew about the ingots! But why didn't you tell
me?'

The four children stared at him and didn't answer. They
couldn't very well say, 'Well, firstly, you wouldn't have
believed us. Secondly, you are bad-tempered and unjust
and we are frightened of you. Thirdly, we didn't trust you
enough to do the right thing.'

'Why don't you answer?' said their uncle. His wife
answered for them, in a gentle voice.

'Quentin, you scare the children, you know, and I don't
expect they liked to go to you. But now that they have, you
will be able to take matters into your own hands. The
children cannot do any more. You must ring up the police
and see what they have to say about all this.'

'Right,' said Uncle Quentin, and he got up at once. He
patted Julian on the back. 'You have all done well,' he
said. Then he ruffled George's short curly hair. 'And I'm
proud of you, too, George,' he said.

'Oh, Father!' said George, going red with surprise and
pleasure. She smiled at him and he smiled back. The
children noticed that he had a very nice face when he
smiled. He and George were really very alike to look at.
Both looked ugly when they sulked and frowned – and
both were good to look at when they laughed or smiled!

George's father went off to telephone the police and his

160

lawyer too. The children sat and ate biscuits and plums, telling their aunt a great many little details they had forgotten when telling the story before.

As they sat there, there came a loud and angry bark from the front garden. George looked up. 'That's Tim,' she said, with an anxious look at her mother. 'I hadn't time to take him to Alf, who keeps him for me. Mother, Tim was such a comfort to us on the island, you know. I'm sorry he's barking now – but I expect he's hungry.'

'Well, fetch him in,' said her mother, unexpectedly. 'He's quite a hero, too – we must give him a good dinner.'

George smiled in delight. She sped out of the door and went to Tim. She set him free and he came bounding indoors, wagging his long tail. He licked George's mother and cocked his ears at her.

'Good dog,' she said, and actually patted him. 'I'll get you some dinner!'

Tim trotted out to the kitchen with her. Julian grinned at George. 'Well, look at that,' he said. 'Your mother's a brick, isn't she?'

'Yes – but I don't know what Father will say when he sees Tim in the house again,' said George, doubtfully.

Her father came back at that minute, his face grave. 'The police take a serious view of all this,' he said, 'and so does my lawyer. They all agree in thinking that you children have been remarkably clever and brave. And George – my lawyer says that the ingots definitely belong to us. Are there really a lot?'

'Father! There are hundreds!' cried George. 'Simply hundreds – all in a big pile in the dungeon. Oh, Father – shall we be rich now?'

'Yes,' said her father. 'We shall. Rich enough to give

you and your mother all the things I've longed to give you for so many years and couldn't. I've worked hard enough for you – but it's not the kind of work that brings in a lot of money, and so I've become irritable and bad-tempered. But now you shall have everything you want!'

'I don't really want anything I haven't already got,' said George. 'But Father, there is one thing I'd like more than anything else in the world – and it won't cost you a penny!'

THE END OF THE GREAT ADVENTURE

'You shall have it, my dear!' said her father, slipping his arm around George, much to her surprise. 'Just say what it is – and even if it costs a hundred pounds you shall have it!'

Just then there came the pattering of big feet down the passage to the room they were in. A big hairy head pushed itself through the door and looked inquiringly at everyone there. It was Tim, of course!

Uncle Quentin stared at him in surprise. 'Why, isn't that Tim?' he asked. 'Hallo, Tim!'

'Father! Tim is the thing I want most in all the world,' said George, squeezing her father's arm. 'You can't think what a friend he was to us on the island – and he wanted to fly at those men and fight them. Oh, Father, I don't want any other present – I only want to keep Tim and have him here for my very own. We could afford to give him a proper kennel to sleep in now, and I'd see that he didn't disturb you, I really would.'

'Well, of course you can have him!' said her father – and Tim came right into the room at once, wagging his tail, looking for all the world as if he had understood every word that had been said. He actually licked Uncle Quentin's hand! Anne thought that was very brave of him.

But Uncle Quentin was quite different now. It seemed as if a great weight had been lifted off his shoulders. They were rich now – George could go to a good school – and his wife could have the things he had so much wanted her to have – and he would be able to go on with the work he loved without feeling that he was not earning enough to keep his family in comfort. He beamed round at everyone, looking as jolly a person as anyone could wish!

George was overjoyed about Tim. She flung her arms

163

round her father's neck and hugged him, a thing she had not done for a long time. He looked astonished but very pleased. 'Well, well,' he said, 'this is all very pleasant. Hallo – is this the police already?'

It was. They came up to the door and had a few words with Uncle Quentin. Then one stayed behind to take down the children's story in his notebook and the others went off to get a boat to the island.

The men had gone from there! The boat from the fishing-smack had fetched them away! – and now both ship and boat had disappeared! The motor-boat was still there, quite unusable. The inspector looked at it with a grin.

'Fierce young lady, isn't she, that Miss Georgina?' he said. 'Done this job pretty well – no one could get away in this boat. We'll have to get it towed into harbour.'

The police brought back with them some of the ingots of gold to show Uncle Quentin. They had sealed up the door of the dungeon so that no one else could get in until the children's uncle was ready to go and fetch the gold. Everything was being done thoroughly and properly – though far too slowly for the children! They had hoped that the men would have been caught and taken to prison – and that the police would bring back the whole of the gold at once!

They were all very tired that night and didn't make any fuss at all when their aunt said that they must go to bed early. They undressed and then the boys went to eat their supper in the girls' bedroom. Tim was there, ready to lick up any fallen crumbs.

'Well, I must say we've had a wonderful adventure,' said Julian, sleepily. 'In a way I'm sorry it's ended – though at times I didn't enjoy it very much – especially when you and I, George, were prisoners in that dungeon. That was awful.'

George was looking very happy as she nibbled her gingerbread biscuits. She grinned at Julian.

'And to think I hated the idea of you all coming here to stay!' she said. 'I was going to be such a beast to you! I was going to make you wish you were all home again! And now the only thing that makes me sad is the idea of you going away – which you will do, of course, when the holidays end. And then, after having three friends with me, enjoying adventures like this, I'll be all on my own again. I've never been lonely before – but I know I shall be now.'

'No, you won't,' said Anne, suddenly. 'You can do something that will stop you being lonely ever again.'

'What?' said George in surprise.

'You can ask to go to the same boarding-school as I go to,' said Anne. 'It's such a lovely one – and we are allowed to keep our pets, so Tim could come too!'

'Gracious! Could he really?' said George, her eyes shining. 'Well, I'll go then. I always said I wouldn't – but I will because I see now how much better and happier it is to be with others than all by myself. And if I can have Tim, well that's simply wonderful!'

'You'd better go back to your own bedroom now, boys,' said Aunt Fanny, appearing at the doorway. 'Look at Dick, almost dropping with sleep! Well, you should all have pleasant dreams tonight, for you've had an adventure to be proud of. George – is that Tim under your bed?'

'Well, yes it is, Mother,' said George, pretending to be surprised. 'Dear me! Tim, what are you doing here?'

165

Tim crawled out and went over to George's mother. He lay flat on his tummy and looked up at her most appealingly out of his soft brown eyes.

'Do you want to sleep in the girls' room tonight?' said George's mother, with a laugh. 'All right – just for once!'

'*Mother!*' yelled George, overjoyed. 'Oh, thank you, thank you, thank you! How did you guess that I just didn't want to be parted from Tim tonight? Oh, Mother! Tim, you can sleep on the rug over there.'

Four happy children snuggled down into their beds. Their wonderful adventure had come to a happy end. They had plenty of holidays still in front of them – and now that Uncle Quentin was no longer poor, he would give them the little presents he wanted to. George was going to school with Anne – and she had Tim for her own again! The island and castle still belonged to George – everything was marvellous!

'I'm so glad Kirrin Island wasn't sold, George,' said Anne, sleepily. 'I'm so glad it still belongs to you.'

'It belongs to three other people too,' said George. 'It belongs to me – and to you and Julian and Dick. I've discovered that it's fun to share things. So tomorrow I am going to draw up a deed, or whatever it's called, and put in it that I give you and the others a quarter-share each. Kirrin Island and Castle shall belong to us all!'

'Oh, George – how lovely!' said Anne, delighted. 'Won't the boys be pleased? I do feel so ha . . .'

But before she could finish, the little girl was asleep. So was George. In the other room the two boys slept, too, dreaming of ingots and dungeons and all kinds of exciting things.

Only one person was awake – and that was Tim. He had

one ear up and was listening to the children's breathing. As soon as he knew they were asleep he got up quietly from his rug. He crept softly over to George's bed. He put his front paws up and sniffed at the sleeping girl.

Then, with a bound he was on the bed, and snuggled himself down into the crook of her legs. He gave a sigh, and shut his eyes. The four children might be happy – but Tim was happiest of all.

'Oh, Tim,' murmured George, half waking up as she felt him against her. 'Oh, Tim, you mustn't – but you do feel so nice. Tim – we'll have other adventures together, the five of us – won't we?'

They will – but that's another story!

FIVE GO ADVENTURING AGAIN

CONTENTS

1 CHRISTMAS HOLIDAYS   173
2 ALL TOGETHER AGAIN   182
3 THE NEW TUTOR   190
4 AN EXCITING DISCOVERY   200
5 AN UNPLEASANT WALK   209
6 LESSONS WITH MR ROLAND   218
7 DIRECTIONS FOR THE SECRET WAY   228
8 WHAT HAPPENED ON
    CHRISTMAS NIGHT   238
9 A HUNT FOR THE SECRET WAY   247
10 A SHOCK FOR GEORGE AND TIM   258
11 STOLEN PAPERS   268
12 GEORGE IN TROUBLE   277
13 JULIAN HAS A SURPRISE   287
14 THE SECRET WAY AT LAST!   299
15 AN EXCITING JOURNEY AND HUNT   308
16 THE CHILDREN ARE DISCOVERED   318
17 GOOD OLD TIM!   326

CHAPTER ONE

Christmas holidays

IT WAS the last week of the Christmas term, and all the girls at Gaylands School were looking forward to the Christmas Holidays. Anne sat down at the breakfast-table and picked up a letter addressed to her.

'Hallo, look at this!' she said to her cousin Georgina, who was sitting beside her. 'A letter from Daddy – and I only had one from him and Mummy yesterday.'

'I hope it's not bad news,' said George. She would not allow anyone to call her Georgina, and now even the mistresses called her George. She really was very like a boy with her short curly hair, and her boyish ways. She looked anxiously at Anne as her cousin read the letter.

'Oh, George – we can't go home for the holidays!' said Anne, with tears in her eyes. 'Mummy's got scarlet fever – and Daddy is in quarantine for it – so they can't have us back. Isn't it just too bad?'

'Oh, I *am* sorry,' said George. She was just as disappointed for herself as for Anne, because Anne's mother had invited George, and her dog Timothy, to stay for the Christmas holidays with them. She had been promised many things she had never seen before – the pantomime, and the circus – and a big party with a fine Christmas tree! Now it wouldn't happen.

'Whatever will the two boys say?' said Anne, thinking of Julian and Dick, her two brothers. 'They won't be able to go home either.'

173

'Well – what are you going to do for the holidays then?' asked George. 'Won't you come and stay at Kirrin Cottage with *me*? I'm sure my mother would love to have you again. We had such fun when you came to stay for the summer hols.'

'Wait a minute – let me finish the letter and see what Daddy says,' said Anne, picking up the note again. 'Poor Mummy – I do hope she isn't feeling very ill.'

She read a few more lines and then gave such a delighted exclamation that George and the other girls waited impatiently for her to explain.

'George! We *are* to come to you again – but oh blow, blow, blow! – we've got to have a tutor for the hols, partly to look after us so that your mother doesn't have too much bother with us, and partly because both Julian and Dick have been ill with 'flu twice this term and have got behind in their work.'

'A tutor! How sickening! That means I'll have to do lessons too, I'll bet!' said George, in dismay. 'When my mother and father see my report I guess they'll find out how little I know. After all, this is the first time I've ever been to a proper school, and there are heaps of things I don't know.'

'What horrid hols they'll be, if we have a tutor running after us all the time,' said Anne, gloomily. 'I expect I'll have quite a good report, because I've done well in the exams – but it won't be any fun for me not doing lessons with you three in the hols. Though, of course, I could go off with Timothy, I suppose. *He* won't be doing lessons!'

'Yes, he will,' said George, at once. She could not bear the idea of her beloved dog Timothy going off each

174

morning with Anne, while she, George, sat and worked hard with Julian and Dick.

'Timothy can't do lessons, don't be silly, George,' said Anne.

'He can sit under my feet while *I'm* doing them,' said George. 'It will be a great help to feel him there. For goodness' sake eat up your sausages, Anne. We've all nearly finished. The bell will be going in a minute and you won't have had any breakfast.'

'I am glad Mummy isn't very bad,' said Anne, hurriedly finishing her letter. 'Daddy says he's written to Dick and Julian – and to your father to ask him to engage a tutor for us. Oh dash – this is an awful disappointment, isn't it? I don't mean I shan't enjoy going to Kirrin Cottage again – and seeing Kirrin Island – but after all there are no pantomimes or circuses or parties to look forward to at Kirrin.'

The end of the term came quickly. Anne and George packed up their trunks, and put on the labels, enjoying the noise and excitement of the last two days. The big school coaches rolled up to the door, and the girls clambered in.

'Off to Kirrin again!' said Anne. 'Come on, Timothy darling, you can sit between me and George.'

Gaylands School allowed the children to keep their own pets, and Timothy, George's big mongrel dog, had been a great success. Except for the time when he had run after the dustman, and dragged the dustbin away from him, all the way up the school grounds and into George's class-room, he had really behaved extremely well.

'I'm sure *you'll* have a good report, Tim,' said George, giving the dog a hug. 'We're going home again. Will you like that?'

'Woof,' said Tim, in his deep voice. He stood up, wagging his tail, and there was a squeal from the seat behind.

'George! Make Tim sit down. He's wagging my hat off!'

It was not very long before the two girls and Timothy were in London, being put into the train for Kirrin.

'I do wish the boys broke up today too,' sighed Anne. 'Then we could all have gone down to Kirrin together. That would have been fun.'

Julian and Dick broke up the next day and were to join the girls then at Kirrin Cottage. Anne was very much looking forward to seeing them again. A term was a long time to be away from one another. She had been glad to have her cousin George with her. The three of them had stayed with George in the summer, and had had some exciting adventures together on the little island off the coast. An old castle stood on the island and in the dungeons the children had made all kinds of wonderful discoveries.

'It will be lovely to go across to Kirrin Island again, George,' said Anne, as the train sped off towards the west.

'We shan't be able to,' said George. 'The sea is terribly rough round the island in the winter. It would be too dangerous to try and row there.'

'Oh, what a pity,' said Anne disappointed. 'I was looking forward to some more adventures there.'

'There won't be any adventures at Kirrin in the winter,' said George. 'It's cold down there – and when it snows we sometimes get frozen up completely – can't even walk to the village because the sea-wind blows the snow-drifts so high.'

'Oooh – that sounds rather exciting!' said Anne.

'Well, it isn't really,' said George. 'It's awfully boring –

176

nothing to do but sit at home all day, or turn out with a spade and dig the snow away.'

It was a long time before the train reached the little station that served Kirrin. But at last it was there pulling in slowly and stopping at the tiny platform. The two girls jumped out eagerly, and looked to see if anyone had met them. Yes – there was George's mother!

'Hallo, George darling – hallo, Anne!' said George's mother, and gave both children a hug. 'Anne, I'm so sorry about your mother, but she's getting on all right, you'll be glad to know.'

'Oh, good!' said Anne. 'It's nice of you to have us, Aunt Fanny. We'll try and be good! What about Uncle Quentin? Will he mind having four children in the house in the winter-time? We won't be able to go out and leave him in peace as often as we did in the summer!'

George's father was a scientist, a very clever man, but rather frightening. He had little patience with children, and the four of them had felt very much afraid of him at times in the summer.

'Oh, your uncle is still working very hard at his book,' said Aunt Fanny. 'You know, he has been working out a secret theory – a secret idea – and putting it all into his book. He says that once it is all explained and finished, he is to take it to some high authority, and then his idea will be used for the good of the country.'

'Oh, Aunt Fanny – it does sound exciting,' said Anne. 'What's the secret?'

'I can't tell you that, silly,' said her aunt, laughing. 'Why, even I myself don't know it. Come along, now – it's cold standing here. Timothy looks very fat and well, George dear.'

'Oh Mother, he's had a marvellous time at school,' said George. 'He really has. He chewed up the cook's old slippers . . .'

'And he chased the cat that lives in the stables every time he saw her,' said Anne.

'And he once got into the larder and ate a whole steak pie,' said George; 'and once . . .'

'Good gracious, George, I should think the school will refuse to have Timothy next term,' said her mother, in horror. 'Wasn't he well punished? I hope he was.'

'No – he wasn't,' said George, going rather red. 'You see, Mother, we are responsible for our pets and their behaviour ourselves – so if ever Timothy does anything bad *I'm* punished for it, because I haven't shut him up properly, or something like that.'

'Well, you must have had quite a lot of punishments then,' said her mother, as she drove the little pony-trap along the frosty roads. 'I really think that's rather a good idea!' There was a twinkle in her eyes as she spoke. 'I think I'll keep on with the same idea – punish you every time Timothy misbehaves himself!'

The girls laughed. They felt happy and excited. Holidays were fun. Going back to Kirrin was lovely. Tomorrow the boys would come – and then Christmas would be there!

'Good old Kirrin Cottage!' said Anne, as they came in sight of the pretty old house. 'Oh – look, there's Kirrin Island!' The two looked out to sea, where the old ruined castle stood on the little island of Kirrin – what adventures they had had there in the summer!

The girls went into the house. 'Quentin!' called George's mother. 'Quentin! The girls are here.'

Uncle Quentin came out of his study at the other side of the house. Anne thought he looked taller and darker than ever. 'And frownier!' she said to herself. Uncle Quentin

might be very clever, but Anne preferred someone jolly and smiling like her own father. She shook hands with her uncle politely, and watched George kiss him.

'Well!' said Uncle Quentin to Anne. 'I hear I've got to get a tutor for you! At least, for the two boys. My word, you *will* have to behave yourself with a tutor, I can tell you!'

This was meant to be a joke, but it didn't sound very nice to Anne and George. People you had to behave well with were usually very strict and tiresome. Both girls were glad when George's father had gone back into his study.

'Your father has been working far too hard lately,' said George's mother to her. 'He is tired out. Thank goodness his book is nearly finished. He had hoped to finish it by Christmas so that he could join in the fun and games – but now he says he can't.'

'What a pity,' said Anne, politely, though secretly she thought it was a good thing. It wouldn't be much fun having Uncle Quentin to play charades and things like that! 'Oh, Aunt Fanny, I'm so looking forward to seeing Julian and Dick – and won't they be pleased to see Tim and George? Aunt Fanny, nobody calls George Georgina at school, not even our form mistress. I was rather hoping they would, because I wanted to see what would happen when she refused to answer to Georgina! George, you liked school, didn't you?'

'Yes,' said George, 'I did. I thought I'd hate being with a lot of others, but it's fun, after all. But Mother, you won't find my report very good, I'm afraid. There were such a lot of things I was bad at because I'd never done them before.'

'Well, you'd never been to school before!' said her mother. 'I'll explain it to your father if he gets upset. Now go along and get ready for a late tea. You must be very hungry.'

The girls went upstairs to their little room. 'I'm glad I'm not spending my hols by myself,' said George. 'I've had much more fun since I've known you and the boys. Hey, Timothy, where have you gone?'

'He's gone to smell all around the house to make sure

it's his proper home!' said Anne, with a giggle. 'He wants to know if the kitchen smells the same – and the bathroom – and his basket. It must be just as exciting for him to come home for the holidays as it is for us!'

Anne was right. Timothy was thrilled to be back again. He ran round George's mother, sniffing at her legs in friendliness, pleased to see her again. He ran into the kitchen but soon came out again because someone new was there – Joanna the cook – a fat, panting person who eyed him with suspicion.

'You can come into this kitchen once a day for your dinner,' said Joanna. 'And that's all. I'm not having meat and sausages and chicken disappearing under my nose if I can help it. I know what dogs are, I do!'

Timothy ran into the scullery and sniffed round there. He ran into the dining-room and the sitting-room, and was pleased to find they had the same old smell. He put his nose to the door of the study where George's father worked, and sniffed very cautiously. He didn't mean to go in. Timothy was just as wary of George's father as the others were!

He ran upstairs to the girl's bedroom again. Where was his basket? Ah, there it was by the window-seat. Good! That meant he was to sleep in the girls' bedroom once more. He curled himself up in his basket, and thumped loudly with his tail.

'Glad to be back,' said his tail, 'glad – to – be – back!'

CHAPTER TWO

All together again

THE NEXT day the boys came back. Anne and George went to meet them with Timothy. George drove the pony-trap, and Tim sat beside her. Anne could hardly wait for the train to stop at the station. She ran along the platform, looking for Julian and Dick in the carriages that passed.

Then she saw them. They were looking out of a window at the back of the train, waving and yelling.

'Anne! Anne! Here we are! Hallo, George! Oh, there's Timothy!'

'Julian! Dick!' yelled Anne. Timothy began to bark and leap about. It was most exciting.

'Oh, Julian! It's lovely to see you both again!' cried Anne, giving her two brothers a hug each. Timothy leapt up and licked them both. He was beside himself with joy. Now he had all the children around him that he loved.

The three children and the dog stood happily together, all talking at once while the porter got the luggage out of the train. Anne suddenly remembered George. She looked round her. She was nowhere to be seen, although she had come on the station platform with Anne.

'Where's old George?' said Julian. 'I saw her here when I waved out of the window.'

'She must have gone back to the pony-trap,' said Anne. 'Tell the porter to bring your trunks out to the trap, Julian. Come along! We'll go and find George.'

George was standing by the pony, holding his head. She

looked rather gloomy, Anne thought. The boys went up to her.

'Hallo, George, old thing!' cried Julian, and gave her a hug. Dick did the same.

'What's up?' asked Anne, wondering at George's sudden silence.

'I believe George felt left-out!' said Julian with a grin. 'Funny old Georgina!'

'*Don't* call me Georgina!' said the little girl fiercely. The boys laughed.

'Ah, it's the same fierce old George, all right,' said Dick, and gave the girl a friendly slap on the shoulder. 'Oh, George – it's good to see you again. Do you remember our marvellous adventures in the summer?'

George felt her awkwardness slipping away from her. She *had* felt left-out when she had seen the great welcome that the two boys gave to their small sister – but no one could sulk for long with Julian and Dick. They just wouldn't let anyone feel left-out or awkward or sulky.

The four children climbed into the trap. The porter heaved in the two trunks. There was only just room for them. Timothy sat on top of the trunks, his tail wagging nineteen to the dozen, and his tongue hanging out because he was panting with delight.

'You two girls were lucky to be able to take Tim to school with you,' said Dick, patting the big dog lovingly. 'No pets are allowed at our school. Awfully hard on those fellows who like live things.'

'Thompson Minor kept white mice,' said Julian. 'And one day they escaped and met Matron round a corner of the passage. She squealed the place down.'

The girls laughed. The boys always had funny tales to tell when they got home.

'And Kennedy keeps snails,' said Dick. 'You know, snails sleep for the winter – but Kennedy kept his in far too warm a place, and they all crawled out of their box and went up the walls. You should have heard how we laughed when the geography master asked Thompson to point out Cape Town on the map – and there was one of the snails in the very place!'

Everyone laughed again. It was so good to be all together once more. They were very much of an age –

Julian was twelve. George and Dick were eleven, and Anne was ten. Holidays and Christmas time were in front of them. No wonder they laughed at everything, even the silliest little joke!

'It's good that Mummy is getting on all right, isn't it?' said Dick, as the pony went along the road at a great pace. 'I was disappointed not to go home, I must say – I did want to go to see Aladdin and the Lamp, and the circus – but still, it's good to be back at Kirrin Cottage again. I wish we could have some more exciting adventures. Not a hope of that this time, though.'

'There's one snag about these hols,' said Julian. 'And that's the tutor. I hear we've got to have one because Dick and I missed so much school this term, and we've got to take important exams next summer.'

'Yes,' said Anne. 'I wonder what he'll be like. I do hope he will be a sport. Uncle Quentin is going to choose one today.'

Julian and Dick made faces at one another. They felt sure that any tutor chosen by Uncle Quentin would be anything but a sport. Uncle Quentin's idea of a tutor would be somebody strict and gloomy and forbidding.

Never mind! He wouldn't come for a day or two. And he *might* be fun. The boys cheered up and pulled Timothy's thick coat. The dog pretended to growl and bite. *He* wasn't worried about tutors. Lucky Timothy!

They all arrived at Kirrin Cottage. The boys were really pleased to see their aunt, and rather relieved when she said that their uncle had not yet come back.

'He's gone to see two or three men who have answered the advertisement for a tutor,' she said. 'It won't be long before he's back.'

185

'Mother, I haven't got to do lessons in the hols too, have I?' asked George. Nothing had yet been said to her about this, and she longed to know.

'Oh yes, George,' said her mother. 'Your father has seen your report, and although it isn't really a bad one, and we certainly didn't expect a marvellous one, still it does show that you are behind your age in some things. A little extra coaching will soon help you along.'

George looked gloomy. She had expected this but it was tiresome all the same. 'Anne's the only one who won't have to do lessons,' she said.

'I'll do some too,' promised Anne. 'Perhaps not always, George, if it's a very fine day, for instance – but sometimes, just to keep you company.'

'Thanks,' said George. 'But you needn't. I shall have Timmy.'

George's mother looked doubtful about this. 'We'll have to see what the tutor says about that,' she said.

'Mother! If the tutor says I can't have Timothy in the room, I jolly well won't do holiday lessons!' began George, fiercely.

Her mother laughed. 'Well, well – here's our fierce, hot-tempered George again!' she said. 'Go along, you two boys, and wash your hands and do your hair. You seem to have collected all the grime on the railway.'

The children and Timothy went upstairs. It was such fun to be five again. They always counted Tim as one of themselves. He went everywhere with them, and really seemed to understand every single word they said.

'I wonder what sort of a tutor Uncle Quentin will choose,' said Dick, as he scrubbed his nails. 'If only he would choose the right kind – someone jolly and full of fun, who knows that holiday lessons are sickening to have, and tries to make up for them by being a sport out of lesson-time. I suppose we'll have to work every morning.'

'Hurry up. I want my tea,' said Julian. 'Come on down, Dick. We'll know about the tutor soon enough!'

They all went down together, and sat round the table. Joanna the cook had made a lovely lot of buns and a great big cake. There was not much left of either by the time the four children had finished!

Uncle Quentin returned just as they were finishing. He seemed rather pleased with himself. He shook hands with the two boys and asked them if they had had a good term.

'Did you get a tutor, Uncle Quentin?' asked Anne, who could see that everyone was simply bursting to know this.

'Ah – yes, I did,' said her uncle. He sat down, while Aunt Fanny poured him out a cup of tea. 'I interviewed three applicants, and had almost chosen the last one, when another fellow came in, all in a hurry. Said he had only just seen the advertisement, and hoped he wasn't too late.'

'Did you choose him?' asked Dick.

'I did,' said his uncle. 'He seemed a most intelligent fellow. Even knew about me and my work! And he had the most wonderful letters of recommendation.'

'I don't think the children need to know all these details,' murmured Aunt Fanny. 'Anyway – you asked him to come?'

'Oh yes,' said Uncle Quentin. 'He's a good bit older than the others – they were rather young fellows – this one seems very responsible and intelligent. I'm sure you'll like him, Fanny. He'll fit in here very well. I feel I would like to have him to talk to me sometimes in the evening.'

The children couldn't help feeling that the new tutor

sounded rather alarming. Their uncle smiled at the gloomy faces.

'You'll like Mr Roland,' he said. 'He knows how to handle youngsters – knows he's got to be very firm, and to see that you know a good bit more at the end of the holidays than you did at the beginning.'

This sounded even more alarming. All four children wished heartily that Aunt Fanny had been to choose the tutor, and not Uncle Quentin.

'When is he coming?' asked George.

'Tomorrow,' said her father. 'You can all go to meet him at the station. That will make a nice welcome for him.'

'We *had* thought of taking the bus and going to do a bit of Christmas shopping,' said Julian, seeing Anne looked very disappointed.

'Oh, no, you must certainly go and meet Mr Roland,' said his uncle. 'I told him you would. And mind you, you four – no nonsense with him! You've to do as you're told, and you must work hard with him, because your father is paying very high fees for his coaching. I'm paying a third, because I want him to coach George a little too – so George, you must do your best.'

'I'll try,' said George. 'If he's nice, I'll do my very best.'

'You'll do your best whether you think him nice or not!' said her father, frowning. 'He will arrive by the ten-thirty train. Be sure to be there in time.'

'I do hope he won't be too strict,' said Dick, that evening, when the five of them were alone for a minute or two. 'It's going to spoil the hols, if we have someone down on us all the time. And I do hope he'll like Timothy.'

George looked up at once. 'Like Timothy!' she said. 'Of course he'll like Timothy! How couldn't he?'

'Well – your father didn't like Timothy very much last summer,' said Dick. 'I don't see how anyone could *dislike* darling Tim – but there are people who don't like dogs, you know, George.'

'If Mr Roland doesn't like Timothy, I'll not do a single thing for him,' said George. 'Not one single thing!'

'She's gone all fierce again!' said Dick, with a laugh. 'My word – the sparks will fly if Mr Roland dares to dislike our Timothy!'

CHAPTER THREE

The new tutor

NEXT MORNING the sun was out, all the sea-mist that had hung about for the last two days had disappeared, and Kirrin Island showed plainly at the mouth of Kirrin Bay. The children stared longingly at the ruined castle on it.

'I do wish we could get over to the castle,' said Dick. 'It looks quite calm enough, George.'

'It's very rough by the island,' said George. 'It always is at this time of year. I know Mother wouldn't let us go.'

'It's a lovely island, and it's all our own!' said Anne. 'You said you would share it with us for ever and ever, didn't you, George?'

'Yes, I did,' said George. 'And so I will, dungeons and all. Come on – we must get the trap out. We shall be late meeting the train if we stand here all day looking at the island.'

They got the pony and trap and set off down the hard lanes. Kirrin Island disappeared behind the cliffs as they turned inland to the station.

'Did all this land round about belong to your family once upon a time?' asked Julian.

'Yes, all of it,' said George. 'Now we don't own any- thing except Kirrin Island, our own house and that farm away over there - Kirrin Farm.'

She pointed with her whip. The children saw a fine old farmhouse standing on a hill a good way off, over the heather-clad common.

190

THE NEW TUTOR

'Who lives there?' asked Julian.

'Oh, an old farmer and his wife,' said George. 'They were nice to me when I was smaller. We'll go over there one day, if you like. Mother says they don't make the farm pay any more, and in the summertime they take in people who want a holiday.'

'Listen! That's the train whistling in the tunnel!' said Julian, suddenly. 'Buck up, for goodness' sake, George. We shan't be there in time!'

The four children and Timothy looked at the train coming out of the tunnel and drawing in at the station. The pony cantered along swiftly. They would be just in time.

'Who's going on to the platform to meet him?' asked George, as they drew into the little station yard. 'I'm not. I must look after Tim and the pony.'

'I don't want to,' said Anne. 'I'll stay with George.'

'Well, we'd better go, then,' said Julian, and he and Dick leapt out of the trap. They ran on to the platform just as the train pulled up.

Not many people got out. A woman clambered out with a basket. A young man leapt out, whistling, the son of the baker in the village. An old man climbed down with difficulty. The tutor could be none of those!

Then, right at the front of the train, rather an odd-looking man got out. He was short and burly, and he had a beard rather like a sailor. His eyes were piercingly blue, and his thick hair was sprinkled with grey. He glanced up and down the platform, and then beckoned to the porter.

'That must be Mr Roland,' said Julian to Dick.

'Come on – let's ask him. There's no one else it could be.'

The boys went up to the bearded man. 'Are you Mr Roland, sir?' he asked.

'I am,' said the man. 'I suppose you are Julian and Dick?'

'Yes, sir,' answered the boys together. 'We brought the pony-trap for your luggage.'

'Oh, fine,' said Mr Roland. His bright blue eyes looked the boys up and down, and he smiled. Julian and Dick liked him. He seemed sensible and jolly.

'Are the other two here as well?' said Mr Roland, walking down the platform, with the porter trailing behind with his luggage.

'Yes – George and Anne are outside with the trap,' said Julian.

'George and Anne,' said Mr Roland, in a puzzled voice. 'I thought the others were girls. I didn't know there was a third boy.'

'Oh, George is a girl,' said Dick, with a laugh. 'Her real name is Georgina.'

'And a very nice name, too,' said Mr Roland.

'George doesn't think so,' said Julian. 'She won't answer if she's called Georgina. You'd better call her George, sir!'

'Really?' said Mr Roland, in rather a chilly tone. Julian took a glance at him.

'Not quite so jolly as he looks!' thought the boy.

'Tim's out there too,' said Dick.

'Oh – and is Tim a boy or a girl?' inquired Mr Roland, cautiously.

'A dog, sir!' said Dick, with a grin.

Mr Roland seemed rather taken aback. 'A dog?' he said. 'I didn't know there was a dog in the household. Your uncle said nothing to me about a dog.'

THE NEW TUTOR

'Don't you like dogs?' asked Julian, in surprise.

'No,' said Mr Roland, shortly. 'But I dare say your dog won't worry me much. Hallo, hallo – so here are the little girls! How do you do?'

George was not very pleased at being called a little girl. For one thing she hated to be spoken of as little, and for another thing she always tried to be a boy. She held out her hand to Mr Roland and said nothing. Anne smiled at him, and Mr Roland thought she was much the nicer of the two.

'Tim! Shake hands with Mr Roland!' said Julian to Timothy. This was one of Tim's really good tricks. He could hold out his right paw in a very polite manner. Mr Roland looked down at the big dog, and Tim looked back at him.

Then, very slowly and deliberately, Timothy turned his back on Mr Roland and climbed up into the pony-trap! Usually he put out his paw at once when told to, and the children stared at him in amazement.

'Timothy! What's come over you?' cried Dick. Tim put his ears down and did not move.

'He doesn't like you,' said George, looking at Mr Roland. 'That's very strange. He usually likes people. But perhaps you don't like dogs?'

'No, I don't, as a matter of fact,' said Mr Roland. 'I was once very badly bitten as a boy, and somehow or other I've never managed to like dogs since. But I dare say your Tim will take to me sooner or later.'

They all got into the trap. It was a tight squeeze. Timothy looked at Mr Roland's ankles as if he would rather like to nibble them. Anne laughed.

'Tim *is* behaving strangely!' she said. 'It's a good thing

you haven't come to teach him, Mr Roland!' She smiled up at the tutor, and he smiled back, showing very white teeth. His eyes were as brilliant a blue as George's.

Anne liked him. He joked with the boys as they drove him, and both of them began to feel that their Uncle Quentin hadn't made such a bad choice after all.

Only George said nothing. She sensed that the tutor disliked Timothy, and George was not prepared to like anyone who didn't take to Timothy at first sight. She thought it was very peculiar too, that Tim would not shake paws with the tutor. 'He's a clever dog,' she thought. 'He knows Mr Roland doesn't like him, so he won't shake hands. I don't blame you, Tim darling, I wouldn't shake hands with anyone who didn't like *me*!'

Mr Roland was shown up to his room when he arrived. Aunt Fanny came down and spoke to the children. 'Well! He seems very nice, youngish and jolly.'

'Youngish!' exclaimed Julian. 'Why, he's awfully old! Must be forty at the very least!'

Aunt Fanny laughed. 'Does he seem so old to you?' she said. 'Well, old or not, he'll be quite nice to you, I'm sure.'

'Aunt Fanny, we shan't begin lessons until after Christmas, shall we?' asked Julian, anxiously.

'Of course you will!' said his aunt. 'It is almost a week till Christmas – you don't suppose we have asked Mr Roland to come and do nothing till Christmas is over, do you?'

The children groaned. 'We wanted to do some Christmas shopping,' said Anne.

'Well, you can do that in the afternoon,' said her aunt. 'You will only do lessons in the morning, for three hours. That won't hurt any of you!'

The new tutor came downstairs at that moment, and Aunt Fanny took him to see Uncle Quentin. She came out after a while, looking very pleased.

'Mr Roland will be nice company for your uncle,' she said to Julian. 'I think they will get on very well together. Mr Roland seems to understand quite a bit about your uncle's work.'

'Let's hope he spends most of his time with him then!' said George, in a low voice.

'Come on out for a walk,' said Dick. 'It's so fine today. We shan't have lessons this morning, shall we, Aunt Fanny?'

'Oh, no,' said his aunt. 'You'll begin tomorrow. Go for a walk now, all of you – we shan't often get sunny days like this!'

'Let's go over to Kirrin Farm,' said Julian. 'It looks such a nice place. Show us the way, George.'

'Right!' said George. She whistled to Timothy, and he came bounding up. The five of them set off together, going down the lane, and then on to a rough road over the common that led to the farm on the distant hill.

It was lovely walking in the December sun. Their feet rang on the frosty path, and Tim's blunt claws made quite a noise as he pattered up and down, overjoyed at being with his four friends again.

After a good long walk across the common the children came to the farmhouse. It was built of white stone, and stood strong and lovely on the hillside. George opened the farm-gate and went into the farm-yard. She kept her hand on Tim's collar for there were two farm-dogs somewhere about.

Someone clattered round the barn near-by. It was an old man, and George hailed him loudly.

'Hallo, Mr Sanders! How are you?'

'Why, if it isn't Master George!' said the old fellow with a grin. George grinned too. She loved being called Master instead of Miss.

'These are my cousins,' shouted George. She turned to the others. 'He's deaf,' she said. 'You'll have to shout to make him hear.'

'I'm Julian,' said Julian in a loud voice and the others said their names too. The farmer beamed at them.

'You come along in and see the Missis,' he said. 'She'll be rare pleased to see you all. We've known Master

George since she was a baby, and we knew her mother when *she* was a baby too, and we knew her granny as well.'

'You must be very, very old,' said Anne.

The farmer smiled down at her.

'As old as my tongue and a little older than my teeth!' he said, chuckling. 'Come away in now.'

They all went into the big, warm farmhouse kitchen, where a little old woman, as lively as a bantam hen, was bustling about. She was just as pleased to see the four children as her husband was.

'Well, there now!' she said. 'I haven't seen you for months, Master George. I did hear that you'd gone away to school.'

'Yes, I did,' said George. 'But I'm home for the holidays now. Does it matter if I let Timothy loose, Mrs Sanders? I think he'll be friendly if your dogs are, too.'

'Yes, you let him loose,' said the old lady. 'He'll have a fine time in the farmyard with Ben and Rikky. Now what would you like to drink? Hot milk? Cocoa? Coffee? And I've some new shortbread baked yesterday. You shall have some of that.'

'Ah, my wife's very busy this week, cooking up all sorts of things,' said the old farmer, as his wife bustled off to the larder. 'We've company this Christmas!'

'Have you?' said George, surprised, for she knew that the old pair had never had any children of their own. 'Who is coming? Anyone I know?'

'Two artists from London Town!' said the old farmer. 'Wrote and asked us to take them for three weeks over Christmas – and offered us good money too. So my old wife's as busy as a bee.'

'Are they going to paint pictures?' asked Julian, who rather fancied himself as an artist, too. 'I wonder if I could come and talk to them some day. I'm rather good at pictures myself. They might give me a few hints.'

'You come along whenever you like,' said old Mrs Sanders, making cocoa in a big jug. She set out a plate of most delicious-looking shortbreads, and the children ate them hungrily.

'I should think the two artists will be rather lonely down here, in the depths of the country at Christmastime,' said George. 'Do they know anyone?'

'They say they don't know a soul,' said Mrs Sanders. 'But there – artists can be peculiar folk. I've had some here before. They seemed to like mooning about all alone. These two will be happy enough, I'll be bound.'

'They should be, with all the good things you're cooking up for them,' said her old husband. 'Well, I must be out after the sheep. Good-day to you, youngsters. Come again and see us sometime.'

He went out. Old Mrs Sanders chattered on to the children as she bustled about the big kitchen. Timothy ran in and settled down on the rug by the fire.

He suddenly saw a tabby cat slinking along by the wall, all her hairs on end with fear of the strange dog. He gave a delighted wuff and sprang at the cat. She fled out of the kitchen into the old panelled hall. Tim flew after her, taking no notice at all of George's stern shout.

The cat tried to leap on top of an old grandfather clock in the hall. With a joyous bark Tim sprang too. He flung himself against a polished panel – and then a most extraordinary thing happened!

The panel disappeared – and a dark hole showed in the old wall! George, who had followed Tim out into the hall, gave a loud cry of surprise. 'Look! Mrs Sanders, come and look!'

CHAPTER FOUR

An exciting discovery

OLD MRS Sanders and the other three children rushed out into the hall when they heard George's shout.

'What's up?' cried Julian. 'What's happened?'

'Tim sprang at the cat, missed her, and fell hard against the panelled wall,' said George, 'and the panel moved, and look – there's a hole in the wall!'

'It's a secret panel!' cried Dick, in excitement, peering into the hole. 'Golly! Did you know there was one here, Mrs Sanders?'

'Oh yes,' said the old lady. 'This house is full of funny things like that. I'm very careful when I polish that panel, because if I rub too hard in the top corner, it always slides back.'

'What's behind the panel?' asked Julian. The hole was only about the width of his head, and when he stuck his head inside, he could see only darkness. The wall itself was about eight inches behind the panelling, and was of stone.

'Get a candle, do get a candle!' said Anne, thrilled. 'You haven't got a torch, have you, Mrs Sanders?'

'No,' said the old woman. 'But you can get a candle if you like. There's one on the kitchen mantelpiece.'

Anne shot off to get it. Julian lit it and put it into the hole behind the panel. The others pushed against him to try and peep inside.

'Don't,' said Julian, impatiently. 'Wait your turn, sillies! Let me have a look.'

200

He had a good look, but there didn't really seem anything to see. It was all darkness behind, and stone wall. He gave the candle to Dick, and then each of the children had a turn at peeping. Old Mrs Sanders had gone back to the kitchen. She was used to the sliding panel!

'She said this house was full of strange things like that,' said Anne. 'What other things are there, do you think? Let's ask her.'

They slid the panel back into place and went to find Mrs Sanders. 'Mrs Sanders, what other funny things are there in Kirrin Farmhouse?' asked Julian.

'There's a cupboard upstairs with a false back,' said Mrs Sanders. 'Don't look so excited! There's nothing in it at all! And there's a big stone over there by the fireplace that pulls up to show a hidey-hole. I suppose in the old days people wanted good hiding-places for things.'

The children ran to the stone she pointed out. It had an iron ring in it, and was easily pulled up. Below was a hollowed-out place, big enough to take a small box. It was empty now, but all the same it looked exciting.

'Where's the cupboard?' asked Julian.

'My old legs are too tired to go traipsing upstairs this morning,' said the farmer's wife. 'But you can go yourselves. Up the stairs, turn to the right, and go into the second door you see. The cupboard is at the farther end. Open the door and feel about at the bottom till you come across a dent in the wood. Press it hard, and the false back slides to the side.'

The four children and Timothy ran upstairs as fast as they could, munching shortbread as they went. This really was a very exciting morning!

They found the cupboard and opened the door. All four

201

went down on hands and knees to press round the bottom of the cupboard to find the dented place. Anne found it.

'I've got it!' she cried. She pressed hard, but her little fingers were not strong enough to work the mechanism of the sliding back. Julian had to help her.

There was a creaking noise, and the children saw the false back of the cupboard sliding sideways. A big space showed behind, large enough to take a fairly thin man.

'A jolly good hiding-place,' said Julian. 'Anyone could hide there and no one would ever know!'

'I'll get in and you shut me up,' said Dick. 'It would be exciting.'

He got into the space. Julian slid the back across, and Dick could no longer be seen!

'Bit of a tight fit!' he called. 'And awfully dark! Let me out again.'

The children all took turns at going into the space behind the back of the cupboard and being shut up. Anne didn't like it very much.

They went down to the warm kitchen again. 'It's a most exciting cupboard, Mrs Sanders,' said Julian. 'I do wish we lived in a house like this, full of secrets!'

'Can we come and play in that cupboard again?' asked George.

'No, I'm afraid you can't, George,' said Mrs Sanders. 'That room where the cupboard is, is one the two gentlemen are going to have.'

'Oh!' said Julian, disappointed. 'Shall you tell them about the sliding back, Mrs Sanders?'

'I don't expect so,' said the old lady. 'It's only you children that get excited about things like that, bless you. Two gentlemen wouldn't think twice about it.'

'How funny grown-ups are!' said Anne, puzzled. 'I'm quite certain I shall be thrilled to see a sliding panel or a trapdoor even when I'm a hundred.'

'Same here,' said Dick. 'Could I just go and look into the sliding panel in the hall once more, Mrs Sanders? I'll take the candle.'

Dick never knew why he suddenly wanted to have another look. It was just an idea he had. The others didn't bother to go with him, for there really was nothing to see behind the panelling except the old stone wall.

Dick took the candle and went into the hall. He pressed on the panel at the top and it slid back. He put the candle inside and had another good look. There was nothing at all to be seen. Dick took out his head and put in his arm, stretching along the wall as far as his hand would reach. He was just about to take it back when his fingers found a hole in the wall.

'Funny!' said Dick. 'Why should there be a hole in the stone wall just there?'

He stuck in his finger and thumb and worked them about. He felt a little ridge inside the wall, rather like a bird's perch, and was able to get hold of it. He wriggled his fingers about the perch, but nothing happened. Then he got a good hold and pulled.

The stone came right out! Dick was so surprised that he let go the heavy stone and it fell to the ground behind the panelling with a crash!

The noise brought the others out into the hall. 'Whatever are you doing, Dick?' said Julian. 'Have you broken something?'

'No,' said Dick, his face reddening with excitement. 'I say – I put my hand in here – and found a hole in one of the stones the wall is made of – and I got hold of a sort of ridge with my finger and thumb and pulled. The stone came right out, and I got such a surprise I let go. It fell, and that's what you heard!'

'Golly!' said Julian, trying to push Dick away from the open panel. 'Let me see.'

'No, Julian,' said Dick, pushing him away. 'This is *my* discovery. Wait till I see if I can feel anything in the hole. It's difficult to get at!'

The others waited impatiently. Julian could hardly prevent himself from pushing Dick right away. Dick put his arm in as far as he could, and curved his hand round to get into the space behind where the stone had been. His fingers felt about and he closed them round something that felt like a book. Cautiously and carefully he brought it out.

'An old book!' he said.

'What's in it?' cried Anne.

They turned the pages carefully. They were so dry and brittle that some of them fell into dust.

'I think it's a book of recipes,' said Anne, as her sharp eyes read a few words in the old brown, faded handwriting. 'Let's take it to Mrs Sanders.'

The children carried the book to the old lady. She laughed at their beaming faces. She took the book and looked at it, not at all excited.

'Yes,' she said. 'It's a book of recipes, that's all it is. See the name in the front – Alice Mary Sanders – that must have been my husband's great-grandmother. She was famous for her medicines, I know. It was said she could cure any ill in man or animal, no matter what it was.'

'It's a pity it's so hard to read her writing,' said Julian,

204

disappointed. 'The whole book is falling to pieces too. It must be very old.'

'Do you think there's anything else in that hidy-hole?' asked Anne. 'Julian, you go and put *your* arm in, it's longer than Dick's.'

'There didn't seem to be anything else at all,' said Dick. 'It's a very small place – just a few inches of hollow space behind that brick or stone that fell down.'

'Well, I'll just put my hand in and see,' said Julian. They all went back into the hall. Julian put his arm into the open panel, and slid it along the wall to where the stone had fallen out. His hand went into the space there, and his long

205

fingers groped about, feeling for anything else that might be there.

There was something else, something soft and flat that felt like leather. Eagerly the boy's fingers closed over it and he drew it out carefully, half afraid that it might fall to pieces with age.

'I've got something!' he said, his eyes gleaming brightly. 'Look – what is it?'

The others crowded round. 'It's rather like Daddy's tobacco pouch,' said Anne, feeling it. 'The same shape. Is there anything inside?'

It was a tobacco pouch, very dark brown, made of soft leather and very much worn. Carefully Julian undid the flap, and unrolled the leather.

A few bits of black tobacco were still in the pouch but there was something else, too! Tightly rolled up in the last bit of pouch was a piece of linen. Julian took it out and unrolled it. He put it flat on the hall-table.

The children stared at it. There were marks and signs on the linen, done in black ink that had hardly faded. But the four of them could not make head or tail of the marks.

'It's not a map,' said Julian. 'It seems a sort of code, or something. I do wonder what it means. I wish we could make it out. It must be some sort of secret.'

The children stared at the piece of linen, very thrilled. It was so old – and contained some kind of secret. Whatever could it be?

They ran to show it to Mrs Sanders. She was studying the old recipe book, and her face glowed with pleasure as she raised it to look at the excited children.

'This book's a wonder!' she said. 'I can hardly read the writing, but here's a recipe for backache. I shall try it myself. My back aches so much at the end of the day. Now, you listen . . .'

But the children didn't want to listen to recipes for backache. They pushed the piece of linen on to Mrs Sanders's lap.

'Look! What's this about, Mrs Sanders? Do you know? We found it in a kind of tobacco pouch in that place behind the panel.'

Mrs Sanders took off her glasses, polished them, and put them on again. She looked carefully at the piece of linen with its strange marks.

She shook her head. 'No – this doesn't make any sense to me. And what's this now? – it looks like an old tobacco pouch. Ah, my John would like that, I guess. He's got such an old one that it won't hold his tobacco any more! This is old too – but there's a lot of wear in it yet.'

'Mrs Sanders, do you want this piece of linen too?' asked Julian, anxiously. He was longing to take it home and study it. He felt certain there was some kind of exciting secret hidden there, and he could not bear the thought of leaving it with Mrs Sanders.

'You take it, Julian, if you want it,' said Mrs Sanders, with a laugh. 'I'll keep the recipes for myself, and John shall have the pouch. You can have the old rag if you want it, though it beats me why you think it's so fascinating! Ah, here's John!'

She raised her voice and shouted to the deaf old man. 'Hey, John, here's a tobacco pouch for you. The children found it somewhere behind that panel that opens in the hall.'

John took it and fingered it. 'It's a strange one,' he said, 'but better than mine. Well, youngsters, I don't want to hurry you, but it's one o'clock now, and you'd better be going if it's near your dinner-time!'

'Gracious!' said Julian. 'We shall be late! Goodbye, Mrs Sanders, and thanks awfully for the shortbread and this old rag. We'll try our best to make out what's on it and tell you. Hurry, everyone! Where's Tim? Come on, Timothy, we're late!'

The five of them ran off quickly. They really were late, and had to run most of the way, which meant that it was difficult to talk. But they were so excited about their morning that they panted remarks to one another as they went.

'I wonder what this old rag says!' panted Julian. 'I mean to find out. I'm sure it's something mysterious.'

'Shall we tell anyone?' asked Dick.

'No!' said George. 'Let's keep it a secret.'

'If Anne starts to give away anything, kick her under the table, like we did last summer,' said Julian, with a grin. Poor Anne always found it difficult to keep a secret, and often had to be nudged or kicked when she began to give things away.

'I won't say a word,' said Anne, indignantly. 'And don't you dare to kick me. It only makes me cry out and then the grown-ups want to know why.'

'We'll have a good old puzzle over this piece of linen after dinner,' said Julian. 'I bet we'll find out what it says, if we really make up our minds to!'

'Here we are,' said George. 'Not too late. Hallo Mother! We won't be a minute washing our hands! We've had a lovely time.'

CHAPTER FIVE

An unpleasant walk

AFTER DINNER the four children went upstairs to the boys' bedroom and spread out the bit of linen on a table there. There were words here and there, scrawled in rough printing. There was the sign of a compass, with E marked clearly for East. There were eight rough squares, and in one of them, right in the middle, was a cross. It was all very mysterious.

'You know, I believe these words are Latin,' said Julian, trying to make them out. 'But I can't read them properly. And I expect if I *could* read them, I wouldn't know what they meant. I wish we knew someone who could read Latin like this.'

'Could your father, George?' asked Anne.

'I expect so,' said George. But nobody wanted to ask George's father. He might take the curious old rag away. He might forget all about it, he might even burn it. Scientists were such peculiar people.

'What about Mr Roland?' said Dick. 'He's a tutor. He knows Latin.'

'We won't ask him till we know a bit more about him,' said Julian, cautiously. 'He *seems* jolly and nice – but you never know. Oh, blow – I wish we could make this out, I really do.'

'There are two words at the top,' said Dick, and he tried to spell them out. 'VIA OCCULTA.' What do you think they could mean, Julian?'

209

'Well – the only thing I can think of that they can mean is – Secret Way, or something like that,' said Julian, screwing up his forehead into a frown.

'Secret Way!' said Anne, her eyes shining. 'Oh, I hope it's that! Secret Way! How exciting. What sort of secret way would it be, Julian?'

'How do I know, Anne, silly?' said Julian. 'I don't even know that the words are meant to mean "Secret Way". It's really a guess on my part.'

'If they did mean that – the linen might have directions to find the Secret Way, whatever it is,' said Dick. 'Oh Julian, isn't it exasperating that we can't read it? Do, do try. You know more Latin than I do.'

'It's so hard to read the funny old letters,' said Julian, trying again. 'No – it's no good at all. I can't make them out.'

Steps came up the stairs, and the door opened. Mr Roland looked in.

'Hallo, hallo!' he said. 'I wondered where you all were. What about a walk over the cliffs?'

'We'll come,' said Julian, rolling up the old rag.

'What have you got there? Anything interesting?' asked Mr Roland.

'It's a—' began Anne, and at once all the others began to talk, afraid that Anne was going to give the secret away.

'It's a wonderful afternoon for a walk.'

'Come on, let's get our things on!'

'Tim, Tim, where are you?' George gave a piercing whistle. Tim was under the bed and came bounding out. Anne went red as she guessed why all the others had interrupted her so quickly.

'Idiot,' said Julian, under his breath. 'Baby.'

Fortunately Mr Roland said no more about the piece of linen he had seen Julian rolling up. He was looking at Tim.

'I suppose he must come,' he said. George stared at him in indignation.

'Of course he must!' she said. 'We never never go anywhere without Timothy.'

Mr Roland went downstairs, and the children got ready to go out. George was scowling. The very idea of leaving Tim behind made her angry.

'You nearly gave our secret away, you silly,' said Dick to Anne.

'I didn't think,' said the little girl, looking ashamed of herself. 'Anyway, Mr Roland seems very nice. I think we

211

might ask him if he could help us to understand those funny words.'

'You leave that to me to decide,' said Julian, crossly. 'Now don't you dare to say a word.'

They all set out, Timothy too. Mr Roland need not have worried about the dog, for Timothy would not go near him. It was very strange, really. He kept away from the tutor, and took not the slightest notice of him even when Mr Roland spoke to him.

'He's not usually like that,' said Dick. 'He's a most friendly dog, really.'

'Well, as I've got to live in the same house with him, I must try and make him friends with me,' said the tutor. 'Hi, Timothy! Come here! I've got a biscuit in my pocket.'

Timothy pricked up his ears at the word 'biscuit', but did not even look towards Mr Roland. He put his tail down and went to George. She patted him.

'If he doesn't like anyone, not even a biscuit or a bone will make him go to them when he is called,' she said.

Mr Roland gave it up. He put the biscuit back into his pocket. 'He's a peculiar-looking dog, isn't he?' he said. 'A terrible mongrel! I must say I prefer well-bred dogs.'

George went purple in the face. 'He's *not* peculiar-looking!' she spluttered. 'He's not nearly so peculiar-looking as you! He's not a terrible mongrel. He's the best dog in the world!'

'I think you are being a little rude,' said Mr Roland, stiffly. 'I don't allow my pupils to be cheeky, Georgina.'

Calling her Georgina made George still more furious. She lagged behind with Tim, looking as black as a thundercloud. The others felt uncomfortable. They knew what tempers George got into, and how difficult she could be. She had been so much better and happier since the summer, when they had come to stay for the first time. They did hope she wasn't going to be silly and get into rows. It would spoil the Christmas holidays.

Mr Roland took no more notice of George. He did not speak to her, but strode on ahead with the others, doing his best to be jolly. He could really be very funny, and the boys began to laugh at him. He took Anne's hand, and the little girl jumped along beside him, enjoying the walk.

Julian felt sorry for George. It wasn't nice to be left out of things, and he knew how George hated anything like

213

that. He wondered if he dared to put in a good word for her. It might make things easier.

'Mr Roland, sir,' he began. 'Could you call my cousin by the name she likes – George – she simply hates Georgina. And she's very fond of Tim. She can't bear anyone to say horrid things about him.'

Mr Roland looked surprised. 'My dear boy, I am sure you mean well,' he said, in rather a dry sort of voice, 'but I hardly think I want your advice about any of my pupils. I shall follow my own wishes in my treatment of Georgina, not yours. I want to be friends with you all, and I am sure we shall be – but Georgina has got to be sensible, as you three are.'

Julian felt rather squashed. He went red and looked at Dick. Dick gave him a squeeze on his arm. The boys knew George could be silly and difficult, especially if anyone didn't like her beloved dog – but they thought Mr Roland might try to be a bit more understanding too. Dick slipped behind and walked with George.

'You needn't walk with me,' said George at once, her blue eyes glinting. 'Walk with your friend Mr Roland.'

'He isn't my friend,' said Dick. 'Don't be silly.'

'I'm not silly,' said George, in a tight sort of voice. 'I heard you all laughing and joking with him. You go on and have a good laugh again. I've got Timothy.'

'George, it's Christmas holidays,' said Dick. 'Do let's all be friends. Do. Don't let's spoil Christmas.'

'I can't like anyone who doesn't like Tim,' said George, obstinately.

'Well, after all, Mr Roland did offer him a biscuit,' said Dick, trying to make peace as hard as he could.

George said nothing. Her small face looked fierce. Dick tried again.

AN UNPLEASANT WALK

'George! Promise to try and be nice till Christmas is over, anyway. Don't let's spoil Christmas, for goodness' sake! Come on, George.'

'All right,' said George, at last. 'I'll try.'

'Come and walk with us then,' said Dick. So George caught up the others, and tried not to look too sulky. Mr Roland guessed that Dick had been trying to make George behave, and he included her in his talk. He could not make her laugh, but she did at least answer politely.

'Is that Kirrin Farmhouse?' asked Mr Roland, as they came in sight of the farm.

'Yes. Do you know it?' asked Julian, in surprise.

'No, no,' said Mr Roland, at once, 'I've heard of it, and wondered if that was the place.'

'We went there this morning,' said Anne. 'It's an exciting place.' She looked at the others, wondering if they would mind if she said anything about the things they had seen that morning. Julian thought for a moment. After all, it couldn't matter telling him about the stone in the kitchen and the false back to the cupboard. Mrs Sanders would tell anyone that. He could speak about the sliding panel in the hall too, and say they had found an old recipe book there. He did not need to say anything about the old bit of marked linen.

So he told their tutor about the exciting things there had been at the old farmhouse, but said nothing at all about the linen and its strange markings. Mr Roland listened with the greatest interest.

'This is all very remarkable,' he said. 'Very remarkable indeed. Most interesting. You say the old couple live there quite alone?'

'Well, they are having two people to stay over Christ-

215

mas,' said Dick. 'Artists. Julian thought he would go over and talk to them. He can paint awfully well, you know.'

'Can he really?' said Mr Roland. 'Well, he must show me some of his pictures. But I don't think he'd better go and worry the artists at the farmhouse. They might not like it.'

This remark made Julian feel obstinate. He made up his mind at once that he *would* go and talk to the two artists when he got the chance!

It was quite a pleasant walk on the whole except that

George was quiet, and Timothy would not go anywhere near Mr Roland. When they came to a frozen pond Dick threw sticks on it for Tim to fetch. It was so funny to see him go slithering about on his long legs, trying to run properly!

Everyone threw sticks for the dog, and Tim fetched all the sticks except Mr Roland's. When the tutor threw a stick the dog looked at it and took no more notice. It was almost as if he had said, 'What, *your* stick! No, thank you!'

'Now, home we go,' said Mr Roland, trying not to look annoyed with Tim. 'We shall just be in time for tea!'

CHAPTER SIX

Lessons with Mr Roland

NEXT MORNING the children felt a little gloomy. Lessons! How horrid in the holidays! Still, Mr Roland wasn't so bad. The children had not had him with them in the sitting-room the night before, because he had gone to talk to their uncle. So they were able to get out the mysterious bit of linen again and pore over it.

But it wasn't a bit of good. Nobody could make anything of it at all. Secret Way! What did it mean? Was it really directions for a Secret Way? And where was the way, and why was it secret? It was most exasperating not to be able to find out.

'I really feel we'll have to ask someone soon,' Julian had said with a sigh. 'I can't bear this mystery much longer. I keep on and on thinking of it.'

He had dreamt of it too that night, and now it was morning, with lessons ahead. He wondered what lesson Mr Roland would take – Latin perhaps. Then he could ask him what the words 'VIA OCCULTA' meant.

Mr Roland had seen all their reports and had noted the subjects they were weak in. One was Latin, and another was French. Maths were very weak in both Dick's report and George's. Both children must be helped on in those. Geometry was Julian's weakest spot.

Anne was not supposed to need any coaching. 'But if you like to come along and join us, I'll give you some painting to do,' said Mr Roland, his blue eyes twinkling at

218

her. He liked Anne. She was not difficult and sulky like George.

Anne loved painting. 'Oh, yes,' she said, happily, 'I'd love to do some painting. I can paint flowers, Mr Roland. I'll paint you some red poppies and blue cornflowers out of my head.'

'We will start at half-past nine,' said Mr Roland. 'We are to work in the sitting-room. Take your schoolbooks there, and be ready punctually.'

So all the children were there, sitting round a table, their books in front of them, at half-past nine. Anne had some painting water and her painting-box. The others looked at her enviously. Lucky Anne, to be doing painting while they worked hard at difficult things like Latin and Maths!

'Where's Timothy?' asked Julian in a low voice, as they waited for their tutor to come in.

'Under the table,' said George, defiantly. 'I'm sure he'll lie still. Don't any of you say anything about him. I want him there. I'm not going to do lessons without Tim here.'

'I don't see why he shouldn't be here with us,' said Dick. 'He's very very good. Sh! Here comes Mr Roland.'

The tutor came in, his black beard bristling round his mouth and chin. His eyes looked very piercing in the pale winter sunlight that filtered into the room. He told the children to sit down.

'I'll have a look at your exercise books first,' he said, 'and see what you were doing last term. You come first, Julian.'

Soon the little class were working quietly together. Anne was very busy painting a bright picture of poppies and cornflowers. Mr Roland admired it very much. Anne thought he really was very nice.

Suddenly there was a huge sigh from under the table. It was Tim, tired of lying so still. Mr Roland looked up, surprised. George at once sighed heavily, hoping that Mr Roland would think it was she who had sighed before.

'You sound tired, Georgina,' said Mr Roland. 'You shall all have a little break at eleven.'

George frowned. She hated being called Georgina. She put her foot cautiously on Timothy to warn him not to make any more noises. Tim licked her foot.

After a while, just when the class was at its very quietest, Tim felt a great wish to scratch himself very hard on his back. He got up. He sat down again with a thump, gave a grunt, and began to scratch himself furiously. The children all began to make noises to hide the sounds that Tim was making.

George clattered her feet on the floor. Julian began to cough, and let one of his books slip to the ground. Dick jiggled the table and spoke to Mr Roland.

'Oh dear, this sum is so hard; it really is! I keep doing it and doing it, and it simply *won't* come right!'

'Why all this sudden noise?' said Mr Roland in surprise. 'Stop tapping the floor with your feet, Georgina.'

Tim settled down quietly again. The children gave a sigh of relief. They became quiet, and Mr Roland told Dick to come to him with his Maths book.

The tutor took it, and stretched his legs out under the table, leaning back to speak to Dick. To his enormous surprise his feet struck something soft and warm – and then something nipped him sharply on the ankle! He drew in his feet with a cry of pain.

The children stared at him. He bent down and looked under the table. 'It's that dog,' he said, in disgust. 'The brute snapped at my ankles. He has made a hole in my trousers. Take him out, Georgina.'

Georgina said nothing. She sat as though she had not heard.

'She won't answer if you call her Georgina,' Julian reminded him.

'She'll answer me whatever I call her,' said Mr Roland, in a low and angry voice. 'I won't have that dog in here. If you don't take him out this very minute, Georgina, I will go to your father.'

George looked at him. She knew perfectly well that if she didn't take Tim out, and Mr Roland went to her father, he would order Timothy to live in the garden kennel, and that would be dreadful. There was absolutely nothing to be done but obey. Red in the face, a huge frown almost hiding her eyes, she got up and spoke to Tim.

'Come on, Tim! I'm not surprised you bit him. I would, too, if I were a dog!'

'There is no need to be rude, Georgina,' said Mr Roland, angrily.

The others stared at George. They wondered how she dared to say things like that. When she got fierce it seemed as if she didn't care for anyone at all!

'Come back as soon as you have put the dog out,' said Mr Roland.

George scowled, but came back in a few minutes. She felt caught. Her father was friendly with Mr Roland, and knew how difficult George was – if she behaved as badly as she felt she would like to, it would be Tim who would suffer, for he would certainly be banished from the house. So for Tim's sake George obeyed the tutor – but from that moment she disliked him and resented him bitterly with all her fierce little heart.

The others were sorry for George and Timothy, but they did not share the little girl's intense dislike of the new tutor. He often made them laugh. He was patient with their mistakes. He was willing to show them how to make paper darts and ships, and to do funny little tricks. Julian and Dick thought these were fun, and stored them up to try on the other boys when they went back to school.

After lessons that morning the children went out for half an hour in the frosty sunshine. George called Tim.

'Poor old boy!' she said. 'What a shame to turn you out of the room! Whatever did you snap at Mr Roland for? I think it was a very good idea, Tim – but I really don't know what made you!'

'George, you can't play about with Mr Roland,' said Julian. 'You'll only get into trouble. He's tough. He won't stand much from any of us. But I think he'll be quite a good sport if we get on the right side of him.'

'Well, get on the right side of him if you like,' said George, in rather a sneering voice. 'I'm not going to. If I don't like a person, I don't – and I don't like *him*.'

'Why? Just because he doesn't like Tim?' asked Dick.

'Mostly because of that – but because he makes me feel prickly down my back,' said George. 'I don't like his nasty mouth.'

'But you can't see it,' said Julian. 'It's covered with his moustache and beard.'

'I've seen his lips through them,' said George, obstinately. 'They're thin and cruel. You look and see. I don't like thin-lipped people. They are always spiteful and hard. And I don't like his cold eyes either. You can suck up to him all you like. *I* shan't.'

Julian refused to get angry with the stubborn little girl. He laughed at her. 'We're not going to suck up to him,' he said. 'We're just going to be sensible, that's all. You be sensible too, George, old thing.'

But once George had made up her mind about something nothing would alter her. She cheered up when she heard that they were all to go Christmas shopping on the bus that afternoon – without Mr Roland! He was going to watch an experiment that her father was going to show him.

'I will take you into the nearest town and you shall shop to your hearts' content,' said Aunt Fanny to the children. 'Then we will have tea in a tea-shop and catch the six o'clock bus home.'

This was fun. They caught the afternoon bus and rumbled along the deep country lanes till they got to the town. The shops looked very colourful and bright. The children had brought their money with them, and were very busy indeed, buying all kinds of things. There were so many people to get presents for!

'I suppose we'd better get something for Mr Roland, hadn't we?' said Julian.

'I'm going to,' said Anne.

'Fancy buying Mr *Roland* a present!' said George, in her scornful voice.

'Why shouldn't she, George?' asked her mother, in surprise. 'Oh dear, I hope you are going to be sensible about him, and not take a violent dislike to the poor man. I don't want him to complain to your father about you.'

'What are you going to buy for Tim, George?' asked Julian, changing the subject quickly.

'The largest bone the butcher has got,' said George. 'What are *you* going to buy him?'

'I guess if Tim had money, he would buy us each a present,' said Anne, taking hold of the thick hair round Tim's neck, and pulling it lovingly, 'He's the best dog in the world!'

George forgave Anne for saying she would buy Mr Roland a present, when the little girl said that about Tim! She cheered up again and began to plan what she would buy for everyone.

They had a fine tea, and caught the six o'clock bus back.

Aunt Fanny went to see if the cook had given the two men their tea. She came out of the study beaming.

'Really, I've never seen your uncle so jolly,' she said to Julian and Dick. 'He and Mr Roland are getting on like a house on fire. He has been showing your tutor quite a lot of his experiments. It's nice for him to have someone to talk to that knows a little about these things.'

Mr Roland played games with the children that evening. Tim was in the room, and the tutor tried again to make friends with him, but the dog refused to take any notice of him.

'As sulky as his little mistress!' said the tutor, with a laughing look at George, who was watching Tim refuse to go to Mr Roland, and looking rather pleased about it. She gave the tutor a scowl and said nothing.

'Shall we ask him whether "VIA OCCULTA" really does mean "Secret Way" or not, tomorrow?' said Julian to Dick, as they undressed that night. 'I'm just longing to know if it does. What do you think of Mr Roland, Dick?'

'I don't really quite know,' said Dick. 'I like lots of things about him, but then I suddenly don't like him at all. I don't like his eyes. And George is quite right about his lips. They are so thin there's hardly anything of them at all.'

'I think he's all right,' said Julian. 'He won't stand any nonsense, that's all. I wouldn't mind showing him the whole piece of rag and asking him to make out its meaning for us.'

'I thought you said it was to be a proper secret,' said Dick.

'I know – but what's the use of a secret we don't know the meaning of ourselves?' said Julian. 'I'll tell you what we *could* do – ask him to explain the words to us, and not show him the bit of linen.

'But we can't read some of the words ourselves,' said Dick. 'So that's no use. You'd have to show him the whole thing, and tell him where we got it.'

'Well, I'll see,' said Julian, getting into bed.

The next day there were lessons again from half-past nine to half-past twelve. George appeared without Tim. She was angry at having to do this, but it was no good being defiant and refusing to come to lessons without Tim. Now that he had snapped at Mr Roland, he had definitely put himself in the wrong, and the tutor had every right to refuse to allow him to come. But George looked very sulky indeed.

In the Latin lesson Julian took the chance of asking what he wanted to know. 'Please, Mr Roland,' he said, 'could you tell me what "VIA OCCULTA" means?'

'"VIA OCCULTA"' said Mr Roland, frowning. 'Yes – it means "Secret Path" or, "Secret Road". A hidden way – something like that. Why do you want to know?'

All the children were listening eagerly. Their hearts thumped with excitement. So Julian had been right. That funny bit of rag contained directions for some hidden way, some secret path – but where to! Where did it begin, and end?

'Oh – I just wanted to know,' said Julian. 'Thank you, sir.'

He winked at the others. He was as excited as they were. If only they could make out the rest of the markings, they might be able to solve the mystery. Well – perhaps he would ask Mr Roland in a day or two. The secret must be solved somehow.

'The "Secret Way",' said Julian to himself, as he worked out a problem in geometry. 'The "Secret Way". I'll find it somehow.'

CHAPTER SEVEN

Directions for the Secret Way

FOR THE next day or two the four children did not really have much time to think about the Secret Way, because Christmas was coming near, and there was a good deal to do.

There were Christmas cards to draw and paint for their mothers and fathers and friends. There was the house to decorate. They went out with Mr Roland to find sprays of holly, and came home laden.

'You look like a Christmas card yourselves,' said Aunt Fanny, as they walked up the garden path, carrying the red-berried holly over their shoulders. Mr Roland had found a group of trees with tufts of mistletoe growing from the top branches, and they had brought some of that too. Its berries shone like pale green pearls.

'Mr Roland had to climb the tree to get this,' said Anne. 'He's a good climber – as good as a monkey.'

Everyone laughed except George. She never laughed at anything to do with the tutor. They all dumped their loads down in the porch, and went to wash. They were to decorate the house that evening.

'Is Uncle going to let his study be decorated too?' asked Anne. There were all kinds of strange instruments and glass tubes in the study now, and the children looked at them with wonder whenever they ventured into the study, which was very seldom.

'No, my study is certainly not to be messed about,' said Uncle Quentin, at once. 'I wouldn't hear of it.'

DIRECTIONS FOR THE SECRET WAY

'Uncle, why do you have all these funny things in your study?' asked Anne, looking round with wide eyes.

Uncle Quentin laughed. 'I'm looking for a secret formula!' he said.

'What's that?' said Anne.

'You wouldn't understand,' said her uncle. 'All these "funny things" as you call them, help me in my experiments, and I put down in my book what they tell me – and from all I learn I work out a secret formula, that will be of great use when it is finished.'

'You want to know a secret formula, and we want to know a secret way,' said Anne, quite forgetting that she was not supposed to talk about this.

Julian was standing by the door. He frowned at Anne. Luckily Uncle Quentin was not paying any more attention to the little girl's chatter. Julian pulled her out of the room.

'Anne, the only way to stop you giving away secrets is to sew up your mouth, like Brer Rabbit wanted to do to Mister Dog!' he said.

Joanna the cook was busy baking Christmas cakes. An enormous turkey had been sent over from Kirrin Farm, and was hanging up in the larder. Timothy thought it smelt glorious, and Joanna was always shooing him out of the kitchen.

There were boxes of crackers on the shelf in the sitting-room, and mysterious parcels everywhere. It was very, very Christmassy! The children were happy and excited.

Mr Roland went out and dug up a little spruce fir tree. 'We must have a Christmas tree,' he said. 'Have you any tree-ornaments, children?'

'No,' said Julian, seeing George shake her head.

'I'll go into the town this afternoon and get some for

you,' promised the tutor. 'It will be fun dressing the tree. We'll put it in the hall, and light candles on it on Christmas Day after tea. Who's coming with me to get the candles and the ornaments?'

'I am!' cried three children. But the fourth said nothing. That was George. Not even to buy tree-ornaments would the obstinate little girl go with Mr Roland. She had never had a Christmas tree before, and she was very much looking forward to it – but it was spoilt for her because Mr Roland bought the things that made it so beautiful.

Now it stood in the hall, with coloured candles in holders clipped to the branches, and bright shining ornaments hanging from top to bottom. Silver strands of frosted string hung down from the branches like icicles, and Anne had put bits of white cotton-wool here and there to look like snow. It really was a lovely sight to see.

'Beautiful!' said Uncle Quentin, as he passed through the hall, and saw Mr Roland hanging the last ornaments on the tree. 'I say – look at the fairy doll on the top! Who's that for? A good girl?'

Anne secretly hoped that Mr Roland would give her the doll. She was sure it wasn't for George – and anyway, George wouldn't accept it. It was such a pretty doll, with its gauzy frock and silvery wings.

Julian, Dick and Anne had quite accepted the tutor now as teacher and friend. In fact, everyone had, their uncle and aunt too, and even Joanna the cook. George, of course, was the only exception, and she and Timothy kept away from Mr Roland, each looking as sulky as the other whenever the tutor was in the room.

'You know, I never knew a dog could look so sulky!'

230

said Julian, watching Timothy. 'Really, he scowls almost like George.'

'And I always feel as if George puts her tail down like Tim, when Mr Roland is in the room,' giggled Anne.

'Laugh all you like,' said George, in a low tone. 'I think you're beastly to me. I know I'm right about Mr Roland. I've got a feeling about him. And so has Tim.'

'You're silly, George,' said Dick. 'You haven't *really* got a Feeling – it's only that Mr Roland will keep calling you Georgina and putting you in your place, and that he doesn't like Tim. I dare say he can't help disliking dogs. After all, there was once a famous man called Lord Roberts who couldn't bear cats.'

'Oh well, cats are different,' said George. 'If a person doesn't like dogs, especially a dog like our Timothy, then there really *must* be something wrong with him.'

'It's no use arguing with George,' said Julian. 'Once she's made up her mind about something, she won't budge!'

George went out of the room in a huff. The others thought she was behaving rather stupidly.

'I'm surprised really,' said Anne. 'She was so jolly last term at school. Now she's gone all strange, rather like she was when we first knew her last summer.'

'I do think Mr Roland has been decent digging up the Christmas tree and everything,' said Dick. 'I still don't like him awfully much sometimes, but I think he's a sport. What about asking him if he can read that old linen rag for us – I don't think I'd mind him sharing our secret, really.'

'I would *love* him to share it,' said Anne, who was busy doing a marvellous Christmas card for the tutor. 'He's most awfully clever. I'm sure he could tell us what the Secret Way is. Do let's ask him.'

'All right,' said Julian. 'I'll show him the piece of linen. It's Christmas Eve tonight. He will be with us in the sitting-room, because Aunt Fanny is going into the study with Uncle Quentin to wrap up presents for all of us!'

So, that evening, before Mr Roland came in to sit with them, Julian took out the little roll of linen and stroked it out flat on the table. George looked at it in surprise.

'Mr Roland will be here in a minute,' she said. 'You'd better put it away quickly.'

'We're going to ask him if he can tell us what the old Latin words mean,' said Julian.

'You're not!' cried George, in dismay. 'Ask him to share our secret! How ever can you?'

'Well, we want to know what the secret is, don't we?' said Julian. 'We don't need to tell him where we got this or anything about it except that we want to know what the markings mean. We're not exactly sharing the secret with him – only asking him to use his brains to help us.'

'Well, I never thought you'd ask *him*,' said George. 'And he'll want to know simply everything about it, you just see if he won't! He's terribly snoopy.'

'Whatever do you mean?' said Julian, in surprise. 'I don't think he's a bit snoopy.'

'I saw him yesterday snooping round the study when no one was there,' said George. 'He didn't see me outside the window with Tim. He was having a real poke round.'

'You know how interested he is in your father's work,' said Julian. 'Why shouldn't he look at it? Your father likes him too. You're just seeing what horrid things you can find to say about Mr Roland.'

'Oh shut up, you two,' said Dick. 'It's Christmas Eve. Don't let's argue or quarrel or say beastly things.'

Just at that moment the tutor came into the room. 'All as busy as bees?' he said, his mouth smiling beneath its moustache. 'Too busy to have a game of cards, I suppose?'

'Mr Roland, sir,' began Julian, 'could you help us with something? We've got an old bit of linen here with odd markings on it. The words seem to be in some sort of Latin and we can't make them out.'

George gave an angry exclamation as she saw Julian push the piece of linen over towards the tutor. She went out of the room and shut the door with a bang. Tim was with her.

'Our sweet-tempered Georgina doesn't seem to be very friendly tonight,' remarked Mr Roland, pulling the bit of linen towards him. 'Where in the world did you get this? What an odd thing!'

Nobody answered. Mr Roland studied the roll of linen, and then gave an exclamation. 'Ah – I see why you wanted to know the meaning of those Latin words the other day – the ones that meant "hidden path", you remember. They are at the top of this linen roll.'

'Yes,' said Dick. All the children leaned over towards Mr Roland, hoping he would be able to unravel a little of the mystery for them.

'We just want to know the meaning of the words, sir,' said Julian.

'This is really very interesting,' said the tutor, puzzling over the linen. 'Apparently there are directions here for finding the opening or entrance of a secret path or road.'

'That's what we thought!' cried Julian, excitedly. 'That's exactly what we thought. Oh sir, do read the directions and see what you make of them.'

'Well, these eight squares are meant to represent wooden boards or panels, I think,' said the tutor, pointing to the eight rough squares drawn on the linen. 'Wait a minute – I can hardly read some of the words. This is most fascinating. *Solum lapideum – paries ligneus –* and what's this? – *cellula* – yes, *cellula!*'

The children hung on his words. 'Wooden panels!' That must mean panels somewhere at Kirrin Farmhouse.

Mr Roland frowned down at the old printed words. Then he sent Anne to borrow a magnifying glass from her uncle. She came back with it, and the four of them looked through the glass, seeing the words three times as clearly now.

'Well,' said the tutor at last, 'as far as I can make out the directions mean this: a room facing east; eight wooden panels, with an opening somewhere to be found in that marked one; a stone floor – yes, I think that's right, a stone floor, and a cupboard. It all sounds most extraordinary and very thrilling. Where *did* you get this from?'

'We just found it,' said Julian, after a pause. 'Oh Mr Roland, thanks awfully. We could never have made it out by ourselves. I suppose the entrance to the Secret Way is in a room facing east then.'

'It looks like it,' said Mr Roland, poring over the linen roll again. 'Where did you say you found this?'

'We didn't say,' said Dick. 'It's a secret really, you see.'

'I think you might tell me,' said the tutor, looking at Dick with his brilliant blue eyes. 'I can be trusted with secrets. You've no idea how many strange secrets I know.'

'Well,' said Julian, 'I don't really see why you shouldn't know where we found this, Mr Roland. We found it at Kirrin Farmhouse, in an old tobacco pouch. I suppose the Secret Way begins somewhere there! I wonder where and wherever can it lead to?'

'You found it at Kirrin Farmhouse!' exclaimed Mr Roland. 'Well, well – I must say that seems to be an interesting old place. I shall have to go over there one day.'

Julian rolled up the piece of linen and put it into his pocket. 'Well, thank you, sir,' he said. 'You've solved a bit of the mystery for us but set another puzzle! We must look for the entrance of the Secret Way after Christmas, when we can walk over to Kirrin Farmhouse.'

'I'll come with you,' said Mr Roland. 'I may be able to help a little. That is – if you don't mind me having a little share in this exciting secret.'

'Well – you've been such a help in telling us what the words mean,' said Julian, 'we'd like you to come if you want to, sir.'

'Yes, we *would*,' said Anne.

'We'll go and look for the Secret Way, then,' said Mr Roland. 'What fun we shall have, tapping round the panels, waiting for a mysterious dark entrance to appear!'

'I don't suppose George will go,' Dick murmured to Julian. 'You shouldn't have said Mr Roland could go with us, Ju. That means that old George will have to be left out of it. You know how she hates that.'

'I know,' said Julian, feeling uncomfortable. 'Don't let's worry about that now though. George may feel different after Christmas. She can't keep up this kind of behaviour for ever!'

CHAPTER EIGHT

What happened on Christmas night

IT WAS great fun on Christmas morning. The children awoke early and tumbled out of bed to look at the presents that were stacked on chairs near-by. Squeals and yells of delight came from everyone.

'Oh! a railway station! Just what I wanted! Who gave me this marvellous station?'

'A new doll – with eyes that shut! I shall call her Betsy-May. She looks just like a Betsy-May!'

'I say – what a whopping great book – all about aeroplanes. From Aunt Fanny! How decent of her!'

'Timothy! Look what Julian has given you – a collar with big brass studs all round – you *will* be grand. Go and lick him to say thank you!'

'Who's this from? I say, who gave me this? Where's the label? Oh – from Mr Roland. How decent of him! Look, Julian, a pocket-knife with three blades!'

So the cries and exclamations went on, and the four excited children and the equally-excited dog spent a glorious hour before a late Christmas breakfast, opening all kinds and shapes of parcels. The bedrooms were in a fine mess when the children had finished!

'Who gave you that book about dogs, George?' asked Julian, seeing rather a nice dog-book lying on George's pile.

'Mr Roland,' said George, rather shortly. Julian wondered if George was going to accept it. He rather thought

238

she wouldn't. But the little girl, defiant and obstinate as she was, had made up her mind not to spoil Christmas Day by being 'difficult'. So, when the others thanked the tutor for their things she too added her thanks, though in rather a stiff little voice.

George had not given the tutor anything, but the others had, and Mr Roland thanked them all very heartily, appearing to be very pleased indeed. He told Anne that her Christmas card was the nicest he had ever had, and she beamed at him with joy.

'Well, I must say it's nice to be here for Christmas!' said Mr Roland, when he and the others were sitting round a loaded Christmas table, at the mid-day dinner. 'Shall I carve for you, Mr Quentin? I'm good at that!'

Uncle Quentin handed him the carving knife and fork gladly. 'It's nice to have you here,' he said warmly. 'I must say you've settled in well – I'm sure we all feel as if we've known you for ages!'

It really was a jolly Christmas Day. There were no lessons, of course, and there were to be none the next day either. The children gave themselves up to the enjoyment of eating a great deal, sucking sweets, and looking forward to the lighting of the Christmas tree.

It looked beautiful when the candles were lighted. They twinkled in the darkness of the hall, and the bright ornaments shone and glowed. Tim sat and looked at it, quite entranced.

'He likes it as much as we do,' said George. And indeed Tim had enjoyed the day just as much as any of them.

They were all tired out when they went to bed. 'I shan't be long before I'm asleep,' yawned Anne. 'Oh, George – it's been fun, hasn't it? I did like the Christmas tree.'

'Yes, it's been lovely,' said George, jumping into bed. 'Here comes Mother to say good-night. Basket, Tim, basket!'

Tim leapt into his basket by the window. He was always there when George's mother came into say good-night to the girls but as soon as she had gone downstairs, the dog took a flying leap and landed on George's bed. There he slept, his head curled round her feet.

'Don't you think Tim ought to sleep downstairs to-night?' said George's mother. 'Joanna says he ate such an enormous meal in the kitchen that she is sure he will be sick.'

'Oh *no*, Mother!' said George, at once. 'Make Tim sleep downstairs on Christmas night? Whatever would he think?'

'Oh, very well,' said her mother, with a laugh. 'I might have known it was useless to suggest it. Now to sleep quickly, Anne and George – it's late and you are all tired.'

She went into the boys' room and said good-night to them too. They were almost asleep.

Two hours later everyone else was in bed. The house was still and dark. George and Anne slept peacefully in their small beds. Timothy slept too, lying heavily on George's feet.

Suddenly George awoke with a jump. Tim was growling softly! He had raised his big shaggy head and George knew that he was listening.

'What is it, Tim?' she whispered. Anne did not wake. Tim went on growling softly. George sat up and put her hand on his collar to stop him. She knew that if he awoke her father, he would be cross.

Timothy stopped growling now that he had roused

George. The girl sat and wondered what to do. It wasn't any good waking Anne. The little girl would be frightened. Why was Tim growling? He never did that at night!

'Perhaps I'd better go and see if everything is all right,' thought George. She was quite fearless, and the thought of creeping through the still, dark house did not disturb her at all. Besides she had Tim! Who could be afraid with Tim beside them!

She slipped on her dressing-gown. 'Perhaps a log has fallen out of one of the fire-places and a rug is burning,' she thought, sniffing as she went down the stairs. 'It would be just like Tim to smell it and warn us!'

With her hand on Tim's head to warn him to be quite quiet, George crept softly through the hall to the sitting-room. The fire was quite all right there, just a red glow. In the kitchen all was peace too. Tim's feet made a noise there, as his claws rattled against the linoleum.

A slight sound came from the other side of the house. Tim growled quite loudly, and the hairs on the back of his neck rose up. George stood still. Could it possibly be burglars?

Suddenly Timothy shook himself free from her fingers and leapt across the hall, down a passage, and into the study beyond! There was the sound of an exclamation, and a noise as if someone was falling over.

'It *is* a burglar!' said George, and she ran to the study. She saw a torch shining on the floor, dropped by someone who was even now struggling with Tim.

George switched on the light, and then looked with the greatest astonishment into the study. Mr Roland was there in his dressing-gown, rolling on the floor, trying to get away from Timothy, who, although not biting him, was holding him firmly by his dressing-gown.

'Oh – it's you, George! Call your beastly dog off!' said Mr Roland, in a low and angry voice. 'Do you want to rouse all the household?'

'Why are you creeping about with a torch?' demanded George.

'I heard a noise down here, and came to see what it was,' said Mr Roland, sitting up and trying to fend off the angry dog. 'For goodness' sake, call your beast off.'

'Why didn't you put on the light?' asked George, not

attempting to take Tim away. She was very much enjoying the sight of an angry and frightened Mr Roland.

'I couldn't find it,' said the tutor. 'It's on the wrong side of the door, as you see.'

This was true. The switch was an awkward one to find if you didn't know it. Mr Roland tried to push Tim away again, and the dog suddenly barked.

'Well – he'll wake everyone!' said the tutor, angrily. 'I didn't want to rouse the house. I thought I could find out for myself if there was anyone about – a burglar perhaps. Here comes your father!'

George's father appeared, carrying a large poker. He stood still in astonishment when he saw Mr Roland on the ground and Timothy standing over him.

'What's all this?' he exclaimed. Mr Roland tried to get up, but Tim would not let him. George's father called to him sternly.

'Tim! Come here, sir!'

Timothy glanced at George to see if his mistress agreed with her father's command. She said nothing. So Timothy took no notice of the order and merely made a snap at Mr Roland's ankles.

'That dog's mad!' said Mr Roland, from the floor. 'He's already bitten me once before, and now he's trying to do it again!'

'Tim! Will you come here, sir!' shouted George's father. 'George, that dog is really disobedient. Call him off at once.'

'Come here, Tim!' said George, in a low voice. The dog at once came to her, standing by her side with the hairs on his neck still rising up stiffly. He growled softly as if to say, 'Be careful, Mr Roland, be careful!'

The tutor got up. He was very angry indeed. He spoke to George's father.

'I heard some sort of noise and came down with my torch to see what it was,' he said. 'I thought it came from your study, and knowing you kept your valuable books and instruments here, I wondered if some thief was about. I had just got down, and into the room, when that dog appeared from somewhere and got me down on the ground! George came along too, and would not call him off.'

'I can't understand your behaviour, George; I really can't,' said her father, angrily. 'I hope you are not going to behave stupidly, as you used to behave before your cousins came last summer. And what is this I hear about Tim biting Mr Roland before?'

'George had him under the table during lessons,' said Mr Roland. 'I didn't know that, and when I stretched out my legs, they touched Tim, and he bit me. I didn't tell you before, sir, because I didn't want to trouble you. Both George and the dog have tried to annoy me ever since I have been here.'

'Well, Tim must go outside and live in the kennel,' said George's father. 'I won't have him in the house. It will be a punishment for him, and a punishment for you too, George. I will not have this kind of behaviour. Mr Roland has been extremely kind to you all.'

'I won't let Tim live outside,' said George furiously. 'It's such cold weather, and it would simply break his heart.'

'Well, his heart must be broken then,' said her father. 'It will depend entirely on your behaviour from now on whether Tim is allowed in the house at all these holidays. I shall ask Mr Roland each day how you have behaved. If you have a bad report, then Tim stays outside. Now you know! Go back to bed but first apologise to Mr Roland!'

'I won't!' said George, and choked by feelings of anger and dismay, she tore out of the room and up the stairs. The two men stared after her.

'Let her be,' said Mr Roland. 'She's a very difficult child – and has made up her mind not to like me, that's quite plain. But I shall be very glad to know that that dog isn't in the house. I'm not at all certain that Georgina wouldn't set him on me, if she could!'

'I'm sorry about all this,' said George's father. 'I wonder what the noise was that you heard? – a log falling in the grate I expect. Now – what am I to do about that tiresome dog tonight? Go and take him outside, I suppose!'

'Leave him tonight,' said Mr Roland. 'I can hear noises upstairs – the others are awake by now! Don't let's make any more disturbance tonight.'

'Perhaps you are right,' said George's father, thankfully. He didn't at all want to tackle a defiant little girl and an angry big dog in the middle of a cold night!

The two men went to bed and slept. George did not sleep. The others had been awake when she got upstairs, and she had told them what had happened.

'George! You really are an idiot!' said Dick. 'After all, why shouldn't Mr Roland go down if he heard a noise! *You* went down! Now we shan't have darling old Tim in the house this cold weather!'

Anne began to cry. She didn't like hearing that the tutor she liked so much had been knocked down by Tim, and she hated hearing that Tim was to be punished.

'Don't be a baby,' said George. '*I'm* not crying, and it's *my* dog!'

But, when everyone had settled down again in bed, and slept peacefully, George's pillow was very wet indeed. Tim crept up beside her and licked the salt tears off her cheek. He whined softly. Tim was always unhappy when his little mistress was sad.

CHAPTER NINE

A hunt for the Secret Way

THERE WERE no lessons the next day. George looked rather pale, and was very quiet. Tim was already out in the yard-kennel, and the children could hear him whining unhappily. They were all upset to hear him.

'Oh, George, I'm awfully sorry about it all,' said Dick. 'I wish you wouldn't get so fierce about things. You only get yourself into trouble – and poor old Tim.'

George was full of mixed feelings. She disliked Mr Roland so much now that she could hardly bear to look at him – and yet she did not dare to be openly rude and rebellious because she was afraid that if she was, the tutor would give her a bad report, and perhaps she would not be allowed even to *see* Timothy. It was very hard for a defiant nature like hers to force herself to behave properly.

Mr Roland took no notice of her at all. The other children tried to bring George into their talks and plans, but she remained quiet and uninterested.

'George! We're going over to Kirrin Farmhouse today,' said Dick. 'Coming? We're going to try and find the entrance to the Secret Way. It must start somewhere there.'

The children had told George what Mr Roland had said about the piece of marked linen. They had all been thrilled about this, though the excitements of Christmas Day had made them forget about it for a while.

247

'Yes – of course I'll come,' said George, looking more cheerful. 'Timothy can come too. He wants a walk.'

But when the little girl found that Mr Roland was also going, she changed her mind at once. Not for anything would she go with the tutor! No – she would go for a walk alone with Timothy.

'But, George, think of the excitement we'll have trying to find the Secret Way,' said Julian, taking hold of her arm. George wrenched it away.

'I'm not going if Mr Roland is,' she said, obstinately, and the others knew that it was no good trying to coax her.

'I shall go alone with Tim,' said George. 'You go off together with your dear Mr Roland!'

She set out with Timothy, a lonely little figure going down the garden path. The others stared after her. This was horrid. George was being more and more left out, but what could they do about it?

'Well, children, are you ready?' asked Mr Roland. 'You start off by yourselves, will you? I'll meet you at the farmhouse later. I want to run down to the village first to get something.'

So the three children set off by themselves, wishing that George was with them. She was nowhere to be seen.

Old Mr and Mrs Sanders were pleased to see the three children, and sat them down in the big kitchen to eat ginger buns and drink hot milk.

'Well, have you come to find a few more secret things?' asked Mrs Sanders, with a smile.

'May we try?' asked Julian. 'We're looking for a room that's facing east, with a stone floor, and panelling!'

'All the rooms downstairs have stone floors,' said Mrs Sanders. 'You hunt all you like, my dears. You won't do any damage, I know. But don't go into the room upstairs with the cupboard that has a false back, will you, or the one next to it! Those are the rooms the two artists have.'

'All right,' said Julian, rather sorry that they were unable to fiddle about with the exciting cupboard again. 'Are the artists here, Mrs Sanders? I'd like to talk to them about pictures. I hope one day I'll be an artist too.'

'Dear me, is that so?' said Mrs Sanders. 'Well, well – it's always a marvel to me how people make any money at painting pictures.'

'It isn't making money that artists like, so much as the painting of the pictures,' said Julian, looking rather wise. That seemed to puzzle Mrs Sanders even more. She shook her head and laughed.

'They're peculiar folk!' she said. 'Ah well – you go along and have a hunt for whatever it is you want to find. You can't talk to the two artists today though, Master Julian – they're out.'

The children finished their buns and milk and then stood up, wondering where to begin their search. They must look for a room or rooms facing east. That would be the first thing to do.

'Which side of the house faces east, Mrs Sanders?' asked Julian. 'Do you know?'

'The kitchen faces due north,' said Mrs Sanders. 'So east will be over there,' she pointed to the left.

'Thanks,' said Julian. 'Come on, everyone!' The three children went out of the kitchen, and turned to the left. There were three rooms there – a kind of scullery, not much used now, a tiny room used as a den by old Mr Sanders, and a room that had once been a drawing-room, but which was now cold and unused.

'They've all got stone floors,' said Julian.

'So we'll have to hunt through all of the three rooms,' said Anne.

'No, we won't,' said Julian. 'We shan't have to look in this scullery, for one thing!'

'Why not?' asked Anne.

'Because the walls are of stone, silly, and we want panelling,' said Julian. 'Use your brains, Anne!'

'Well, that's one room we needn't bother with, then,' said Dick. 'Look – both this little room and

250

the drawing-room have panelling, Julian. We must search in both.'

'There must be some reason for putting *eight* squares of panelling in the directions,' said Julian, looking at the roll of linen again. 'It would be a good idea to see whether there's a place with eight squares only – you know, over a window, or something.'

It was tremendously exciting to look round the two rooms! The children began with the smaller room. It was panelled all the way round in dark oak, but there was no place where only eight panels showed. So the children went into the next room.

The panelling there was different. It did not look so old, and was not so dark. The squares were rather a different size, too. The children tried each panel, tapping and pressing as they went, expecting at any moment to see one slide back as the one in the hall had done.

But they were disappointed. Nothing happened at all. They were still in the middle of trying when they heard footsteps in the hall, and voices. Somebody looked into the drawing-room. It was a man, thin and tall, wearing glasses on his long nose.

'Hallo!' he said. 'Mrs Sanders told me you were treasure-hunting, or something. How are you getting on?'

'Not very well,' said Julian, politely. He looked at the man, and saw behind him another one, younger, with rather screwed-up eyes and a big mouth. 'I suppose you are the two artists?' he asked.

'We are!' said the first man, coming into the room. 'Now, just exactly what are you looking for?'

Julian did not really want to tell him, but it was difficult not to. 'Well – we're just seeing if there's a sliding panel

here,' he said at last. 'There's one in the hall, you know.
It's exciting to hunt round.'

'Shall we help?' said the first artist, coming into the
room. 'What are your names? Mine's Thomas, and my
friend's name is Wilton.'

The children talked politely for a minute or two, not at
all wanting the two men to help. If there was anything to
be found, *they* wanted to find it. It would spoil everything
if grown-ups solved the puzzle!

Soon everyone was tap-tap-tapping round the wooden

panels. They were in the middle of this when a voice hailed them.

'Hallo! My word, we *are* all busy!'

The children turned, and saw their tutor standing in the doorway, smiling at them. The two artists looked at him.

'Is this a friend of yours?' asked Mr Thomas.

'Yes – he's our tutor, and he's very nice!' said Anne, running to Mr Roland and putting her hand in his.

'Perhaps you will introduce me, Anne,' said Mr Roland, smiling at the little girl.

Anne knew how to introduce people. She had often seen her mother doing it. 'This is Mr Roland,' she said to the two artists. Then she turned to Mr Roland. 'This is Mr Thomas,' she said, waving her hand towards him, 'and the other one is Mr Wilton.'

The men half-bowed to one another and nodded. 'Are you staying here?' asked Mr Roland. 'A very nice old farmhouse, isn't it?'

'It isn't time to go yet, is it?' asked Julian, hearing a clock strike.

'Yes, I'm afraid it is,' said Mr Roland. 'I'm later meeting you than I expected. We must go in about five minutes – no later. I'll just give you a hand in trying to find this mysterious secret way!'

But no matter how any one of them pressed and tapped around the panels in either of the two rooms, they could not find anything exciting. It really was most disappointing.

'Well, we really must go now,' said Mr Roland. 'Come and say good-bye to Mrs Sanders.'

They all went into the warm kitchen, where Mrs Sanders was cooking something that smelt most delicious.

'Something for our lunch, Mrs Sanders?' said Mr Wilton. 'My word, you really are a wonderful cook!'

Mrs Sanders smiled. She turned to the children. 'Well, dearies, did you find what you wanted?' she asked.

'No,' said Mr Roland, answering for them. 'We haven't been able to find the secret way, after all!'

'The secret way?' said Mrs Sanders, in surprise. 'What do you know about that now? I thought it had all been forgotten – in fact, I haven't believed in that secret way for many a year!'

'Oh, Mrs Sanders – do you know about it?' cried Julian. 'Where is it?'

'I don't know, dear – the secret of it has been lost for many a day,' said the old lady. 'I remember my old grandmother telling me something about it when I was smaller than any of you. But I wasn't interested in things like that when I was little. I was all for cows and hens and sheep.'

'Oh, Mrs Sanders – do, do try and remember something!' begged Dick. 'What *was* the secret way?'

'Well, it was supposed to be a hidden way from Kirrin Farmhouse to somewhere else,' said Mrs Sanders. 'I don't know where, I'm sure. It was used in the olden days when people wanted to hide from enemies.'

It was disappointing that Mrs Sanders knew so little. The children said good-bye and went off with their tutor, feeling that their morning had been wasted.

George was indoors when they got to Kirrin Cottage. Her cheeks were not so pale, now, and she greeted the children eagerly.

'Did you discover anything? Tell me all about it!' she said.

'There's nothing to tell,' said Dick, rather gloomily. 'We found three rooms facing east, with stone floors, but only two of them had wooden panelling, so we hunted round those, tapping and punching – but there wasn't anything to be discovered at all.'

'We saw the two artists,' said Anne. 'One was tall and thin and had a long nose with glasses on. He was called Mr Thomas. The other was younger, with little piggy eyes and an enormous mouth.'

'I met them out this morning,' said George. 'It must have been them. Mr Roland was with them, and they were all talking together. They didn't see me.'

'Oh, it couldn't have been the artists you saw,' said Anne, at once. 'Mr Roland didn't know them, I had to introduce them.'

'Well, I'm sure I heard Mr Roland call one of them Wilton,' said George, puzzled. 'He *must* have known them.'

'It couldn't have been the artists,' said Anne, again. 'They really didn't know Mr Roland. Mr Thomas asked if he was a friend of ours.'

'I'm sure I'm not mistaken,' said George, looking obstinate. 'If Mr Roland said he didn't know the two artists, he was telling lies.'

'Oh, you're always making out that he is doing something horrid!' cried Anne, indignantly. 'You just make up things about him!'

'Sh!' said Julian. 'Here he is.'

The door opened and the tutor came in. 'Well,' he said, 'it *was* disappointing that we couldn't find the secret way, wasn't it? Anyway, we were rather foolish to hunt about that drawing-room as we did – the

255

panelling there wasn't really old – it must have been put in years after the other.'

'Oh – well, it's no good looking there again,' said Julian, disappointed. 'And I'm pretty sure there's nothing to be found in that other little room. We went all over it so thoroughly. Isn't it disappointing?'

'It is,' said Mr Roland. 'Well, Julian, how did you like the two artists? I was pleased to meet them – they seemed nice fellows, and I shall like to know them.'

George looked at the tutor. Could he possibly be telling untruths in such a truthful voice? The little girl was very puzzled. She felt sure it was the artists she had seen him with. But why should he pretend he didn't know them? She must be mistaken. But all the same, she felt uncomfortable about it, and made up her mind to find out the truth, if she could.

CHAPTER TEN

A shock for George and Tim

NEXT MORNING there were lessons again – and no Timothy under the table! George felt very much inclined to refuse to work, but what would be the good of that? Grown-ups were so powerful, and could dole out all kinds of punishments. She didn't care how much she was punished herself but she couldn't bear to think that Timothy might have to share in the punishments too.

So, pale and sullen, the little girl sat down at the table with the others. Anne was eager to join in the lessons – in fact she was eager to do anything to please Mr Roland, because he had given her the fairy doll from the top of the Christmas tree! Anne thought it was the prettiest doll she had ever seen.

George had scowled at the doll when Anne showed it to her. She didn't like dolls, and she certainly wasn't going to like one that Mr Roland had chosen, and given to Anne! But Anne loved it, and had made up her mind to do lessons with the others, and work as well as she could.

George did as little as she could without getting into trouble. Mr Roland took no interest in her or in her work. He praised the others, and took a lot of trouble to show Julian something he found difficult.

The children heard Tim whining outside as they worked. This troubled them very much, for Timothy was such a companion, and so dear to them all. They could not bear to think of him left out of everything, cold and miserable in the yard-kennel. When the ten minutes' break came, and Mr Roland went out of the room for a few minutes, Julian spoke to George.

'George! It's awful for us to hear poor old Tim whining out there in the cold. And I'm sure I heard him cough. Let me speak to Mr Roland about him. You must feel simply dreadful knowing that Tim is out there.'

'I thought I heard him cough, too,' said George, looking worried. 'I hope he won't get a cold. He simply doesn't understand why I have to put him there. He thinks I'm terribly unkind.'

The little girl turned her head away, afraid that tears might come into her eyes. She always boasted that she never cried – but it was very difficult to keep the tears away when she thought of Timothy out there in the cold.

Dick took her arm. 'Listen, George – you just hate Mr Roland, and I suppose you can't help it. But we can none of us bear Timothy being out there all alone – and it looks like snow today, which would be awful for him. Could you be awfully, awfully good today, and forget your dislike, so that when your father asks Mr Roland for your report, he can say you were very good – and then we'll ask Mr Roland if he wouldn't let Timmy come back into the house.'

'See?'

Timothy coughed again, out in the yard, and George's heart went cold. Suppose he got that awful illness called pneumonia – and she couldn't nurse him because he had to live in the kennel? She would die of unhappiness! She turned to Julian and Dick.

'All right,' she said. 'I do hate Mr Roland – but I love Timothy more than I hate the tutor – so for Tim's sake I'll

259

pretend to be good and sweet and hard-working. And then you can beg him to let Timothy come back.'

'Good girl!' said Julian. 'Now here he comes – so do your best.'

To the tutor's enormous surprise, George gave him a smile when he came into the room. This was so unexpected that it puzzled him. He was even more puzzled to find that George worked harder than anyone for the rest of the morning, and she answered politely and cheerfully when he spoke to her. He gave her a word of praise.

'Well done, Georgina! I can see you've got brains.'

'Thank you,' said George, and gave him another wan smile – a very watery, poor affair, compared with the happy smiles the others had been used to – but still, it *was* a smile!

At dinner-time George looked after Mr Roland most politely – passed him the salt, offered him more bread, got up to fill his glass when it was empty! The others looked at her in admiration. George had plenty of pluck. She must be finding it very difficult to behave as if Mr Roland was a great friend, when she really disliked him so much!

Mr Roland seemed very pleased, and appeared to be quite willing to respond to George's friendliness. He made a little joke with her, and offered to lend her a book he had about a dog. George's mother was delighted to find that her difficult daughter seemed to be turning over a new leaf. Altogether things were very much happier that day.

'George, you go out of the room before your father comes in to ask Mr Roland about your behaviour to-night,' said Julian. 'Then, when the tutor gives you a splendid report, we will all ask if Timothy can come back. It will be easier if you are not there.'

'All right,' said George. She was longing for this difficult day to be over. It was very hard for her to pretend to be friendly, when she was not. She could never never do it, if it wasn't for Timothy's sake!

George disappeared out of the room just before six o'clock, when she heard her father coming. He walked into the room and nodded to Mr Roland.

'Well? Have your pupils worked well today?' he asked.

'Very well indeed,' said Mr Roland. 'Julian has really mastered something he didn't understand today. Dick has done well in Latin. Anne has written out a French exercise without a single mistake!'

'And what about George?' asked Uncle Quentin.

'I was coming to Georgina,' said Mr Roland, looking round and seeing that she was gone. 'She has worked better than anyone else today! I am really pleased with her. She has tried hard – and she has really been polite and friendly. I feel she is trying to turn over a new leaf.'

'She's been a brick today,' said Julian, warmly. 'Uncle Quentin, she has tried awfully hard, she really has. And, you know, she's terribly unhappy.'

'Why?' asked Uncle Quentin in surprise.

'Because of Timothy,' said Julian. 'He's out in the cold, you see. And he's got a dreadful cough.'

'Oh, Uncle Quentin, please do let poor Timmy come indoors,' begged Anne.

'Yes, please do,' said Dick. 'Not only for George's sake, because she loves him so, but for us too. We hate to hear him whining outside. And George does deserve a reward, Uncle – she's been marvellous today.'

'Well,' said Uncle Quentin, looking doubtfully at the three eager faces before him, 'well – I hardly know what to say. If George is going to be sensible – and the weather gets colder – well . . .'

He looked at Mr Roland, expecting to hear him say something in favour of Timothy. But the tutor said nothing. He looked annoyed.

'What do you think, Mr Roland?' asked Uncle Quentin.

'I think you should keep to what you said and let the dog stay outside,' said the tutor. 'George is spoilt, and needs firm handling. You should really keep to your decision about the dog. There is no reason to give way about it just because she tried to be good for once!'

The three children stared at Mr Roland in surprise and dismay. It had never entered their heads that he would not back them up!

'Oh, Mr Roland, you *are* horrid!' cried Anne. 'Oh do, do say you'll have Timothy back.'

The tutor did not look at Anne. He pursed up his mouth beneath its thick moustache and looked straight at Uncle Quentin.

'Well,' said Uncle Quentin, 'perhaps we had better see how George behaves for a whole week. After all – just one day isn't much.'

The children stared at him in disgust. They thought he was weak and unkind. Mr Roland nodded his head.

'Yes,' he said, 'a week will be a better test. If Georgina behaves well for a whole week, we'll have another word about the dog. But at present I feel it would be better to keep him outside.'

'Very well,' said Uncle Quentin, and went out of the room. He paused to look back. 'Come along into my study sometime,' he said. 'I've got a bit further with my formula. It's at a very interesting stage.'

The three children looked at one another but said
nothing. How mean of the tutor to stop Uncle Quentin
from having Timothy indoors again! They all felt disappointed in him. The tutor saw their faces.

'I'm sorry to disappoint you,' he said. 'But I think if
you'd been bitten by Timothy once and snapped at all over
when he got you on the floor, you would not be very keen
on having him in either!'

He went out of the room. The children wondered what to say to George. She came in a moment later, her face eager. But when she saw the gloomy looks of the other three, she stopped short.

'Isn't Tim to come in?' she asked, quickly. 'What's happened? Tell me!'

They told her. The little girl's face grew dark and angry when she heard how the tutor had put his foot down about Timothy, even when her father had himself suggested that the dog might come indoors.

'Oh, what a beast he is!' she cried. 'How I do hate him! I'll pay him back for this. I will, I will, I will!'

She rushed out of the room. They heard her fumbling in the hall, and then the front door banged.

'She's gone out into the dark,' said Julian. 'I bet she's gone to Timmy. Poor old George. Now she'll be worse than ever!'

That night George could not sleep. She lay and tossed in her bed, listening for Timothy. She heard him cough. She heard him whine. He was cold, she knew he was. She had put plenty of fresh straw into his kennel and had turned it away from the cold north wind – but he must feel the bitter night terribly, after sleeping for so long on her bed!

Timothy gave such a hollow cough that George could bear it no longer. She must, she simply must, get up and go down to him. 'I shall bring him into the house for a little while and rub his chest with some of that stuff Mother uses for herself when she's got a cold on her chest,' thought the girl. 'Perhaps that will do him good.'

She quickly put a few clothes on and crept downstairs. The whole house was quiet. She slipped out into the yard and undid Tim's chain. He was delighted to see her and licked her hands and face lovingly.

'Come along into the warm for a little while,' whispered the little girl. 'I'll rub your poor chest with some oil I've got.'

Timmy pattered behind her into the house. She took him to the kitchen – but the fire was out and the room was cold. George went to look at the other rooms.

There was quite a nice fire still in her father's study. She and Tim went in there. She did not put on the light, because the firelight was fairly bright. She had with her the little bottle of oil from the bathroom cupboard. She put it down by the fire to warm.

Then she rubbed the dog's hairy chest with the oil, hoping it would do him good. 'Don't cough now if you can help it, Tim,' she whispered. 'If you do, someone may hear you. Lie down here by the fire, darling, and get nice and warm. Your cold will soon be better.'

Timothy lay down on the rug. He was glad to be out of his kennel and with his beloved mistress. He put his head on her knee. She stroked him and whispered to him.

The firelight glinted on the curious instruments and glass tubes that stood around on shelves in her father's study. A log shifted a little in the fire and settled lower, sending up a cloud of sparks. It was warm and peaceful there.

The little girl almost fell asleep. The big dog closed his eyes too, and rested peacefully, happy and warm. George settled down with her head on his neck.

She awoke to hear the study clock striking six! The room was cold now, and she shivered. Goodness! Six o'clock! Joanna the cook would soon be awake. She must not find Timmy and George in the study!

'Tim darling! Wake up! We must put you back into your kennel,' whispered George. 'I'm sure your cold is better, because you haven't coughed once since you've been indoors. Get up – and don't make a noise. Sh!'

Tim stood up and shook himself. He licked George's hand. He understood perfectly that he must be quite quiet. The two of them slipped out of the study, went into the hall and out of the front door.

In a minute or two Timothy was on the chain, and in his kennel, cuddled down among the straw. George wished she could cuddle there with him. She gave him a pat and slipped back indoors again.

A SHOCK FOR GEORGE AND TIM

She went up to bed, sleepy and cold. She forgot that she was partly dressed and got into bed just as she was. She was asleep in a moment!

In the morning Anne was most amazed to find that George had on vest, knickers, jeans and jersey, when she got out of bed to dress.

'Look!' she said. 'You're half-dressed! But I *saw* you undressing last night.'

'Be quiet,' said George. 'I went down and let Tim in last night. We sat in front of the study fire and I rubbed him with oil. Now don't you dare to say a word to anyone! Promise!'

Anne promised – and she faithfully kept her word. Well, well – to think that George dared to roam about like that all night – what an extraordinary girl she was!

CHAPTER ELEVEN

Stolen papers

'GEORGE, DON'T behave fiercely today, will you?' said Julian, after breakfast. 'It won't do you or Timothy any good at all.'

'Do you suppose I'm going to behave well when I know perfectly well that Mr Roland will never let me have Tim indoors all these holidays?' said George.

'Well – they said a week,' said Dick. 'Can't you try for a week?'

'No. At the end of a week Mr Roland will say I must try for another week,' said George. 'He's got a real dislike for poor Tim. And for me too. I'm not surprised at that, because I know that when I try to be horrid, I really *am* horrid. But he shouldn't hate poor Timmy.'

'Oh George – you'll spoil the whole hols if you are silly, and keep getting into trouble,' said Anne.

'Well, I'll spoil them then,' said George, the sulky look coming back on her face.

'I don't see why you have to spoil them for us, as well as for yourself,' said Julian.

'They don't need to be spoilt for you,' said George. 'You can have all the fun you want – go for walks with your dear Mr Roland, play games with him in the evening, and laugh and talk as much as you like. You don't need to take any notice of me.'

'You are a funny girl, George,' said Julian, with a sigh. 'We like you, and we hate you to be unhappy – so how can we have fun if we know you're miserable – and Timmy too?'

'Don't worry about *me*,' said George, in rather a choky voice. 'I'm going out to Tim. I'm not coming in to lessons today.'

'George! But you must!' said Dick and Julian together.

'There's no "must" about it,' said George. 'I'm just not coming. I won't work with Mr Roland till he says I can have Timothy indoors again.'

'But you know you can't do things like that – you'll be told off or something,' said Dick.

'I shall run away if things get too bad,' said George, in a shaky voice. 'I shall run away with Tim.'

She went out of the room and shut the door with a bang. The others stared after her. What could you do with a person like George? Anyone could rule her with kindness and understanding – but as soon as she came up against anyone who disliked her, or whom she disliked, she shied away like a frightened horse – and kicked like a frightened horse, too!

Mr Roland came into the sitting-room, his books in his hand. He smiled at the three children.

'Well? All ready for me, I see. Where's Georgina?'

Nobody answered. Nobody was going to give George away!

'Don't you know where she is?' asked Mr Roland in surprise. He looked at Julian.

'No, sir,' said Julian, truthfully. 'I've no idea where she is.'

'Well – perhaps she will come along in a few minutes,' said Mr Roland. 'Gone to feed that dog of hers, I suppose.'

They all settled down to work. The time went on and George did not come in. Mr Roland glanced at the clock and made an impatient clicking noise with his tongue.

'Really, it's too bad of Georgina to be so late! Anne, go and see if you can find her.'

Anne went. She looked in the bedroom. There was no George there. She looked in the kitchen. Joanna was there, making cakes. She gave the little girl a hot piece to eat. She had no idea where George was.

Anne couldn't find her anywhere. She went back and told Mr Roland. He looked angry.

'I shall have to report this to her father,' he said. 'I have never had to deal with such a rebellious child before. She seems to do everything she possibly can to get herself into trouble.'

Lessons went on. Break came, and still George did not appear. Julian slipped out and saw that the yard-kennel was empty. So George had gone out with Timmy! What a row she would get into when she got back!

No sooner had the children settled down after break to do the rest of the morning's lessons, than a big disturbance came.

Uncle Quentin burst in looking upset and worried.

'Have any of you children been into my study?' he asked.

'No, Uncle Quentin,' they all answered.

'You said we weren't to,' said Julian.

'Why? Has something been broken?' asked Mr Roland.

'Yes – the test-tubes I set yesterday for an experiment have been broken – and what is worse, three most important pages of my book have gone,' said Uncle Quentin. 'I can write them out again, but only after a great deal of

270

work. I can't understand it. Are you *sure*, children, that none of you has been meddling with things in my study?'

'Quite sure,' they answered. Anne went very red – she suddenly remembered what George had told her. George said she had taken Timmy into Uncle Quentin's study last night, and rubbed his chest with oil! But George couldn't possibly have broken the test-tubes, and taken pages from her father's book!

Mr Roland noticed that Anne had gone red.

'Do you know anything about this, Anne?' he asked.

'No, Mr Roland,' said Anne, blushing even redder, and looking very uncomfortable indeed.

'Where's George?' suddenly said Uncle Quentin.

The children said nothing, and it was Mr Roland who answered:

'We don't know. She didn't come to lessons this morning.'

'Didn't come to lessons! Why not?' demanded Uncle Quentin, beginning to frown.

'She didn't say,' said Mr Roland dryly. 'I imagine she was upset because we were firm about Timothy last night, and this is her way of being defiant.'

'The naughty girl!' said George's father, angrily. 'I don't know what's come over her lately. Fanny! Come here! Did you know that George hasn't been in to her lessons today?'

Aunt Fanny came into the room. She looked very worried. She had a little bottle in her hand. The children wondered what it was.

'Didn't come in to lessons!' repeated Aunt Fanny. 'How extraordinary! Then where is she?'

'I don't think you need to worry about her,' said Mr Roland, smoothly. 'She's probably gone off with Timothy in a fit of temper. What is very much more important, is the fact that your work appears to have been spoilt by someone. I only hope it is not George, who has been spiteful enough to get back at you for not allowing her to have her dog in the house.'

'Of *course* it wasn't George!' cried Dick, angry that anyone should even think such a thing of his cousin.

'George would never, never do a thing like that,' said Julian.

'No, she never would,' said Anne, sticking up valiantly for her cousin, although a horrid doubt was in her mind. After all – George *had* been in the study last night!

'Quentin, I am sure George would not even *think* of such a thing,' said Aunt Fanny. 'You will find those pages somewhere – and as for the test-tubes that were broken, well, perhaps the wind blew the curtain against them, or something! When did you last see those pages?'

'Last night,' said Uncle Quentin. 'I read them over again, and checked my figures to make sure they were right. Those pages contain the very heart of my formula! If they got into anyone else's hands, they could use my secret. This is a terrible thing for me! I *must* know what has happened to them.'

'I found this in your study, Quentin,' said Aunt Fanny, and she held up the little bottle she carried. 'Did you put it there? It was in the fender.'

Uncle Quentin took the bottle and stared at it. 'Camphorated oil!' he said. 'Of course I didn't take it there. Why should I?'

'Well – who took it there, then?' asked Aunt Fanny, puzzled. 'None of the children has a cold – and anyway, they wouldn't think of the camphorated oil, and take it into the study to use! It's most extraordinary!'

Everyone was astonished. Why should a bottle of camphorated oil appear in the study fender?

Only one person could think why. It suddenly came into Anne's mind in a flash. George had said she had taken Timmy into the study, and rubbed him with oil! He had had a cough, that was why. And she had left the oil in the study. Oh dear, oh dear – now what would happen? What a pity George had forgotten the oil!

Anne went very red again as she looked at the oil. Mr Roland, whose eyes seemed very sharp this morning, looked hard at the little girl.

'Anne! You know something about that oil!' he said suddenly. 'What do you know? Did you put it there?'

'No,' said Anne. 'I haven't been into the study. I said I hadn't.'

'Do you know anything about the oil?' said Mr Roland, again. 'You *do* know something.'

Everyone stared at Anne. She stared back. This was simply dreadful. She could not give George away. She could *not*. George was in quite enough trouble as it was, without getting into any more. She pursed up her little mouth and did not answer.

'Anne!' said Mr Roland, sternly. 'Answer when you are spoken to.'

Anne said nothing. The two boys stared at her, guessing that it was something to do with George. They did not know that George had brought Timothy in the night before.

'Anne, dear,' said her aunt, gently. 'Tell us if you know something. It might help us to find out what has happened to Uncle Quentin's papers. It is very, very, important.'

Still Anne said nothing. Her eyes filled with tears. Julian squeezed her arm.

'Don't bother Anne,' he said to the grown-ups. 'If she thinks she can't tell you, she's got some very good reason.'

'I think she's shielding George,' said Mr Roland. 'Is that it, Anne?'

Anne burst into tears. Julian put his arms round his little sister, and spoke again to the three grown-ups.

'*Don't* bother Anne! Can't you see she's upset?'

'We'll let George speak for herself, when she thinks she will come in,' said Mr Roland. 'I'm sure she knows how that bottle got there – and if she put it there herself she must have been into the study – and she's the only person that *has* been there.'

The boys could not think for one moment that George would do such a thing as spoil her father's work. Anne feared it, and it upset her. She sobbed in Julian's arms.

'When George comes in, send her to me in my study,' said Uncle Quentin, irritably. 'How can a man work when these upsets go on? I was always against having children in the house.'

He stamped out, tall, cross and frowning. The children were glad to see him go. Mr Roland shut the books on the table with a snap.

'We can't do any more lessons this morning,' he said. 'Put on your things and go out for a walk till dinner-time.'

'Yes, do,' said Aunt Fanny, looking white and worried. 'That's a good idea.'

Mr Roland and their aunt went out of the room. 'I don't know if Mr Roland thinks he's coming out with us,' said Julian, in a low voice, 'but we've got to get out first and give him the slip. We've got to find George and warn her what's up.'

'Right!' said Dick. 'Dry your eyes, Anne darling. Hurry and get your things. We'll slip out of the garden door before Mr Roland comes down. I bet George has gone for her favourite walk over the cliffs. We'll meet her!' The three children threw on their outdoor things and crept out of the garden door quietly. They raced down the garden path, and out of the gate before Mr Roland even knew they were gone! They made their way to the cliffs, and looked to see if George was coming.

'There she is – and Timothy, too!' cried Julian, pointing. 'George! George! Quick, we've got something to tell you!'

CHAPTER TWELVE

George in trouble

'WHAT'S THE matter?' asked George, as the three children tore up to her. 'Has something happened?'

'Yes, George. Someone has taken three most important pages out of your father's book!' panted Julian. 'And broken the test-tubes he was making an experiment with. Mr Roland thinks you might have had something to do with it!'

'The beast!' said George, her blue eyes deepening with anger. 'As if I'd do a thing like that! Why should he think it's me, anyway?'

'Well, George, you left that bottle of oil in the study fender,' said Anne. 'I haven't told anyone at all what you told me happened last night – but somehow Mr Roland guessed you had something to do with the bottle of oil.'

'Didn't you tell the boys how I got Timmy indoors?' asked George. 'Well, there's nothing much to tell, Julian. I just heard poor old Tim coughing in the night, and I half-dressed, went down, and took him into the study, where there was a fire. Mother keeps a bottle of oil that she used to rub her chest with when she has a cough – so I thought it might do Timmy's cold good, too. I got the oil and rubbed him well – and we both fell asleep by the fire till six o'clock. I was sleepy when I woke up, and forgot the oil. That's all.'

'And you didn't take any pages from the book Uncle Quentin is writing, and you didn't break anything in the study, did you?' said Anne.

'Of course not, silly,' said George, indignantly. 'How can you ask me a thing like that? You must be mad.'

George never told a lie, and the others always believed her, whatever she said. They stared at her, and she stared back.

'I wonder who could have taken those pages then?' said Julian. 'Maybe your father will come across them, after all. I expect he put them into some safe place and then forgot all about them. And the test-tubes might easily have over-balanced and broken themselves. Some of them look very shaky to me.'

'I suppose I shall get into trouble now for taking Tim into the study,' said George.

'And for not coming into lessons this morning,' said Dick. 'You really are an idiot, George. I never knew anyone like you for walking right into trouble.'

'Hadn't you better stay out a bit longer, till everyone has calmed down a bit?' said Anne.

'No,' said George at once. 'If I'm going to get into a row, I'll get into it now! I'm not afraid!'

She marched over the cliff path, with Timmy running round her as usual. The others followed. It wasn't nice to think that George was going to get into such trouble.

They came to the house and went up the path.

Mr Roland saw them from the window and opened the door. He glanced at George.

'Your father wants to see you in the study,' said the tutor. Then he turned to the others, looking annoyed.

'Why did you go out without me? I meant to go with you.'

'Oh did you, sir? I'm sorry,' said Julian, politely, not looking at Mr Roland. 'We just went out on the cliff a little way.'

'Georgina, did you go into the study last night?' asked Mr Roland, watching George as she took off her hat and coat.

'I'll answer my father's questions, not yours,' said George.

'What you want is a good telling off,' said Mr Roland. 'And if I were your father I'd give it to you!'

'You're not my father,' answered George. She went to the study door and opened it. There was no one there.

'Father isn't here,' said George.

'He'll be there in a minute,' said Mr Roland. 'Go in and wait. And you others, go up and wash for lunch.'

The other three children felt almost as if they were deserting George as they went up the stairs. They could hear Timmy whining from the yard outside. He knew his little mistress was in trouble, and he wanted to be with her.

George sat down on a chair, and gazed at the fire, remembering how she had sat on the rug there with Tim last night, rubbing his hairy chest. How silly of her to have forgotten the bottle of oil!

Her father came into the room, frowning and angry. He looked sternly at George.

'Were you in here last night, George?' he asked.

'Yes, I was,' answered George at once.

'What were you doing in here?' asked her father. 'You know you children are forbidden to come into my study.'

'I know,' said George. 'But you see Timmy had a dreadful cough, and I couldn't bear it. So I crept down about one o'clock and let him in. This was the only room that was really warm, so I sat here and rubbed his chest with the oil Mother uses when she has a cold.'

'Rubbed the dog's chest with camphorated oil!' exclaimed her father, in amazement. 'What a mad thing to do! As if it would do him any good.'

'It didn't seem mad to me,' said George. 'It seemed sensible. And Timmy's cough is much better today. I'm sorry for coming into the study. I didn't touch a thing, of course.'

'George, something very serious has happened,' said her father, looking gravely at her. 'Some of my test-tubes with which I was doing an important experiment, have been broken – and, worse than that, three pages of my book have gone. Tell me on your honour that you know nothing of these things.'

'I know nothing of them,' said George, looking her father straight in the eyes. Her own eyes shone very blue and clear as she gazed at him. He felt quite certain that George was speaking the truth. She could know nothing of the damage done. Then where were those pages?

'George, last night when I went to bed at eleven o'clock, everything was in order,' he said. 'I read over those three important pages and checked them once more myself. This morning they are gone.'

'Then they must have been taken between eleven o'clock and one o'clock,' said George. 'I was here from that time until six.'

'But *who* could have taken them?' said her father. 'The window was fastened, as far as I know. And nobody knows that those three pages were so important but myself. It is most extraordinary.'

'Mr Roland probably knew,' said George, slowly.

'Don't be absurd,' said her father. 'Even if he did realise they were important, he would not have taken them. He's a very decent fellow. And that reminds me – why were you not at lessons this morning, George?'

'I'm not going to do lessons any more with Mr Roland,'
said George. 'I simply hate him!'

'George! I will *not* have you talking like this!' said her
father. 'Do you want me to say you are to lose Tim
altogether?'

'No,' said George, feeling shaky about the knees. 'And I
don't think it's fair to keep trying to force me to do things

by threatening me with losing Timothy. If – if – you do a thing like that – I'll – I'll run away or something!'

There were no tears in George's eyes. She sat bolt upright on her chair, gazing defiantly at her father. How difficult she was! Her father sighed, and remembered that he too in his own childhood had been called 'difficult'. Perhaps George took after him. She could be so good and sweet – and here she was being perfectly impossible!

Her father did not know what to do with George. He thought he had better have a word with his wife. He got up and went to the door.

'Stay here. I shall be back in a moment. I want to speak to your mother about you.'

'Don't speak to Mr Roland about me, will you?' said George, who felt quite certain that the tutor would urge terrible punishments for her and Timmy. 'Oh, Father, if only Timothy had been in the house last night, sleeping in my room as usual, he would have heard whoever it was that stole your secret – and he would have barked and roused the house!'

Her father said nothing, but he knew that what George had said was true. Timmy wouldn't have let anyone get into the study. It was funny he hadn't barked in the night, if anyone from outside had climbed in at the study window. Still, it was the other side of the house. Maybe he had heard nothing.

The door closed. George sat still on her chair, gazing up at the mantelpiece, where a clock ticked away the time. She felt very miserable. Everything was going wrong, every single thing!

As she gazed at the panelled overmantel, she counted

the wooden panels. There were eight. Now, where had she heard of eight panels before? Of course – in that Secret Way. There were eight panels marked on the roll of linen. What a pity there had not been eight panels in a wooden overmantel at Kirrin Farmhouse!

George glanced out of the window, and wondered if it faced east. She looked to see where the sun was – it was not shining into the room – but it did in the early morning – so it must face east. Fancy – here was a room facing east and with eight wooden panels. She wondered if it had a stone floor.

The floor was covered with a large thick carpet. George got up and went to the wall. She pulled up the edge of the carpet there – and saw that the floor underneath was made of large flat stones. The study had a stone floor too!

She sat down again and gazed at the wooden panels, trying to remember which one in the roll of linen was marked with a cross. But of course it couldn't be a room in Kirrin Cottage – it must be in Kirrin Farmhouse where the Secret Way began.

But just suppose it *was* Kirrin Cottage! Certainly the directions had been found in Kirrin Farmhouse – but that was not to say that the Secret Way had to begin there, even though Mrs Sanders seemed to think it did.

George was feeling excited. 'I must tap round about those eight panels and try to find the one that is marked on the linen roll,' she thought. 'It may slide back or some-thing, and I shall suddenly see the entrance opening!'

She got up to try her luck – but at that moment the door opened again and her father came in looking very grave.

'I have been talking to your mother,' he said. 'She agrees with me that you have been very disobedient, rude and defiant. We can't let behaviour like that pass, George. You will have to be punished.'

George looked anxiously at her father. If only her punishment had nothing to do with Timothy! But, of course, it had.

'You will go to bed for the rest of the day, and you will not see Timothy for three days,' said her father. 'I will get Julian to feed him and take him for a walk. If you persist in being defiant, Timothy will have to go away altogether. I am afraid, strange as it may seem, that that dog has a bad influence on you.'

'He hasn't, he hasn't!' cried George. 'Oh, he'll be so miserable if I don't see him for three whole days.'

'There's nothing more to be said,' said her father. 'Go straight upstairs to bed, and think over all I have said to you, George. I am very disappointed in your behaviour these holidays. I really did think the influence of your three cousins had made you into a normal, sensible girl. Now you are worse then you have ever been.'

He held open the door and George walked out, holding her head high. She heard the others having their dinner in the dining-room. She went straight upstairs and undressed. She got into bed and thought miserably of not seeing Tim for three days. She couldn't bear it! Nobody could possibly know how much she loved Timothy!

Joanna came up with a tray of dinner. 'Well, it's a pity to see you in bed,' she said cheerfully. 'Now you be a sensible girl and behave properly and you'll soon be downstairs again.'

George picked at her dinner. She did not feel at all hungry. She lay back on the bed, thinking of Tim and thinking of the eight panels over the mantelpiece. Could

they possibly be the ones shown in the Secret Way directions? She gazed out of the window and thought hard.

'Golly, it's snowing!' she said suddenly, sitting up. 'I
thought it would when I saw that leaden sky this morning.
It's snowing hard! It will be quite thick by tonight – inches
deep. Oh, poor Timothy. I hope Julian will see that his
kennel is kept clear of the drifting snow.'

George had plenty of time to think as she lay in bed.
Joanna came and took the tray away. No one else came to
see her. George felt sure the other children had been

forbidden to go up and speak to her. She felt lonely and left-out.

She thought of her father's lost pages. Could Mr Roland have taken them? After all, he was very interested in her father's work and seemed to understand it. The thief must have been someone who knew which were the important pages. Surely Timothy would have barked if a thief had come in from outside, even though the study was the other side of the house. Timmy had such sharp ears.

'I think it must have been someone *in*side the house,' said George. 'None of us children, that's certain – and not Mother or Joanna. So that only leaves Mr Roland. And I did find him in the study that other night when Timmy woke me by growling.'

She sat up in bed suddenly. 'I believe Mr Roland had Timothy put out of the house because he wanted to go poking round the study again and was afraid Tim would bark!' she thought. 'He was so very insistent that Tim should go out of doors – even when everyone else begged for me to have him indoors. I believe – I really do believe – that Mr Roland is the thief!'

The little girl felt very excited. Could it be that the tutor had stolen the pages – and broken those important test-tubes? How she wished that the others would come and see her, so that she could talk things over with them!

CHAPTER THIRTEEN

Julian has a surprise

THE THREE children downstairs felt very sorry for George. Uncle Quentin had forbidden them to go up and see her.

'A little time for thinking out things all alone may do George good,' he said.

'Poor old George,' said Julian. 'It's too bad, isn't it? I say – look at the snow!'

The snow was falling very thickly. Julian went to the window and looked out. 'I shall have to go and see that Timmy's kennel is all right,' he said. 'We don't want the poor old fellow to be snowed up! I expect he is wondering what the snow is!'

Timothy was certainly very puzzled to see everywhere covered with soft white stuff. He sat in his kennel and stared out at the falling flakes, his big brown eyes following them as they fell to the ground. He was puzzled and unhappy. Why was he living out here by himself in the cold? Why didn't George come to him? Didn't she love him any more? The big dog was very miserable, as miserable as George!

He was delighted to see Julian. He jumped up at the boy and licked his face. 'Good old Tim!' said Julian. 'Are you all right? Let me sweep away some of this snow and swing your kennel round a bit so that no flakes fly inside. There – that's better. No, we're not going for a walk, old thing – not now.'

The boy patted the dog and fussed him a bit, then went indoors. The others met him at the sitting-room door.

287

'Julian! Mr Roland is going out for a walk by himself. Aunt Fanny is lying down, and Uncle Quentin is in his study. Can't we go up and see George?'

'We were forbidden to,' said Julian, doubtfully.

'I know,' said Dick. 'But I don't mind risking it for the sake of making George feel a bit happier. It must be so awful for her, lying up there all alone, knowing she can't see Tim for days.'

'Well – let me go up, as I'm the eldest,' said Julian. 'You two stay down here in the sitting-room and talk. Then Uncle Quentin will think we're all here. I'll slip up and see George for a few minutes.'

'All right,' said Dick. 'Give her our love and tell her we'll look after Timmy.'

Julian slipped quietly up the stairs. He opened George's door and crept inside. He shut the door, and saw George sitting up in bed, looking at him in delight.

'Sh!' said Julian. 'I'm not supposed to be here!'

'Oh Julian!' said George joyfully. 'How good of you to come. I was so lonely. Come this side of the bed. Then if anyone comes in suddenly, you can duck down and hide.'

Julian went to the other side of the bed. George began to pour out to him all she had been thinking of.

'I believe Mr Roland is the thief, I really do!' she said. 'I'm not saying that because I hate him, Julian, really I'm not. After all, I *did* find him snooping round the study one afternoon – and again in the middle of the night. He may have got to hear of my father's work, and come to see if he could steal it. It was just lucky for him that we needed a tutor. I'm sure he stole those pages, and I'm sure he wanted Timmy out of the house so that he could do his stealing without Tim hearing him and growling.'

'Oh, George – I don't think so,' said Julian, who really could not approve of the idea of the tutor doing such a thing. 'It all sounds so far-fetched and unbelievable.'

'Lots of unbelievable things happen,' said George. 'Lots. And this is one of them.'

'Well, if Mr Roland *did* steal the pages, they must be somewhere in the house,' said Julian. 'He hasn't been out all day. They must be somewhere in his bedroom.'

'Of course!' said George, looking thrilled. 'I wish he'd go out! Then I'd search his room.'

'George, you can't do things like that,' said Julian, quite shocked.

'You simply don't know what things I can do, if I really want to,' said George, setting her mouth in a firm line. 'Oh – what's that noise?'

There was the bang of a door. Julian went cautiously to the window and peeped out. The snow had stopped falling for a time, and Mr Roland had taken the chance of going out.

'It's Mr Roland,' said Julian.

'Oooh – I could search his room now, if you'll keep watch at the window and tell me if he comes back,' said George, throwing back the bedclothes at once.

'No, George, don't,' said Julian. 'Honestly and truly, it's awful to search somebody's room like that. And anyway, I dare say he's got the pages with him. He may even be going to give them to somebody!'

'I never thought of that,' said George, and she looked at Julian with wide eyes. 'Isn't that sickening? Of course he may be doing that. He knows those two artists at Kirrin Farmhouse, for instance. They may be in the plot too.'

'Oh, George, don't be silly,' said Julian. 'You are making a mountain out of a mole-hill, talking of plots and goodness knows what! Anyone would think we were in the middle of a big adventure.'

'Well, I think we are,' said George, unexpectedly, and she looked rather solemn. 'I sort of feel it all round me – a Big Adventure!'

Julian stared at his cousin thoughtfully. Could there possibly be anything in what she said?

'Julian, will you do something for me?' said George.

'Of course,' said the boy, at once.

JULIAN HAS A SURPRISE

'Go out and follow Mr Roland,' said George. 'Don't let him see you. There's a white macintosh in the hall cupboard. Put it on and you won't be easily seen against the snow. Follow him and see if he meets anyone and gives them anything that looks like the pages of my father's book – you know those big pages he writes on. They're very large.'

'All right,' said Julian. 'But if I do, promise you won't go and search his room. You can't do things like that, George.'

'I can,' said George. 'But I won't, if you'll just follow Mr Roland for me. I'm sure he's going to hand over what he has stolen to others who are in the plot! And I bet those others will be the two artists at Kirrin Farmhouse that he pretended not to know!'

'You'll find you're quite wrong,' said Julian, going to the door. 'I'm sure I shan't be able to follow Mr Roland, anyway – he's been gone five minutes now!'

'Yes, you will, silly – he'll have left his footmarks in the snow,' said George. 'And oh, Julian – I quite forgot to tell you something else exciting. Oh dear, there isn't time now. I'll tell you when you come back, if you can come up again then. It's about the Secret Way.'

'Really?' said Julian, in delight. It had been a great disappointment to him that all their hunting and searching had come to nothing. 'All right – I'll try and creep up again later. If I don't come, you'll know I can't, and you must wait till bed-time.'

He disappeared and shut the door quietly. He slipped downstairs, popped his head into the sitting-room and whispered to the others that he was going out after the tutor.

'Tell you why, later,' he said. He put the white macintosh around him and went out into the garden. Snow was beginning to fall again, but not yet heavily enough to hide Mr Roland's deep footsteps. He had had big wellington boots on, and the footmarks showed up well in the six-inch-deep snow.

The boy followed them quickly. The countryside was very wintry-looking now. The sky was low and leaden, and he could see there was much more snow to come. He hurried on after Mr Roland, though he could not see a sign of the tutor.

Down the lane and over the path that led across the common went the double row of footmarks. Julian stumbled on, his eyes glued to the foot-prints. Suddenly he heard the sound of voices and stopped. A big gorse bush lay to the right and the voices came from there. The boy went nearer to the bush. He heard his tutor's voice, talking in low tones. He could not hear a word that was said.

'Whoever can he be talking to?' he wondered. He crept up closer to the bush. There was a hollow space inside. Julian thought he could creep right into it, though it would be very prickly, and peer out of the other side. Carefully the boy crept into the prickly hollow, where the branches were bare and brown.

He parted the prickly branches slowly and cautiously – and to his amazement he saw Mr Roland talking to the two artists from Kirrin Farmhouse – Mr Thomas and Mr Wilton! So George was right. The tutor had met them – and, as Julian watched, Mr Roland handed over to Mr Thomas a doubled-up sheaf of papers.

'They look just like pages from Uncle Quentin's book,'

said Julian to himself. 'I say – this is mighty strange. It does begin to look like a plot – with Mr Roland at the centre of it!'

Mr Thomas put the papers into the pocket of his overcoat. The men muttered a few more words, which even Julian's sharp ears could not catch, and then parted. The artists went off towards Kirrin Farmhouse, and

Mr Roland took the path back over the common. Julian crouched down in the hollow of the prickly gorse bush, hoping the tutor would not turn and see him. Luckily he didn't. He went straight on and disappeared into the snow, which was now falling thickly. It was also beginning to get dark and Julian, unable to see the path very clearly, hurried after Mr Roland, half-afraid of being lost in the snowstorm.

Mr Roland was not anxious to be out longer than he could help, either. He almost ran back to Kirrin Cottage. He came to the gate at last, and Julian watched him go into the house. He gave him a little time to take off his things and then, giving Timothy a pat as he went by, he went to the garden door. He took off his macintosh, changed his boots, and slipped into the sitting-room before Mr Roland had come down from his bedroom.

'What's happened?' asked Dick and Anne, seeing that Julian was in a great state of excitement. But he could not tell them, for just then Joanna came in to lay the tea.

Much to Julian's disappointment, he could not say a word to the others all that evening, because one or other of the grown-ups was always in the room. Neither could he go up to see George. He could hardly wait to tell his news, but it was no good, he had to.

'Is it still snowing, Aunt Fanny?' asked Anne.

Her aunt went to the front door and looked out. The snow was piled high against the step!

'Yes,' she said, when she came back. 'It is snowing fast and thickly. If it goes on like this we shall be completely snowed up, as we were two winters ago! We couldn't get out of the house for five days then. The milkman couldn't get to us, nor the baker. Fortunately we had plenty of tinned milk, and I can bake my own bread. You poor children, you will not be able to go out tomorrow – the snow will be too thick!'

'Will Kirrin Farmhouse be snowed up too?' asked Mr Roland.

'Oh yes – worse than we shall be,' said Aunt Fanny. 'But they won't mind! They have plenty of food there. They will be prisoners just as much, and more, as we shall.'

Julian wondered why Mr Roland had asked that question. Was he afraid that his friends would not be able to send those pages away by the post – or take them anywhere by bus or car? The boy felt certain this was the reason for the question. How he longed to be able to talk over everything with the others.

'I'm tired!' he said, about eight o'clock. 'Let's go to bed.'

Dick and Anne stared at him in astonishment. Usually, as he was the eldest, he went to bed last of all. Tonight he was actually *asking* to go! Julian winked quickly at them, and they backed him up at once.

Dick yawned widely, and so did Anne. Their aunt put down the sewing she was doing. 'You *do* sound tired!' she said. 'I think you'd better all go to bed.'

'Could I just go out and see if Timmy is all right?' asked Julian. His aunt nodded. The boy put on his rubber boots and coat, and slipped out through the garden door into the yard. It was very deep in snow, too. Tim's kennel was half-hidden in it. The dog had trampled a space in front of the kennel door, and stood there, looking for Julian as he came out of the house.

'Poor old boy, out here in the snow all alone,' said Julian. He patted the dog, and Timmy whined. He was asking to go back with the boy.

'I wish I *could* take you back with me,' said Julian. 'Never mind, Timothy. I'll come and see you tomorrow.'

He went indoors again. The children said good-night to their aunt and Mr Roland, and went upstairs.

'Undress quickly, put on dressing-gowns and meet in George's room,' whispered Julian to the others. 'Don't make a sound or we'll have Aunt Fanny up. Quick now!'

In less than three minutes the children were undressed, and were sitting on George's bed. She was very pleased to see them. Anne slipped into bed with her, because her feet were cold.

'Julian! Did you follow Mr Roland all right?' whispered George.

'Why did he follow him?' asked Dick, who had been dying to know.

Julian told them everything as quickly as he could – all that George suspected – and how he had followed the tutor – and what he had seen. When George heard how Julian had watched him giving a sheaf of papers to the two artists, her eyes gleamed angrily.

'The thief! They must have been the lost pages! And to think my father has been so friendly to him. Oh, what can we do? Those men will get the papers away as quickly as they can, and the secret Father has been working on for ages will be used by someone else – for some other country, probably!'

'They can't get the papers away,' said Julian. 'You've no idea how thick the snow is now, George. We shall be prisoners here for a few days, if this snow goes on, and so will the people in Kirrin Farmhouse. If they want to hide the papers, they will have to hide them in the farmhouse! If only we could get over there and hunt round!'

296

'Well, we can't,' said Dick. 'That's quite certain. We'd be up to our necks in snow!'

The four children looked gloomily at one another. Dick and Anne could hardly believe that the jolly Mr Roland was a thief – a spy perhaps, trying to steal a valuable secret from a friendly scientist. And they couldn't stop it.

'We'd better tell your father,' said Julian at last.

'No,' said Anne. 'He wouldn't believe it, would he, George?'

'He'd laugh at us and go straight and tell Mr Roland,' said George. 'That would warn him, and he mustn't be warned. He mustn't know that we guess anything.'

'Sh! Aunt Fanny's coming!' whispered Dick, suddenly. The boys slipped out of the room and into bed. Anne hopped across to her own little bed. All was peace and quiet when the children's aunt came into the bedroom.

She said good-night and tucked them up. As soon as she had gone down, the four children met together again in George's room.

'George, tell me now what you were going to say about the Secret Way,' said Julian.

'Oh, yes,' said George. 'Well, there may be nothing in my idea at all – but in the study downstairs, there are eight wooden panels over the mantelpiece – and the floor is of stone – and the room faces east! A bit odd, isn't it? Just what the directions said.'

'Is there a cupboard there too?' asked Julian.

'No. But there is everything else,' said George. 'And I was just wondering if by any chance the entrance to the Secret Way is in this house, not in the farmhouse. After all, they both belonged to my family at one time, you know. The people living in the farmhouse years ago must have known all about this cottage.'

'Golly, George – suppose the entrance *was* here!' said Dick. 'Wouldn't it be simply marvellous! Let's go straight down and look!'

'Don't be silly,' said Julian. 'Go down to the study when Uncle Quentin is there? I'd rather meet twenty lions than face Uncle! Especially after what has happened!'

'Well, we simply MUST find out if George's idea is right; we simply must,' said Dick, forgetting to whisper.

'Shut up, idiot!' said Julian, giving him a punch. 'Do you want to bring the whole household up here?'

'Sorry!' said Dick. 'But, oh golly, this *is* exciting. It's an Adventure again.'

'Just what I said,' said George, eagerly. 'Listen, shall we wait till midnight, and then creep down to the study when everyone is asleep, and try our luck? There may be nothing in my idea at all – but we'll have to find out now. I don't believe I could go to sleep till I've tried each one of those panels over the mantelpiece to see if something happens.'

'Well, I know I can't sleep a wink either,' said Dick. 'Listen – is that someone coming up? We'd better go. Come on, Julian! We'll meet in George's room at midnight – and creep down and try out George's idea!'

The two boys went off to their own room. Neither of them could sleep a wink. Nor could George. She lay awake, and went over and over in her mind all that had happened those holidays. 'It's like a jigsaw puzzle,' she thought. 'I couldn't understand a lot of things at first – but now they are fitting together, and making a picture.'

Anne was fast asleep. She had to be awakened at midnight. 'Come on!' whispered Julian, shaking her. 'Don't you want to share in this adventure?'

CHAPTER FOURTEEN

The Secret Way at last!

THE FOUR children crept downstairs through the dark and silent night. Nobody made a sound at all. They made their way to the study. George softly closed the door and then switched on the light.

The children stared at the eight panels over the mantelpiece. Yes – there were exactly eight, four in one row and four in the row above. Julian spread the linen roll out on the table, and the children pored over it.

'The cross is in the middle of the second panel in the top row,' said Julian in a low voice. 'I'll try pressing it. Watch, all of you!'

He went to the fireplace. The others followed him, their hearts beating fast with excitement. Julian stood on tiptoe and began to press hard in the middle of the second panel. Nothing happened.

'Press harder! Tap it!' said Dick.

'I daren't make too much noise,' said Julian, feeling all over the panel to see if there was any roughness that might tell of a hidden spring or lever.

Suddenly, under his hands, the panel slid silently back, just as the one had done at Kirrin Farmhouse in the hall! The children stared at the space behind, thrilled.

'It's not big enough to get into,' said George. 'It can't be the entrance to the Secret Way.'

Julian got out his torch from his dressing-gown pocket. He put it inside the opening, and gave a low exclamation.

'There's a sort of handle here – with strong wire or something attached to it. I'll pull it and see what happens.'

He pulled – but he was not strong enough to move the handle that seemed to be embedded in the wall. Dick put his hand in and the two boys then pulled together.

'It's moving – it's giving way a bit,' panted Julian. 'Go on, Dick, pull hard!'

The handle suddenly came away from the wall, and behind it came thick wire, rusty and old. At the same time a curious grating noise came from below the hearthrug in front of the fireplace, and Anne almost fell.

'Julian! Something is moving under the rug!' she said, frightened. 'I felt it. Under the rug, quick!'

The handle could not be pulled out any farther. The boys let go, and looked down. To the right of the fireplace, under the rug, something had moved. There was no doubt of that. The rug sagged down instead of being flat and straight.

'A stone has moved in the floor,' said Julian, his voice shaking with excitement. 'This handle works a lever, which is attached to this wire. Quick – pull up the rug, and roll back the carpet.'

With trembling hands the children pulled back the rug and the carpet – and then stood staring at a very strange thing. A big flat stone laid in the floor had slipped downwards, pulled in some manner by the wire attached to the handle hidden behind the panel! There was now a black space where the stone had been.

'Look at that!' said George, in a thrilling whisper.

'The entrance to the Secret Way!'

'It's here after all!' said Julian.

'Let's go down!' said Dick.

'No!' said Anne, shivering at the thought of disappearing into the black hole.

Julian flashed his torch into the black space. The stone had slid down and then sideways. Below was a space just big enough to take a man, bending down.

'I expect there's a passage or something leading from here, under the house, and out,' said Julian. 'Golly, I wonder where it leads to?'

'We simply must find out,' said George.

'Not now,' said Dick. 'It's dark and cold. I don't fancy going along the Secret Way at midnight. I don't mind just hopping down to see what it's like – but don't let's go along any passage till tomorrow.'

'Uncle Quentin will be working here tomorrow,' said Julian.

'He said he was going to sweep the snow away from the front door in the morning,' said George. 'We could slip into the study then. It's Saturday. There may be no lessons.'

'All right,' said Julian, who badly wanted to explore everything then and there. 'But for goodness' sake let's have a look and see if there *is* a passage down there. At present all we can see is a hole!'

'I'll help you down,' said Dick. So he gave his brother a hand and the boy dropped lightly down into the black space, holding his torch. He gave a loud exclamation.

'It's the entrance to the Secret Way all right! There's a passage leading from here under the house – awfully low and narrow – but I can see it's a passage. I do wonder where it leads to!'

He shivered. It was cold and damp down there. 'Give me a hand up, Dick,' he said. He was soon out of the hole and in the warm study again.

The children looked at one another in the greatest joy and excitement. This *was* an Adventure, a real Adventure. It was a pity they couldn't go on with it now.

'We'll try and take Timmy with us tomorrow,' said George. 'Oh, I say – how are we going to shut the entrance up?'

'We can't leave the rug and carpet sagging over that hole,' said Dick. 'Nor can we leave the panel open.'

'We'll see if we can get the stone back,' said Julian. He stood on tiptoe and felt about inside the panel. His hand closed on a kind of knob, set deep in a stone. He pulled it, and at once the handle slid back, pulled by the wire. At the same time the sunk stone glided to the surface of the floor again, making a slight grating sound as it did so.

'Well, it's like magic!' said Dick. 'It really is! Fancy the mechanism working so smoothly after years of not being used. This is the most exciting thing I've ever seen!'

There was a noise in the bedroom above. The children stood still and listened.

'It's Mr Roland!' whispered Dick. 'He's heard us. Quick, slip upstairs before he comes down.'

They switched out the light and opened the study door softly. Up the stairs they fled, as quietly as church mice, their hearts thumping so loudly that it seemed as if everyone in the house must hear the beat.

The girls got safely to their rooms and Dick was able to slip into his. But Julian was seen by Mr Roland as he came out of his room with a torch.

'What are you doing, Julian!' asked the tutor, in surprise. 'Did you hear a noise downstairs? I thought I did.'

'Yes – I heard quite a lot of noise downstairs,' said Julian, truthfully. 'But perhaps it's snow falling off the roof, landing with a plop in the ground, sir. Do you think that's it?'

'I don't know,' said the tutor doubtfully. 'We'll go down and see.'

They went down, but of course there was nothing to be seen. Julian was glad they had been able to shut the panel and make the stone come back to its proper place again. Mr Roland was the very last person he wanted to tell his secret to.

They went upstairs and Julian slipped into his room. 'Is it all right?' whispered Dick.

'Yes,' said Julian. 'Don't let's talk. Mr Roland's awake, and I don't want him to suspect anything.'

The boys fell asleep. When they awoke in the morning,

there was a completely white world outside. Snow covered everything and covered it deeply. Timothy's kennel could not be seen! But there were footmarks round about it.

George gave a squeal when she saw how deep the snow was. 'Poor Timothy! I'm going to get him in. I don't care what anyone says! I won't let him be buried in the snow!'

She dressed and tore downstairs. She went out to the kennel, floundering knee deep in the snow. But there was no Timmy there!

A loud bark from the kitchen made her jump. Joanna the cook knocked on the kitchen window. 'It's all right! I couldn't bear the dog out there in the snow, so I fetched him in, poor thing. Your mother says I can have him in the kitchen but you're not to come and see him.'

'Oh, good – Timmy's in the warmth!' said George, gladly. She yelled to Joanna, 'Thanks awfully! You *are* kind!'

She went indoors and told the others. They were very glad. 'And *I've* got a bit of news for *you*,' said Dick. 'Mr Roland is in bed with a bad cold, so there are to be no lessons today. Cheers!'

'Golly, that *is* good news,' said George, cheering up tremendously. 'Timmy in the warm kitchen and Mr Roland kept in bed. I do feel pleased!'

'We shall be able to explore the Secret Way safely now,' said Julian. 'Aunt Fanny is going to do something in the kitchen this morning with Joanna, and Uncle is going to tackle the snow. I vote we say we'll do lessons by ourselves in the sitting-room, and then, when everything is safe, we'll explore the Secret Way!'

'But why must we do lessons?' asked George in dismay.

'Because if we don't, silly, we'll have to help your father dig away the snow,' said Julian.

305

So, to his uncle's surprise, Julian suggested that the four children should do lessons by themselves in the sitting-room. 'Well, I thought you'd like to come and help dig away the snow,' said Uncle Quentin. 'But perhaps you had better get on with your work.'

The children sat themselves down as good as gold in the sitting-room, their books before them. They heard Mr Roland coughing in his room. They heard their aunt go into the kitchen and talk to Joanna. They heard Timmy scratching at the kitchen door – then paws pattering down the passage – then a big, inquiring nose came round the door, and there was old Timmy, looking anxiously for his beloved mistress!

'Timmy!' squealed George, and ran to him. She flung her arms round his neck and hugged him.

'You act as if you hadn't seen Tim for a year,' said Julian.

'It seems like a year,' said George. 'I say, there's my father digging away like mad. Can't we go to the study now? We ought to be safe for a good while.'

They left the sitting-room and went to the study. Julian was soon pulling the handle behind the secret panel. George had already turned back the rug and the carpet. The stone slid downward and sideways. The Secret Way was open!

'Come on!' said Julian. 'Hurry!'

He jumped down into the hole. Dick followed, then Anne, then George. Julian pushed them all into the narrow, low passage. Then he looked up. Perhaps he had better pull the carpet and rug over the hole, in case anyone came into the room and looked around. It took him a few seconds to do it. Then he bent down and joined the others in the passage. They were going to explore the Secret Way at last!

CHAPTER FIFTEEN

An exciting journey and hunt

TIMOTHY HAD leapt down into the hole when George had jumped. He now ran ahead of the children, puzzled at their wanting to explore such a cold, dark place. Both Julian and Dick had torches, which threw broad beams before them.

There was not much to be seen. The Secret Way under the old house was narrow and low, so that the children were forced to go in single file, and to stoop almost double. It was a great relief to them when the passage became a little wider, and the room a little higher. It was very tiring to stoop all the time.

'Have you any idea where the Secret Way is going?' Dick asked Julian. 'I mean – is it going towards the sea, or away from it?'

'Oh, not towards the sea!' said Julian, who had a very good sense of direction. 'As far as I can make out the passage is going towards the common. Look at the walls – they are rather sandy in places, and we know the common has sandy soil. I hope we shan't find that the passage has fallen in anywhere.'

They went on and on. The Secret Way was very straight, though occasionally it would round a rocky part in a curve.

'Isn't it dark and cold?' said Anne, shivering. 'I wish I had put on a coat. How many miles have we come, Julian?'

'Not even one, silly!' said Julian. 'Hallo – look here – the passage has fallen in a bit there!'

Two bright torches shone in front of them and the children saw that the sandy roof had fallen in. Julian kicked at the pile of sandy soil with his foot.

'It's all right,' he said. 'We can force our way through easily. It isn't much of a fall, and it's mostly sand. I'll do a bit of kicking!'

After some trampling and kicking, the roof-fall no longer blocked the way. There was now enough room for the children to climb over it, bending their heads low to avoid knocking them against the top of the passage. Julian shone his torch forward, and saw that the way was clear.

'The Secret Way is very wide just here!' he said suddenly, and flashed his torch around to show the others.

'It's been widened out to make a sort of little room,' said George. 'Look, there's a kind of bench at the back, made out of the rock. I believe it's a resting-place.'

George was right. It was very tiring to creep along the narrow passage for so long. The little wide place with its rocky bench made a very good resting-place. The four tired children, cold but excited, huddled together on the funny seat and took a welcome rest. Timmy put his head on George's knee. He was delighted to be with her again.

'Well, come on,' said Julian, after a few minutes. 'I'm getting awfully cold. I do wonder where this passage comes out!'

'Julian – do you think it could come out at Kirrin Farmhouse?' asked George, suddenly. 'You know what Mrs Sanders said – that there was a secret passage leading from the farmhouse somewhere. Well, this may be the one – and it leads to Kirrin Cottage!'

'George, I believe you're right!' said Julian. 'Yes – the two houses belonged to your family years ago! And in the

309

old days there were often secret passages joining houses, so it's quite plain this secret way joins them up together! Why didn't I think of that before?'

'I say!' squealed Anne, in a high, excited voice, 'I say! I've thought of something too!'

'What?' asked everyone.

'Well – if those two artists have got Uncle's papers, we may be able to get them away before the men can send them off by post, or take them away themselves!' squeaked Anne, so thrilled with her idea that she could hardly get the words out quickly enough. 'They're prisoners at the farmhouse because of the snow, just as we were at the cottage.'

'*Anne*! You're right!' said Julian.

'Clever girl!' said Dick.

'I *say* – if we *could* get those papers again – how wonderful it would be!' said George. Timmy joined in the general excitement, and jumped up and down in joy. Something had pleased the children, so he was pleased too!

'Come on!' said Julian, taking Anne's hand. 'This is thrilling. If George is right, and this Secret Way comes out at Kirrin Farmhouse somewhere, we'll somehow hunt through those men's rooms and find the papers.'

'You said that searching people's rooms was a shocking thing to do,' said George.

'Well, I didn't know then all I know now,' said Julian. 'We're doing this for your father – and maybe for our country too, if his secret formula is valuable. We've got to set our wits to work now, to outwit dangerous enemies.'

'Do you really think they are dangerous?' asked Anne rather afraid.

'Yes, I should think so,' said Julian. 'But you needn't worry, Anne, you've got me and Dick and Tim to protect you.'

'I can protect her too,' said George, indignantly.

'You're fiercer than any boy I know!' said Dick.

'Come on,' said Julian, impatiently. 'I'm longing to get to the end of this passage.'

They all went on again, Anne following behind Julian, and Dick behind George. Timmy ran up and down the line, squeezing by them whenever he wanted to. He thought it was a very peculiar way to spend a morning!

Julian stopped suddenly, after they had gone a good way. 'What's up?' asked Dick, from the back. 'Not another roof-fall, I hope!'

'No – but I think we've come to the end of the passage!' said Julian, thrilled. The others crowded as close to him as they could. The passage certainly had come to an end. There was a rocky wall in front of them, and set firmly in it were iron staples intended for footholds. These went up the wall and when Julian turned his torch upwards, the children saw that there was a square opening in the roof of the passage.

'We have to climb up this rocky wall now,' said Julian, 'go through that dark hole there, keep on climbing – and goodness knows where we come out! I'll go first. You wait here, everyone, and I'll come back and tell you what I've seen.'

The boy put his torch between his teeth, and then pulled himself up by the iron staples set in the wall. He set his feet on them, and then climbed up through the square dark hole, feeling for the staples as he went.

He went up for a good way. It was almost like going up

311

a chimney shaft, he thought. It was cold and smelt musty.

Suddenly he came to a ledge, and he stepped on to it. He took his torch from his teeth and flashed it around him.

There was a stone wall behind him, at the side of him and stone above him. The black hole up which he had come, yawned by his feet. Julian shone his torch in front of him, and a shock of surprise went through him.

There was no stone wall in front of him, but a big wooden door, made of black oak. A handle was set about waist-high; Julian turned it with trembling fingers. What was he going to see?

The door opened outwards, over the ledge, and it was difficult to get round it without falling back into the hole. Julian managed to open it wide, squeezed round it without losing his footing, and stepped beyond it, expecting to find himself in a room.

But his hand felt more wood in front of him! He shone his torch round, and found that he was up against what looked like yet another door. Under his searching fingers it suddenly moved sideways, and slid silently away!

And then Julian knew where he was! 'I'm in the cupboard at Kirrin Farmhouse – the one that has a false back!' he thought. 'The Secret Way comes up behind it! How clever! Little did we know when we played about in this cupboard that not only did it have a sliding back, but that it was the entrance to the Secret Way, hidden behind it!'

The cupboard was now full of clothes belonging to the artists. Julian stood and listened. There was no sound of anyone in the room. Should he just take a quick look round, and see if those lost papers were anywhere about?

Then he remembered the other four, waiting patiently

below in the cold. He had better go and tell them what had happened. They could all come and help in the search.

He stepped into the space behind the sliding back. The sliding door slipped across again, and Julian was left standing on the narrow ledge, with the old oak door wide open to one side of him. He did not bother to shut it. He felt about his feet, and found the iron staples in the hole below him. Down he went, clinging with his hands and feet, his torch in his teeth again.

'Julian! What a time you've been! Quick, tell us all about it!' cried George.

'It's most terribly thrilling,' said Julian. 'Absolutely super! Where do you suppose all this leads to? Into the cupboard at Kirrin Farmhouse – the one that's got a false back!'

'Golly!' said Dick.

'I *say*!' said George.

'Did you go into the room?' cried Anne.

'I climbed as far as I could and came to a big oak door,' said Julian. 'It has a handle this side, so I swung it wide open. Then I saw another wooden door in front of me – at least, I thought it was a door, I didn't know it was just the false back of that cupboard. It was quite easy to slide back and I stepped through, and found myself among a whole lot of clothes hanging in the cupboard! Then I hurried back to tell you.'

'Julian! We can hunt for those papers now,' said George, eagerly. 'Was there anyone in the room?'

'I couldn't *hear* anyone,' said Julian. 'Now what I propose is this – we'll all go up, and have a hunt round those two rooms. The men have the room next to the cupboard one too.'

'Oh good!' said Dick, thrilled at the thought of such an adventure. 'Let's go now. You go first, Ju. Then Anne, then George and then me.'

'What about Tim?' asked George.

'He can't climb, silly,' said Julian. 'He's a simply mar-vellous dog, but he certainly can't climb, George. We'll have to leave him down here.'

'He won't like that,' said George.

'Well, we can't carry him up,' said Dick. 'You won't mind staying here for a bit, will you, Tim, old fellow?'

Tim wagged his tail. But, as he saw the four children mysteriously disappearing up the wall, he put his big tail down at once. What! Going without him? How could they?

He jumped up at the wall, and fell back. He jumped again and whined. George called down in a low voice.

'Be quiet, Tim dear! We shan't be long.'

Tim stopped whining. He lay down at the bottom of the wall, his ears well-cocked. This adventure was becoming more and more peculiar!

Soon the children were on the narrow ledge. The old oak door was still wide open. Julian shone his torch and the others saw the false back of the cupboard. Julian put his hands on it and it slid silently sideways. Then the torch shone on coats and dressing-gowns!

The children stood quite still, listening. There was no sound from the room. 'I'll open the cupboard door and peep into the room,' whispered Julian. 'Don't make a sound!'

The boy pushed between the clothes and felt for the outer cupboard door with his hand. He found it, and pushed it slightly. It opened a little and a shaft of daylight came into the cupboard. He peeped cautiously into the room.

There was no one there at all. That was good. 'Come on!' he whispered to the others. 'The room's empty!'

One by one the children crept out of the clothes cupboard and into the room. There was a big bed there, a wash-stand, chest of drawers, small table and two chairs. Nothing else. It would be easy to search the whole room.

'Look, Julian, there's a door between the two rooms,' said George, suddenly. 'Two of us can go and hunt there and two here – and we can lock the doors that lead on to the landing, so that no one can come in and catch us!'

'Good idea!' said Julian, who was afraid that at any moment someone might come in and catch them in their search. 'Anne and I will go into the next room, and you and Dick can search this one. Lock the door that opens on to the landing, Dick, and I'll lock the one in the other room. We'll leave the connecting-door open, so that we can whisper to one another.'

Quietly the boy and girl slipped through the connecting door into the second room, which was very like the first. That was empty too. Julian went over to the door that led to the landing, and turned the key in the lock. He heard Dick doing the same to the door in the other room. He heaved a big sigh. Now he felt safe!

'Anne, turn up the rugs and see if any papers are hidden there,' he said. 'Then look under the chair-cushions and strip the bed to see if anything is hidden under the mattress.'

Anne set to work, and Julian began to hunt too. He started on the chest of drawers, which he thought would be a very likely place to hide things in. The children's hands were shaking, as they felt here and there for the lost papers. It was so terribly exciting.

They wondered where the two men were. Down in the warm kitchen, perhaps. It was cold up here in the bedrooms, and they would not want to be away from the warmth. They could not go out because the snow was piled in great drifts round Kirrin Farmhouse!

Dick and George were searching hard in the other room. They looked in every drawer. They stripped the bed. They turned up rugs and carpet. They even put their hands up the big chimney-place!

'Julian? Have you found anything?' asked Dick in a low voice, appearing at the door between the two rooms.

'Not a thing,' said Julian, rather gloomily. 'They've hidden the papers well! I only hope they haven't got them on them – in their pockets, or something!'

Dick stared at him in dismay. He hadn't thought of that. 'That *would* be sickening!' he said.

'You go back and hunt *everywhere* – simply *everywhere!*' ordered Julian. 'Punch the pillows to see if they've stuck them under the pillow-case!'

Dick disappeared. Rather a lot of noise came from his room. It sounded as if he were doing a good deal of punching!

Anne and Julian went on hunting too. There was simply nowhere that they did not look. They even turned the pictures round to see if the papers had been stuck behind one of them. But there was nothing to be found. It was bitterly disappointing.

'We can't go without finding them,' said Julian, in desperation. 'It was such a bit of luck to get here like this, down the Secret Way – right into the bedrooms! We simply *must* find those papers!'

'I say,' said Dick, appearing again, 'I can hear voices! Listen!'

All four children listened. Yes – there were men's voices – just outside the bedroom doors!

317

CHAPTER SIXTEEN

The children are discovered

'WHAT SHALL we do?' whispered George. They had all tiptoed to the first room, and were standing together, listening.

'We'd better go down the Secret Way again,' said Julian.

'Oh no, we . . .' began George, when she heard the handle of the door being turned. Whoever was trying to get in, could not open the door. There was an angry exclamation, and then the children heard Mr Wilton's voice. 'My door seems to have stuck. Do you mind If I come through your bedroom and see what's the matter with this handle?'

'Come right along!' came the voice of Mr Thomas. There was the sound of footsteps going to the outer door of the second room. Then there was the noise of a handle being turned and shaken.

'What's this!' said Mr Wilton, in exasperation. 'This won't open, either. Can the doors be locked?'

'It looks like it!' said Mr Thomas.

There was a pause. Then the children distinctly heard a few words uttered in a low voice. 'Are the papers safe? Is anyone after them?'

'They're in your room, aren't they?' said Mr Thomas. There was another pause. The children looked at one another. So the men *had* got the papers – and what was more, they *were* in the room! The very room the

318

children stood in! They looked round it eagerly, racking their brains to think of some place they had not yet explored.

'Quick! Hunt round again while we've time,' whispered Julian. 'Don't make a noise.'

On tiptoe the children began a thorough hunt once more. How they searched! They even opened the pages of the books on the table, thinking that the papers might have been slipped in there. But they could find nothing.

'Hi, Mrs Sanders!' came Mr Wilton's voice. 'Have you by any chance locked these two doors? We can't get in!'

'Dear me!' said the voice of Mrs Sanders from the stairs. 'I'll come along and see. I certainly haven't locked any doors!'

Once again the handles were turned, but the doors would not open. The men began to get very impatient.

'Do you suppose anyone is in our rooms?' Mr Wilton asked Mrs Sanders.

She laughed.

'Well now, who would be in your rooms? There's only me and Mr Sanders in the house, and you know as well as I do that no one can come in from outside, for we're quite snowed up. I don't understand it – the locks of the doors must have slipped.'

Anne was lifting up the wash-stand jug to look under-neath, at that moment. It was heavier than she thought, and she had to let it down again suddenly. It struck the marble wash-stand with a crash, and water slopped out all over the place!

Everyone outside the door heard the noise. Mr Wilton banged on the door and rattled the handle.

319

'Who's there? Let us in or you'll be sorry! What are you doing in there?'

'Idiot, Anne!' said Dick. 'Now they'll break the door down!'

That was exactly what the two men intended to do! Afraid that someone was mysteriously in their room, trying to find the stolen papers, they went quite mad, and began to put their shoulders to the door, and heave hard. The door shook and creaked.

'Now you be careful what you're doing!' cried the indignant voice of Mrs Sanders. The men took no notice. There came a crash as they both tried out their double strength on the door.

'Quick! We must go!' said Julian. 'We mustn't let the men know how we got here, or we shan't be able to come and hunt another time. Anne, George, Dick – get back to the cupboard quickly!'

The children raced for the clothes cupboard. 'I'll go first and help you down,' said Julian. He got out on to the narrow ledge and found the iron foot-holds with his feet. Down he went, torch held between his teeth as usual.

'Anne, come next,' he called. 'And Dick, you come third, and give a hand to Anne if she wants it. George is a good climber – she can easily get down herself.'

Anne was slow at climbing down. She was terribly excited, rather frightened, and so afraid of falling that she hardly dared to feel for each iron staple as she went down.

'Buck up, Anne!' whispered Dick, above her. 'The men have almost got the door down!'

There were tremendous sounds coming from the bedroom door. At any moment now it might break down, and the men would come racing in. Dick was thankful when he could begin to climb down the wall! Once they were all out, George could shut the big oak door, and they would be safe.

George was hidden among the clothes in the cupboard, waiting her turn to climb down. As she stood there, trying in vain to go over any likely hiding-place in her mind, her hands felt something rustly in the pocket of a coat she was standing against. It was a macintosh coat, with big pockets. The little girl's heart gave a leap.

Suppose the papers had been left in the pocket of the coat the man had on when he took them from Mr Roland? That was the only place the children had not searched – the pockets of the coats in the cupboard! With trembling fingers the girl felt in the pocket where the rustling was.

She drew out a sheaf of papers. It was dark in the cupboard, and she could not see if they were the ones she was hunting for, or not – but how she hoped they were! She stuffed them up the front of her jersey, for she had no big pocket, and whispered to Dick:

'Can I come now?'

CRASH! The door fell in with a terrific noise, and the two men leapt into the room. They looked round. It was empty! But there was the water spilt on the wash-stand and on the floor. Someone must be there somewhere!

'Look in the cupboard!' said Mr Thomas.

George crept out of the clothes cupboard and on to the narrow ledge, beyond the place where the false back of the cupboard used to be. It was still hidden sideways in the wall. The girl climbed down the hole a few steps and then shut the oak door which was now above her head. She had not enough strength to close it completely, but she hoped that now she was safe!

The men went to the cupboard and felt about in the clothes for anyone who might possibly be hiding there. Mr Wilton gave a loud cry.

'The papers are gone! They were in this pocket! There's not a sign of them. Quick, we must find the thief and get them back!'

The men did not notice that the cupboard seemed to go farther back than usual. They stepped away from it now that they were sure no one was there, and began to hunt round the room.

By now all the children except George were at the bottom of the hole, standing in the Secret Way, waiting impatiently for George to come down. Poor George was in such a hurry to get down that she caught her clothing on one of the staples, and had to stand in a very dangerous position trying to disentangle it.

'Come on, George, for goodness' sake!' said Julian.

Timothy jumped up at the wall. He could feel the fear and excitement of the waiting children, and it upset him. He wanted George. Why didn't she come? Why was she up that dark hole? Tim was unhappy about her.

He threw back his head and gave such a loud and mournful howl that all the children jumped violently.

'Shut up, Tim!' said Julian.

Tim howled again, and the weird sound echoed round and about in a strange manner. Anne was terrified, and she began to cry. Timothy howled again and again. Once he began to howl it was difficult to stop him.

The men in the bedroom above heard the extraordinary noise, and stopped in amazement.

'Whatever's that?' said one.

'Sounds like a dog howling in the depths of the earth,' said the other.

'Funny!' said Mr Wilton. 'It seems to be coming from the direction of that cupboard.'

He went over to it and opened the door. Tim chose that moment to give a specially mournful howl, and Mr Wilton jumped. He got into the cupboard and felt about at the back. The oak door there gave way beneath his hand, and he felt it open.

'There's something weird here,' called Mr Wilton. 'Bring my torch off the table.'

Tim howled again and the noise made Mr Wilton shiver! Tim had a peculiarly horrible howl. It came echoing up the hole, and burst out into the cupboard.

Mr Thomas got the torch. The men shone it at the back of the cupboard, and gave an exclamation.

'Look at that! There's a door here! Where does it lead to?'

Mrs Sanders, who had been watching everything in surprise and indignation, angry that her door should have been broken down, came up to the cupboard.

'My!' she said. 'I knew there was a false back to that cupboard – but I didn't know there was another door behind it too! That must be the entrance to the Secret Way that people used in the old days.'

'Where does it lead to?' rapped out Mr Wilton.

'Goodness knows!' said Mrs Sanders. 'I never took much interest in such things.'

'Come on, we must go down,' said Mr Wilton, shining his torch into the square black hole, and seeing the iron foot-holds set in the stone. 'This is where the thief went. He can't have got far. We'll go after him. We've got to get those papers back!'

It was not long before the two men had swung themselves over the narrow ledge and down into the hole, feeling with their feet for the iron staples. Down they went and down, wondering where they were coming to. There was no sound below them. Clearly the thief had got away!

THE CHILDREN ARE DISCOVERED

George had got down at last. Tim almost knocked her over in his joy. She put her hand on his head. 'You old silly!' she said. 'I believe you've given our secret away! Quick, Ju – we must go, because those men will be after us in a minute. They could easily hear Tim's howling!'

Julian took Anne's hand. 'Come along, Anne,' he said. 'You must run as fast as you can. Hurry now! Dick, keep with George.'

The four of them hurried down the dark, narrow passage. What a long way they had to go home! If only the passage wasn't such a long one! The children's hearts were beating painfully as they made haste, stumbling as they went.

Julian shone his light steadily in front of him, and Dick shone his at the back. Half-leading, half-dragging Anne, Julian hurried along. Behind them they heard a shout.

'Look! There's a light ahead! That's the thief! Come on, we'll soon get him!'

CHAPTER SEVENTEEN

Good old Tim!

'HURRY, ANNE. Do hurry!' shouted Dick, who was just behind.

Poor Anne was finding it very difficult to get along quickly. Pulled by Julian and pushed by Dick, she almost fell two or three times. Her breath came in loud pants, and she felt as if she would burst.

'Let me have a rest!' she panted. But there was no time for that, with the two men hurrying after them! They came to the piece that was widened out, where the rocky bench was, and Anne looked longingly at it. But the boys hurried her on.

Suddenly the little girl caught her foot on a stone and fell heavily, almost dragging Julian down with her. She tried to get up, and began to cry.

'I've hurt my foot! I've twisted it! Oh, Julian, it hurts me to walk.'

'Well, you've just *got* to come along, darling,' said Julian, sorry for his little sister, but knowing that they would all be caught if he was not firm. 'Hurry as much as you can.'

But now it was impossible for Anne to go fast. She cried with pain as her foot hurt her, and hobbled along so slowly that Dick almost fell over her. Dick cast a look behind him and saw the light of the men's torches coming nearer and nearer. Whatever were they to do?

'I'll stay here with Tim and keep them off,' said George,

326

suddenly. 'Here, take these papers, Dick! I believe they're the ones we want, but I'm not sure till we get a good light to see them. I found them in a pocket of one of the coats in the cupboard.'

'Golly!' said Dick, surprised. He took the sheaf of papers and stuffed them up his jersey, just as George had stuffed them up hers. They were too big to go into his

327

trouser pockets. 'I'll stay with you, George, and let the other two go on ahead.'

'No. I want the papers taken to safety, in case they are my father's,' said George. 'Go on, Dick! I'll be all right here with Tim. I shall stay here just where the passage curves round this rocky bit. I'll make Tim bark like mad.'

'Suppose the men have got revolvers?' said Dick doubtfully. 'They might shoot him.'

'I bet they haven't,' said George. '*Do* go, Dick! The men are almost here. There's the light of their torch.'

Dick sped after the stumbling Anne. He told Julian what George had suggested. 'Good for George!' said Julian. 'She really is marvellous – not afraid of anything! She will keep the men off till I get poor old Anne back.'

George was crouching behind the rocky bit, her hand on Tim's collar, waiting. 'Now, Tim!' she whispered. 'Bark your loudest. Now!'

Timothy had been growling up till now, but at George's command he opened his big mouth and barked. How he barked! He had a simply enormous voice, and the barks went echoing all down the dark and narrow passage. The hurrying men, who were near the rocky piece of the passage, stopped.

'If you come round this bend, I'll set my dog on you!' cried George.

'It's a child shouting,' said one man to another. 'Only a child! Come on!'

Timothy barked again, and pulled at his collar. He was longing to get at the men. The light of their torch shone round the bend. George let Tim go, and the big dog sprang joyfully round the curve to meet his enemies.

They suddenly saw him by the light of their torch, and he

was a very terrifying sight! To begin with, he was a big dog, and now that he was angry all the hairs on the back of his neck had risen up, making him look even more enormous. His teeth were bared and glinted in the torch-light.

The men did not like the look of him at all. 'If you move one step nearer I'll tell my dog to fly at you!' shouted George. 'Wait, Tim, wait! Stand there till I give the word.'

The dog stood in the light of the torch, growling deeply. He looked an extremely fierce animal. The men looked at him doubtfully. One man took a step forward and George heard him. At once she shouted to Tim.

'Go for him, Tim, go for him!'

Tim leapt at the man's throat. He took him completely by surprise and the man fell to the ground with a thud, trying to beat off the dog. The other man helped.

'Call off your dog or we'll hurt him!' cried the second man.

'It's much more likely he'll hurt *you*!' said George, coming out from behind the rock and enjoying the fun. 'Tim, come off.'

Tim came away from the man he was worrying, looking up at his mistress as if to say, 'I was having *such* a good time! Why did you spoil it?'

'Who are you?' said the man on the ground.

'I'm not answering any of your questions,' said George. 'Go back to Kirrin Farmhouse, that's my advice to you. If you dare to come along this passage I'll set my dog on to you again – and next time he'll do more damage.'

The men turned and went back the way they had come. They neither of them wanted to face Tim again. George waited until she could no longer see the light of their torch, then she bent down and patted Timothy.

'Brave, good dog!' she said. 'I love you, darling Tim, and you don't know how proud I am of you! Come along – we'll hurry after the others now. I expect those two men will explore this passage some time tonight, and won't they get a shock when they find out where it leads to, and see who is waiting for them!'

George hurried along the rest of the long passage, with Tim running beside her. She had Dick's torch, and it did not take her long to catch the others up. She panted out to them what had happened, and even poor Anne chuckled in delight when she heard how Tim had flung Mr Wilton to the ground.

'Here we are,' said Julian, as the passage came to a stop below the hole in the study floor. 'Hallo – what's this?'

A bright light was shining down the hole, and the rug and carpet, so carefully pulled over the hole by Julian, were now pulled back again. The children gazed up in surprise.

Uncle Quentin was there, and Aunt Fanny, and when they saw the children's faces looking up at them from the hole, they were so astonished that they very nearly fell down the hole too!

'Julian! Anne! What in the wide world are you doing down there?' cried Uncle Quentin. He gave them each a hand up, and the four children and Timothy were at last safe in the warm study. How good it was to feel warm again! They got as near the fire as they could.

'Children – what *is* the meaning of this?' asked Aunt Fanny. She looked white and worried. 'I came into the study to do some dusting, and when I stood on that bit of the rug, it seemed to give way beneath me. When I pulled it up and turned back the carpet, I saw that hole – and the hole in the panelling too! And then I found that all of you had disappeared, and went to fetch your uncle. What *has* been happening – and where does that hole lead to?'

Dick took the sheaf of papers from under his jersey and gave them to George. She took them and handed them to her father. 'Are these the missing pages?' she asked.

Her father fell on them as if they had been worth more than a hundred times their weight in gold. 'Yes! Yes! They're the pages – all three of them! Thank goodness

331

they're back. They took me three years to bring to perfection, and contained the heart of my secret formula. George, where did you get them?'

'It's a very long story,' said George. 'You tell it all, Julian, I feel tired.'

Julian began to tell the tale. He left out nothing. He told how George had found Mr Roland snooping about the study – how she had felt sure that the tutor had not wanted Timmy in the house because the dog gave warning of his movements at night – how George had seen him talking to the two artists, although he had said he did not know them. As the tale went on, Uncle Quentin and Aunt Fanny looked more and more amazed. They simply could not believe it all.

But after all, there were the missing papers, safely back. That was marvellous. Uncle Quentin hugged the papers as if they were a precious baby. He would not put them down for a moment.

George told the bit about Timmy keeping the men off the escaping children. 'So you see, although you made poor Tim live out in the cold, away from me, he really saved us all, and your papers too,' she said to her father, fixing her brilliant blue eyes on him.

Her father looked most uncomfortable. He felt very guilty for having punished George and Timothy. They had been right about Mr Roland and he had been wrong.

'Poor George,' he said, 'and poor Timmy. I'm sorry about all that.'

George did not bear malice once anyone had owned themselves to be in the wrong. She smiled at her father.

'It's all right,' she said. 'But don't you think that as I was punished unfairly, Mr Roland might be punished well and truly? He deserves it!'

'Oh, he shall be, certainly he shall be,' promised her father. 'He's up in bed with a cold, as you know. I hope he doesn't hear any of this, or he may try to escape.'

'He can't,' said George. 'We're snowed up. You could ring up the police, and arrange for them to come here as soon as ever they can manage it, when the snow has cleared. And I rather think those other two men will try to explore the Secret Way as soon as possible, to get the papers back. Could we catch them when they arrive, do you think?'

'Rather!' said Uncle Quentin, though Aunt Fanny looked as if she didn't want any more exciting things to happen! 'Now look here, you seem really frozen all of you, and you must be hungry too, because it's almost lunch-time. Go into the dining-room and sit by the fire, and Joanna shall bring us all a hot lunch. Then we'll talk about what to do.'

Nobody said a word to Mr Roland, of course. He lay in bed, coughing now and then. George had slipped up and locked his door. She wasn't going to have him wandering out and overhearing anything!

They all enjoyed their hot lunch, and became warm and cosy. It was nice to sit there together, talking over their adventure, and planning what to do.

'I will telephone to the police, of course,' said Uncle Quentin. 'And tonight we will put Timmy into the study to give the two artists a good welcome if they arrive!'

Mr Roland was most annoyed to find his door locked that afternoon when he took it into his head to dress and go downstairs. He banged on it indignantly. George grinned and went upstairs. She had told the other children how she had locked the door.

'What's the matter, Mr Roland?' she asked, in a polite voice.

'Oh, it's you, George, is it?' said the tutor. 'See what's the matter with my door, will you? I can't open it.'

George had pocketed the key when she had locked the door. She answered Mr Roland in a cheerful voice.

'Oh Mr Roland, there's no key in your door, so I can't unlock it. I'll see if I can find it!'

Mr Roland was angry and puzzled. He couldn't understand why his door was locked and the key gone. He did not guess that everyone knew about him now. Uncle Quentin laughed when George went down and told him about the locked door.

'He may as well be kept a prisoner,' he said. 'He can't escape now.'

'That night, everyone went to bed early, and Timmy was left in the study, guarding the hole. Mr Roland had become more and more angry and puzzled when his door was not unlocked. He had shouted for Uncle Quentin, but only George had come. He could not understand it. George, of course, was enjoying herself. She made Timothy bark outside Mr Roland's door, and this puzzled him too, for he knew that George was not supposed to see Timmy for three days. Wild thoughts raced through his head. Had that fierce, impossible child locked up her father and mother and Joanna, as well as himself? He could not imagine what had happened.

In the middle of the night Timmy awoke everyone by barking madly. Uncle Quentin and the children hurried downstairs, followed by Aunt Fanny, and the amazed Joanna. A fine sight met their eyes!

Mr Wilton and Mr Thomas were in the study crouching behind the sofa, terrified of Timothy, who was barking for all he was worth! Timmy was standing by the hole in the stone floor, so that the two men could not escape down there. Artful Timmy! He had waited in silence until the men had crept up the hole into the study, and were exploring it, wondering where they were – and then the dog had leapt to the hole to guard it, preventing the men from escaping.

'Good evening, Mr Wilton, good evening, Mr Thomas,' said George, in a polite voice. 'Have you come to see our tutor Mr Roland?'

'So this is where he lives!' said Mr Wilton. 'Was it you in the passage today?'

'Yes – and my cousins,' said George. 'Have you come to look for the papers you stole from my father?'

The two men were silent. They knew they were caught. Mr Wilton spoke after a moment.

'Where's Mr Roland?'

'Shall we take these men to Mr Roland, Uncle?' asked Julian, winking at George. 'Although it's in the middle of the night I'm sure he would love to see them.'

'Yes,' said his uncle, jumping at once to what the boy meant to do. 'Take them up. Timmy, you go too.'

The men followed Julian upstairs, Timmy close at their heels. George followed too, grinning. She handed Julian the key. He unlocked the door and the men went in, just as Julian switched on the light. Mr Roland was wide awake and gave an exclamation of complete amazement when he saw his friends.

Before they had time to say a word Julian locked the door again and threw the key to George.

'A nice little bag of prisoners,' he said. 'We will leave old Tim outside the door to guard them. It's impossible to get out of that window, and anyway, we're snowed up if they could escape that way.'

Everyone went to bed again, but the children found it difficult to sleep after such an exciting time. Anne and George whispered together and so did Julian and Dick. There was such a lot to talk about.

Next day there was a surprise for everyone. The police

did arrive after all! The snow did not stop them, for somewhere or other they had got skis and had come skimming along valiantly to see the prisoners! It was a great excitement for everyone.

'We won't take the men away, sir, till the snow has gone,' said the Inspector. 'We'll just put the handcuffs on them, so that they don't try any funny tricks. You keep the door locked too, and that dog outside. They'll be safe there for a day or two. We've taken them enough food till we come back again. If they go a bit short, it will serve them right!'

The snow melted two days later, and the police took away Mr Roland and the others. The children watched.

'No more lessons *these* hols!' said Anne gleefully.

'No more shutting Timothy out of the house,' said George.

'You were right and we were wrong, George,' said Julian. 'You were fierce, weren't you? – but it's a jolly good thing you were!'

'She is fierce, isn't she?' said Dick, giving the girl a sudden hug. 'But I rather like her when she's fierce, don't you, Julian? Oh George, we do have marvellous adventures with you! I wonder if we'll have any more?'

They will – there isn't a doubt of that!

FIVE GO TO BILLYCOCK HILL

CONTENTS

1 A WEEK'S HOLIDAY   343

2 OFF TO BILLYCOCK HILL   350

3 BILLYCOCK FARM   358

4 A FINE CAMPING PLACE   367

5 THE FIRST NIGHT –
  AND A MORNING VISITOR   374

6 THE BUTTERFLY FARM   382

7 MRS JANES – A SPIDER – AND A POOL   389

8 A SPOT OF TROUBLE   397

9 COUSIN JEFF   405

10 BUTTERFLY FARM AGAIN   413

11 A STORMY NIGHT   420

12 WHAT HAPPENED IN BILLYCOCK
   CAVES   428

13 A DREADFUL SHOCK   435

14 MR GRINGLE IS ANNOYED   442

15 MORE NEWS – AND A NIGHT TRIP   449

16 LOOKING THROUGH WINDOWS   456

17 QUITE A LOT HAPPENS   465

18 NOBODY KNOWS WHERE TO LOOK   473

19 A MORNING OF WORK   480

20 A PECULIAR MESSAGE   487

21 AN EXCITING FINISH   496

CHAPTER ONE

A week's holiday

'WHERE'S THE map?' said Julian. 'Is that it, George? Good! Now – where shall we spread it?'

'On the floor,' said Anne. 'A map is always easiest to read on the floor. I'll push the table out of the way.'

'Well, be careful, for goodness sake,' said George. 'Father's in his study, and you know what happened before when someone pushed the table right over!'

Everyone laughed. George's father so often came pouncing out of his study if any sudden noise was made when he was working.

The table was pushed out of the way and the big map unfolded and spread out over the floor. Timmy was surprised to see the four children kneeling down around it, and barked, imagining this was some kind of new game.

'Be quiet, Timmy!' said Dick. 'You've got into trouble once this morning already for making a row. And stop brushing my face with your tail.'

'Wuff,' said Timmy and lay down heavily on the map.

'Get up, idiot,' said Dick. 'Don't you know we're in a hurry? We want to trace our route to Billycock Hill . . .'

'Billycock Hill – what a lovely name!' said Anne. 'Is that where we're going?'

'Yes,' said Julian, poring over the map. 'It's near some caves we want to see – and there's a butterfly farm not far off, and . . .'

'A butterfly farm!' said George, surprised. 'Whatever's that?'

'Just what it sounds like!' said Dick. 'A farm for butterflies! Toby, a friend of ours at school, told me about it. He lives quite near it and he says it's a most interesting place – they breed butterflies – and moths, too – from eggs, and sell them to collectors.'

'Do they really?' said Anne. 'Well, I must say I used to enjoy keeping caterpillars and seeing what they turned into – it was like magic to see a lovely butterfly or moth creep out of the chrysalis. But a *farm* for them – can we really go and see it?'

'Oh yes – Toby says the men who run it are very happy to show anyone round,' said Julian. 'Apparently Billycock Hill is a good place for rare butterflies too – that's why they've got their farm there. They rush about with nets half the time – and at night they go moth-hunting.'

'It sounds exciting,' said Dick. 'Well, what with caves to see, and a butterfly farm, and Toby to visit, and . . .'

'And just Five together again on a sunny week's holiday!' said George, giving Timmy a sudden thump of joy. 'Hurrah for Whitsun – and thank goodness our two schools had a week's holiday at the same time!'

The four cousins sprawled on the floor, looking with great interest at the map, following out a route with their fingers. As they traced out the way, there came an angry noise from the study, where George's father was at work.

'Who's been tidying my desk? Where are those papers I left here? Fanny, Fanny – come here!'

'He wants Mother – I'll get her,' said George. 'No, I can't – she's gone shopping.'

'Why can't people leave my papers alone?' came her father's voice again. 'Fanny! FANNY!'

Then the study door was flung open and Mr Kirrin came striding out, muttering to himself. He didn't see the four children on the floor and fell right over them. Timmy barked in delight and leapt at him, thinking that for once George's father was actually having a game with them!

'Oooh!' said George, as her father's hand came over her face. 'Don't! What *are* you doing, Father?'

'Uncle Quentin – sorry you fell over us!' said Julian. 'Shut up, Timmy – this isn't a game!'

He helped his uncle up and waited for the explosion. His uncle brushed himself down and glared at Julian. 'Have you *got* to lie on the floor? Get down, will you, Timmy! Where's your mother, George? Get up, for goodness sake! Where's Joanna? If she's been tidying my desk again I'll give her her notice!'

Joanna the cook appeared at the doorway, wiping her floury hands on her apron. 'Whatever's all this noise about?' she began. 'Oh sorry – I didn't know it was you. I . . .'

'Joanna – have you been tidying my desk again?' barked George's father.

'No. Have you lost something? Never you mind, I'll come along and find it,' said Joanna, who was used to Mr Kirrin's ways. 'Pick up that map, you four – and put the table back. Stop barking, Timmy. George, take him out for goodness' sake, or your father will go mad.'

'He's only excited because we're all together again,' said George, and took Timmy into the garden. The others followed, Julian folding up the map, grinning.

'We ought to put Uncle Quentin into a play,' said Dick. 'He'd bring the house down! Well – do we know the way, Julian? And when do we start?'

'Here's Mother,' said George as someone came to the front gate with a basket.

Julian ran to open it. He was very fond of his kindly, pleasant-faced aunt. She smiled round at them all.

'Well – have you decided where to go – and what to take

346

with you? You'll be able to camp out this beautiful weather – what a lovely Whitsun it's going to be!'

'Yes,' said Julian, taking his aunt's basket from her and carrying it indoors. 'We're going to Billycock Hill, and as our friend Toby lives at the bottom of it, at Billycock Farm, he's going to lend us all the camping gear we need.'

'So we shan't need to load our bikes with tents and mattresses and things,' said Dick.

'Oh – good!' said his aunt. 'What about food? You can get it at Toby's farm, I suppose?'

'You bet! We shan't *eat* there, of course,' said Julian. 'But we shall buy any eggs or milk or bread we need – and Toby says the strawberries are already ripening!'

Aunt Fanny smiled. 'Well, I needn't worry about your meals, then. And you'll have Timmy with you, too. He'll look after you all, won't you, Timmy? You won't let them get into any trouble, will you?'

'Woof,' said Timmy, in his deepest voice, and wagged his tail. 'Woof.'

'Good old Tim,' said George, patting him. 'If it wasn't for you we'd never be allowed to go off so much on our own, *I* bet!'

'Uncle Quentin's a bit on the warpath, Aunt Fanny,' said Dick. 'He wants to know who's been tidying his desk. He came rushing out of the study, didn't see us lying on the floor round our map – and fell right over us.'

'Oh dear – I'd better go and find out what papers he's lost *now*,' said his aunt. 'I expect he forgot that he had a tidying fit last night, and tidied his desk himself. He's probably put a lot of his most precious papers into the waste-paper basket!'

Everyone laughed as Mrs Kirrin hurried into the study.

'Well, let's get ready,' said Julian. 'We won't need to take much, as old Toby's going to help us. Anoraks, of course – and don't forget yours, Timmy! And sweaters. And one or two maps.'

'And torches,' said Anne, 'because we want to explore those caves. Oh, and let's take our swimsuits in *case* we find somewhere to bathe. It's warm enough!'

'And candles and matches,' said George, slapping the pocket of her jeans. 'I've got those. I got Joanna to give me three boxes. And let's take some sweets.'

'Yes. That tin of humbugs,' said Julian. 'And I vote we take our little portable radio!'

'Oh yes – that's a good idea,' said Anne, pleased. 'We can hear our favourite programmes then – and the news. I don't suppose we shall be able to buy newspapers.'

'I'll get out the bikes from the shed,' said Julian.

'Dick, get the sandwiches from Joanna – she said she'd make us some because we shan't get to Toby's farm till after our dinner-time – and I bet we'll be hungry!'

'Wuff,' said Timmy, who knew that word very well.

'He says remember biscuits for him,' said Anne with a laugh. 'I'll go and get some now, Tim – though I expect you can share meals with the dogs at Billycock Farm.'

Joanna had two large packets of sandwiches and cake ready for them, and two bottles of orangeade. 'There you are,' she said, handing them over. 'And if you get through all those you'll no longer feel hungry. And here are Timmy's biscuits – *and* a bone.'

'You're a star, Joanna,' said Dick, and put his arm round her to give her one of the sudden hugs she liked. 'Well, you'll soon be rid of us – a whole week at Whitsun – isn't that luck – and with such glorious weather, too.'

'Buck up!' called Julian. 'I've got the bikes – and no one's had a puncture, for a change. Bring my anorak, Dick.'

In three minutes everything was packed into the bicycle carriers. Timmy made sure that his biscuits and bone were packed by sniffing at each pack until he came to the smell he was hoping for. Then he wagged his tail and bounded round excitedly. The Five were together again – and who knew what might happen? Timmy was ready for anything!

'Goodbye, dears,' said Mrs Kirrin, standing at the gate to see them go. 'Julian, take care of the girls – and Tim, take care of everyone!'

Uncle Quentin suddenly appeared at the window. 'What's all the noise about?' he began impatiently. 'Oh – they're off at last, are they? Now we'll have a little peace and quiet! Goodbye – and behave yourselves!'

'Grown ups always say that,' said Anne as the Five set off happily, ringing their bells in farewell. 'Hurrah – we're off on our own again – yes, you too, Timmy. What fun!'

CHAPTER TWO

Off to Billycock Hill

THE SUN shone down hotly as the Five sped down the
sandy road that ran alongside Kirrin Bay. Timmy loped
easily beside them, his tongue hanging out quite a long
way. Anne always said that he had the longest tongue of
any dog she had ever known!

The sea was as blue as forget-me-nots as they cycled
along beside it. Across the bay they could see little Kirrin
Island, with Kirrin Castle towering up.

'Doesn't it look fine?' said Dick. 'I half wish we were
going to spend Whitsun at Kirrin Cottage, and were going
bathing, and rowing across to George's little island over
there.'

'We can do that in the summer hols,' said Julian. 'It's fun to explore other parts of the country when we can. Toby says the caves in Billycock Hill are marvellous.'

'What's Toby like?' asked George. 'We've never seen him, Anne and I.'

'He's a bit of a joker,' said Dick. 'Likes to put caterpillars down people's necks and so on – and beware if he has a magnificent rose in his buttonhole and asks you to smell it.'

'Why?' asked Anne, surprised.

'Because when you bend down to smell it you'll get a squirt of water in your face,' said Dick. 'It's a trick rose.'

'I don't think I'm going to like him much,' said George, who didn't take kindly to tricks of this sort. 'I'll probably bash him on the head if he does things like that to me.'

'That won't be any good,' said Dick cheerfully. 'He won't bash you back – he'll just think up some worse trick. Don't scowl, George – we're on holiday! Toby's all right – a bit of an ass, that's all.'

They had now left Kirrin Bay behind and were cycling down a country lane, set with hawthorn hedges each side. The may was over now, and the first wild roses were showing pink here and there. A little breeze got up, and was very welcome indeed.

'We'll have an ice when we come to a village,' said Julian after they had cycled about six miles.

'*Two* ices,' said Anne. 'Oh dear – this hill – what a steep one we've come to. I don't know whether it's worse to ride up slowly and painfully, or to get off and push my bike to the top.'

Timmy tore up to the top in front of them and then sat down to wait in the cool breeze there, his tongue hanging

351

out longer than ever. Julian came to the top first and looked down the other side.

'There's a village there,' he said. 'Right at the bottom. Let's see – yes, it's Tennick village – we'll stop and ask if it sells ices.'

It did, of course, strawberry and vanilla. The four children sat on a seat under a tree outside the small village shop, and dug little wooden spoons into ice-tubs. Timmy sat nearby, watching hopefully. He knew that at least he would be able to lick out the empty tubs.

'Oh, Tim – I didn't mean to buy you one, because you really are a bit fat,' said George, looking at the beseeching brown eyes fixed on her ice-cream. 'But as you'll probably get very thin running so far while we're cycling, I'll buy you a whole one for yourself.'

'Wuff,' said Timmy, bounding into the little shop at once and putting his great paws up on the counter, much to the surprise of the woman behind it.

'It's a waste, really, giving Timmy an ice,' said Anne when George and the dog came out. 'He just loosens it with his tongue and gulps it down. I sometimes wonder he doesn't chew up the cardboard tub, too!'

After ten minutes' rest they all set off again, feeling nice and cool inside. It really was lovely cycling through the June countryside – the trees were so fresh and green still, and the fields they passed were golden with buttercups – thousands and thousands of them, nodding their polished heads in the wind.

There was very little traffic on these deserted country roads – an occasional farm-cart, and sometimes a car, but little else. The Five kept to the lanes as much as they could, for they all preferred their quaint winding curves set with hedges of all kinds to the wide, dusty main roads, straight and uninteresting.

'We ought to get to Billycock Farm about four o'clock,' said Dick. 'Or maybe sooner. What time do we have our lunch, Julian? And where?'

'We'll find a good place about one o'clock,' said Julian. 'And not a minute before. So it's no good anyone saying they are hungry yet. It's only twelve.'

'I'm more thirsty than hungry,' said Anne. 'And I'm sure old Timmy must be dying of thirst! Let's stop at the next stream so that he can have a drink.'

'There's one,' said Dick, pointing to where a stream wound across a nearby field. 'Hey, Tim – go and have a drink, old fellow!'

Timmy shot through the hedge to the stream and began to lap. The others dismounted and stood waiting. Anne picked a spray of honeysuckle and put it through a buttonhole of her blouse. 'Now I can sniff it all the time,' she said. 'Delicious!'

'Hey, Tim – leave some water for the fishes!' shouted Dick. 'George, stop him drinking any more. He's swelling up like a balloon.'

'He's *not*,' said George. 'Timmy! That's enough! Here, boy, here!'

Timmy took one last lap and then raced over to George. He pranced round her, barking joyfully.

'There – he feels much better now,' said George, and away they all went again, groaning as they cycled slowly up the many hills in that part of the country, and shouting with delight as they sped furiously down the other side.

Julian had decided where to have their midday meal – on the top of a high hill! Then they could see all the country for miles around, and there would also be a nice cooling breeze.

'Cheer up,' he said as they came to the steepest hill they had so far encountered. 'We'll have our lunch at the top of this hill – and a good long rest!'

'Thank goodness,' panted Anne. 'We'll be as stiff as anything tomorrow!'

It really was lovely at the top of the hill! It was so high that they could see the countryside spreading for miles and miles around them.

'You can see five counties from here,' said Julian. 'But don't ask me which – I've forgotten! Let's lie in this heather and have a bit of a rest before we have our lunch.'

It was soft and comfortable lying in the springy heather, but Timmy did not approve of a rest before lunch. He wanted his bone! He went to where George had put her bicycle down, and sniffed in her carrier. Yes – his bone was most certainly there! He glanced round to make sure that everyone was resting, and nobody watching him. Then he began to nuzzle a paper parcel.

Anne was lying nearest to him, and she heard the crackling of the paper and sat up. '*Timmy!*' she said, shocked. 'Oh, Timmy – fancy helping yourself to our sandwiches!'

George sat up at once, and Timmy put his tail down, still wagging it a little as if to say, 'Sorry – but after all, it *is* my bone!'

'Oh – he just wants his bone,' said George. 'He's not after our sandwiches. As if he *would* take them, Anne! You might have known he wouldn't!'

'I feel rather like having mine now,' said Anne. 'Julian, can't we have some? – and I *do* really want a drink.'

The idea of a drink made everyone long to begin lunch and soon they were unwrapping ham and tomato sandwiches, and enormous slices of Joanna's fruit cake. Julian found the little cardboard drinking cups, and poured out the orangeade carefully.

'This is fine,' said Dick, munching his sandwiches and gazing out over the rolling countryside, with its moorlands, its stretches of farmland with the fields of green corn, and its sloping hills. 'Look – see that hill far away in the distance, Julian – over there – would that be Billycock Hill, do you think? It's rather a funny shape.'

'I'll look through my field-glasses,' said Julian, and took them from their leather case. He put them to his eyes and stared hard at the faraway hill that lay to the north of them.

'Yes – I think it probably is Billycock Hill,' he said. 'It's got such an odd-shaped top; it looks a bit like an old Billycock hat.'

He handed the glasses round, and everyone looked at the far-off hill. George put the glasses to Timmy's eyes. 'There you are!' she said. 'Have a squint, Timmy! Julian, it doesn't look so very far away.'

'It's not, as the crow flies,' said Julian, taking back his glasses and surveying the countryside around them again. 'But it's a long, long way through those hundreds of little winding lanes. Any more sandwiches, anyone?'

'There aren't any more left,' said Dick. 'Or fruit cake either. Have a humbug if you're still hungry.'

The humbugs were passed round and Timmy waited hopefully for his turn. George gave him one. 'Not that it's much use to you,' she said. 'You just swallow it without even one suck!'

'We'll rest for half an hour more,' said Julian. 'Gosh, I do feel sleepy!'

They all snuggled down into the soft clumps of heather, and soon they were asleep in the warm sun. Even Timmy snoozed, with one ear half up just in case someone came by. But nobody did. In fact it was so very quiet on the top of the hill that three-quarters of an hour went by before anyone awoke. Anne felt something crawling up her arm and woke with a jump.

'Ugh – a big beetle!' she said, and shook it off. She glanced at her watch. 'Dick! Ju! Wake up! We must get on, or we'll never be there by tea-time!'

Soon they were once more on their way, tearing down the hill at top speed, shouting as they went, with Timmy barking madly beside them. Really, the start of a holiday was the happiest thing in the world!

CHAPTER THREE

Billycock Farm

THE FIVE certainly cycled fast that afternoon, and would have arrived at Billycock Hill even sooner than they did if it hadn't been for Timmy. He panted so much in the heat that they stopped for brief rests every fifteen minutes.

'It's a pity he's so big and heavy,' said Anne. 'If he had been a small dog we could have taken turns at carrying him on our bikes.'

Billycock Hill was soon very near. It certainly was a strange shape, very like an old-fashioned hat. It was partly heather-clad and partly sloping meadow land. Cows grazed in the meadows, and farther up the hill, where there was shorter, wiry grass, the farmer had put a good many sheep.

Nestling down at the foot of the hill was a rambling old farm-building, with out-houses and stables and a big greenhouse. 'That must be Billycock Farm,' said Julian. 'Well, we've made very good time, you know – it's only half past three. Let's wash our faces in that stream over there – we all look rather hot and dirty. Timmy, you can have a bathe if you want to!'

The water was cool and silky to the touch, and the children splashed it over their faces and necks, wishing they could do as Timmy was doing – lying down in the stream and letting the water flow over him!

'That's better,' said Dick, mopping his face with an enormous handkerchief. 'Now let's go and present ourselves at Billycock Farm. I hope Toby's remembered that we're coming – he *promised* to lend us all we wanted for camping out.'

They combed their hair, brushed down their clothes with their hands, and then, feeling more respectable, made their way across a field-path to a farm gate. The field was bumpy, so they rode slowly.

Soon they were in a big farmyard, with hens pecking around them, and ducks swimming on a round duck-pond. Farm dogs began barking from somewhere – and then something ran round the corner of the old house – something very small and pink.

'Whatever is it?' said Anne. 'Oh – it's a pigling! What a pet! Oh, it's come right up to us – little pigling, have you escaped from your sty? How clean you are!'

The tiny pig gave funny little squeals, and ran up to Timmy, who sat back on his haunches in surprise, staring at this unexpected little creature. He thought it must be some sort of dog without any hair.

The pigling butted Timmy gently and Timmy retreated backwards. Julian laughed. 'Tim can't make it out!' he said. 'No don't growl, Timmy – it's quite harmless!'

'Hallo – who's this?' said Dick as a small figure came round the house. It stopped when it saw the Five.

'What a dear little boy!' said Anne. 'Is he Toby's brother?'

The child didn't look more than five years old. He had a head of bright yellow curls, big brown eyes, and a grin just like his big brother's.

'That's my pig,' he said, coming slowly towards them. 'He runned away from me.'

Anne laughed. 'What's your pig's name?' she said.

'Curly,' said the small boy, and pointed at the pigling's tail. 'He's got a curly tail. It won't go straight.'

'It's a nice tail,' said Anne. The pigling ran to the small boy, and he grabbed it by its tail. 'You runned away again,' he said. Then he picked up the pig and walked off.

'Hey! Is this Billycock Farm?' called Julian. 'Have you got a brother called Toby?'

'Toby? Yes, Toby's over there,' said the boy, and he pointed to a big barn. 'Toby's ratting with Binky.'

'Right,' said Julian. The little boy disappeared with his funny pet, and Julian laughed. 'He's rather a pet himself,' he said. 'Come on – let's go and find Toby and Binky. Perhaps Binky is another brother.'

'Or a dog,' said George, and put her hand on Timmy's collar. 'Better be careful. He might go for Tim.'

'Yes – Binky might be a dog, of course – probably a good ratter,' said Julian. 'Dick and I will go to the barn and you two girls stay here with Timmy.'

They went off to the barn. A great noise came from inside as the two boys approached. Shouts and barks and the rap of a stick came to their ears.

'Get him, Binky – look, he went under that sack! Oh, you fathead, you've lost him again!'

Wuff-wuff-wuff! Rap-rap! More yells! In great curiosity Julian and Dick peered into the rather dark old barn. They saw Toby there, prodding under sacks, with a most excited collie beside him, barking incessantly.

'Hey, Toby!' yelled Julian, and Toby stood up and turned a red and perspiring face towards the two boys.

'Oh – you've arrived!' he said, going quickly to the door. 'I thought you were never coming. Glad to see you! But are there only two of you? I got out tents and things for four.'

'There *are* four of us – five counting Timmy,' said Julian. 'We've left the two girls over there with him – he's our dog. Will yours be friendly or not?'

'Oh, yes, so long as I introduce them,' said Toby and they all went out of the barn. As soon as Binky, Toby's dog, saw Timmy, he stood still, made himself stiff, and growled, while the hackles on his neck slowly rose up.

'It's all right,' shouted Toby to the girls. 'Bring your dog here. He'll be all right with Binky in half a minute.'

Rather doubtfully George brought Timmy across. Timmy was a bit doubtful himself of this big collie! Toby bent down and spoke into Binky's ear.

'Binky, shake paws with this nice girl – she's a friend.'

He nodded at George. 'Hold out your hand,' he said.

George bent down to the collie and held out her hand. At once the dog put up his paw and allowed her to shake it solemnly.

361

'Now you,' said Toby to Anne, and she did the same. She liked this dog Binky, with his bright brown eyes and long, sleek nose.

'Does *your* dog shake hands, too?' asked Toby. George nodded. 'He does? Right – tell him to shake paws with Binky. Binky, shake!'

'Timmy, shake,' commanded George, and very politely and solemnly the two dogs shook paws, eyeing each other cautiously. Timmy gave a sudden little whine – and then the two were tearing round the yard together, barking furiously, chasing one another, rolling over, and having a wonderful game.

'That's all right, then,' said Toby, pleased. 'Binky's quite all right with anyone, human or animal, so long as he can shake hands with them. I've taught him that. But he's a dud ratter! He just can't seem to nip a rat. Well – let's go and see my mother. She's expecting you. She's got a whopping great tea.'

This was all very satisfactory! Just the kind of welcome the Five liked. Anne looked sideways at Toby. She thought he was rather nice. George wasn't so sure. He had a rose in his button-hole – was it a trick one, and was he going to ask her to smell it?

'We saw a little yellow-haired boy just now,' said Anne. 'With a tiny pigling.'

'Oh, that's Benny with his pet pig,' said Toby, laughing. 'He calls it Curly – and he adores it! We've offered him a kitten or a puppy – but no, he wants that pigling. They go everywhere together – like Mary and her lamb! Benny's a pet – he really is. Kid brothers are usually a nuisance, you know, but Benny isn't.'

'Kid sisters are a bit of a nuisance sometimes too,' said Dick, glancing slyly at Anne, who at once gave him a determined punch. 'Still – Anne's not too bad, is she, Ju?'

Toby's mother, Mrs Thomas, was a plump and jolly woman, with a smile as wide as Toby's and Benny's. She made them all very welcome.

'Come along in,' she said. 'Toby's pleased you're going

to camp hereabouts – he's got all the tents and rugs you'll need – and you can come every day and get eggs and milk and bread and butter and anything else you need from here. Don't be afraid to ask!'

There was suddenly the scamper of little hooves and Curly the pigling came running indoors.

'There, now!' said Toby's mother. 'There's that pigling again. Benny, Benny – you are NOT to let Curly come indoors. Cats I don't mind, nor dogs – but pigs I won't have. Benny!'

Benny appeared, looking most apologetic. 'Sorry, Mum – but he's lively today. Oooh, I say – what a tea! Can we have some yet?'

'I'll just make the tea – unless you'd rather have some of our creamy milk?' said Toby's mother.

'Oh, milk, please, Mrs Thomas,' said Anne, and they all said the same. Nothing could be nicer than icy-cold, creamy farm milk from the dairy on a hot day like this.

They all sat down to tea, and the four visitors wished they had not had such a big lunch! A large ham sat on the table, and there were crusty loaves of new bread. Crisp lettuces, dewy and cool, and red radishes were side by side in a big glass dish. On the sideboard was an enormous cake, and beside it a dish of scones. Great slabs of butter and jugs of creamy milk were there, too, with honey and home-made jam.

'I wish I was hungry, *really* hungry,' said Dick. 'This is just the kind of meal for a hungry day.'

'I didn't think you'd have had much lunch,' said Mrs Thomas. 'Now then, Toby – you're the host. See to your guests, please – and, Benny, take the pigling off your knee. I will *not* have him at the table.'

'Curly will be very upset if he sees that ham,' said Toby slyly. 'That's his grandfather!'

Benny put Curly down hurriedly, afraid that his feelings might be hurt. The pigling went to sit beside Timmy, who, very much surprised, but rather pleased, at once made room for him.

It was a very happy meal, and Toby was a good host. Anne sat beside little Benny, and found herself liking him more than ever. 'He's like a little boy out of a story,' she said to George. 'He and Curly ought to be put into a book!'

'Well now,' said Mrs Thomas after everyone had eaten their fill, 'what are your plans? Toby, show them where you have put their tents and everything. Then they can decide where they are going to camp.'

'Come on, then,' said Toby, and Benny and Curly and Binky all came along, too. 'You can help to carry everything – and we'll go up on Billycock Hill and find a fine camping place. How I wish I could camp out with you too!'

Away they all went, feeling rather full but very happy. Where should they camp? How lovely to sleep out at nights, and see the stars through the opening in the tent!

CHAPTER FOUR

A fine camping place

TOBY HAD put all the camping-out gear in a nearby barn.
He took the Five there, with Benny and the pigling trailing
after. Binky came, too, so friendly now with Timmy that
they trotted along side by side, occasionally pushing
against each other like schoolboys!

Julian and Dick looked at the pile of canvas, the pegs
and the ropes. Yes, these two tents would do very well,
though if the weather stayed like this they would hardly
need tents! They could lay their rugs out on the springy
heather.

'This is fine, Toby,' said Julian gratefully. 'You've even
provided a kettle and a frying-pan.'

'Well, you might want to cook a meal,' said Toby. 'Or
boil soup. There's a saucepan for that – ah, here it is!'

He picked it up and promptly put it on Benny's head,
where it stuck tightly on his yellow curls. Benny yelled and
ran at Toby, hitting him with his fists. The little pig rushed
away in fright and disappeared round a corner.

Anne took the saucepan off poor Benny's head. 'You're
all right!' she said. 'It was a funny hat to wear, wasn't it?'

'Curly runned away again!' wept Benny, and he pummelled the laughing Toby. 'I hate you, I hate you!'

'You go and find him,' said Toby, fending off the angry
small boy, and Benny ran off on his fat little legs.

'Well, we've got rid of him for a few minutes,' said
Toby. 'Now – is there anything I've forgotten? You've got

torches, I suppose? What about candles – and matches?'

'We've got those, too,' said Dick. 'And we've brought sweaters and swimsuits – but that's about all. I see you've put a couple of rugs here as well in case we're cold!'

'Well, it *might* turn wet and chilly,' said Toby. 'Of course, if it snows, or anything like that, you'll have to come and borrow some more rugs! Now, shall I help you to fix them on your bikes?'

It was too difficult to fix anything on to the four bikes, and in the end Toby found a hand-cart and the children piled everything into that.

'We'll fetch our bikes some other time,' said Julian.

'Leave them here!' said Toby. 'They'll be all right. Are you going now? Well, I'll get a package Mother's got ready for you – you know, ham and new-laid eggs and bread and butter and the rest.'

'It's most awfully good of her,' said Julian gratefully. 'Well, let's start – we've got everything in the hand-cart now. We'll just wait for the food. Dick, you and I can push this hand-cart together. It will need two of us up the hill – and I vote we camp on the side of the slope somewhere, so that we can get a good view.'

Toby came back with an enormous package of food. Benny came with him, Curly trotting behind. Benny carried a basket of ripe strawberries.

'I picked them for you,' he said, and handed them to Anne.

'What beauties!' she said, and gave the smiling child a hug. 'We shall enjoy them, Benny.'

'Can I come and see your camp when you've built it?' he asked. 'Can I bring Curly? He's never seen a camp.'

'Yes, of course you can,' said Anne. 'Are we ready now,

Julian? What about milk? Mrs Thomas said we could take some.'

'Oh yes – I forgot that,' said Toby. 'It's in the dairy.' He sped off with Binky, and the others arranged everything neatly in the useful little hand-cart. Toby came back with the milk – two big bottles. They were stacked carefully in a corner of the cart.

'Well, we're ready now, I think,' said Julian, and he and Dick began to push the cart down the path to the gate. Timmy and Binky trotted on ahead, and everyone else followed. Benny came as far as the gate with Curly, then Toby sent him back.

'You know what Mother said, Benny,' he said. 'You're not to come with us now – it'll be too late when Binky and I come back.'

Benny's mouth went down, but he didn't attempt to follow them. He picked Curly up in his arms in case the pigling should run away after the others.

'Benny's a pet,' said Anne. 'I wish I had a little brother like that.'

'He's all right,' said Toby. 'A bit of a cry-baby, though. I'm *trying* to bring him up properly – teasing him out of his babyishness, and making him stand on his own feet.'

'He seems to be able to do that all right,' said Dick. 'My word – the way he went for you when you put that saucepan on his head! He pummelled you right and left!'

'Benny's a funny little kid,' said Toby, giving a hand with the cart as they reached the slope of the hill. 'He's always having funny pets. Two years ago he had a lamb that followed him everywhere. Last year he had two goslings that followed him about – and when they grew

369

into geese they still followed him! They waddled all the way upstairs one day!'

'And this year he's got a pig!' said George, who, like Anne, was very much amused with Benny. 'Don't you think Timmy was very funny with Curly? I'm sure he still thinks it's a puppy without any hair!'

They made their way up the hill, following a narrow sheep-path. The hand-cart bumped and wobbled, and soon it needed four or five pairs of hands to push it.

'How much farther?' panted Toby at last. 'Surely you're not going right to the top?'

'No,' said Julian. 'About halfway up. We do want to have a good view, Toby. Not very much farther up, I should think. But let's have a bit of rest, shall we?'

They sat down, glad to get their breath. Certainly the view was magnificent. Far away on the horizon were purplish hills, and in front of them stretched miles and miles of green and golden countryside. Green for growing corn and grass – gold for the buttercups, which were at their best in this sunny week of June.

'I like those silvery threads here and there winding about the green fields,' said Anne. 'Little streams – or rivers – curving like snakes all about! And I like the dark green patches that are woods.'

'What's that just down there?' asked George, pointing to what looked like an enormous field with great sheds in the centre.

'That's an airfield,' said Toby promptly. 'A bit hush-hush. Secret planes tried out, and all that. I know all about it because a cousin of mine is there – he's a flight-lieutenant. He comes to see us sometimes and tells me things. It's an experimental place.'

'What's that, exactly?' asked Anne.

'Well – where new ideas are tried out,' said Toby. 'They deal mostly with very small planes down there – one-man fighter planes, I think. Don't be scared if you hear noises from the airfield sometimes – bangs and bursts. I don't know what they are, of course – it's all to do with their experiments.'

'I wish I could visit the airfield,' said Dick. 'I'm keen on planes. I'm going to fly one when I'm older.'

'You'd better meet my cousin, then,' said Toby. 'He might take you up in one.'

'I *should* like to meet him,' said Dick, delighted. 'So would Julian.'

'We'd better get on now,' said Julian, standing up. 'We won't go much higher – the view can't be much better anywhere else!'

George and Anne went on ahead to find a good camping place, while the three boys pushed the cart slowly over the heather. But it was Timmy who found the right place! He ran on ahead, feeling thirsty, so when he heard the sound of running water he ran to it at once.

From under a jutting rock gushed a little spring. It rippled down a rocky shelf and lost itself in a mass of lush greenery below. Rushes grew to mark the way it went, and George's sharp eyes could follow its path for quite a long way down the hill, outlined by the dark line of rushes.

'Julian! Look what Timmy's found!' she called as she watched him lap from the clear spring water. 'A little spring gushing out of the hillside! Hadn't we better camp near it?'

'Good idea!' shouted back Julian, and left the hand-cart to come and see. 'Yes, this is just the place! A fine view – plenty of springy heather to camp on – and water laid on quite near!'

Everyone agreed that it was a fine place, and soon all the gear was taken from the hand-cart. The tents were not erected, for everyone meant to sleep under the stars that night, the evening was so warm. Nobody wanted to lie in a stuffy tent!

372

A FINE CAMPING PLACE

Anne unpacked the food parcel, wondering where would be the coolest place for a 'larder'. She went over to the rock from which gushed the crystal-clear spring water. She pushed away the rushes around and discovered a kind of small cave hollowed out of the rock below the spring.

'It would be as cool as anything in there,' thought Anne, and put her hand through the falling water into the cave-like hole. Yes, it was icy cold! Was it big enough to hold the milk bottles and everything? Just about, she thought.

Anne loved arranging anything, and she was soon at work putting away the food and the milk into her odd larder. George laughed when she saw it.

'Just like you, Anne!' she said. 'Well, we'd better put a towel by the spring, for certainly we shall get soaked every time we get out any food!'

'Tell Timmy he's *not* to try and poke his head into my larder,' said Anne, pushing Timmy away. 'Oh, now he's all wet. Go and shake yourself somewhere else, Timmy – you're showering me with drops of water!'

Toby had to leave them, for it was already past his supper-time. 'See you tomorrow!' he said. 'How I wish I was staying up here with you! So long!'

Away he went down the hill with Binky at his heels. The Five looked at one another and grinned.

'He's nice – but it's good to be alone again – just us Five,' said George. 'Come on – let's settle in. This is the best camp we've ever had!'

CHAPTER FIVE

The first night – and a morning visitor

'WHAT'S THE time?' said Julian, looking at his watch. 'Good gracious – it's almost eight o'clock. Anyone feel tired?'

'Yes,' said Dick, Anne and George, and even Timmy joined in with his deepest 'Woof'.

'With all that bicycling and then pushing that heavy cart up the hill, I can hardly move!' said Dick. 'I vote we have a simple supper – something out of Anne's little larder – and then spread our rugs over some thick heather and sleep under the sky. Even up here, with a breeze, it's warm. I should be stifled in a tent.'

'Well, we're all agreed on that,' said Julian. 'Anne, what do you suggest for a light supper?'

'Bread, butter and some of Mrs Thomas's farm cheese,' said Anne promptly. 'With a tomato or two if you like and icy-cold milk and Benny's strawberries to finish with. That is – if the milk has had time to get cold in the little hole under the spring.'

'Sounds jolly good,' said Julian. 'What do *you* think, Timmy? Anne, if you and George get the supper ready, Dick and I will prepare our heathery beds. Then we can all turn in as soon as possible. I honestly feel that once I sit down or lie down I'll not be able to get up again!'

'Same here,' said Dick, and went off with Julian to find the best place for sleeping. They soon found one. They came across a giant of a gorse bush, thick, prickly and still full of golden blooms. In front of it was a stretch of very close-set heather, as springy as the best mattress in the world. Dick sat down on it and grinned at Julian.

'Just made for us!' he said. 'We shall sleep like logs here. We hardly need a rug to lie on, it's so close-grown. Help me up – legs won't do anything now I've sat down!'

Julian pulled him up and they called to the girls: 'Anne! George! Bring the supper here. We've found a good place. It's by this giant gorse bush.'

The girls came along with the meal, and the boys fetched a couple of rugs from the pile of things that they had brought in the hand-cart. They spread them on the heather.

'I say! This certainly is a good place,' said George, coming up with Anne and Timmy carrying a loaf of bread, a pat of butter and tomatoes. Anne had the milk and the cheese. Timmy was carrying a little bag of his own biscuits.

'The gorse bush will shelter us from too much wind,' said Dick, taking the milk from Anne. 'It's an ideal spot – and the view is superb.'

It was a very happy supper they had, sitting in the heather, while the sun sank lower and lower in the west. The evenings were very light now, and certainly they would not need candles! They finished up everything, and then went to wash at the little spring that bubbled out so cheerfully.

They lay down on their rugs in the heather while it was still daylight. 'Good-night!' said Dick, and promptly fell fast asleep. 'Good-night!' called Julian and lay for a few seconds looking at the view which was now becoming dim and blue.

Timmy kept the two girls awake for a minute or two,

trying to squeeze in between them. 'Do keep still, Timmy,' said George. 'And just remember you're on guard, even though I don't expect there is anyone nearer than a mile – and that will be at Billycock Farm! Lie still now, or I'll push you off the rug! Good-night, Anne.'

George was soon asleep, and so was Timmy, tired out with so many miles of running. Anne lay awake for a few minutes, looking at the evening star which shone large and golden in the sky. She felt very happy. 'I don't want to grow up,' she thought. 'There can't be anything nicer in the world than this – being with the others, having fun with them. No – I don't want to grow up!'

Then she, too, fell asleep, and night came quietly down, with stars brilliant in the sky, and very little noise to be heard anywhere – just the gurgling of the spring some way away, and the far-off bark of some dog – perhaps Binky at the farm. The breeze died down, so that even that could not be heard.

No one except Timmy awoke at all that night. Timmy put up one ear when he heard a squeak just above his head. It came again and he opened one eye. It was a small black bat circling and swooping, hunting for insects. Its squeak was so high that only Timmy's quick ear caught it. He put down his listening ear and went to sleep again.

Nobody stirred until a very loud noise awakened them. R-r-r-r-r-r-r-r-r! R-r-r-r-r-r-r-r-r! They all woke up with a jump and the boys sat up straight, startled. What could it be?

'It's a plane,' said Julian, staring up at a small aeroplane flying over the hill. 'It must be one from that airfield down there! I say – it's five past nine! Five past nine – we've slept for nearly twelve hours!'

'Well, I'm going to sleep for some more,' said Dick, snuggling down into his heathery bed again and shutting his eyes.

'No, you're not,' said Julian, giving him a shove. 'It's too good a day to waste in any more sleep. Hey, you girls – are you awake?'

'Yes,' called George, sitting up, rubbing her eyes. 'That aeroplane woke me. Anne's awake, too – and you can see that Timmy is; he's gone after a rabbit or something.'

'We'll go and wash at the spring,' said Anne, scrambling off the rug. 'And George and I will get breakfast. Anyone like a boiled egg?'

The sun shone down out of a blue sky, and the little breeze awoke and began to blow again. They washed in the cold water, and Timmy drank it, lapping it thirstily as it splashed down over his nose. Then they had their breakfast.

It was easy to make a little fire in the shelter of the giant

377

gorse bush, and boil the eggs in the saucepan. Bread and butter and tomatoes completed the simple meal, with cold creamy milk to wash it down.

In the middle of this Timmy began to bark frantically, but as his tail was wagging all the time, the others guessed that it must be Toby coming. They heard Binky's answering bark, and then the dog himself appeared, panting and excited. He greeted Timmy first of all, and then ran round to give everyone a lick.

'Hallo, hallo, hallo!' came Toby's voice, and he appeared round the gorse bush. 'Had a good night? I say, aren't you late – *still* having your breakfast? My word, you're sleepy-heads! I've been up since six. I've milked cows and cleaned out a shed, and fed the hens and collected the eggs.'

The Five immediately felt ashamed of themselves! They gazed at Toby in admiration – why, he was quite a farmer!

'I've brought you some more milk, bread and eggs and cake,' he said, and put down a basket.

'Jolly good of you,' said Julian. 'We must pay for any food we get from your farm, you know that. Any idea of how much we owe for yesterday's food and for what you've brought today?'

'Well, my mother says you don't *need* to pay her,' said Toby. 'But I know you mean to – so I suggest that you pay *me* each time and I'll put the money into a box and buy my mother a smashing present at the end – from you all. Will that do?'

'That's a good idea,' said Julian. 'We couldn't possibly accept food if we didn't pay for it – but I know what mothers are – they don't like being paid in money for their kindness! So we'll do what you say. Now, reckon up what we owe so far, and I'll pay you.'

'Right,' said Toby in a business-like way. 'I'll charge you market prices, not top prices. I'll just tot up the bill while you're clearing up and putting away what I've brought.'

The girls washed up in the spring, and the boys carried everything there for Anne to put in her 'larder'. Toby presented Julian with a neatly written bill, which he at once paid. Toby receipted the bill and gave it back.

'There you are – all business-like,' he said. 'Thanks very much. What are you going to do today? There are super caves to be explored if you like – or there's the butterfly farm – or you can just come down to *our* farm for the day.'

'No, not today,' said Julian, afraid that they might make themselves a nuisance to Mrs Thomas. 'I don't feel like seeing caves this morning either – so dark and eerie on such a sunny day. What shall we do, girls?'

But before they could decide Binky and Timmy began to bark, each dog standing quite still, facing the same way – towards the giant gorse bush.

'Who is it, Tim?' asked George. 'Go and see! Go on then!'

Timmy ran behind the bush, followed by Binky, and then the children heard a surprised voice.

'Hallo, Binky! What are *you* doing all the way up here? And who's your friend?'

'It's Mr Gringle,' said Toby. 'One of the men who own the butterfly farm. He's often up here with his net, because it's a wonderful place for butterflies.'

A man came round the gorse bush – rather a peculiar figure, untidy, with glasses slipping down his nose, and his hair much too long. He carried a big butterfly net and stopped when he saw the five children.

'Hallo!' he said. 'Who are all these, Toby? Quite a crowd!'

'Friends of mine, Mr Gringle,' said Toby solemnly. 'Allow me to introduce them. Julian Kirrin, Dick Kirrin, Anne Kirrin, George Kirrin, their cousin – and their dog Timothy.'

'Ha – pleased to meet you!' said Mr Gringle, and came shambling forward, his big butterfly net over his shoulder. Behind his glasses shone curiously bright eyes. He nodded his head to each of the four cousins. 'Three boys – and a girl. Very nice lot, too. You don't look as if you'll leave litter about or start fires in this lovely countryside.'

'We shouldn't dream of it,' said George, delighted that he had thought she was a boy. Nothing pleased George as much as that! 'Mr Gringle – *could* we see your butterfly farm, please? We would so like to!'

'Of course, my dear boy, of course,' said Mr Gringle, and his eyes shone as if he were pleased. 'We don't often have visitors, so it's quite an event when somebody comes along. This way, this way!'

CHAPTER SIX

The butterfly farm

MR GRINGLE led the way down the hill by a little path so overgrown that it was hardly possible to see it. Halfway down the little company heard a squealing noise – and then an excited little voice.

'Toby, Toby! I'm here! Can I come with you?'

'It's Benny – and the pigling!' said Anne, amused at the little couple making their way excitedly towards them. Timmy ran to Curly and sniffed him all over, still not quite sure that he wasn't some kind of strange puppy.

'What are you doing up here?' said Toby sternly. 'You know you're not supposed to wander too far from the farm. You'll get lost one of these days, Benny.'

'Curly runned away,' said Benny, looking up at his big brother with wide brown eyes.

'You mean you wanted to find out where I'd gone so you came after me with Curly,' said Toby.

'Curly runned away, he runned fast!' said Benny, looking as if he was going to cry.

'You're a scoundrel, Benny,' said Toby. 'You make that pigling of yours an excuse for getting about all over the place. You wait till Dad hears it – you'll get such a spanking. Well – tail on to us now – we're going to the butterfly farm. And if Curly runs away, let him! I'm tired of that pig.'

'I'll carry him,' said Benny, and picked up the little creature in his arms. But he soon had to put him down, for

382

Curly squealed so loudly that Timmy and Binky both leapt round him in great concern.

'Hm – well – shall we proceed?' asked Mr Gringle, walking on in front. 'Quite a party we have today.'

'Are your butterflies afraid of pigs or dogs?' asked Benny, trotting beside him. 'Shall we leave them outside?'

'Don't ask idiotic questions, Benny,' said Toby. Then he gave a cry and caught Mr Gringle's arm. 'I say – look at that butterfly. Don't you want to catch it? Is it rare?'

'No,' said Mr Gringle rather coldly. 'It's a meadow-brown – very common indeed. Don't they teach you anything at school? Fancy not knowing that!'

'Julian, do we have any butterfly lessons?' asked Toby with a grin. 'I say, Mr Gringle, what about you coming and teaching us about Cabbage butterflies and Cauli-flower moths, and Red Admirals and Blue Captains and Peacock butterflies and Ostrich moths and . . .'

'Don't be an ass, Toby,' said Julian, seeing that Mr Gringle had no sense of humour at all, and did not think this in the least funny. 'Mr Gringle, are there many rare butterflies about here?'

'Oh, yes, yes,' said the butterfly man. 'But not only that – there are so many of *all* kinds here, and it is easy to catch as many as I want for breeding purposes. One butterfly means hundreds of eggs, you know – and we hatch them out and sell them.'

He suddenly made a dart to one side, almost knocking George over. 'Sorry, boy!' he said, making the others smile. 'Sorry! There's a Brown Argus there – a lovely specimen, first I've seen this year! Stand clear, will you.'

The children – and the dogs too – stood still as he tiptoed towards a small dark brown butterfly spreading its tiny wings as it sat on a flowering plant. With a swift downwards swoop the net closed over the plant, and in a trice the butterfly man had caught the fluttering insect. He pinched the net inwards, and showed the children the tiny creature.

'There you are – a female Brown Argus, one of the family of the Blue butterflies you see so often in full summer. She'll lay me plenty of eggs and they'll all hatch into fat little slug-like caterpillars, and . . .'

'But this isn't a blue butterfly,' said Anne, looking through the fine net. 'It's dark brown, with a row of pretty orange spots along the margins of its wings.'

'All the same, it belongs to the Blue butterfly family,' said Mr Gringle, taking it out with the gentlest of fingers and putting it into a tin case slung round his shoulders. 'It's probably come up from one of those hay meadows down in the valley there. In you go, my little beauty!'

'Mr Gringle, quick – here's a most lovely butterfly!' called George. 'It's got greeny-black front wings with red spots, and lovely red back wings with dark green borders. Oh, quick – I'm sure you want this one!'

'That's not a butterfly,' said Dick, who knew a good deal about them.

'I should think not!' said Mr Gringle, getting his net poised ready to swoop. 'It's a moth – a lovely little thing!' Down went his net and the pretty little red and green insect fluttered in surprise inside it.

'But moths don't fly in the daytime,' argued George. 'Only at night.'

'Rubbish!' said Mr Gringle, looking at the moth through the thick lenses of his glasses. 'What are boys coming to nowadays? In *my* boyhood nearly every boy knew that there are nighttime *and* daytime ones as well!'

'But,' began George again, and stopped as Mr Gringle gave her quite a glare.

'This is a Six-Spot Burnet Day-Flying moth,' he said speaking slowly as if he were addressing a very small child. 'It loves to fly in the hot sunshine. Please do not argue with me. I don't like ignorance of this sort.'

George looked rather mutinous and Dick nudged her. 'He's right, fathead,' he said in a low voice. 'You don't know much about moths, so say nothing, George, or he won't let us go with him.'

'I'd like two or three more of these Six-Spots highly coloured and unusually large. Perhaps you would see if you can find any more, all of you.'

Everybody began to look here and there, and to shake any little bush or clump of grass they passed. Timmy and Binky were most interested in this and began a hunt on their own, sniffing and snuffling everywhere, not quite sure what they were looking for, but enjoying it all the same.

Mr Gringle took a long time to get to his butterfly farm, and the children began to wish they hadn't asked to go. There was so much side-stepping to see this and that, so much examining when a specimen was caught, so much 'talky-talk', as Dick whispered to Anne.

'Do you keep your butterflies and moths in those glasshouses?' asked Julian.

'Yes,' said Mr Gringle. 'Come along – I'll show you what I and my friend Mr Brent do. He's away today, so you can't meet him.'

It was certainly a strange place. The cottage looked as if it were about to fall down at any moment. Two of the windows were broken and some tiles had fallen off the roof. But the glasshouses were in good repair, and the glass panes were perfectly clean. Evidently the butterfly men thought more of their butterflies and moths than they did of themselves.

'Do you live here all alone with Mr Brent, your friend?' asked Dick curiously, thinking that it must be a strange and lonely life.

'Oh, no. Old Mrs Janes lives here too,' said Mr Gringle. 'And sometimes her son comes to do my small repairs, and to clean all the glass of the butterfly houses. There's the old lady, look. She can't bear insects of any sort, so she never comes into the glasshouses.'

An old woman, looking exactly like a witch, peered out at them through a window in the cottage. Anne was quite scared to see her. Toby grinned. 'She's quite harmless,' he said to Anne. 'Our cook knows her because she often comes to us for eggs and milk. She's got no teeth at all, so she mutters and mumbles and that makes her seem more like a witch than ever.'

'I don't much like the look of her,' said Anne, going thankfully into the first of the butterfly houses. 'Oh – what a lot of butterflies!'

There certainly were! Hundreds were flying about loose, and many others were in little compartments either by themselves or with another butterfly to match.

The children saw that many bushes and plants were growing in the glasshouse, and on some of them were placed long sleeves made of muslin, tied in at each end.

'What's in these long sleeves of fine muslin?' asked Dick. 'Oh – I see. They are full of caterpillars! My word, how they are eating, too!'

'Yes. I told you we breed butterflies and moths,' said Mr Gringle, and he opened the end of one of the muslin bags, so that the visitors could see the caterpillars better. 'These are the caterpillars of one kind of butterfly; they feed on this particular plant.'

The children gazed at scores of green caterpillars, marked with red and yellow spots, all eating greedily on the leaves of the twig enclosed there. Mr Gringle undid another of the muslin bags and showed them some huge caterpillars, each of them green, with purple stripes on the side and a curious black horn on the tail end.

'Privet-Hawk moth caterpillars,' said Mr Gringle, and Julian and Dick nodded. They knew these big green caterpillars quite well.

'Why is the moth called Privet-*Hawk*?' asked Anne. 'There are so many different Hawk moths, I know. I've often wondered why they are all called *Hawk*.'

Mr Gringle beamed at Anne, evidently thinking that this was a quite intelligent question. 'Haven't you ever seen a Hawk moth flying?' he said. 'No? Well, it flies very strongly indeed. Oh, a most striking flight – like the flight of the *bird* called a hawk, you know.'

'You're not feeding the caterpillars on privet, though,' said George. 'But you *said* they were Privete Hawks.'

'There isn't any privet growing near here,' said Mr Gringle. 'So I give them elder – this is an elder bush which I planted in the glasshouse. They like it just as much.'

The butterfly farm was certainly interesting, and the children wandered about the glasshouse watching caterpillars of all kinds, admiring the lovely specimens of butterflies, and marvelling at the collection of curious-shaped chrysalides and cocoons that Mr Gringle kept carefully in boxes, waiting for the perfect insect, moth or butterfly, to emerge.

'Like magic,' he said in an awed voice, his eyes shining behind his glasses. 'Sometimes, you know, I feel like a magician myself – and my butterfly net is a wand!'

The children felt rather uncomfortable as he said this, waving his butterfly net to and fro like a wand. He really was rather an odd person.

'It's terribly hot in here,' said Julian suddenly. 'Let's get into the fresh air. I've had enough. Goodbye, Mr Gringle, and thank you!'

Out they all went and drew in deep breaths of fresh air. And then they heard a croaking voice behind them.

'Get out of here!' said the voice. 'Get out!'

CHAPTER SEVEN

Mrs Janes – a spider – and a pool

TIMMY GROWLED, and so did Binky. The children swung round and saw the old witch-like woman standing there, her wispy grey hair hanging over her face.

'What's the matter, Mrs – er – Mrs Janes?' said Julian, fortunately remembering the name Mr Gringle had told them. 'We're not doing any harm.'

'My son doesn't like strangers here,' said Mrs Janes, mumbling so much that the children could hardly understand what she was saying.

'But this place belongs to Mr Gringle surely, and his friend,' said Dick, puzzled.

'I tell you my son doesn't like strangers here,' mumbled the old woman again and shook her fist at them.

Timmy didn't like this, and growled. She at once pointed her finger at him and muttered a long string of strange-sounding words so that Anne shrank back, afraid. Really, Mrs Janes did look exactly like a witch – and sounded like one, too.

Timmy acted strangely. He put his tail down, stopped growling and crept close to George. She was most astonished.

'It looks as if she's trying to put a spell on old Tim,' said Dick, half laughing, but that was too much for Anne and George.

Taking Timmy by the collar, George rushed off quickly with Anne following. The boys laughed. Binky ran after Timmy, and Toby spoke boldly to the funny old woman.

'Your son isn't even here – so what business is it of his to tell you to give orders to visitors?'

Tears suddenly began to pour down the old woman's face and she wrung her bony hands together. 'He'll hit me,' she wept. 'He'll twist my arm! Go away! Do go away! If he comes, he'll chase you off. He's a bad man, my son!'

'She's mad, poor old thing,' said Toby, feeling sorry for old Mrs Janes. 'Our cook often says so, though she's harmless enough. Her son's not too bad – he's quite handy at repairs, and we used to have him come to the farm to mend roofs and things like that. But he's not so good as he used to be. Come on – let's go. Mr Gringle's a bit peculiar, too, isn't he?'

They went off after the two girls, Toby still feeling uncomfortable and distressed.

'What's Mr Gringle's friend like – the one who helps him?' Julian asked.

'I don't know. I've never seen him,' said Toby. 'He's away mostly, doing the business side, I think – selling specimens of eggs, caterpillars and so on – and the perfect moths and butterflies too, of course.'

'I'd like to see that butterfly house again, but Mr Gringle gets on my nerves,' said Dick. 'Those brilliant eyes behind those thick glasses. You'd think that if they were as bright and piercing as that he wouldn't need to wear any glasses at all!'

'Hey, George – Anne!' shouted Julian. 'Wait for us – we're just coming.' They caught up with the girls and Julian grinned at George.

390

'You thought old Timmy was going to be changed into a black beetle or something, didn't you?' he said.

'No, of course not,' said George, going red. 'I just didn't like her very much – pointing her finger like that at Timmy. No wonder he growled.'

'You didn't hear what she said about her son,' said Dick. 'She began to cry like anything after you'd gone, and say that her son would beat her and twist her arm if we didn't go – and he's not even there!'

391

'She's mad,' said George. 'I don't want to go there again. What are we going to do now?'

'Go up to our camping place and have our lunch,' said Julian promptly. 'Come with us, Toby – or have you got jobs to do at the farm?'

'No. I've done them all,' said Toby. 'I'd love to have a meal with you up on the hill.'

It wasn't very long before they were back at their camping place. Everything was as they had left it – anoraks neatly under the gorse bush with the rugs and other little things – and the food in Anne's 'larder' waiting for them.

The meal was very hilarious, as Toby was in one of his silly moods, and produced some idiotic jokes. The most successful one was a large imitation spider with shaky legs, which, while Anne and George had gone to get the food, he hung by a thin nylon thread to a spray on the nearby gorse bush. Dick grinned broadly.

'Wait till Anne sees that!' he said. 'George always says *she* doesn't mind spiders, but a big one like that is distinctly creepy.'

It certainly was. Anne didn't spot it until she was eating her strawberries, covered with some of the cream that Toby's mother had generously sent. Then she suddenly spied it, shaking slightly in the breeze, hanging by its thread just over George's head.

'Ooooooooh!' she squealed. 'Ooooh, George – be careful! There's a MONSTER spider just over your head!'

'What – is George scared of spiders?' cried Toby at once. 'Just like a girl!'

George glared at him. 'I don't mind them at all,' she said coldly.

'*George* – do move!' cried Anne, upsetting her strawberries in her anxiety. 'It's almost on your head, I tell you
– its legs are wobbling as if they are going to settle on your
hair. George, it's an ENORMOUS one! It might even be
one of those foreign things – a tarantula or something!'

The wind blew a little just then and the spider moved
about on the thread most realistically. Even Dick was glad
it wasn't alive!

George couldn't resist looking up, pretending to be quite
unmoved – but when she saw the enormous creature just
above her she shot straight out of her place and landed on
Toby's legs, making him spill his strawberries and cream.

'Now, now, Georgina,' said the annoying Toby, picking
up his strawberries. 'You said you didn't *mind* spiders. I'll
remove it for you, and you can go back to your place.'

'No, no – don't touch it – ugh!' cried Anne. But Toby,
putting on a very brave face, leaned over and neatly took
the spider off the gorse bush, still swinging by its thread.
He swung it near to Anne, who scrambled up at once.

Then he made it 'walk' over Dick's knee, and Timmy
came to investigate at once. Binky came too, and snapped
at it, breaking the nylon thread that held it.

'Ass!' said Toby, giving him a smack. 'My beautiful
spider – my spinner of webs – my tame catcher of flies!'

'What – is it a *tame* one?' said Anne in horror.

'More or less,' said Toby, and put it carefully into his
pocket, grinning all over his round face.

'That's enough, Toby,' said Julian. 'Joke's finished.'

George stared at Toby, her face growing crimson. 'A
joke? A JOKE! You wait till I pay you back, Toby! I don't
call that a joke . . . I call it a mean trick. You knew Anne
hated spiders.'

'Let's change the subject,' said Dick hastily. 'What are we going to do this afternoon?'

'I know what I'd *like* to do,' said Julian longingly. 'I'd like a bathe. It's so jolly hot. If we were at Kirrin I'd be in the sea all the afternoon.'

'I wish we *were* at Kirrin,' said George sulkily.

'Well – if you really do want a bathe, I can take you to a pool,' said Toby, anxious to get into everyone's good books again.

'A pool? Where?' said Dick eagerly.

'Well – see that airfield down there?' said Toby pointing. 'And see this spring here, where you get your water? It goes on and on running down the hill, joins two or three more little rivulets, and ends in a smashing pool not far from the airfield. Cold as ice it is, too. I've often bathed there.'

'It sounds jolly good,' said Julian, pleased. 'Well, we can't bathe immediately after a meal. We'll do the washing-up, and put the rest of the food away. Then we'll sit here and have a bit of a rest, and then go and find this pool.'

Everyone agreed to this and they all set to work. The girls hurried off to the little spring.

'If Toby has any more idiotic tricks like that I'll play a few on *him*!' said George. 'In fact I've a good mind to pull him under in the pool.'

'He's all right, George,' said Anne. 'He's just like that at school, Dick says. He must drive the masters mad!'

They soon joined the boys and had a short rest, while Timmy and Binky went off amiably together to do a little hunting – sniffing down holes and under bushes, looking very serious indeed. They came back immediately George whistled.

'We're going, Timmy,' said George. 'Here's your swimsuit, Dick, and yours, Julian. Good thing we brought them with us!'

'What about you, Toby? You haven't a swimsuit with you,' said Julian.

'We have to pass fairly near the farm,' said Toby. 'I'll leave you when we're near there and get mine – it won't take more than five minutes if I run all the way back.'

They set off down the hill towards the airfield. Except for the plane they had heard that morning, they had heard and seen none. It seemed a very quiet airfield.

'Wait till they start experimenting with the new fighter planes my cousin told me about!' said Toby. 'You'll hear a noise then – they're so fast they break the sound barrier every time they go up!'

'Would your cousin let us look over the airfield one day?' asked Julian. 'I'd like to do that. Look – isn't that your farm, Toby? We've got here jolly quickly – but it's all downhill, of course.'

'Yes,' said Toby. 'Come on, Binky – race you home and back. Shan't be long, Julian! Keep straight ahead and walk towards that big pine tree you can see in the distance. I'll be with you by the time you're there.'

He raced off at top speed, while the others went on slowly towards the pine trees in the distance. It would be heavenly to bathe in a cool pool!

Toby was certainly a fast runner! Just before they reached the pine tree he came up behind them, his swimsuit over his shoulder, so out of breath that he could hardly speak!

'It's over there,' he panted. 'Look – the pool!'

And sure enough, there was the pool – deep blue, cool and as smooth as glass. Trees surrounded it on one side, and heather grew right down to the edge.

The five children went towards it gladly – but suddenly they came to a big notice, nailed to a tree:

KEEP OUT

DANGER

CROWN PROPERTY

'I say – what does *that* mean?' said Dick in dismay. 'We can't bathe after all!'

'Oh, take no notice of that,' said Toby. 'It doesn't mean a thing!'

But it did as they were very soon to find out!

CHAPTER EIGHT

A spot of trouble

'WHAT DO you mean by saying that the notice doesn't mean a thing?' said Julian. 'Why put it up, then?'

'Oh, there are notices like that all round the airfield,' said Toby airily. 'Telling you to KEEP OUT, there's DANGER. But there isn't. Only aeroplanes are here, no guns, no bombs, nothing. It's a jolly lonely place, too, tucked away at the foot of this hill.'

'Why don't you ask your cousin *why* they put up the notices?' asked Dick. 'There must be *some* reason!'

'I tell you those notices have been up for ages,' said Toby, sounding cross. 'Ages! They might have been some use at some time or other, but not now. We can bathe here and do what we like.'

'All right – but I hope you know what you're talking about,' said Julian. 'I must say I can't see any sense myself in putting notices here – there's no wire or fencing to keep anyone out.'

'Let's get into our bathing things, then,' said Dick. 'You girls can have that bush over there and we'll have this one. Buck up!'

They were soon changed into their swimsuits, and dived into the pool, which was surprisingly deep. It was also deliciously cool, and silky to the touch, just as the spring water had been. The two dogs leapt in gladly and swam vigorously round and round. The children splashed them, and Timmy began to bark excitedly.

397

'Shut up, Timmy!' said Toby at once.

'Why should he?' demanded George, swimming up.

'Well – someone at the airfield might hear him,' said Toby.

'You said it didn't matter us being here!' said George. 'Look out for yourself!' She dived underwater and got hold of Toby's legs, pulling him down. He yelled and kicked and spluttered, but George was strong and she gave him a very, very good ducking! He came up purple in the face.

'I said I'd pay you back for the spider!' yelled George, and swam strongly away. Toby swam after her, and she led him a fine dance round the pool, for she was a splendid swimmer. The others laughed at the contest.

'I back old George,' said Dick. 'She'd outswim most boys. Well, she's put Toby in his place all right. He won't be so free with spiders and silly jokes for a while!'

Timmy began to bark again when he saw Toby chasing George, and Binky joined in.

'Shut up, Binky!' shouted Toby, 'I tell you *stop barking*!'

Before Binky had obeyed, something happened. A very loud voice came across the pool.

'What's all this! You're trespassing on Crown property. Didn't you see the notice?'

The dogs stopped barking and the five children looked round to see who was shouting. Their heads bobbed on the surface of the water as they gazed about to find the shouter.

It was a man in Air Force uniform, a big man, burly and red-faced.

'What's the matter?' called Julian, swimming towards him. 'We're only bathing. We're not doing any harm.'

'Didn't you see the notice?' shouted the man, pointing over to it.

'Yes. But we couldn't see much danger here,' called back Julian, wishing now that he hadn't believed Toby.

'You come on out!' roared the man. 'All of you. Come on.'

They all waded out of the cool pond, Anne feeling scared. The dogs splashed out, too, and stood eyeing the man grimly. He calmed down a little when he saw them.

'Those your dogs I heard barking? Well, now, I see you're all kids – though one of you's big enough to know better!' and he pointed to Julian. 'I thought maybe you were trippers – thinking you could come wandering on the airfield and not get into trouble!'

'Trippers don't come here,' said Toby, squeezing the water out of his hair.

'Nor do sensible children,' retorted the man. 'I've had trouble from you before, haven't I? Yes. Didn't you come walking round the hangars bold as brass one day? And that dog with you, too?'

'I only went to see my cousin, Flight-Lieutenant Thomas,' said Toby. 'I wasn't doing any harm – I wasn't spying. I tell you I only went to see my cousin!'

'Well, I shall report you to him,' said the man, 'and tell him to give you a proper ticking off. We've strict instructions to warn off anyone – there's notices everywhere.'

'Is something hush-hush going on then?' said Toby with a sudden grin.

'As if I'd tell you if there was!' said the man in disgust. 'Far as I can see, there's nothing much doing here – dull as ditch-water this place – and as far as I'm concerned I'd welcome a *horde* of trippers – it would liven up the place no end. But orders are orders, as you very well know.'

Julian thought it was about time that he should join in. The man was only doing his duty, and Toby was an ass to have said that the notices meant nothing.

'Well, we apologise for trespassing,' he said in his clear, pleasant voice. 'We shan't bathe here again, I promise you. Sorry to have made you come all this way to warn us off.'

The RAF guard looked at Julian with respect.

There was something about the boy that reassured people, and the man now felt quite sure that it was all Toby's fault. He smiled.

'That's all right,' he said. 'Sorry to cut your bathe short this hot day. And – er-if that rogue of a boy here' – he pointed to Toby – 'if he cares to ask Flight-Lieutenant Thomas for permission to bathe in this pool at certain hours, it's okay by me. I shan't come running then when I hear dogs barking and a lot of shouting if I know you're allowed here at certain hours.'

'Thanks,' said Julian. 'But anyway we're only here for a few days.'

'So long,' said the man and walked off smartly.

'Well,' said Toby, quite unashamed, 'what did he want to come messing about here for, spoiling our bathe? He *said* there wasn't anything secret going on, so why . . .'

'Oh shut up!' said Dick. 'You heard what he said about orders being orders? He's not a silly schoolboy trying to be clever and getting out of doing his work – yes, like *you* do at school, Toby, and a good many of the others! He's a man in uniform. You'd better grow up a bit, young Toby.'

'I agree,' said Julian. 'So don't let's hear any more about it. You slipped up, Toby, and that's all there is to it. Now let's dry ourselves and go to the farm and ask your nice kind mother if she'll let us have some more food to take back to our camp with us. I'm as hungry as a hunter after our bathe.'

Toby was rather subdued after all this. He glanced at George to see if she was gloating over his ticking off, but

George was never one to exult over anyone's downfall, and Toby felt relieved.

'*Shall* I ask my cousin if he'll get permission for us to bathe in the pool?' he said as they went away from the water, dry and dressed again.

'I think not,' said Julian. 'But I'd like to meet your cousin some time all the same.'

'He *might* take us up in a plane,' said Toby hopefully, his spirits rising at the thought. 'Oh, look there – here's that little wretch Benny again – *and* the pigling!'

Benny panted up, carrying the little pig. 'You look like Tom, Tom the Piper's Son,' said Julian, ruffling the yellow curls. 'He stole a pig and ran away, carrying it under his arm.'

'But this is my own pig,' said Benny, surprised. 'I didn't steal him. I came to find you, because my mother says come to tea.'

'You *have* got a nice mother!' said Anne, taking the small boy's hand. 'Why don't you put the pig down? He must be so heavy.'

'He runned away again,' said Benny severely. 'So I carried him.'

'Put a collar on his neck, with a lead,' suggested Dick.

'He hasn't got a neck,' said Benny, and indeed the pigling was so plump that his head joined his body without any neck at all.

The little procession made its way to the farm, and the pigling at once ran in front, squealing. It seemed surprised and delighted to find it was home again. Timmy pricked up his ears when it squealed. He thought that it must be in pain, and he was worried! He ran beside the little creature, trying to nuzzle it.

402

Mrs Thomas saw them through the window. 'Come along in!' she said. 'I thought you might like to have tea here again today, because I've a visitor you'd like to meet!'

'Who is it?' cried Toby, running indoors. 'Oh! it's you, Cousin Jeff. Hey, Julian, Dick – look, it's my Cousin Jeff from the airfield – Flight-Lieutenant Thomas! The one I told you about! Cousin Jeff, meet my friends – Julian, Dick, Anne, Georgina – er, I mean George – and Timmy!'

A tall, good-looking young man stood up, smiling. The Five gazed at him, liking him very much indeed. They all envied Toby at that moment. No wonder he had boasted about him so much!

'Hallo to you!' said Cousin Jeff. 'Glad to see you all. 'Hey – look at this dog!'

And well might everyone look, for Timmy had marched straight up to him and then held up a paw. 'Wuff!' he said, which, of course, meant 'Shake'!

'How do you do?' said Cousin Jeff solemnly, and shook paws with Timmy at once.

'Timmy's *never* done that before!' said George, astonished. 'Well – what a surprising thing! He must like you *very* much!'

CHAPTER NINE

Cousin Jeff

'I LIKE dogs,' said Jeff, and patted Timmy on the head. 'This is a fine one – as smart as can be, too, isn't he?'

George nodded, pleased. She loved anyone to praise Timmy. 'Yes, he's very clever. He's been in heaps of adventures with us. He can be very fierce if he thinks anyone is going to attack us. Oh, look – he wants to shake hands *again*! Isn't he funny!'

Jeff shook paws once more and then Timmy settled down beside him, almost as if he considered himself to be his dog. George didn't mind. She liked Cousin Jeff as much as Timmy did!

'Tell us about your job,' begged Dick. 'It's such a strange airfield, the one you're at – no fencing round it, hardly any planes, nobody about the field! Do you do much flying?'

'Not much at the moment,' said Cousin Jeff. 'But don't be misled by the fact that there's no fencing round the airfield! Believe me, the commanding officer knows immediately if any stranger comes into the district, and – er – well, let us say that extra precautions are taken.'

'*Really?*' said George. 'Do you mean to say, for instance, that your commanding officer knows *we've* arrived?'

'You bet he does,' said Jeff, laughing. 'You've probably been given the once-over already, though you didn't know it. I expect someone has been detailed to find out who you are and why you're here, and you may even have been watched for a few hours – though you had no idea of it.'

This was rather a creepy thought. Watched? How? By whom? And where did they hide to watch? Dick asked Jeff these questions, but the young airman shook his head.

'Sorry. Can't answer,' he said. 'But you needn't worry, *you're* all right. Maybe my aunt here has said a few words about you – you never know!'

Mrs Thomas smiled, but said nothing. She beckoned to Anne and George to help her to bring in the tea – just as good a one as they had had before. The girls bustled about, setting out cups and saucers, while the boys talked to Cousin Jeff and asked him eager questions about planes and flying and how this was done and that.

'I suppose you wouldn't take us up some time, Cousin Jeff, would you?' asked Toby at last.

'I don't think I'd be allowed to,' said Jeff. 'In fact I don't think I can even ask. You see, the planes there are pretty special – you can't go joy-riding in them and . . .'

'Of course we see,' said Julian hurriedly, afraid of embarrassing the friendly young airman. 'We wouldn't *dream* of bothering you. When are you going up next? Can we watch you from our camping place?'

'Yes, I should think you could see me with fieldglasses,' said Jeff, considering. 'I'll tell you the number of my plane – it's painted underneath it, of course, so you'll know it's me if you see it circling over the hill. But I shan't do any stunts, I'm afraid – like coming down low to you, or anything like that. Only silly beginners do that.'

'We'll look out for you,' said Dick, quite envious of Toby for having such a fine young cousin. 'I don't expect you'll see us – but we'll wave anyway!'

Tea was now ready and they all drew up their chairs. Benny wandered in with his pigling under his arm, and set it down in the cat's basket, where it stayed quite peacefully, falling asleep and making tiny, grunting snores.

'Does the cat mind?' asked George, astonished, looking at the basket.

'Not a bit,' said Mrs Thomas. 'It had to put up with two goslings last year in its basket – and something the year before . . .'

'A lamb,' said Toby.

'Oh yes – and old Tinky – that's the cat – didn't seem to worry at all,' said Mrs Thomas, pouring out creamy milk for everyone, even Cousin Jeff. 'I once found her curled up round the goslings one morning, purring loudly.'

'Good old Tinky!' said Toby. 'Where is she? I'd like to see what she thinks of Curly. She couldn't cuddle *him* – he takes up nearly all the basket, he's so plump.'

Tea was a merry meal, with Toby playing the fool, putting a spoonful of sifted sugar on the side of Anne's plate to eat with her crisp radishes instead of salt, and offering the salt to George to eat with her strawberries.

Both girls were listening so intently to Cousin Jeff that they didn't even notice what Toby had done, and he almost fell off his chair with laughing when he saw their faces. Salt with strawberries – ugh! Sugar and radishes – ugh!

'Funny boy, aren't you?' said George, annoyed at being tricked. 'You wait!' But Toby was too wily to be tricked and George had to give it up. Anyway, she couldn't bother with Toby when Cousin Jeff was talking about planes, his eyes shining with pleasure. Flying was his great love, and in listening to him all three boys there made up their minds to take it up as soon as ever they could!

Benny didn't listen much. He was more interested in animals than in planes. He ate his tea solemnly and watched his pigling in the cat's basket, occasionally leaning over to tap his mother's hand when he wanted to speak to her.

'Curly runned away again,' he told her solemnly. 'Right up to the horse-pond.'

'I thought I had told you not to go there,' said his mother. 'You fell in last time.'

'But Curly *runned* there,' said Benny, his big eyes looking very wide and innocent. 'I had to go after him, didn't I? He's my pigling.'

'Well, I shall spank Curly if he takes you to places you've been told not to go to,' said his mother. 'I can't let him grow up disobedient, can I?'

This needed thinking over, and Benny ate his tea with a serious face, ignoring the others. Anne looked at him several times, delighted with the solemn little boy and his funny ways. How nice it would be to have a small brother like that!

'Well, I must be off,' said Jeff when the meal was finished. 'Thanks most awfully for a super tea, Aunt Sarah – but then your teas always *are* super! I was jolly lucky to be stationed here so near to Billycock Farm! Well, so long, everyone! So long, Timmy!'

Everyone went with him to the gate, Timmy and Binky as well, and Benny awoke his little pig and carried him to the gate too, squealing and kicking. They all watched the tall, sturdy young airman striding away round the hill.

'Do you like him?' asked Toby proudly. 'Isn't he super? I'm awfully proud of him. He's supposed to be one of the cleverest flying men in the kingdom – did you know?'

'No, we didn't,' said Dick. 'But I'm not surprised. He's got eyes as keen as a hawk's, and he's heart and soul in his work! How lucky for you that he is stationed so near!'

'We'd better get back to our camp when we've helped your mother to clear away and wash-up,' said Julian, anxious not to outstay his welcome at the farm. 'Toby, can you pack us up a bit more food in case we don't see you tomorrow?'

'Right,' said Toby, and went off, whistling.

Benny appeared again with Curly running round his feet.

'Hallo!' said Dick with a grin. 'Is that pigling of yours running away again?'

Benny grinned back. 'If he runned away to your camp, would you be cross?' he asked, looking most innocently up at Dick.

'He mustn't do that,' said Dick seriously, guessing what was in the little boy's mind; he meant to go to find the camp himself, and then say that it was Curly who had 'runned away' there! 'You see, you might lose your way if you went so far.'

Benny said no more, but wandered off with his comical pet running in front of him. The boys went to find Toby to see if they could help him to pack food into a basket. 'We must pay his bill, too,' said Julian, feeling for his purse. 'It was a good idea of his to save up the money to buy his mother a present. She really is a darling.'

Soon the Five were on their way back to their camp again. Toby was left behind to do his usual jobs of collecting the eggs, washing them and grading them into sizes for the market. 'I'll be up tomorrow!' he called after them. 'We'll plan something good to do – maybe visit the caves if you like!'

The four children went up the steep slope of Billycock Hill, talking, while Timmy ranged in front, sniffing everywhere as usual. And then suddenly a large butterfly sailed through the air, and came to rest on a flower of a blossoming elder bush, just in front of George – a butterfly that none of them had ever seen before.

'Look at that! What is it?' cried Anne in delight. 'Oh, what a beauty! Julian, what is it?'

'I've absolutely no idea!' said Julian, astonished. 'It may be an unusual Fritillary, though it's early in the year for those. That butterfly man – what's his name now? – Mr Gringle – said that this hill was famous for rare butterflies, and I imagine this is pretty uncommon. It *is* a beauty, isn't it?'

They watched the butterfly opening and shutting its magnificent wings on the white blossom. 'We ought to try and catch it,' said Dick. 'I'm sure that Mr Gringle would be thrilled. It might lay eggs for him and start a whole breed of uncommon butterflies in this country.'

'I've got a very thin hanky,' said Anne. 'I think I can catch it without harming its wings – and we'll put it into the little box that Toby filled with sugar lumps for us. Get it and empty it, Dick.'

In half a minute the butterfly was inside the box, quite unharmed, for Anne had been very deft in catching it.

'What a magnificent creature!' said Dick, shutting the box. 'Now come on – we'll give Mr Gringle a surprise!'

'What about that witch woman – you know, Mrs Janes, who looks exactly like a witch?' said Anne. 'I don't want to meet her again.'

'I'll tell her to jump on her broomstick and fly away!' said Julian with a laugh. 'Don't be silly, Anne – she can't hurt you.'

They went off round the hill, taking the little path down which Mr Gringle had guided them. Soon they saw the reflection of the sun glittering on the glasshouses. Anne and George hesitated as they came near, and Timmy stopped, too, his tail down.

'Well, stay there, then,' said Dick impatiently. 'Ju and I won't be long!' And off went the two boys together, while George and Anne waited in the distance.

'I hope they *won't* be long!' said Anne, worried. 'I don't know *why* I feel creepy here, but I do!'

CHAPTER TEN

Butterfly farm again

DICK AND Julian went to the glasshouses where the butterflies and caterpillars lived. They peered through the panes, but could see nobody there.

'Mr Gringle must be in the cottage,' said Julian. 'Let's stand outside and call – he'll come out then. I don't much like Mrs Janes.'

So they stood outside the tumbledown cottage and shouted: 'Mr Gringle! Mr Gringle!'

Nobody answered. No Mr Gringle came out, but somebody pulled aside the corner of a window curtain upstairs and peeped out. The boys shouted again, waving at the window.

'Mr Gringle! We've got a rare butterfly for you!'

The window opened and old Mrs Janes looked out, seeming more witch-like than ever.

'Mr Gringle's away!' she mumbled.

'What about his friend Mr Brent – the one we didn't see?' shouted Dick. 'Is he in?'

The old woman stared at them, mumbled something else, and then disappeared very suddenly indeed from the window.

Dick looked at Julian in surprise.

'Why did she go so suddenly? Almost as if somebody pulled her roughly away? Julian, I don't like it.'

'Why? Do you think that son of hers is here – the one she said was cruel to her?' asked Julian, who was puzzled, too.

'I don't know,' said Dick. 'Let's snoop round a bit. Perhaps Mr Gringle *is* somewhere about, whatever old Mrs Janes says!'

They went round the corner of the house and peered into a shed. Nobody there. Then they heard footsteps and turned round hurriedly. A man was coming towards them, small and thin, with a pinched-looking face, and dark glasses. He carried a butterfly net, and nodded at the two boys.

'My friend Gringle is away,' he said. 'Can I do anything for you?'

'Oh – you're Mr Brent then?' said Dick. 'Look – we've found a rare butterfly. That's why we came!'

He undid the box in which the butterfly was peacefully resting, having found a tiny grain of sugar to feed on. Mr Brent looked at it through his dark glasses.

'Hm! Hm!' he said, peering closely at it. 'Yes, very fine indeed. I'll buy it off you for fifty pence.'

'Oh, you can have it for nothing,' said Dick. 'What is it?'

'Can't say without examining it closely,' said Mr Brent, and took the box and put the lid on again.

'But isn't it some kind of Fritillary?' asked Julian. 'We thought it was.'

'Quite likely,' said Mr Brent, and suddenly produced a fifty pence piece and shoved it at Dick. 'Here you are. Much obliged. I'll tell Mr Gringle you came.'

He turned abruptly and went off, his butterfly net still over his shoulder.

Dick stared at the fifty pence piece in his hand, then at the receding back of Mr Brent.

'What a peculiar fellow!' he said. 'Well, I must say that he and Mr Gringle are a pair! What are we to do with this money, Julian? I don't want it!'

'Let's see if we can give it to that poor Mrs Janes,' said Julian, always generous. 'She looks as if they paid her only about ten pence a week, poor soul.'

They went round to the front of the house, hoping to find the old woman, and after a little hesitation knocked at the door. It opened and she stood there, mumbling as before.

'You go away! My son's coming back. He'll hit me. He doesn't like strangers. You go away, I say!'

'All right,' said Dick. 'Look – here's something for you,' and he pressed the fifty pence into her clawlike hand. She looked at it as if she couldn't believe her eyes, and then, amazingly quickly she slipped the money into one of her broken-down shoes. When she stood up her eyes were full of tears.

'You're kind,' she whispered, and gave them a little

push. 'Yes, you're kind. Keep away from here. My son's a bad man. Keep away!'

The boys went off silently, not knowing what to make of it. After all, Toby knew the son – they had employed him at the farm. Why did the old woman keep saying he was bad and cruel? She must be at least a little mad to talk like that!

'It must be a strange household,' said Julian as they went to join the waiting girls. 'Two butterfly men, both rather peculiar. One old witch-like woman, *very* peculiar. And a son who seems to terrify her out of her wits! I vote we don't go there again.'

'So do I,' said Dick. 'Hallo, you two – did we keep you waiting for long?'

'You did rather,' said Anne. 'We were just about to send Timmy to look for you! We thought you might have been turned into mice, or something!'

The boys told the two girls about Mr Brent and the fifty pence and old Mrs Janes. 'A funny household alto-gether,' said Dick. 'We think we'll give it a miss now, however many rare butterflies we spot! I'm pretty certain that the one we found was a kind of Fritillary, aren't you, Julian?'

'Yes, I was surprised Mr Brent didn't say so,' said Julian. 'I have a feeling that Mr Gringle is the expert of the two. Mr Brent probably does the donkey-work – sees to the caterpillars and so on.'

They came to their camp at last, and Timmy at once went to the 'larder'. But Anne shook her head. 'No, Tim – it's not nearly supper-time. Bad luck!'

'What shall we do?' asked Dick, flinging himself down on the heather. 'It's another heavenly evening!'

'Yes – but I don't much like the look of the sky over to the west tonight,' said Julian. 'See those clouds there coming up slowly against the wind? It looks like rain tomorrow to me!'

'Blow!' said George. 'The weather might have lasted for just one week! Whatever shall we do if it pours? Sit in our tents all day, I suppose!'

'Cheer up – we could go and see the caves,' said Dick. 'I know what we'll do now! We'll get out our portable radio and turn it on. If there's some decent music, it will sound glorious up here!'

'All right. But for goodness sake have it on softly,' said Anne. 'I *loathe* people who take radios out into the country with them, and switch them on loudly, so that it spoils the peace and quiet for everyone else. I could go and kick their radios to pieces!'

'Gracious, Anne – you do sound fierce!' said George, looking at her cousin in surprise.

'You don't know our quiet sister Anne quite as well as we do, George,' said Julian, with a twinkle in his eyes. 'She can be really fierce if she thinks anyone is spoiling things for others. I had to stop her once from going up to scold people at a picnic – they actually had a gramophone going full-pelt, in spite of the angry looks from people all round. I do believe she meant to take off the gramophone record and break it over somebody's head!'

'Oh, *Julian*! How can you say such a thing!' said Anne. 'I did feel like it – but I didn't do it.'

'All right, young Anne!' said Julian affectionately and patted her head. Both he and Dick thought the world of their quiet, kind little sister and looked after her well. She smiled at them.

417

'Well – let's have some music, then,' she said. 'There's the Pastoral Symphony on sometime this evening, I know, because I made a note of it. It would sound beautiful out here in this lovely countryside with that view spreading for miles in front of us. But softly, *please*.'

Julian fetched the little radio set and took it out of its waterproof case. He switched on, and a voice came loudly from the set. Julian lowered the volume to make it softer. 'It's the seven o'clock news,' he said. 'We'll hear it, shall we?'

But it was almost the end of the news, and the voice soon stopped to give way to an announcer. Yes – it was going to be the Pastoral Symphony now. Soon the first notes came softly from the little radio, and it seemed to set the countryside around to music. The four settled down in the heather to listen, lying half-propped up to watch the changing colours of the view in front of them as the sun sank lower.

The bank of cloud on the horizon was higher now, and the sun would soon slip behind it, for it was coming up fast. What a pity!

And then, cutting across the music, came another sound – the sound of an aeroplane.

R-r-r-r-r-r-r! R-r-r-r-r-r-r! R-r-r-r-r-r-r!

It sounded so very loud that Dick and Julian leapt to their feet, and Timmy began to bark loudly.

'Where is it?' said Dick, puzzled. 'It sounds so jolly near. I wonder if it's Cousin Jeff's!'

'There it is – coming up over the back of the hill!' said Julian, and as he spoke a small aeroplane appeared over the brow of the hill, and circled once before it flew down to the airfield.

BUTTERFLY FARM AGAIN

The four children could plainly see the number painted underneath. '5–6–9,' began Julian, and Dick gave a shout.

'It's Jeff's plane! It is – that's his number! Wave, everybody, wave!'

So they all waved madly, though they felt sure that Jeff wouldn't see them, tucked away in their camp on the hillside. They watched the plane fly down to the airfield, circle round, and land neatly on the runway. It came to a stop.

Julian looked through his glasses and saw a small figure leap from the plane. 'I bet it's Jeff,' he said. 'Gosh – I do wish *I* had a plane to fly over the hills and far away!'

CHAPTER ELEVEN

A stormy night

THE FIVE soon began to prepare for their evening meal and Timmy trotted about pretending to help, always hopeful of being allowed to carry a loaf of bread or piece of cold ham in his mouth. But he was never lucky!

As they sat eating their meal, Julian glanced uneasily at the western sky again. 'The rain's certainly coming,' he said. 'That cloud has covered half the sky now, and swallowed up the evening sun. I think we ought to put up the tents.'

'Blow! I suppose we ought,' said George.

'*And* we'd better do it quickly,' said Dick. 'I distinctly felt a nasty cold wind just then – the first really cold air since we came here. We shall certainly want to roll up in our rugs tonight!'

'Well, let's get the things out from under the old gorse bush,' said Julian. 'It won't take long to put up the tents if we all get to work.'

In three-quarters of an hour the tents were up, set nicely in the shelter of the giant gorse bush. 'A good, business-like job,' said Dick, pleased. 'It would take a hurricane to blow the tents away – we'll be quite all right here. Let's pull up some more heather and pile it in the tents. We shall want our rugs to wrap ourselves in, not to lie on tonight, so we might as well make our beds as soft as possible.'

They piled heather into the tents, spread their anoraks there, too, and then looked at the sky. Yes, there was no

420

doubt about it – there was rain coming and probably a storm! Still, it might clear tomorrow, and be as fine as ever. If it wasn't they would go and explore the caves that Toby had told them about.

It was now almost dark and the children decided that they would all get into one tent and have the radio on again. They called Timmy, but he preferred to be outside.

They set the radio going – but almost immediately Timmy began to bark. George switched off at once.

'That's the bark he gives when somebody is coming,' she said. 'I wonder who it is?'

'Toby, to say we'd better go to the farm for the night,' guessed Dick.

'Mr Gringle hunting for moths!' said Anne with a giggle.

'Old Mrs Janes looking for things to make spells with!' said George.

Everyone laughed. 'Idiot!' said Dick. 'Though I must say this looks a night for witches!'

Timmy went on barking, and Julian put his head out of the tent. 'What's up, Tim?' he said. 'Who's coming?'

'Wuff, wuff,' said Timmy, not turning his head to Julian, but seeming to watch something or someone in the half-light.

'It may be a hedgehog he's seen,' said George from inside the tent. 'He always barks at them because he knows he can't pick them up.'

'Well – maybe you're right,' said Julian. 'But I think I'll just go out and get Timmy to take me to whatever it is he's barking at. I feel I'd like to know. He obviously hears or sees something!'

He slid out of the tent opening and went to Timmy.

'Come on, Tim,' he said. 'Who is it? What's upsetting you?'

Timmy wagged his tail and ran in front of Julian. He obviously had no doubts about where he was going. Julian followed him, stumbling over the heather and wishing he had brought his torch, for it was now half-dark.

Timmy ran some way down the hill towards the airfield, then rounded a clump of birch trees and stopped. He barked loudly again. Julian saw a dark shadow moving there and called out.

'Who's there? Who is it?'

'It's only me – Mr Brent,' said an annoyed voice, and Julian caught sight of a long stick with a shadowy net on the end. 'I've come out to examine our honey-traps before the rain comes and washes away the moths feeding there.'

'Oh,' said Julian. 'I might have thought of that when Timmy barked. Is Mr Gringle about, too?'

'Yes – so if your dog barks again you'll know it's only us,' said Mr Brent. 'We're often prowling around at night – this is just as good a hill for moths at night as it is for butterflies by day. Can't you stop that dog barking at me? Really, he's very badly trained.'

'Shut up, Tim,' ordered Julian, and Timmy obediently closed his mouth, but still stood stiffly, staring at the man in the darkness.

'I'm going on to our next honey-trap,' said the man. 'So you can take that noisy dog back to wherever you are camping.' Mr Brent began to move away, flashing a torch in front of him.

'We're just up the hill,' said Julian. 'About a hundred yards. Oh – you've got a torch, I see. I wish I'd brought mine.'

The man said nothing more, but went slowly on his way, the beam of his torch growing fainter. Julian began to climb back up the hill to the tents, but in the growing darkness it was not easy! He missed his way and went much too far to the right. Timmy was puzzled and went to him, tugging gently at his sleeve.

'Am I going wrong?' said Julian. 'Blow! I'd soon get lost

on this lonely hillside. Dick! George! Anne! Give a shout, will you? I don't know where I am.'

But he had wandered so far off the path that the three didn't hear him – and Timmy had to guide him for a good way before he saw the torches of the others flashing up above. He felt most relieved. He had no wish to be caught in a heavy rainstorm on the exposed side of Billycock Hill!

'Is that you, Julian?' called Anne's anxious voice. 'What a long time you've been! Did you get lost?'

'Almost!' said Julian. 'Like an idiot I went without my torch – but Timmy here knew the way all right. I'm glad I'm back – it's just beginning to rain!'

'Who was Tim barking at?' asked George.

'One of the butterfly men – Mr Brent, the one Dick and I saw today,' said Julian. 'I just caught the glint of his dark glasses in the half-light, and saw the butterfly net he carried. He said Mr Gringle was out, too.'

'But whatever for, with a storm coming?' marvelled Anne. 'All the moths would be well in hiding.'

'They've come out to examine their moth-traps, as they call them,' said Julian. 'They spread sticky stuff like honey or something round the trunks of trees – and the moths fly down to it by the score. Then they come along and collect any they want to take back.'

'I see – and I suppose Mr Brent was afraid the rain might wash away the clinging moths,' said Dick. 'Well, they'll both be caught in the storm, that's certain. Listen to the rain pelting down on the tent now!'

Timmy squeezed into the tent, not liking the sting of the heavy raindrops. He sat down by George and Anne.

'You do take up a lot of room in a small tent, Tim,' said George. 'Can't you make yourself a bit smaller?'

Timmy couldn't. He was a big dog, and rather a sprawly one. He put his wet head on George's knee and heaved a heavy sigh. George patted him.

'Humbug!' she said. 'What are you sighing about? Because you've finished your bone? Because it's raining and you can't go and sit and bark at anything moving on the hill?'

'What shall we do now?' said Julian, setting his torch on the radio set, so that it more or less lit up the tent. 'There's nothing on the radio we want to hear.'

'I've got a pack of cards somewhere,' said George, much to everybody's joy, and she found them and got them out. 'Let's have a game of some sort.'

It was rather difficult in the small tent, with Timmy sometimes getting up just when all the cards were neatly dealt, and upsetting the piles. The storm grew fiercer and the rain tried its best to lash its way through the canvas of the little tent.

Then Timmy began to bark again, startling everyone very much. He climbed over legs and knees and poked his head out of the tent opening, barking loudly.

'Good gracious – you almost gave me a heart attack!' said Dick, pulling him back. 'You'll get soaked out there, Tim. Come back – it's only those mad mothmen out there picking moths off rain-soaked honey-traps. Don't worry about *them*. They're probably enjoying themselves enormously.'

But Timmy simply would NOT stop barking, and even growled when Julian tried to drag him into the tent.

'Whatever's up with him?' said Julian, bewildered. 'Oh, stop it, Timmy! You're deafening us!'

'Something's upsetting him – something unusual,' said George. 'Listen – was that a yell?'

Everyone listened, but the rain was pelting down so hard that it was impossible to hear anything but the slashing rain and the wind.

'Well, we can't do much about it, whatever it is that's upsetting Timmy,' said Dick. 'We can't possibly go wandering about in this storm – we'd get soaked through and probably lost!'

Timmy was still barking, and George grew cross. 'Timmy! Stop! Do you hear me? I won't have it.'

It was so seldom that George was angry with him that Timmy turned in surprise. George pounced at his collar and dragged him forcibly into the tent. 'Now – be QUIET!' she commanded. 'Whatever it is, we can't do anything about it!'

Just then another noise rose above the howling of the wind and the torrents of rain, and the Five pricked up their ears at once, sitting absolutely still.

A STORMY NIGHT

'R-r-r-r-r-r-r-r! R-r-r-r-r-r-r-r-r-r! R-R-R-R-R-R-R-R-R-R-R! R-R-R-R-R-R-R-R-R-R!'

They all looked round at one another. 'Aeroplanes!' said Dick. '*Aeroplanes*! In this weather, too. Whatever *is* going on?'

CHAPTER TWELVE

What happened in Billycock Caves

THE LITTLE company in the tent were amazed. Why should aeroplanes take off from the airfield in the middle of a stormy night?

'For experiments in storms, perhaps?' said Dick. 'No – that would be rather unnecessary.'

'Perhaps they were aeroplanes *landing* there, not leaving,' suggested Anne.

'Possibly – perhaps seeking the shelter of the airfield when they were caught in this storm,' said Dick. But Julian shook his head.

'No,' he said. 'This airfield is too far off the ordinary air-routes – nobody would bother about it; it's so small for one thing – more a little experimental station than anything else. Any aeroplane in difficulties could easily go to a first-class airfield for shelter or help.'

'I wonder if Jeff went up in one of the two we heard,' said George.

Anne yawned. 'What about bedding down?' she said. 'This tent is so hot and stuffy that I feel half-asleep.'

'Yes – it's getting late,' said Julian, looking at his watch. 'You two girls and Timmy can have this tent – it will save you going out into the rain. Fasten the flap after we've gone – and yell if you want anything.'

'Right. Goodnight, Ju, goodnight, Dick,' said the girls, and the boys scrambled out into the rain. Anne fastened the flap of the tent, and wrapped her rug round her. She

428

burrowed into her heathery bed and made herself comfortable. George did the same.

'Goodnight,' said Anne, sleepily. 'Keep Tim on your side. I can't bear him on my legs, he's so heavy.'

The Five slept soundly and awoke the next morning to a dismal scene of rain and dark clouds.

'*How* disappointing!' said Dick, peering out of his tent. 'We ought to have listened to the weather forecast to see if it would clear today. What's the time, Julian?'

'Just gone eight,' said Julian. 'My word, we *are* sleepy these days! Well, it's not raining so very hard now – let's see if the girls are awake, and put on our anoraks and go and wash at the spring.'

They all had breakfast – not quite so merry as usual, because it was a bit of a crowd in the tent and not nearly so much fun as having it in the sunshine. Still, the day might clear, and then they could go down to see Toby at the farm.

'I suppose we'd better go and explore those caves this morning,' said Dick, after breakfast. 'There's nothing else to do, and I refuse to play cards all morning.'

'We *all* refuse!' said George. 'Let's put on our anoraks and see if we can find the caves.'

'We can look at the map,' said Julian. 'It's a large-scale one. There must be a road or lane to them – they are quite well-known. They're probably round the hill – a bit lower down.'

'Well, never mind – we'll see if we can find them, and if we can't it won't matter. We shall have been for a walk!' said Dick.

They set off in a fine drizzle, walking through the damp heather, Timmy leaping in front.

'Everyone got torches?' said Dick suddenly. 'I've got mine. We'll need them in the caves!'

Yes, everyone had a torch – except Timmy of course, and he, as Anne pointed out, had eyes that were far better for seeing in the dark than any torch could ever be!

They made their way down the hill and then veered off to the north side – and came suddenly upon a wide rather chalky path, where the heather had been cut well back.

'This rather looks as if it led somewhere,' said Julian, stopping.

'It might lead to an old chalk quarry,' said Dick, kicking some loose white lumps of chalk. 'Like the one near Kirrin.'

'Well, let's follow it up and see,' said George, and they went along it, kicking the lumps of chalk as they went. They rounded a corner and saw a notice.

To Billycock Caves
Warning
Keep only to the roped ways.
Beware of losing your way in the
unroped tunnels.

'This sounds good,' said Julian. 'Let's see – what did Toby tell us about the caves?'

'They're thousands of years old – they've got stalagmites and stalactites,' said George.

'Oh – I know what those are,' said Anne. 'They look like icicles hanging from the roof – while below, on the floor of the cave, other icicles seem to grow upwards to meet them!'

430

'Yes – the roof ones are stalac*tites* and the ground ones are stalag*mites*,' said Dick.

'I simply *never* can remember which is which,' said Anne.

'It's easy!' said Julian. 'The stalac*tite* icicles have to hold *tight* to the roof – and the stalag*mite* ones *might* some day join with the ones above them!'

The others laughed.

'I shall never forget which are which now,' said Anne.

The path they were following altered as they came near to the caves, and lost its chalky look. Just in front of the entrance the way was properly paved, and was no longer rough. The entrance was only about six feet high, and had over it a white board with two words painted very large in black.

BILLYCOCK CAVES

The warning they had read on the first notice they had come to was repeated on another one just inside the entrance. 'Read it, Tim,' said George, seeing him looking at it. 'And keep close to us!'

They went right in, and had to switch on their torches at once. Timmy was amazed to see the walls around him glittering suddenly in the light of the four torches. He began to bark, and the noise echoed all around in a very weird manner.

Timmy didn't like it, and he pressed close to George. She laughed. 'Come on, silly. These are only caves. You've been in plenty in your life, Timmy! Goodness, don't they feel cold! I'm glad of my anorak!'

They passed through one or two small and ordinary

caves and then came to a magnificent one, full of what looked like gleaming icicles. Some hung down from the roof, others rose up from the ground. In some places the one below had reached to the one hanging down, so that they had joined, making it look as if the cave was held up by great shining pillars.

'Oh!' said Anne, catching her breath. 'What a wonderful sight! How they gleam and shine!'

'It reminds me of cathedrals I have seen,' said Julian, looking up at the roof of the cave. 'I don't know why. All these finely wrought pillars . . . come along, let's go into the next cave.'

The next one was smaller, but contained some splendid coloured 'icicles' that shone and gleamed in the light of the torches. 'It's like a cave in Fairyland,' said Anne. 'Full of rainbow colours!'

The following cave had no colour, but was of a dazzling white, walls, roof, floor and pillars. So many stalactites and stalagmites had joined that they almost formed a snow-white screen through which the children peered – only to see even more of the strange 'icicles'.

They came to a threefold forking of the ways. The centre one was roped, but the other two tunnels were not. The children looked down the unroped tunnels, stretching away so dark and quiet, and shivered. How awful to go down one and lose the way, never to be found again, perhaps!

'Let's go down the roped way,' said George. 'Just to see where it leads to – more caves, probably.'

Timmy ran sniffing down one of the other ways, and George called him, 'Tim! You'll get lost! Come back.'

But Timmy didn't come back. He ran off into the

darkness and the others felt cross. 'Blow him,' said Dick. 'What's he after? TIM! TIM!' The echoes took up the last word and sent it repeatedly up and down the passage.

Timmy barked in answer, and at once the place was full of weird barking, echoing everywhere and making Anne put her fingers to her ears.

'Woof-oof-oof-oof!' said the echoes, sounding as if a gang of dogs were barking madly in the caves. Then Timmy appeared in the light of their torches, looking extremely surprised at the enormous noise he had created with his barking.

'I shall put you on the lead, Timmy,' scolded George. 'Keep to heel now. Surely you understand what that word means after all these years?'

Timmy did. He kept faithfully to heel as the little company went along a narrow, roped tunnel and came out into a succession of dazzling caves, all linked together by little passages or tunnels. They kept only to those that were roped. Many of them were not, and the Five longed to see where they led to, but were sensible enough not to try.

And then, as they were examining what looked like a frozen pool, which reflected the snowy roof above like a mirror, a curious noise came to their ears. They straightened themselves and listened.

It was a whistling sound, high-pitched and shrill, that filled the cave, and filled their eardrums, too, until they felt like bursting. It rose high, then died down – then rose again till the children were forced to put their hands to their heads – and died away.

Timmy couldn't bear it. He barked frantically and ran round and round like a mad thing. And then the second noise began – a howling! A howling that seemed to be tossed to and fro, and grew louder as the echoes threw it about from cave to cave! Anne clutched Dick, terrified.

'What is it?' she said. 'Quick, let's go!' And, led by an extremely scared Timmy, the Five raced pell-mell out of Billycock Caves as if a hundred dogs were after them!

CHAPTER THIRTEEN

A dreadful shock

THE FIVE stood panting outside the entrance of the caves, feeling decidedly sheepish at having run away from a noise.

'Whew!' said Julian, mopping his forehead. 'That was decidedly weird. That whistling – it got inside my head. It was like a – like a police whistle gone mad or something. As for the howling . . . well.'

'It was horrible,' said Anne, looking quite pale. 'Like wild animals. I'm not going into those caves again for anything. Let's get back to the camp.'

They walked soberly down the chalk-strewn path that led away from the caves and made their way back to their camp. The rain had stopped now, and the clouds were beginning to break.

The Five sat down inside a tent, and discussed the matter. 'We'll ask Toby if it's usual for noises like that to be heard,' said Dick. 'I wonder anyone ever visits the cave if it *is* infested with horrible whistles and screeches like that.'

'All the same, we were a bit cowardly,' said Julian, now feeling rather ashamed of himself.

'Well, go back and do a bit of howling yourself,' suggested George. 'It may frighten the howler as much as his howling scared *you*.'

'Nothing doing,' said Julian promptly. 'I'm not going in for any howling matches.' He burrowed down under the rug for his field-glasses and slung them round his neck.

'I'm going to have a squint at the airfield,' he said. 'Just to see if I can spot Cousin Jeff.' He put the glasses to his eyes and focused them on the airfield below them. He gave a sudden exclamation.

'There's quite a lot going on at the airfield this morning!' he said in surprise. 'Dozens of people there! I wonder what's up. There are quite a lot of planes, too – they must all have arrived this morning!'

Each of the others took a turn at looking through the glasses. Yes – Julian was right. There was certainly something going on at the airfield today. Men hurried about, and then came the noise of yet another aeroplane, which zoomed neatly down to the runway.

'Gosh – *another* plane!' said Dick. 'Where did all the others come from? We never heard them.'

'They must have arrived while we were in the caves,' said Dick. 'I wish we could ask Toby's Cousin Jeff what all the excitement is about.'

'We could go down to the farm after our lunch and see if he has heard anything,' suggested Anne, and the others agreed.

'Thank goodness the sun's coming out again,' said George, as a shaft of warm sunlight burst out from behind a cloud, and the sun sailed into a patch of blue sky. 'The heather will soon dry now. Let's have the news on – we may just catch the weather forecast. I don't want to carry my anorak about if it's going to clear up.'

They switched on the little radio set – but they had missed the weather news. 'Blow!' said Dick and raised his hand to switch off – and then he heard two words that stopped him. They were 'Billycock Hill'! He left his hand suspended in the air and listened, full of surprise. The announcer's voice came clearly to the four.

'The aeroplanes stolen from Billycock Hill airfield were two valuable ones, into which had been incorporated new devices,' said the voice from the radio. 'It is possible that they were stolen because of these. We regret that it appears that two of our best pilots flew them away – Flight-Lieutenant Jeffrey Thomas and Flight-Lieutenant Ray Wells. No news has been received of either plane. Both disappeared during a storm over Billycock Hill during the night.'

There was a pause, and then the announcer went on to another item of news. Dick switched off the radio and looked blankly at the others. No one had a word to say at first.

'To think that *Jeff* could do a thing like that – Jeff a traitor – flying off with a plane of ours to sell to an enemy!' said Julian at last, voicing the thought of all the others.

'We heard the planes go!' said Dick. 'Two of them. Gosh – we ought to go to the police and tell what we know. Not that it's much. But, I say – fancy JEFF doing that! I liked him so much.'

'So did I,' said Anne, turning her head away.

'So did Timmy,' said George. 'And he hardly ever makes a mistake in anyone.'

'What will poor Toby do?' said Dick. 'He thought the world of Jeff.'

Timmy suddenly ran off a few yards and began barking – a welcoming bark this time. Julian looked to see who was coming. It was Toby!

He came up to them and sat down beside them. He looked pale and shocked, though he tried to smile at them.

'I've got awful news,' he said in a funny, croaking voice.

'We know,' said Dick. 'We've just heard it on the radio. Oh, Toby – fancy – *Jeff*!'

To everyone's horror Toby's face crumpled up and tears poured down his cheeks. He made no attempt to wipe them away; indeed, he hardly seemed to know that they were there. Nobody knew what to do – except Timmy. Dear old Tim scrambled over Julian and most sympathetically licked Toby's wet face, whining as he did so. Toby put his arm round the dog's neck and began to speak.

'It *wasn't* Jeff! Jeff couldn't have done such a thing. He couldn't! You know he couldn't, don't you?' He turned quite fiercely on the others as he spoke.

'*I* can't believe that he did,' said Julian. 'He seemed to

me to be absolutely straight and trustworthy, even though I only met him that once.'

'He was – well – a sort of hero to me,' said Toby, beginning to mop his cheeks with his hanky, and staring in surprise to see it so damp. 'Gosh, I'm a sissy to go on like this! But when the military police came to our farm this morning to ask questions about Jeff – he's my dad's nephew, you know – I couldn't believe my ears. I was so furious with one idiot that I punched him – and Mother sent me out of the room.'

'I suppose both Jeff and the other fellow have definitely *gone*?' asked Julian. 'No other pilots are missing, are they?'

'No, I asked that,' said Toby dismally. 'Everyone answered roll-call at the camp this morning except Jeff and Ray. Ray is Jeff's best friend, you know.'

'It looks bad,' said Dick, after a long pause.

'But it's *not true* that Jeff's a traitor!' cried Toby, up in arms again. 'Are you suggesting that he is?'

'No, I'm not,' said Dick. 'Don't be an ass. I don't . . .' Then he stopped as Timmy ran off and barked fiercely. *Now* who was coming?

A deep voice called to Timmy. 'Down, boy, down! Where are your friends?'

Julian scrambled up and saw two military policemen standing facing the excited Timmy. 'Here, Tim,' called Julian. 'It's all right. Friends!'

Timmy ran to him and the two burly men came up. 'You the children camping on this hill?' asked the first one. 'Well, we want to ask you a few questions about last night. You were here then, weren't you?'

'Yes. We know what you've come about, too,' said

Julian. 'We'll tell you all we know – but we're pretty certain that Flight-Lieutenant Thomas hadn't anything to do with it.'

'That's as may be,' said the man. 'Well, sit down, all of you, and we'll have a little talk.'

Soon they were sitting down in the heather, while Julian told all they knew, which wasn't much – just the sound of the two aeroplanes flying off together.

'And you heard nothing suspicious last night – nothing at all?' asked the first man.

'Nothing,' said Julian.

'Nobody about at all, I suppose?' asked the second man, looking up from his notebook in which he had been writing.

'Oh – well, yes – there were people about,' said Julian, suddenly remembering the butterfly man, Mr Brent, who had said that he and Mr Gringle were out looking at their moth-traps.

The first policeman asked some rapid questions and Julian and the others told them what little they knew – though Julian knew the most, of course.

'You're sure it was Mr Brent you saw?' asked the policeman.

'Well – he *said* he was,' said Julian. 'And he carried a butterfly net on his shoulder – and he wore the same dark glasses I saw him wearing earlier. Of course, it was pretty dark – but I honestly *think* it was Mr Brent. I didn't see or hear Mr Gringle. Mr Brent said he was some way off. They're both mad on moth and butterfly hunting.'

'I see,' said the policeman, and the second one shut his notebook. 'Thanks very much. I think we'll just go and pay a call on these – er – what do you call them – butterfly men? Where do they hang out?'

The children offered to guide them on their way, and the whole company went with the two burly men almost to the butterfly farm.

'Well, thanks a lot,' said the first policeman as they came near the tumbledown cottage. 'We'll go on alone, now. You get back to your camp.'

'Will you send us word as soon as *you* know it wasn't my Cousin Jeff?' asked Toby, forlornly. 'He'll be getting in touch with you, I know, as soon as he hears what he's suspected of.'

'It's bad luck on you, son – he's your cousin, isn't he?' said the big policeman kindly. 'But you'll have to make up your mind to it – it was Jeff Thomas all right that flew off in one of those aeroplanes last night. There isn't a doubt of it!'

CHAPTER FOURTEEN

Mr Gringle is annoyed

THE MILITARY police went off down the hill to the butterfly farm, and the five children stood disconsolately watching them, with Timmy staring, too, tail well down. He didn't quite know what had happened but he was sure it was something dreadful . . .

'Well – it's no good waiting about here, I suppose,' said Julian. 'I bet the police won't get anything useful out of the butterfly men – *they* wouldn't have noticed anything when they were out last night, except their precious moths!'

They were just turning away when they heard someone screaming in a high voice, and they stopped to listen in surprise. 'It must be old Mrs Janes,' said Dick. 'What's up with her?'

'We'd better see,' said Julian, and he and the others, with Timmy at their heels, went quickly down to the cottage. They heard the voices of the two policemen as they came near.

'Now, now, old lady – don't take on so!' one was saying in a kindly voice. 'We've only come to ask a few questions.'

'Go away, go away!' screamed the old woman, and actually battered at the men with her little bony hands. 'Why are you here? Go away, I tell you!'

'Now listen, Ma – don't take on so,' said the other man patiently. 'We want to talk to Mr Gringle and Mr Brent – are they here?'

'Who? Who did you say? Oh, them! They're out with their nets,' mumbled the old woman. 'I'm all alone here, and I'm scared of strangers. You go away.'

'Listen,' said one policeman. 'Were Mr Gringle and Mr Brent out on the hills last night?'

'I'm in my bed at night,' she answered. 'How would *I* know? You go away and leave me in peace.'

The policemen looked at one another, and shook their heads. It was clearly quite useless to find out anything from this frightened old woman.

'Well, we'll go, Ma,' said one, patting her shoulder gently. 'Sorry we've scared you – there's nothing to be afraid of.'

They turned away and came back up the slope of the hill, seeing the children standing silently there. 'We heard old Mrs Janes screaming,' said Julian. 'So we came to see what was happening.'

'The butterfly men, as you call them, are out with their nets,' said one policeman. 'A funny life, I must say – catching insects and looking after their eggs and caterpillars. Well – I don't suppose they know anything about last night's job. Not that there's anything to know! Two pilots flew off with the planes, we know who they were – and that's that!'

'Well, one was NOT my Cousin Jeff,' said Toby, fiercely. The men shrugged their shoulders and went off together.

The five children went off up the hill again, very silent. 'I think we'd better have something to eat,' said Julian at last. 'We've had no lunch – and it's long past our usual time. Toby, stay and have some with us.'

'I couldn't eat a thing,' said Toby. 'Not a thing!'

'Let's get out what we've got,' said Julian, and the girls and Timmy went to the little 'larder'. Nobody really felt like eating – but when the food was there, in front of them, they found that they were quite hungry – except poor Toby, who sat forlorn and pale-faced, trying to chew through a sandwich made for him by Anne, but not making a very good job of it!

Timmy began to bark in the middle of the meal, and everyone looked to see who was coming now. Julian thought he saw a movement some way down the hill, and took his field-glasses and put them to his eyes.

'I *think* it's Mr Gringle,' he said. 'I can see his net too. He's out butterflying, I suppose.'

'Let's shout to him,' said Dick. 'We can tell him why the police went to call at his cottage this morning, when he wasn't there. He'll never get any sense out of old Mrs Janes.'

Julian cooeed, and there came an answering call. 'He's coming up,' said Dick. Timmy ran to meet him, and soon the man was just below them, panting as he made his way up the steep slope.

'I hoped I'd see you,' he said. 'I want you to look out for some special moths for me – another day-flying one like the Six-Spot Burnet you saw the other day. It's the Cinnabar moth – it's got rich crimson underwings, and – and—'

'Yes – I know that one,' said Julian. 'We'll look out for it. We just wanted to tell you that two military policemen went to your cottage a little while ago to ask you some questions about last night – and as we're sure old Mrs Janes won't be able to explain anything to you, we thought we'd better tell you ourselves.'

444

Mr Gringle looked absolutely blank and bewildered. 'But – but why on earth should military policemen come to our cottage?' he said at last.

'For nothing much,' said Julian. 'Only to ask you if you saw anything suspicious when you were out looking at your moth-traps last night – you see, two aeroplanes were—'

Mr Gringle interrupted in a most surprised voice. 'But – but, dear boy, I wasn't out at all last night! It wouldn't have been a bit of good looking for moths anywhere, on our moth-traps or anywhere else, on a night like that.'

'Well,' said Julian, also surprised, 'I saw your friend Mr Brent, and he *said* you were both out looking at your moth-traps.'

Mr Gringle stared at Julian as if he were mad, and his mouth fell open in amazement. 'Mr *Brent*!' he said at last. 'But Peter – that's Mr Brent – was at home with *me*! We were busy writing up our notes together.'

There was a silence after this surprising statement. Julian frowned. What was all this? Was Mr Gringle trying to hide the fact that he and his friend had been out on the hills the night before?

'Well – I certainly saw Mr Brent,' said Julian at last. 'It was very dark, I admit – but I'm sure I saw his butterfly net – and his dark glasses.'

'He doesn't *wear* dark glasses,' said Mr Gringle, still more astonished. 'What *is* this tale? Is it a joke of some sort? If you can't talk better sense than this, I'm going.'

'Wait!' said Dick, something else occurring to him. 'You say that Mr Brent doesn't wear dark glasses – then who was the man that took the moth from us yesterday evening about six o'clock and gave us fifty pence? He *said* he was Mr Brent, your friend!'

'This is all nonsense!' said Mr Gringle, getting up angrily. 'Wasting my time on a poor joke of this kind! Brent doesn't wear dark glasses, I tell you – and he wasn't at home at six o'clock yesterday – we'd been to buy some tackle in the next town. He was with *me*, not at the cottage. You couldn't possibly have seen him! What do you mean by all this nonsense – dark glasses, fifty pence for a moth – and seeing Brent on the hillside last night when he didn't stir out of the house!'

He was now standing up, looking very fierce, his brilliant eyes flashing behind his thick glasses. 'Well,' said Julian, 'all this is extremely puzzling, and . . .'

'Puzzling! You're nothing but a pack of nitwitted, ill-mannered children!' suddenly roared Mr Gringle, quite losing his temper. Timmy gave a warning growl, and stood up – he didn't allow anyone to rave at his friends!

Mr Gringle went off angrily, trampling down the heather as if he were trampling down the children. They heard him muttering to himself as he went off. They looked at one another in really great surprise.

'Well – I simply don't know what to make of all this!' said Julian helplessly. 'Was I dreaming last night? No – I *did* see that fellow – half-see him, anyway – and he *did* say he was Mr Brent, and that Gringle was somewhere near. But – if he wasn't Brent, who was he? And what was he doing on a stormy night, hunting moths?'

Nobody could make even a guess. Toby spoke first.

'Perhaps the man you saw was mixed up in the stealing of those aeroplanes – you never know?'

'Impossible, Toby!' said Julian. 'That's *too* farfetched. I can't say that I understand it at all – but honestly, he didn't seem like a man who could steal an aeroplane!'

'Who was the man that gave us the fifty pence then, if he wasn't Brent?' said Dick, puzzled.

'Could it have been Mrs Janes's son, pretending he was Brent – just for a silly joke?' said George.

'What was he like?' asked Toby at once. 'I know Will Janes – I told you he's often been to our farm. We don't have him now because he drinks so much and he isn't reliable any more. What was this man Brent like – I'd soon know if he was Will Janes pretending to be someone else!'

'He was small and thin, with dark glasses,' began Dick – and Toby interrupted him at once.

'Then it wasn't Will Janes! He's tall and burly – with a thick neck and, anyway, he doesn't wear dark glasses – or any glasses at all!'

'Then who in the world was it? And WHY did he pretend to be Brent, Gringle's friend?' wondered Dick. Everyone frowned and puzzled over the whole thing – but nobody could think of a sensible reason for anyone wanting to pretend to be Mr Brent!

'Well – for goodness sake, let's get on with our meal,' said George at last. 'We stopped in the middle of it – and the rest is still waiting for us. Have another ham sandwich, Julian?'

They all munched in silence, thinking hard. Toby sighed. 'I don't really feel that this mix-up with the butterfly men and somebody else, whoever he is, has anything to do with the stealing of the aeroplanes. I wish it had!'

'All the same – it wants looking into,' said Dick seriously. 'And what's more – I vote we keep our eyes and ears open. *Something's* going on at the butterfly farm!'

CHAPTER FIFTEEN

More news – and a night trip

THE FIVE spent most of the afternoon talking about the mystery of the man who had pretended to be Mr Brent. It really was difficult to understand why anyone should do such a foolish thing, especially as it could be so easily found out.

'I can only think there's a madman about who has got it into his head that he is Mr Brent!' said Dick at last. 'No wonder he didn't seem to recognise that butterfly we took him!'

'Do you know what I think would be a good idea?' suddenly said George. 'Why don't we slip down to the butterfly farm tonight, when it's getting dark, and see if the false Mr Brent is there, *and* the real one – whom we've never seen, by the way, *and* Mr Gringle?'

'Hm – yes – quite an idea,' said Julian, seriously. 'But only Dick and I will go – not you or Anne.'

'I'll come, too,' said Toby.

'Right,' said Julian. 'But we'll have to be jolly careful – because if there *is* something funny going on down there, we don't want to be caught. It wouldn't be at all pleasant, I fear!'

'Take Timmy with you,' said George at once.

'No. He might bark or something,' said Dick. 'We'll be all right, George. Gracious – we've had enough adventures by now to teach us how to go about things like this! Ha – I shall look forward to tonight!'

449

Everyone suddenly felt much more cheerful, even Toby. He managed a very small smile, and stood up to brush the crumbs off his jersey.

'I'm going now,' he said. 'I've a lot of farm jobs to do this afternoon – I'll meet you at the big oak tree behind the butterfly farm – did you notice it?'

'Yes – an enormous one,' said Julian. 'Right. Be there at – say – ten o'clock. No, eleven – it will be dark by then, or almost.'

'So long!' said Toby and plunged down the hill, accompanied for a little way by Timmy.

'Well – I feel much better now we've made a definite plan,' said Dick. 'My goodness, it's half past five already! *Don't* suggest tea, George – we had our lunch so late!'

'I wasn't going to,' said George. 'We'll miss it out and have a really good supper later on. And don't let's forget to listen to the news at six o'clock – there *might* be something about Jeff and his friend Ray – and the aeroplanes.'

So, just before six o'clock, they switched on the little radio set, and listened intently for the news. It came at last – and almost the first piece was about the stolen aeroplanes. The children listened, holding their breath, bending close to the set.

'The two aeroplanes stolen from Billycock airfield last night, flown away by Flight-Lieutenant Jeffrey Thomas and Flight-Lieutenant Ray Wells, have been found. Both planes apparently crashed into the sea, but were seen, and there is a chance of their being salvaged. The pilots were not found, and are presumed to have been drowned. At Edinburgh this afternoon there was a grand rally of . . .'

Julian switched off the news and looked at the others

soberly. 'Well – that's that! Crashed, both of them! That was because of the storm, I suppose. Well, at least no enemy will be able to get hold of the new devices that were incorporated in the planes.'

'But – that means Toby's cousin is drowned – or killed,' said Anne, her face very white.

'Yes. But remember, if he flew away in that plane, he was a traitor,' said Dick gravely.

'But Toby's cousin didn't *seem* like a traitor,' said George. 'He seemed so – well, so *very* honest, and I can't say anything finer than that. I feel as if I shall never trust my judgment of anyone again. I liked him so very much.'

'So did I,' said Dick, frowning. 'Well, these things happen – but I just wish it hadn't been Toby's cousin. He was such a hero to him. I don't feel as if Toby will ever be quite the same after this – it's something so absolutely *beastly*!'

Nobody said anything for a little while. They were all profoundly shocked – not only by the idea of Cousin Jeff being a traitor, but also by the news that he had been drowned. It seemed such a horrible end to come to that bright-eyed smiling young airman they had joked with only the other day.

'Do you think we ought to pack up and go home?' said Anne. 'I mean – won't it be awkward for the Thomases to have us hanging round when they must feel shocked and unhappy?'

'No, we don't need to bother them much at the farm,' said Julian. 'And I don't think we can desert old Toby at the moment. It will help him to have friends around, you know.'

'Yes. You're right,' said Dick. 'This is the sort of time to have good friends – poor old Toby. He'll be knocked out by this last piece of news.'

'Will he be waiting for you at the old oak tree tonight, do you think?' asked George.

'Don't know,' said Julian. 'It doesn't matter if he's not there, anyway – Dick and I can do all the snooping round that is necessary. And it will take our minds off this shock a bit – to try and solve the mystery down at the butterfly farm!'

They went for a walk round the hill, with Timmy leaping over the heather in delight. He couldn't understand the lack of laughter and the unusual solemnity shown by his four friends, and he was pleased to be able to forget any troubles and sniff for rabbits.

They had their suppers at eight o'clock and then turned on the radio to listen to a programme. 'We'll hear the news at nine,' said Dick. 'Just in *case* there might be any more.'

But the nine o'clock news only repeated what had been said about the two planes in the six o'clock broadcast, and not a word more. Dick switched off and gazed down at the airfield below.

There were still quite a lot of planes there, though some of them had taken off and flown away during the day. Julian trained his field-glasses on the field.

'Not so many men scurrying about now,' he said. 'Things are quietening down. My word – what a shock it must have been for everyone there last night, to hear the planes revved up, and then flown away! They *must* have been amazed!'

'Maybe they didn't hear them go, in the storm,' said George.

'They must have,' said Dick. '*We* heard them up here.

452

Well, what about you girls turning in? Dick and I don't want to, in case we fall off to sleep – we've got to slip away about half past ten or we shan't be down at the oak tree at eleven.'

'I wish you'd take Timmy with you,' said George uneasily. 'I don't *like* the butterfly farm – or the witch-like old woman there – or the man you met with dark glasses who wasn't Mr Brent, or the son you haven't seen.'

'Don't be an ass, George,' said Julian. 'We shall be back by twelve, I expect – and Timmy is sure to bark in welcome, so you'll know we're safe.'

The girls wouldn't go to their tent to sleep, so they all sat and talked, and watched the sun slip behind the clear horizon. The weather was now perfect again, and there wasn't a cloud in the sky. It was difficult to imagine the sweeping rain and howling wind of last night's storm.

'Well,' said Julian at last, looking at his watch. 'Time we went. Timmy, look after the girls as usual.'

'Woof,' said Timmy, understanding perfectly.

'And you look after *your*selves,' said Anne. 'We'll come down a little way with you – it's such a lovely evening.'

They all set off together, and the girls went halfway to the butterfly farm and then turned back with Timmy. 'Well, Tim – mind you bark at twelve, when they come back,' said Anne. 'Though somehow I think that both George and I will still be awake!'

The two boys went on down the hill and round to the right across towards the butterfly farm. It was almost dark now, though the June night was very clear and bright. 'Better be careful we're not seen,' muttered Julian. 'It's such a clear night.'

They made their way to the big old oak tree that stood

at the back of the butterfly farm. Toby was not there – but in about two minutes they heard a slight rustling noise, and saw Toby, panting a little, as if he had been hurrying. Then he was close beside them.

'Sorry I'm a bit late,' he whispered. 'I say – did you hear the six o'clock news?'

'Yes – we were awfully sorry about it,' said Julian.

'Well – as I still don't believe that Cousin Jeff stole the aeroplanes with Ray Wells, but that somebody else did, I wasn't any more upset than before,' said Toby. 'If Jeff didn't steal the plane, he wasn't in it when it crashed, so he's not drowned. See?'

'Yes. I see,' said Julian, glad that Toby had taken the news in that way, but convinced himself that there wasn't really much hope.

'What are your plans?' whispered Toby. 'There are lights in the cottage windows – and I don't think any curtains are pulled. We could go and peep into each one and see exactly who is there!'

'Good idea,' said Julian. 'Come on – and, for goodness sake, don't make a noise. Single file, of course. I'll lead the way.'

And silently and slowly they went round the oak tree and down to the tumbledown cottage. What would they see there, when they looked through those lit windows?

CHAPTER SIXTEEN

Looking through windows

THE THREE tiptoed quietly up to the cottage. 'Don't go too near when you look in,' whispered Julian. 'Keep a little distance away. We shall be able to see who is in the rooms, but they mustn't be able to see us outside. I sincerely hope they won't!'

'Look in the downstairs rooms,' said Dick. 'See, that's the kitchen window over there. Old Mrs Janes may be there, if she's still up.'

They crept to the uncurtained window. The room was lit by only a candle, and was full of shadows. The boys gazed in.

Old Mrs Janes *was* there, sitting up in a brown rocking-chair, clad in a dirty dressing-gown. She rocked herself to and fro, and although the boys could not see her face, they sensed that the old woman was frightened and unhappy. Her head was sunk on her chest, and when she put her wispy hair back from her face, her hand shook.

'She's no witch, poor old thing!' whispered Dick, feeling quite sad to see her rocking to and fro all by herself so late at night. 'She's just a poor frightened old woman.'

'Why is she up so late?' wondered Julian. 'She must be waiting for someone.'

'Yes. She might be. We'd better look out then,' said Toby at once, looking behind him as if he expected to see someone creeping up.

'Now let's go round to the front,' said Dick. So they

456

tiptoed there, and saw another lit window – much more brightly lit than the kitchen window had been. They kept a little way from the pane, afraid of being seen. They looked in and saw two men there, sitting at a table, poring over some papers.

'Mr Gringle!' said Julian, in a low voice. 'No doubt

about that – and the other one must be his friend, Mr Brent, I suppose. Certainly he isn't wearing dark glasses, as that man was we gave the butterfly to and who gave us fifty pence. He isn't a *bit* like him!'

They all looked intently at the friend. He was a perfectly ordinary man, with a small moustache, dark hair and a rather big nose. Not in the least like the 'Mr Brent' they had seen the day before.

'What are they doing?' whispered Toby.

'It looks as if they're making lists of something – probably making out bills for their customers,' said Julian. 'Anyway – I must say they look perfectly ordinary sitting there, doing a perfectly ordinary job. I think Mr Gringle was speaking the truth when he said that it wasn't Mr Brent who gave us the fifty pence and it certainly wasn't him either that I saw on the hillside last night with a butterfly net.'

'Then who *was* it?' asked Dick, pulling the others right away from the window, in order to talk more easily. 'And why did he carry the butterfly net and tell that lie about moth-traps? Why was he on the hill, the night the planes were stolen?'

'Yes – why *was* he? I'd like to ask him that!' said Toby in too loud a voice. The others nudged him at once, and he spoke more softly. 'Something funny was going on last night – something people don't know anything about. I'd like to find that phony Mr Brent you met on the hillside, Julian!'

'Well, maybe we shall,' said Julian. 'Now – any other window lit? Yes – one up there, under the roof. Who's there, I wonder?'

'Perhaps it's Mrs Janes's son,' said Dick. 'It would be

just like him to take one of the three bedrooms and make her sleep downstairs in the old rocking-chair! I expect the other two little rooms up there are used by the butterfly men.'

'How can we see into the lit room?' wondered Toby. 'Look – if we got up in that tree there, we'd see in.'

'There's an easier way!' said Julian, switching his torch on and off very quickly, giving the others just half a second to see a ladder leaning against a nearby wood-shed.

'Good – yes, that would be much easier,' said Dick. 'But we'll have to be jolly quiet. Whoever is in there would come to the window at once if he so much as heard the top of the ladder grating against the window-ledge!'

'Well, we'll manage it all right,' said Julian. 'The window isn't very high, and the ladder isn't very heavy. Between us we can place it very gently against the wall without disturbing anyone!'

The ladder was certainly quite light. The boys found no difficulty in carrying it slowly and carefully across to the cottage. They placed it against the wall without a sound.

'I'll go up,' whispered Julian. 'Hold the ladder steady – and for goodness sake keep a lookout! Give me a signal if you hear anything at all, because I don't want to be trapped at the top of the ladder!'

The others held the sides as he climbed the rather rickety rungs. He came to the lit window and very cautiously and slowly lifted his head until he could see right into the room.

It was lit by a candle, a very small and untidy room, poorly furnished. A man sat on the bed there, a big hulking man, with broad shoulders and a neck like a bull.

Julian gazed at him – yes, that must be Mrs Janes's son, who, she said, was so unkind to her. Julian remembered the old mumbling voice saying that her son was cruel. 'He hits me. He twists my arm!' Yes, the man on the bed could be a nasty bully, no doubt about that.

He was reading a newspaper close to the candle.

As Julian looked at him, he pulled out a big watch from his pocket and stared at it, muttering something that Julian couldn't hear. He stood up, and the boy was so afraid that he might come to the window, that he slithered down the ladder as quickly as possible.

'The son's in there,' he whispered to the others. 'I was afraid he was coming to the window to look out; that's why I slid down so quickly. Blow! I've got a splinter in the palm of my hand doing that! Toby – could you creep up to the top in a minute or two and look in – just to make sure I'm right, and that it *is* Will Janes, the old woman's son?'

LOOKING THROUGH WINDOWS

Toby went up the ladder as soon as they were certain that Will Janes was not going to look out. He came down almost at once.

'Yes – that's Will – but, my word, he *has* changed!' whispered Toby. 'He looks a brute now – and yet he was a kind decent fellow not so long ago. Mother said he'd fallen in with some bad men, and had taken to drinking – so I suppose he's quite different now.'

'He looked at his watch as if he was expecting someone,' said Julian. 'I wonder – now, I wonder – if the man who paraded about the hillside last night with a net is coming here tonight? I must say I'd like to get a good look at him. He can't be up to any good.'

'Well – let's hide somewhere and wait,' suggested Toby. 'Nobody knows I've slipped out to be with you, so I shan't be missed. Anyway, Mother wouldn't mind if she knew I was on a night trip with you two!'

'We'll hide in that barn over there,' said Julian, and, on tiptoe again, they crossed to an old ruined barn, whose roof was partly off, and whose walls were falling in. It smelt dirty and there seemed no clean place to sit in, but at last Julian pulled out some dusty sacks and laid them in a corner and they sat there waiting in the dark.

'Pooh!' said Dick. 'What a horrible smell in here – old rotting potatoes, or something. I wish we'd chosen somewhere else.'

'Sh!' said Julian suddenly, giving him a nudge that made him jump. 'I can hear something.'

They all sat silent and listened. They could certainly hear something – yes – quiet footsteps, very quiet – made by rubber-soled shoes. The soft sounds passed by the barn, and they could no longer hear them. Then came a soft, low whistle.

Julian stood up and looked through the broken barn window. 'I think there are two men standing below Will Janes's bedroom,' he whispered. 'They must be the men he was waiting for. He'll be coming down. I hope to goodness they don't come into this barn to talk!'

This was a horrible thought, but there was no chance of going anywhere else, because at that moment the front door opened and Will Janes came out. Julian, still looking through the broken pane, could see him dimly outlined in the light that came from Mr Gringle's front window.

The three men went off very quietly round the cottage. 'Come on,' said Julian. 'Let's shadow them. We might hear something to explain what's up.'

'What's the time?' asked Dick. 'I hope the girls won't start worrying about us. It must be gone twelve by now.'

'Yes. It is,' said Julian, looking at the luminous hands of his watch. 'It can't be helped. They'll guess we're on to something!'

They crept after the three men, who went to a clump of trees on the other side of the glasshouses. There they began to talk, but in such low tones that the three boys could hear nothing but the murmur of the voices.

Then one man raised his voice. It was Will Janes – Toby recognised it at once and told the others. 'It's Will. He's furious about something. He always loses his temper when he thinks people have treated him badly in any way – and it sounds as if he thinks those two men have.'

The two men tried to quiet him, but he would not be pacified. 'I want my money!' the boys heard him say. 'I helped you, didn't I, I hid you here, didn't I, till the job was done. Then give me my money!'

His voice rose almost to a shout, and the two men with him grew frightened. Exactly what happened next the boys never knew, but quite suddenly there was the sound of a blow and a fall – then another blow and a fall – Will Janes laughed. It was not a nice laugh.

In a few seconds there came an anxious voice from the window of the room where Mr Gringle and his friend were at work. 'Who's there? What's happening?'

CRASH! That was the sound of breaking glass! Will Janes had picked up a big stone and flung it at the nearby glasshouse. It made the three boys almost jump out of their skins.

'It's all right! I came out to see who was prowling about!' shouted Will Janes. 'And whoever it was has broken some of the glass in your butterfly house. I've been out here shouting, trying to catch him.'

He came blundering towards the house – and then, as luck would have it, his torch picked out the three crouching boys. He gave a yell!

'Who's this? Here they are, kids who've been trying to smash the glass! Catch them – that's right – I've got two of them – you catch the third!'

CHAPTER SEVENTEEN

Quite a lot happens

THINGS THEN happened so quickly that, to their utter amazement, the three boys found themselves captives quite unable to escape.

Big Will Janes had hold of both Dick and Toby – and he was so strong, and held them in such a vice-like grip, one in each hand, that it was hopeless to try to get away.

Julian had run straight into Mr Gringle and Mr Brent, and the men had captured him between them. They were very angry.

'What do you mean by coming here and snooping around, smashing our glasshouses!' yelled Mr Gringle, shaking Julian in his rage. 'We shall lose all our butterflies through that broken pane!'

'Let me go. We didn't break your glass,' shouted Julian.

'He did! I saw him!' shouted Will Janes.

'You didn't!' cried Toby. 'Let me go, Will. I'm Toby Thomas, from Billycock Farm. You let me go or my father will have something to say!'

'Oho – so it's Toby Thomas, is it?' said Will in a sneering voice. 'Toby Thomas, whose father won't employ Will Janes now because he turns his nose up at him. You wait till I tell the police tomorrow what I've caught you doing – I'll say you're the kids that have been taking our hens!'

Will dragged the angry boys over to a shed, calling out to the other two men. 'Bring them here. Chuck them in and we'll lock the door and let them cool off till tomorrow morning!'

Julian struggled valiantly against the two men, but short of kicking them viciously there was nothing he could do to escape – and he didn't really want to harm them. It was all a mistake!

And then – oh, joy – there came a sound that made Julian's heart leap – the bark of a dog!

'Timmy! It's Timmy!' yelled Julian to the others. 'Call him! He'll soon make Janes drop you!'

'Tim, Tim!' shouted Dick, and Timmy ran to him at once, and began to growl so ferociously that Will Janes stopped dragging the boys to the shed.

'Set us free or he'll spring at you,' warned Dick, Timmy growled again, and nipped Will's ankle just to let him know he had teeth. Will let both boys go, and they staggered away from him in relief. Then Timmy ran to Julian – but Mr Gringle and Mr Brent had already heard his fierce growls and did not wait for any more! They gave Julian a shove away from them, and retreated into the cottage.

Will Janes also went into the cottage and lumbered up the stairs. The boys saw his figure outlined against the candlelight.

'Well, thank goodness he didn't go and scare his poor old mother,' said Julian, shaking his clothes straight. They had been twisted and pulled in the struggle. 'We'd better go and see if Will knocked those two men out – gracious, what a night! Good old Timmy – you just came in time!'

'I bet the girls sent him after us when twelve o'clock came,' said Dick. 'He'd smell our tracks easily. Dear old Tim. Now, go carefully – it's about here that Will floored those two men, whoever they were.'

But there was no sign of them at all. They must have got up from the ground very quickly and made themselves scarce. 'They went while the going was good!' said Toby grimly. 'What do we do next?'

'Get back to the camp,' said Julian. 'We're really not much wiser now than when we came – except that we know that Gringle and Brent *are* butterfly men, and that Janes is a bad lot and in with those two fellows he knocked out . . .'

'And that he helped them in some way, and hid them here – and hasn't been paid,' finished Dick. 'But how did he help them and why?'

'I've no idea,' said Julian. 'I can't think any more tonight – my mind just won't work. Go back home, Toby. We'll talk it all out tomorrow.'

Toby went off to the farm, puzzled and excited. What an evening! What would Cousin Jeff say when he told him – but no, he couldn't tell him. People said he had gone off in that plane, and that he was now at the bottom of the sea.

'But I won't believe it,' thought the tired boy, stoutly. 'I will – not – believe it!'

The girls were most relieved to hear the boys and Timmy coming back. 'What's happened? Why are you so late?' said George. 'Timmy found you all right, of course?'

'Couldn't have come at a better moment,' said Julian, grinning in the light of George's torch. 'I suppose you sent him after us?'

'We did,' said George. 'He wanted to go, anyway. He kept whining and whining as if you needed help – so we sent him off.'

'And we *did* need help!' said Dick, flinging himself down in the heather. 'Listen to our tale!'

He and Julian told it, and the girls listened, astonished. 'What *has* been going on down there?' said George, puzzled. 'What has Will Janes been up to with those fellows? How can we find out?'

'*He* won't talk,' said Julian. 'Nobody can make him, either. But I think maybe if we went down tomorrow morning and found that he'd gone out, we might persuade old Mrs Janes to tell us a few secrets.'

'Yes – that's a good idea,' said George. 'She *must* know what her son has been up to – especially if he has been hiding people there. She would have to feed them of course. Yes – old Mrs Janes would tell you – if she could!'

'But now,' said Julian, snuggling down in the heather on his rug, 'now, you two gabblers, I want to go to sleep. Goodnight!'

'Well! *Who's* been doing the gabbling!' said George. 'We have hardly been able to get a word in! Come on, Anne – we can go to sleep all right now. I wonder if Toby's home safely, and fast asleep in bed!'

Yes, Toby was home, but he wasn't asleep! He was still brooding over his Cousin Jeff. If only he could *do* something – but he couldn't. Cousin Jeff had disappeared, and he, and he only, could clear himself of the hateful charge of traitor . . . but people said he was drowned.

Next morning the Five awoke late, even Timmy. There wasn't a great deal left in the larder, and Julian hoped that Toby would bring up some more food. If not, they must certainly go down to Billycock Farm and get some. They breakfasted on bread and butter and cheese, with water to wash it down and a humbug from the tin to follow!

QUITE A LOT HAPPENS

'We'll go straight down to the butterfly farm, I think,' said Julian, taking the leadership as he always did when there was any quick decision to be made. 'Dick, you'd better take on the asking of questions – the old lady was so touched when you gave her that money! She's probably got a soft spot for you now.'

'Right,' said Dick. 'Well, are we ready?'

They set off to the butterfly farm, Timmy at their heels. When they came near, they slowed their steps, not wanting to run into Will Janes. But there did not seem to be anybody about at all, not even the butterfly men themselves.

'They've probably gone off butterfly-hunting, I should think,' said Dick. 'Look – there's poor old Mrs Janes trying to peg up her washing – dropping half of it on the ground.'

Anne ran over to the little woman. 'I'll peg up the things for you,' she said. 'Here, let me have them.' Mrs Janes turned to her and Anne was shocked to see that her right eye was black and bruised.

'However did you get that black eye?' she began. 'Here give me the whole basket. Gracious, what a lot of washing!'

Mrs Janes seemed a little dazed. She let Anne peg up the things without a word – she just stood and watched her. 'Where are Mr Gringle and Mr Brent?' asked Anne as she pegged.

Mrs Janes mumbled something. Anne made out with some difficulty that they had gone butterfly-hunting. 'And where is your son, Will?' she asked, having been prompted to ask this by signs from Julian.

To her dismay Mrs Janes began to sob. The old woman

lifted her dirty apron and covered her head with it, and then, half-blinded by it, she stumbled towards the kitchen door, her arms stretched out in front of her.

'Gracious – whatever's the matter with her this morning?' said Anne to the others. Dick ran to the kitchen door and guided the old lady in, sitting her down in her rocking-chair. Her apron slid down from her head and she looked at him.

'You're the one that give me fifty pence,' she mumbled, and patted his hand. 'Kind, you are. Nobody's kind to me now. My son's cruel. He hits me.'

'Did he give you that black eye?' asked Dick, gently. 'When? Today?'

'Yes. He wanted money – he always wants money,' wept Mrs Janes. 'And I wasn't going to give him that fifty pence. And he hit me. And then the police came and took him away.'

'What! The police took him – this morning do you mean?' asked Dick astonished. The others came a little closer, astonished, too. Why – it was only last night that Will Janes had captured two of them!

'They said he'd been thieving,' sobbed Mrs Janes. 'Robbed old Farmer Darvil of his ducks. But it's those bad men that changed my son. He was a good son once.'

'What men?' asked Dick, patting the skinny old hand. 'You tell us everything. We understand. We'll help you.'

'You're the one that give me fifty pence, aren't you?' she said once more. 'You'll help a poor old woman, won't you? It was those men, I tell you, that changed my son.'

'Where are they now? Did he hide them here?' asked Dick. Mrs Janes clung to his hand and pulled him closer.

'There were four men,' she mumbled, in such a low voice that Dick could hardly hear. 'And my son, he was promised money if he hid them here, on Billycock Hill. They all had a secret, see? And they only talked about it when they were hiding up in my bedroom there – but I listened and I heard.'

'What was the secret?' asked Dick, his heart beating fast. Now perhaps he would hear what all this mystery was about.

'They were watching something,' whispered Mrs Janes. 'Watching something out on the hills. Sometimes daytime, sometimes nighttime, always watching. And they hid up there in my little old room, and cook for them I did and got nothing for it. Bad men they were.'

She sobbed again, and the four children felt sad and embarrassed. 'Don't worry her any more,' said Anne.

Then there came the sound of feet outside and

Mr Gringle walked by the window. He looked in and was astounded to see such a crowd in the little kitchen.

'What! You again!' he cried, when he saw Julian and Dick. 'You just look out! I told the police about you when they fetched Will Janes this morning. They'll be after *you* next, and you'll be punished for prowling round here at night and smashing my glasshouse! How *dare* you come here again!'

CHAPTER EIGHTEEN

Nobody knows where to look

'LET'S GO,' said George. 'We can't find out any more from the poor old woman. I'm glad that son of hers has been arrested for thieving. At least he won't be here to knock her about any more!'

Mr Gringle began to talk angrily again, but the Five had had enough. Timmy growled and made him retreat.

'We're going, Mr Gringle,' said Julian coldly. 'We shall be very *glad* to see the police, if you have really sent them after us. Quite a lot has been going on here that you don't know anything about. You've noticed nothing but your butterflies and moths.'

'Anything wrong in that, you uncivil boy?' shouted Mr Gringle.

'Well, it would have been a good thing if you had noticed how that fellow Janes knocked his poor mother about,' said Julian. 'I suppose you haven't even seen the bruised black eye she has this morning? No? I thought not. Well, maybe the police will be asking you a few questions soon – about the four strangers that have been hiding in that little bedroom up there!'

'What? What's that you say? What do you mean?' stammered Mr Gringle, astonished. 'Men? Where from? Who?'

'I've no idea,' said Julian. 'I wish I had.' And then the Five walked off together, leaving a very puzzled and worried Mr Gringle behind them.

473

'It serves him right,' said Julian. 'To think that he could make that miserable little woman slave for him, and never even notice how frightened and unhappy she was – or even see that she had a black eye from that scoundrel of a son. Let him get back to his butterflies!'

'What did Mrs Janes mean – mumbling about men hidden in that room – *four* of them she said,' wondered Anne. 'And why did they go and watch on the hillside? What *for*? That must have been one of them you saw that night of the storm, Julian – the one you spotted with the butterfly net, who said he was Mr Brent. I suppose he pretended to be him, so that nobody would ask him why he was prowling out there!'

'Yes, you're right,' said Julian. 'Of course, they may have been watching the airfield, you know – yes, of course that's what they *were* doing! Why didn't I think of that before? They were watching it night and day – two by day, I suppose, and two by night – and paid Janes to keep them hidden in that room. What were they up to?'

'Julian – could it – could it *possibly* be anything to do with the stolen aeroplanes?' asked George, with sudden excitement in her voice.

'It might. It certainly might,' said Julian. 'But I don't know how it ties up with Jeff Thomas and Ray Wells flying them away. That doesn't seem to fit somehow. You know – I do really believe we are on to something here! Let's go down to Billycock Farm and see if Mr Thomas, Toby's father, is about. I think we ought to tell him all we know.'

'Yes, that's a fine idea,' said Anne, pleased. 'We do want a bit of help over this now.'

'Well, come on then,' said Julian, and off they went at

top speed down the hill, taking the path to Billycock Farm. They soon came to the farmyard and called Toby.

'Toby! Where are you? We've got a bit of news.'

Toby appeared at the barn door, looking rather pale for he had had a bad night. 'Oh, hallo – what news? The only news *I* want to hear is about Jeff. I can't get it out of my mind.'

'Where's your father?' asked Julian. 'We think he ought to hear what we've got to say. He'll know what to do. I'm afraid we don't – it's a puzzle we can't seem to fit together!'

'I'll call Dad,' said Toby at once, and sent a shout over the field where red-and-white cows were grazing. 'Da-ad! Da-ad! You're WANTED!'

His father came hurrying over the field. 'What is it? I'm busy.'

'Dad – Julian and Dick have got something to tell you,' said Toby. 'It won't take very long – but they're a bit worried.'

'Oh – well, what is it, lads?' said Mr Thomas, turning his kindly brown face to the boys. 'Got into any trouble?'

'Oh no, not exactly,' said Julian. 'I'll tell you as shortly as I can.' And he began to tell him the tale of the butterfly farm – and of the man he had seen at night on the hill – of the old woman at the butterfly farm, and of Will Janes, who treated her so badly. The farmer nodded at that.

'Ay!' he said. 'Will's changed this last year. Got into bad company, of course.'

'We've met some of the "bad company",' said Julian and told of their adventure the night before – and then ended by telling Mr Thomas what the old woman had said to them that morning.

'*Now* what has Will Janes been up to?' said the farmer.
'Bad enough to get into ill company – but worse to ill-treat
his poor old mother! He'll have to say who these men are
that he's been harbouring up there at the butterfly farm –
and why they go out at night – watching the airfield, as
you say, I don't doubt. Why, maybe they've even had a
hand in the stealing of those planes!'

Toby became very excited at this and his face grew
crimson. 'Dad! Maybe it was those men who took the
planes! There were *four*, weren't there? They would be
strong enough to capture Jeff and Ray and take them off
somewhere – and then two of them could fly off the
planes, and the other two watch poor Jeff and Ray,
wherever they are!'

'You know – you may be right, young Toby,' said his
father. 'This is a matter for the police – and at once, too.
They must get on to Will, and get everything out of him –
make him confess. If Jeff and Ray are held prisoner
anywhere, they must be freed.'

Toby was dancing round in excitement. 'I *knew* it wasn't
Jeff! I knew he couldn't do a thing like that! I'm sure it was
two of those men. Dad, get on to the police at once.'

Mr Thomas hurried indoors to the telephone, and was
soon telling the police all he knew. They listened in
astonishment, and at once saw the tremendous importance of the information the children had given.

'We'll question Will Janes at once,' they said. 'He's held
on a matter of thieving, so we've got him under our
thumb. We'll call you back in about half an hour.'

That half-hour was the very longest the children had
ever known. Julian looked at his watch a score of times
and nobody could sit still, least of all Toby. Anne was

476

fidgety, and thought she would play with Benny. But neither Benny nor the pigling was there, so she had to wait in patience.

When the telephone bell at last shrilled out everyone jumped violently. Mr Thomas ran to it. 'Yes – yes – that's the police speaking, is it? Yes, I'm listening. What's the news? Oh . . . yes . . . yes . . .'

The farmer held the telephone close to his ear, nodding as he listened intently. The children watched him just as intently, trying to glean something from his few words, and from his face.

'I see. Well – that's very disappointing,' they heard Mr Thomas say, and their hearts sank. 'Thank you. Yes, very worrying indeed. Goodbye!'

He put down the receiver and faced the children. Toby called out to him. 'Was it Jeff who stole the plane, Dad? Was it?'

'No!' said his father, and Toby gave a wild yell of joy, and leapt into the air.

'Then nothing else matters!' he cried. 'Oh I *knew* it wasn't Jeff!'

'Wait a minute, wait a minute,' said Mr Thomas. 'There's something very worrying.'

'What?' said Toby, startled.

'Will Janes has confessed that those four men were sent to steal those two planes,' he said. 'Two of them were first-class pilots – foreign, of course. The other two were thugs – bullies – sent to capture Jeff and Ray that night in the storm. They knocked them out and dragged them away from the airfield, and hid them somewhere. Then the pilots got out the two planes, and flew away. When the alarm was raised, it was too late.'

'So – when the planes crashed into the sea, it was the *foreign* pilots who were drowned, not Jeff and Ray?' said Julian.

'Yes. But here's the worrying part. The other two men, the ones who captured Jeff and Ray, have hidden them away, but didn't tell Janes *where*!' said Mr Thomas. 'They refused to pay him any money for his help, because the planes had crashed and their plans had failed – and they also refused to tell him where Jeff and Ray were hidden . . .'

'And now I suppose the two thugs have left the district –

made their escape – and left Jeff and Ray to starve in some place where they may never be found!' said Toby, sitting down heavily and looking suddenly subdued.

'Exactly,' said Mr Thomas. 'And unless we find out where they are pretty quickly, things will go hard with them – they're probably bound hand and foot – and are dependent on the two bullies for food and water. Once the men are gone, there is no one to bring them anything!'

'Oh, I say!' said Toby, horrified. 'Dad, we must find them, we *must*!'

'That's what the police think,' said his father. 'And what I think, too. But nobody knows where to look!'

'Nobody knows where to look!' The words repeated themselves in everyone's mind. Nobody knows where to look!

CHAPTER NINETEEN

A morning of work

THERE WAS a dead silence after Mr Thomas had said those despairing words – 'Nobody knows where to look!' Where *were* Jeff and Ray lying, worried and anxious, knowing their planes to be stolen, picturing them in the hands of an alien country, being dismantled to discover the new and secret devices built into them!

'They must be absolutely furious to think how easily it was all done!' said Dick. 'Taken by surprise like that! Surely there must be someone on the airfield who was in the secret?'

'Bound to be,' said Mr Thomas. 'These things are carefully planned to the very last detail – and, of course, it was a bit of luck for the men to have a storm going on just at the time when they needed something to make their getaway unseen and unheard – unheard, that is, until the planes were actually up in the air, and then it didn't matter!'

'Yes – the rain poured down that night,' said George, remembering. 'Nobody would be out in it – even the guards on the airfield would be under shelter somewhere. It *was* a bit of luck for those fellows!'

'I expect they were delighted to look out of the tiny little window at the cottage and see a storm blowing up on the very night they wanted one!' said Dick.

'It beats me how Mr Gringle and Mr Brent never heard or suspected anything – with four strange men hanging about the butterfly farm,' said Julian.

480

'There can't be *anything* in their heads but butterflies or moths,' said Toby. 'I bet the police will have something to say to *them*!'

'The thing is – what's to be done now?' said Julian, frowning. He turned to Mr Thomas, who was deep in thought. 'What do *you* think? Is there anything we can do?'

'I doubt it,' said Mr Thomas. 'The police have had reports of two men driving a closed van at a fast speed – the number was taken by two or three people who complained – and they think that it might have been the one used to transport Jeff and Ray to some distant hiding place – somewhere in a disused quarry – or in some deserted cellar. Likely places of that sort.'

Everyone groaned. There certainly was absolutely nothing they could do, then – it would be impossible to hunt for miles for old quarries or other hiding places!

'Well – I must get on with my work,' said Mr Thomas. 'Where's your mother, Toby? You'd better tell her about all this.'

'She's gone shopping,' said Toby, looking at the clock. 'She'll be back just before dinner-time.'

'I suppose Benny has gone with her,' said Mr Thomas, going to the door. 'Where's Curly, his pigling? Surely he hasn't taken him, too!'

'I expect he has,' said Toby. He looked at the other four children, suddenly remembering something. 'I say – aren't you a bit short of food up at the camp? Shall I get you some to take back with you?'

'Well – if it isn't a bore,' said Julian, apologetically. It seemed rather dreadful to think about food when probably Jeff and Ray were lying tied up somewhere, hungry and thirsty, with no chance of food of any sort.

'I'll get some. You come with me, Anne, and say what you want,' said Toby, and he and Anne went off together to the kitchen, and opened the door of the immense larder. Soon Anne was choosing what she wanted, trying to cheer up poor, downcast Toby at the same time.

'Can we stay and help you this morning, Toby?' asked Julian, when he and Anne came back. He knew that Toby had many jobs to do on the farm, although it was a holiday week – and he thought, too, that it would be good for the boy to have company that worrying morning.

'Yes. I'd like you to!' said Toby, brightening at once. 'I told Dad I'd limewash the hen-houses today – it's just the kind of day for that, nice and dry with a little breeze. You and Dick could help and we'd get them all done by dinner-time.'

'Right. We'll help you all morning, then we'll go back to our camp and have a picnic lunch,' said Julian. 'If you've finished all the jobs you have to do, you could come back with us – and we could go on a hike or something this afternoon.'

'Oh *yes*!' said Toby, cheering up considerably. 'Come on, then – we'll get the lime and find the brushes. Hey Binky, come and help us – and you, too, Timmy.'

'Wait a minute – can't *we* help?' said George. 'I can limewash hen-houses as well as anyone!'

'Oh, no, George – it's a messy job – a job for *boys* not girls,' said Toby, and went off with Dick and Julian, leaving George looking furious.

'Now you've offended George,' said Dick, grinning. Toby was genuinely surprised.

'Have I really?' he said. 'Oh, of course – I forgot she

482

doesn't like to be girlish! Half a minute!' He ran back to
the window of the sitting-room and called through it.

'Hi, George! What about doing a job for my mother?
She never has time to weed her flower-garden and she is
always upset because it's so untidy. I suppose you and
Anne couldn't do something about that?'

'Yes, of course!' called Anne, going out of the door.
'Let's find a trowel each, and something to put weeds in.
George! Don't look so gloomy! Let's weed the whole bed
and make it marvellous for Mrs Thomas. She's so kind
and generous, I'd like to do something for her.'

'All right. So would I,' said George, more graciously,
and went with her cousin into the garden.

'I wish little Benny was at home,' said Anne, as she and
George began their task a few minutes later, complete with
trowels and two old tin pails for the weeds. 'I'd like him
running round us, asking questions in that dear little high
voice of his. And Curly, his pigling, running about like a
funny little pig-puppy!'

'Yes. I like Benny, too,' said George, pulling up a
handful of weeds. 'My word – there are more weeds than
flowers in this bed.'

'Let's take Benny up to the camp with us this afternoon,
if Toby comes,' said Anne. 'Then Toby can take him back
with him when he goes. I love little Benny – I could look
after him while you and the boys go hiking this afternoon.'

'All right,' said George, torn between wanting to stay
with Anne and little Benny and his pig and going with the
boys. 'Help – I've been stung by a most *vicious* nettle!'

All the children worked hard that morning. The hen-
houses had been scrubbed down and well and truly lime-
washed. Now they were drying quickly, the doors flung

483

open to sun and wind. The girls had practically cleared the big flower-bed of weeds and were feeling rather pleased with it – and with themselves too!

There came the sound of a car at about a quarter to one. 'That must be Mrs Thomas coming back from her shopping,' said George. 'Quick, let's finish this bed before she sees us – we've only about ten minutes' more work.'

'Benny will soon come running to see what we are doing,' said Anne. 'And little Curly, too. My word – I've just filled my ninth pail of weeds!'

The three boys came by just then, swinging their empty pails and carrying their big brushes. Timmy came, too, with quite a few white patches on his coat!

'Hallo, girls!' said Dick. 'My word, you've done a fine job on that bed – you can actually see the flowers now!'

The girls sat back pleased. 'Yes, it looks a bit better,' said Anne, pushing back her hair. 'Your mother's home, I think, Toby. We'd better go now, because you'll soon be having your dinner, and we'll be as hungry as hunters by the time we get back to our camp.'

'Right,' said Toby. 'Here, I'll take those pails of weeds for you – and the trowels!'

'Oh – thanks,' said George. 'Dick, Anne and I will go off to the camp now, with Timmy, and take the salad and stuff that wants washing under the spring – you bring the rest of the food, will you?'

'Of course,' said Dick. 'You take one basket, and we'll take the other.'

They went off with Toby. Anne and George went to look for Mrs Thomas, but she had gone into the dairy and was not to be seen.

'Never mind – she'll be busy,' said Anne. 'We'll go off straight away and get our lunch ready.'

They went off to the farm gate and up the path on to the steep slopes of Billycock Hill, the basket between them. Soon they were out of sight.

The boys washed their hands under a pump in the yard. Toby had gone to see his mother and to tell her what the police had said – but his father had already told her. She was very worried indeed.

'Poor Jeff! Poor Ray!' she said. Then she looked round as she heard the footsteps of Dick and Julian. 'Oh,' she said, 'I thought it was Benny. Where is he?'

'Benny – well, he was with you, wasn't he?' said Toby. 'You didn't leave him in the car, did you?'

'What do you mean, Toby?' said Mrs Thomas, looking startled. 'I left Benny here at the farm. I didn't take him with me – I never do when I have a lot of shopping, he gets so bored!'

'But Mother – I haven't seen him all morning!' said Toby. 'He's not at the farm. I've not seen him for *hours*!'

'Oh, *Toby*!' said his mother, looking frightened. 'Toby, what's happened to him then? I thought you'd look after him, as you usually do!'

'And I thought he'd gone with *you*,' groaned Toby. 'Dick – Julian, have you seen Benny, or Curly?'

'No – we haven't set eyes on him this morning!' said Dick. 'Gosh – where's he got to? He may have gone up Billycock Hill to try and find our camp – I know he wanted to.'

'Toby – the horse-pond!' said Mrs Thomas, looking pale. 'Go there – he may have fallen in. Look in the loft of the barn, too – and go into the machinery shed. Oh, Benny, Benny, where are you?'

She turned to Dick and Julian, standing anxiously beside her. 'Go up to your camp,' she said. 'Hunt and call all the way. He may be lost on the hillside. My little Benny! Perhaps his pigling "runned away" again as he so often tells us – and he followed and got lost! Oh, dear, whatever shall I do?'

CHAPTER TWENTY

A peculiar message

TOBY RACED off to the horse-pond, very frightened. The pond was deep in the middle and Benny couldn't swim. Dick and Julian went off hurriedly through the farm gate and up to Billycock Hill, calling as they went.

'Benny! Benny, where are you? Benny!'

They toiled up the steep, heathery slopes, looking for any sign of the small boy, but there was none. They were both anxious. Benny was such a little wanderer and his pig made such a good excuse for going long distances!

'Benny! BENNY!' they called, and sometimes the echo came back to them, calling the name too.

'Perhaps he will be at the camp,' said Dick. 'I know he wanted to visit it. He *may* be there, the little monkey – with Curly, too.'

'I hope so,' said Julian, soberly. 'But it's a long way for his small legs to go. I don't see how he could possibly find the way without someone to guide him – he has never been there yet!'

'Well, maybe the girls spotted him on their way up,' said Dick. 'My word – this is a day, isn't it? – nobody knows where Jeff and Ray are – and nobody knows where little Benny is either – I don't call this a very good holiday!'

'Exciting – but decidedly worrying,' said Julian. 'Why do we always run into something like this? We *never* seem to have a really peaceful time!'

Dick glanced sideways at Julian and gave a fleeting

smile. 'Would you *like* a really peaceful time, Ju?' he said.
'I don't think you would! Come on – let's shout again!'

They came to the camp at last, not having seen a sign of
Benny or the pigling. He was not at the camp either, that
was quite clear. The girls and Timmy were alone.

They were horrified when they were told about Benny.
Anne went pale. 'Let's go and look for him at once,' she
said. 'We must!'

'Well, can you make some sandwiches very quickly?'
asked Dick. 'We're all hungry, and it won't take a minute.
We can munch them as we go. Let's make a plan of
campaign while you're cutting them.'

George and Anne set to work with the sandwiches.
Anne's fingers were all thumbs, she was so shocked to hear
that little Benny was missing. 'Oh, I hope nothing's
happened to him!' she said. 'Missing all the morning –
for hours! Poor Mrs Thomas!'

'The sandwiches are ready,' said George. 'Now, what's
the plan, Julian? We all separate, I suppose, and search the
hill, shouting all the time?'

'That's it,' said Julian, beginning on his sandwiches
hungrily, and slipping some tomatoes and radishes into
his pocket. 'You go round that side, Anne and George,
one of you high up on the hill, and one lower down, so
that your shouts cover as much distance as possible.
And Dick and I will do the same on this side. We'll go
down to the butterfly farm too, in case he has wandered
there.'

They all set off, and soon the hill echoed to loud shouts.
'BENNY! BE-ENNY! BENNY! Coo-ee Benny! Coo-ee!'

Over the heather scrambled the four, with Timmy
excitedly leaping about, too. He knew that Benny was

lost, and he was sniffing for some smell of the small boy –
but his sharp nose could find nothing.

Julian went to the butterfly farm and searched all about,
but there was no sign of the boy there. In fact there was no
sign of anyone, not even old Mrs Janes. She had gone off
somewhere, and the two men were out butterflying as
usual. In fact, George and Anne saw them as they
searched their side of the hill and called to them.

'Have you seen anything of a small boy and a little pig?'

The two men were curt and unhelpful. 'No. No sign at
all.'

'I suppose they're annoyed because they still think the
boys broke the glass of their butterfly house!' said George.
'Well, I wish they would hunt for Benny instead of
butterflies.'

It was two hours before Benny was found, and the five
had almost given up looking for him. They had met
together as they came round the hill, and were standing
in despair, wondering what to do next, when Timmy
suddenly pricked up his ears. Then he barked – an excited
little bark that said as plainly as possible, 'I've heard
something interesting.'

'What is it then, Tim, what is it?' cried George at once.
'Go find, go find!'

Timmy trotted off, his ears well pricked. He stopped
every now and again and listened, then went on again. The
children listened, too, but they could hear nothing – no
call, no groan, no whimper.

'Why – he's going downhill towards the caves,' said Julian
at last. '*The caves!* Why didn't we think of those? But how
could that tiny little fellow have found the way there – it's a
long and complicated way from Billycock Farm?'

'He might have followed Curly, the pig,' said Anne. 'We always thought that he only *pretended* that the pig ran away, so that he could wander where he liked and blame it on the pig. But this time the pig might *really* have "runned away"!'

'Let's hope it's Benny that Timmy can hear,' said Julian. 'I must say I can't hear a single sound and I've got pretty sharp ears!'

And then the next minute they *all* heard something – a small, tired voice calling high and clear – 'Curly! Curly! I want you!'

'BENNY!' yelled everyone and leapt ahead so fast that the heathery ground shook beneath their trampling feet.

Timmy was there first, of course, and when the four children came up, they saw him gently licking the golden-haired little boy, who had put his arms round the dog's neck in delight. Benny was sitting just outside the entrance of the caves, all by himself – his pigling was not there.

'Benny! Oh, Benny darling, we've found you,' cried Anne, and knelt down beside him. He looked up at the others, not seeming at all surprised to see them.

'Curly runned away,' he said. 'He runned *right* away. Curly went in there,' and he pointed into the caves.

'Thank goodness you didn't follow him!' said George. 'You might never have been found! Come along – we must take you home!'

But as soon as she lifted up the child he began to kick and scream. 'No! No! I want Curly! I want Curly!'

'Darling, he'll come along when he's tired of the caves,' said Anne. 'But your mummy wants you now – and your dinner is waiting for you.'

'I'm hungry,' announced Benny. 'I want my dinner –
but I want Curly, too. Curly! Curly! Come here!'

'We *must* take Benny back,' said Dick. 'His mother will
be so terribly worried. Curly will eventually come out if
he's got sense enough to remember the way – if not well –
it's just too bad! We daren't go wandering down the
unroped paths in case *we* get lost. Come on, bring Benny,
George.'

'Curly will come when he's ready,' George said, as she carried the little boy away from the entrance to the caves. 'But now your mummy wants you, and your dinner's waiting.'

With Timmy jumping up delightedly beside her, she carried the small boy down the chalky path, talking to him. They were all so thankful to have found him that they felt quite cheerful, forgetting Jeff and Ray for a time. They teased little Benny, trying to make him forget his lost pet.

Mrs Thomas was overjoyed to see the small boy again. She cried over him as she took him into her arms. 'Oh, Benny, Benny – what a bad pair you are, you and your pigling.'

'He runned away,' said Benny, of course. He was set down at the table to have his dinner and began to eat very fast indeed because he was so hungry. Everyone sat and watched him, so glad to have him safe again that they hardly took their eyes off him while he gobbled his meal.

He finished at last. 'I'm going to look for Curly,' he announced as he got down from his chair.

'Oh, no, you're not,' said his mother. 'You're going to stay with me. I want you to help me to make some cakes. Curly will come home when he's ready.'

And in an hour's time, when Julian, Dick, Anne, George and Toby were busy at the messy job of cleaning out the duck-pond, Curly did come back. He trotted into the farmyard, making his usual funny little squeals, and everyone looked round at once.

'CURLY! You *have* come back! Oh, you bad little pig!' cried George, and Timmy ran up to the pigling and sniffed him and licked him. The pig turned himself round to look for Benny – and Julian laughed.

'Someone's written something on him – in black! Come here, Curly, and let's see.'

Curly trotted over to him, and Julian examined the rather smudged black lettering. 'Can't make it out,' he said. 'Somebody's printed something on his pink little body – silly thing to do – but it will wash off.'

'Wait!' said Dick sharply, as Julian bent to get one of the rags they were using, to wash the pigling's body. 'WAIT, I say! Look – isn't that a J and a T and below those are letters that look like R and V – no, W, because half that letter has been rubbed off by the heather or something.'

Now everyone was staring in excitement. 'J . . . T, and R . . . W!' said Toby in a breathless voice. Then it rose to a shout. 'They stand for JEFF THOMAS AND RAY WELLS. What does it *mean* – who put those letters there?'

'There are some more letters, smaller and rather smudged,' said Julian. 'Hold the pigling still, Dick. We must, we *must* make out what they are! It's some kind of message from Jeff and Ray. The pigling must have been where they are hidden!'

They all looked earnestly at the smudgy letters, which appeared to be five in number. They were almost unreadable – but Dick's sharp brain got hold of them at last.

'The word is CAVES!' he said. 'See – the first letter might be G or O or C – but the third one is certainly V and last is S. I'm sure it's CAVES – and that's where Curly went, we know.'

'Whew! That's where Jeff and Ray are hidden then,' said Julian. 'Quite near, after all – and we thought they had been taken away by car and hidden miles away! Quick – where's your father, Toby?'

Mr Thomas was found and was shown Curly, with the smudgy black letters on his back. He was astounded. 'So Curly went wandering in the caves, did he – what a pig he is! Can't keep his nose out of anything! And somehow he went to where Jeff and Ray were. What a strange way to send a message – they could surely have tied one on to his tail, or round his neck – these letters are almost unreadable!'

'I nearly washed them off, thinking that somebody had played a silly joke on Curly,' said Julian. 'My word – if I had, we'd not have known where Jeff and Ray were. What shall we do now? Go to the caves at once? Telephone the police?'

'Both!' said Mr Thomas. 'The police must know because they are searching everywhere, of course. Now – you start off to the caves – but take a ball of string with you,

494

because Jeff and Ray won't have been hidden in any of the roped tunnels, where sightseers so often go, and without string you might not be able to find your way back down the unroped ones. You may find that you need to unwind the string in order to get back safely. And take Timmy. He'll be useful.'

'He certainly will!' said Julian. 'And we'll take the little pig, too, so that Timmy can smell him, and then smell the tracks Curly made as he wandered through the caves, and follow them! We shan't have to wander all about wondering where Jeff and Ray are then.'

The Five set off at once, with Toby, too, all as excited as they could possibly be.

'Good old Jeff! Good old Ray!' Toby kept saying. 'We're coming! Hang on, we're coming!'

CHAPTER TWENTY-ONE

An exciting finish

Up THE heathery hill panted the five children and Timmy.
Julian carried the frightened little pig, who was not at all
sure what was happening to him. He kicked and squealed
but nobody took any notice of him – he would be of
importance when they reached the caves, but not till then!

At last they reached the chalky roadway to the caves
and pounded along it, the loose bits of chalk flying
between their feet. They came to the entrance where the
warning notice stood.

'Timmy!' called George as Julian put down the trembling little pig and held him tightly. 'Timmy – come here!
Smell Curly – that's right – smell him all over – now
follow, follow, follow! Smell where he went in the caves –
and follow, Tim, follow!'

Timmy knew perfectly well what tracking meant and
obediently smelt Curly thoroughly, and then put his nose
to the ground to follow the scent of the pigling's footsteps.
He soon picked it up, and began to run into the first cave.

He stopped and looked back enquiringly. 'Go on, Tim,
go on – I know this seems peculiar to you when we've got
Curly here – but we want to know where he *went*!' called
George, afraid that Timmy might think it was just a silly
game and give up. Timmy put his nose to the ground
again.

He came to the magnificent cave, full of gleaming
'icicles', the stalactites and stalagmites, some of them

looking like shining pillars. Then into the next cave, which, with its glowing rainbow colours, had reminded Anne of a Fairyland cave. Then through the next cave they went – and came to the forking of the ways.

'Here we are – at the three tunnels,' said George. 'I bet Timmy won't go down the usual roped one that all visitors would take . . .'

As she spoke the words Timmy, nose to ground, still following the scent of the pigling's footsteps, took the left-hand, unroped way – and everyone followed, torches shining brightly.

'I thought so!' said George, and her voice began to echo round. 'Thought so, thought so, so, so . . .!'

'Do you remember those awful noises we heard the other day – that piercing whistling, and those howls?' said Dick. 'Well, I bet they were made by the bullies who dragged Jeff and Ray here! I expect they heard Timmy barking – *he* must have heard the men, probably, though we didn't – and they were scared in case we were coming. So they made those frightful noises to scare us off, and the echoes magnified them horribly.'

'Well, they certainly scared us away all right,' said Anne, remembering. 'Yes – it must have been those men – there aren't any awful noises today! My word, what a long, winding tunnel this is – and look, it's forking into two!'

'Timmy will know which way to take,' said George – and, of course he did. With his nose to the ground, he chose the left-hand one without any hesitation.

'You didn't really need to bring a ball of string, Julian,' said Toby. 'Timmy will easily be able to take us the right way back, won't he?'

'Yes,' said Julian. 'He's better than any unwinding ball of string! But without Tim we'd *never* find the way back – there are so many caves, and so many tunnels. We must be well into the heart of the hill now.'

Timmy suddenly stopped in his tracking, raised his head, and listened. Could he hear Jeff and Ray? He barked loudly – and from somewhere in the near distance came a shout. 'Hoy! Hoy! This way! This way!'

'It's Jeff!' shouted Toby, dancing in the dark tunnel with excitement. 'JEFF! CAN YOU HEAR ME? JEFF!'

And a voice came back at once. 'Hi, Toby! This way, this way!'

Timmy ran down the passage and stopped. At first the children could not see why – and then they saw that the passage came to an end there – a blank wall faced them just beyond Timmy – and yet Jeff's voice came quite clearly to them!

'Here we are, here!'

'Why – there's a hole in the floor of the tunnel just by Timmy!' cried Julian, shining his torch on it. 'That's where Jeff and Ray are – down that hole. Hey, Cousin Jeff – are you down there?'

Julian shone his torch right through the hole – and there, lying on the floor of a cave below was Ray – and standing beside him, looking up eagerly, was Jeff!

'Thank God you've found us!' he said. 'Those fellows told us they were leaving us here and not coming back. Ray's got a twisted ankle – he can't stand on it. They pushed us down this hole without any warning, and he fell awkwardly. But with your help we can get him up.'

'Jeff, oh, Jeff – I'm so glad we've found you!' yelled Toby, trying to look down into the hole with Julian.

'What's the best way to get you up? This entrance hole isn't very big.'

'If you can manage to pull *me* up, that's the first thing to do,' said Jeff, considering the matter. 'Then two of you boys can go down to Ray, and help him to stand, and I think I could haul *him* up. This is an awful place – no outlet except through that small hole up there, which was too high for me to jump up to – and Ray couldn't stand, of course, to help me!'

There was soon a great deal of acrobatic work on the part of Jeff, Julian and Dick! The two boys managed to haul up Jeff by lying down on the floor above, and putting their arms and shoulders through the hole to drag him up! Toby and George had to hold on to their legs to prevent them from being pulled into the hole! And Anne had to hold the little pig, which did its best to try and get down the hole, too!

At last Jeff was up through the hole, and then the two boys, Julian and Dick, leapt down to Ray. He seemed rather dazed and Jeff said that he thought he had hurt his head as well as his leg when the men pushed them down the hole. Julian pulled him gently to his feet and then he and Dick lifted him until he could reach Jeff's swinging hands as he leaned down through the hole.

Poor Ray was pulled up at last, and then up went Julian and Dick in the same way. Timmy thought the whole procedure was most extraordinary, and produced volleys of excited barks, scaring the little pig almost out of its skin!

'Phew!' said Jeff, when at last Ray was up, and being helped by the others. 'I never thought we'd get out of there. Let's get away from this nightmare place as quickly

as possible. What we want is a little fresh air and food –
and water! Those brutes haven't been near us for what
seems like weeks!'

They made their way back to the cave entrance, Timmy
leading the way confidently, not even troubling to smell it.
He never forgot a path once he had been along it.

They came out into the bright June sunshine, and it was
so very dazzling to the two men who had been so long in
pitch-black darkness that they had to shade their eyes.

'Sit down a bit till you get used to it,' said Julian. 'And

500

tell us how you wrote your message on the pig! Did he suddenly appear down the hole?'

Jeff laughed. 'Well,' he said, 'there we were down in that awful hole, Ray and I – with no watch to tell us the time, no means of knowing if it was night or day, or even if it was last Thursday or next Monday! And suddenly we heard a pitter-pattering noise – and the next thing we knew was that something had fallen down through the hole and landed on top of us! It began to squeal like billy-o, so we guessed it was a little pig – though *why* a pig should suddenly descend on us out of the dark tunnel above us we simply couldn't imagine!'

Everyone laughed, even Ray. 'Go on,' said Dick. 'What did you do?'

'Well, we felt the pig all over and knew it was a baby,' said Jeff, 'but it didn't occur to us for some time that we might use it as a messenger! That was Ray's bright idea!'

'We could hardly read your message,' said Dick. 'It was just touch and go that we made it out.'

'I dare say – but when you consider that we had been robbed of everything – even my pencil and pen – to say nothing of my money, my watch and my torch – and Ray's, too – and that it was pitch-dark in the hole, I'm sure you will agree that we didn't make a bad job of printing that message!' said Jeff.

'But what did you print it with if your pockets had been emptied?' asked George, in wonder.

'Well, Ray found a tiny bit of black chalk at the bottom of his trouser pocket,' said Jeff. 'It's chalk we use to mark out our air-routes, on big maps – and that was all we had to use! Ray held the pigling and I printed our initials and the word CAVES on his back. I couldn't see what I was doing in the dark, but I just hoped for the best. Then I stood up and tossed the poor little pig through the hole! It was a jolly good shot, I must say – I heard him scrambling on the edge, and then away he trotted, the finest little pig in the world!'

'What a tale!' said Julian. 'My word, you're lucky, Jeff, that the pigling came home all right! It's a wanderer, that pig, always running away. And to think that I nearly washed your message off his back before we read it.'

'Whew! It gives me the creeps to hear that,' said Jeff. 'Now tell me what happened when it was discovered that we'd disappeared from the airfield – wasn't there an uproar?'

'Rather! You knew your planes were stolen didn't you?' said Dick.

'I guessed that, when I heard two planes take off, just as some great thugs were hauling us up the hill,' said Jeff. 'I heard a dog barking as we were being kicked and dragged up – was it Timmy? I did hope he would come to our rescue.'

'Oh, *yes* – that must have been the time when he began to bark that night of the storm!' said George, remembering. 'So it was you and those thugs we heard – oh, what a pity we didn't know it!'

'Those two stolen planes crashed into the sea during the storm, Jeff,' said Toby. 'The pilots weren't found.'

'Oh,' said Jeff and was silent for a moment. 'I shall miss my dear old bus – well let's hope I get another plane – and Ray, too. Ray! How do you feel now? Can you hobble along again or not?'

'Yes – if the boys can help me as they did just now,' said Ray, who was already looking much better since he had been in the open air. 'Let's get along.'

502

It was very slow going – but fortunately the police met them halfway, on their way to the caves! Mr Thomas had telephoned them and they had come along immediately. They took Ray in hand, and the little party made better progress.

'Put that pig down, Anne, you must be tired of carrying it,' said Dick. 'You look like Alice in Wonderland. She carried a pig, too!'

Anne laughed. 'I think it's gone to sleep, just like Alice's pig!' she said. And so it had!

They were all very thankful when at last they arrived at Billycock Farm. What a welcome they had from Mrs Thomas, her husband and Benny. The little boy dragged his pigling from Anne's arms and hugged it. 'You runned away, you're bad, you runned fast!' he scolded, and set it down. It immediately scampered over to the barn, with Benny in pursuit and Anne went to fetch them back.

'Now we'll all have tea – I've got it ready, hoping that everyone would be back in time from their extraordinary adventures!' said Mrs Thomas. 'I know Jeff and Ray must be starved – you look quite thin in the face, Jeff.'

They all sat round the big table, Toby next to his hero, Cousin Jeff. They gazed with pleasure at the food there – surely never, never had there been such a spread before!

'Mother!' said Toby, his eyes gleaming. 'Mother, this isn't a meal – it's a BANQUET! Jeff – what will you have?'

'Everything!' said Jeff. 'Some of every single thing. I'll start with two boiled eggs, three slices of ham, two thick pieces of bread and butter, and some of that wonderful salad. My word, it's almost worth being down that hole for ages to end up with a feast like this!'

It was a most hilarious tea, and for once Benny sat at the table throughout the whole meal, and didn't slip from his chair to go and find Curly. Why didn't they have parties like this every day? Why, even his father was there, roaring with laughter! What a pity the two policemen hadn't been able to stop to tea, too – Benny had a lot of questions to ask policemen! Where was Timmy? Yes, he was under the table – Benny could feel him with his foot. And, yes, Binky was there, too, just by Toby.

He slid his hand down with a large piece of cake in it, and immediately it was taken gently from his hand by a hairy mouth – Timmy was having a wonderful time, too!

Everyone was sorry when the grand meal was over. Jeff and Ray now had to report to the airfield, and Mr Thomas offered to take them in his car. The children went to see them off.

'It will seem awfully dull now, up in our camp on the

hillside,' said Dick. 'So many things have happened in the last few days – and now nothing will happen at all!'

'Rubbish!' said Jeff. 'I *promise* you something will happen – something grand!'

'What?' asked everyone eagerly.

'I shall see that you're all given a free flight in a plane as soon as possible – perhaps tomorrow,' said Jeff. 'And – *I* shall pilot it! Now then – anyone want to loop the loop with me?'

What shouts and squeals from everyone! Jeff made a face and put his hands to his ears.

'Me too, me too – and Curly!' came Benny's little high voice.

'Where *is* Curly?' said Jeff, looking out of the car. 'I really must shake hooves with him – he's been a wonderful friend to me and Ray! Wherever is he?'

'I don't know,' said Benny, looking all round. 'He must have . . .'

'Runned away!' chorused everyone, and Timmy barked at the sudden shout. He put his paws up on the car and licked Jeff's hand.

'Thanks, old boy,' said Jeff. 'We couldn't have done without you either! So long, everybody – see you tomorrow – and then whoooops! – up in the clouds we'll go!'